ROMANCING HIS HEART

AVERY MAXWELL

That's What She Said Publishing, Inc.

Copyright © 2021 by Avery Maxwell

All rights reserved.

No part of this book may be reproduced in any form or by any electronic or mechanical means, including information storage and retrieval systems, without written permission from the publisher, except for the use of brief quotations in a book review.

The book is a work of fiction. The characters and events in this book are fictitious. Any similarity to real persons, living or dead, is purely coincidental and not intended by the author.

www.AveryMaxwellBooks.com

ISBN: 978-1-945631-92-4 (ebook)

ISBN: 978-1-945631-93-1 (paperback)

090623

To all the girls who have never felt they were enough, you are.
To all the girls that make others feel like they're not, eat a bag of dicks.
Luvs,
Avery

TRIGGER WARNING

Hello Luv,

Romancing His Heart is a fictional story of learning to love and learning to accept love with a happily ever after. There is a page that discusses an attempted rape which can be triggering for some readers. I do not go into detail, she simply tells Loki it did not happen. I always like to be upfront with you. I never want one of my stories to be a source of pain for anyone.

If you are dealing with, or have dealt with abuse of any kind, I am deeply sorry. There are people that care and I hope you have a phenomenal support system. If you don't, please consider reaching out to one of these national organizations.

RAINN National Sexual Assault Telephone Hotline
NSVRC National Sexual Violence Resource Center
All my LUV,
Avery

PLAYLIST

1. Family, The Chainsmokers
2. Marjorie, Taylor Swift
3. Doom Days, Bastille
4. Kiss Me, Sixpence None The Richer
5. Narcolepsy, Third Eye Blind
6. Hypnotize, The Notorious B.I.G.
7. Torn, Natalie Imbruglia
8. Things I'll Never Say, Avril Lavigne
9. How You Remind Me, Nickelback
10. With Arms Wide Open, Creed
11. Home, Phillip Phillips
12. Exile, Taylor Swift,
13. The Wolf, Mumford & Sons
14. Milkshake, Kelis
15. I'm Too Sexy, Right Said Fred
16. This is the Last Time, The National
17. Flaws, Bastille
18. Don't Swallow the Cap, The National
19. Hey Jealousy, Gin Blossoms
20. Quarter past Midnight, Bastille
21. About Today, The National

22. Takeaway, The Chainsmokers
23. Before You Go, Lewis Capaldi
24. Darkness, Eminem
25. Life for Rent, Dido
26. Day I Die, The National
27. Evermore, Taylor Swift
28. I'm with You, Avril Lavigne
29. Demons, The National
30. Pompeii, Bastille
31. See The Way, The Chainsmokers
32. I Will Wait, Mumford & Sons
33. Fight Song, Rachel Platten

A NOTE FROM AVERY

Hi Luv,

Romancing His Heart is Book #4 in The Westbrooks Series. While it can be read as a standalone, I strongly encourage you to read them in order. Fall in love with Dexter, Trevor, Preston and Loki from the beginning!

Happy reading,
Avery

PROLOGUE

Loki
Twelve Years Ago

"Loki? My name is Michael Anderson. I'm an agent with the FBI, and this is my partner, Margaret Childs. We were wondering if we could speak with you, son?"

"This boy just lost his parents. Is it necessary to do this right now?" Mr. Westbrook's tone is uncharacteristically icy.

"Who are you?" the woman asks, taking a troubling step forward.

"Clinton Westbrook. I'm Loki's acting guardian, and I will ask you again, does this need to happen right now?" Repositioning his body, he attempts to block me from view.

"Sir, I'm afraid it does. Loki's biological father—"

"Yes …" Mr. Westbrook gives me an unreadable look, so I focus on the ground in front of me.

I'm nervous and unable to control my fidgeting as I shift my weight from foot to foot.

"We've known since Loki was a child. We are very aware of what lies ahead."

My head whips to his. *What has he known since I was a child?* There is no way he knows that my biological sperm donor is a lying, murdering piece of mob shit. I move to his side, and Mr. Westbrook puts an arm around me.

"Loki has always been family. Now he's in my care, and I'll treat him as my own. That means I will use everything at my disposal to protect him." Mr. Westbrook's voice doesn't waver or catch. He stands tall in his decision, and I wonder how much he actually knows. Surely he wouldn't put his family at risk by taking me in if he knew everything.

"You can stop all that worrying right now," Mrs. Westbrook whispers, coming up behind me. "We made your parents a promise a long time ago, and we intend to stand by that promise." She wraps me in one of her famous hugs.

"But—"

"No buts." She turns her attention to the agents and narrows her eyes. With one hand on her hip, she points her finger at them. "I have five boys in that building about to riot. Let me get them in the car with my friend, Grace, and then we can have this chat you are insisting on." She turns, then adds, "Even if it is at the most inappropriate time imaginable."

Both agents look down at their feet. If you've never been chastised by Mrs. W, consider yourself lucky.

"Yes, ma'am," they reply in unison.

Mr. W still has an arm around me protectively, and I take comfort in his strength for as long as I can. As soon as these agents tell them my entire story, I can say good-bye to them and my friends. I'll truly be alone in this world, but I will make Antonio Black pay for taking away everything and everyone I have ever cared about.

He will pay for his crimes.

I don't know how long we stand in the funeral home parking lot, but it feels like an eternity. Mr. W must think the same thing.

"Are you planning to discuss his father's misdeeds right here in the parking lot?" He asks pointedly.

The agents straighten but say nothing.

My body goes rigid. "He is not my father," I grind out.

Mr. Westbrook glances down at me with kind eyes. While Preston and I are in the same grade, I am two years younger and have yet to hit the growth spurt my mother assured me was coming.

"No, he isn't. You're right, son. What would you like us to call him?"

It's out of my mouth before I can censor it, "Is *'cocksucker'* too good for him?"

The Westbrooks are a boisterous family, but they're still traditional in many ways, and I immediately want to punch myself when I feel him shake next to me. Gathering all the courage a fifteen-year-old can, I dare a peek and find him chuckling next to me.

"I think cocksucker is probably too good for him. Plus, I don't believe Sylvie would approve. How about if we just call him Black-hole for now? It can be our little secret." He smirks, squeezing my shoulder, and a small smile pulls at the corner of my lips.

"Mr. W?" My voice falters, and he stares straight into my eyes, then gives a brisk nod.

"You know what," he directs this at the agents, but never takes his eyes off me, "I think Loki and I are going to need a few minutes. He just said good-bye to his parents, and it's my duty to ensure he's up to whatever you have planned for him. My address shouldn't be too hard for you to find. You may meet us there in one hour."

I bob back and forth between the bewildered agents and Mr. W, who is very clearly not going to change his mind.

"Come on, Loki. Let's go tell Sylvie to catch a ride with the Knights, too."

My throat is tight, so I nod and follow behind him.

Glancing over my shoulder, I see the agents' body language, and I immediately straighten my spine. If I am to make it through life as Antonio Black's illegitimate son without my mother's protection, I'll have to emulate the hard-ass persona those agents have cultivated. I know whatever they have to tell me is going to change the course of my life, and I'm not sure I'm ready.

∼

"ALRIGHT, Loki. I'm guessing by your reaction back there you know more about Black-hole than your mother thought. Why don't you tell me everything so I can fill in the blanks before the suits show up at the house?"

I appreciate the fact that he never calls Antonio my father again. That's the kind of man Clinton Westbrook is.

"Mr. Westbrook—"

"Well," he releases a long low breath. "That's not going to work now, is it, son? I think it'll be okay for you to call us Clint and Sylvie. You've always been part of our family, Loki. Now we just have the paperwork to go with it. I also meant what I said earlier. We will be there for you for the rest of our lives. You can count on me, I promise."

I'm silent, allowing the sounds of the road to soothe my frazzled nerves.

"You've always been an only child, but now you're one of six. So, welcome to the chaos, officially," he says, breaking the silence with a wink. His grin is genuine, but the sinking feeling persists, and I just want to get this conversation over with.

"Ah, sir? I'm not sure you'll feel that way after I tell you about Black-hole." I can't even look him in the eye. With my stomach in my throat, I attempt to speak, but have to grab the door handle as Mr. W makes a wild stop on the side of the road.

Spinning in my seat, I glance left, then right frantically. *Has he come for me already?*

After putting his truck in park, Mr. W jumps out of the cab and rounds the hood toward me. Shitting bricks comes to mind as he rips open my door and unbuckles my seatbelt before pulling me from the truck. Whatever I was expecting was not the death grip of a hug he is wrapping me in now. The pressure of his embrace constricts my lungs.

"You listen here, Loki." His voice booms over my head. "Your mother sat us down a long time ago and told us everything we needed to know. This was her worst nightmare, but she did everything she could to make sure you would never end up alone. Or with him." Mr. W clears his throat, but his voice sounds strangled when he speaks. "Candace was Sylvie's best friend, and those two didn't hold back when it came to sharing. We have known all about you and the life your mother fought to protect you from since you started school with the boys. We know everything, son, and we are honored to be your guardians. Nothing and no one will take you from us, that I can promise. Black-hole may have millions in dirty money, but I was born a billionaire. If you think for one second I won't spend every dime to keep you with us, you're mistaken."

He pulls back, and I realize for the first time today, I'm crying. I'm crying for the parents I'll never see again, for the family that takes me in with all my baggage, and for the life I know I'll never have. Mr. W lowers his face so we are eye to eye.

"You are my family, Loki. Now and forever, you belong to us, okay?"

I nod in understanding as we stand there, allowing my tears to run dry.

"We'd better get moving, though. We need to talk before the agents come back. I'm not sure how much you know, but I can guarantee it isn't as much as they'll want to tell you."

"Mr. W—"

"Clint."

"Clint?"

"Yes, son?" he says with a smile.

"Th-Thank you. For not turning my mom or me away when you found out." I choke on the last of my words.

"That's where you're a little mixed up, Loki. It's me who should be thanking you. I always wanted a sixth child, but Sylvie told me she'd cut off an appendage I'm rather fond of if I tried." He winks, and I grin, embarrassed. "Thanks to you, I now have six boys. Eight if you count those knuckleheads, Dex and Trevor. I want you to always remember one thing. Family is what you make it, and I'm making you mine. Got it?"

I nod and mumble a thank you as warmth fills my body.

"We may be a crazy bunch, Loki, but we have love to last a lifetime. Now, let's get moving before those agents circle back and pass us again." He points to the black SUV with tinted windows passing by well below the speed limit.

This is all like a bad movie.

"You've seen them pass by already?" I ask as I climb into the cab of his truck.

"Three times since we were standing here. That's something we will need to work on, buddy. I don't want to scare you or make you paranoid, but you will have to learn to be aware of your surroundings at all times. Black-hole is still a dangerous man, and we must be ready for anything he tries to throw at you. I have a feeling that's what the agents want to talk about, too. He won't let you go willingly."

"I'm more worried about his spawn coming after the Princes of Waverley-Cay," I grumble without thinking.

Mr. W lets out a low whistle. "How about if we start there, huh? Your mom told us you've been having nightmares and yelling at someone in your sleep about the Princes since you returned from Boston last month."

"Am ... will they ... will they force me to visit him again?"

"Not if I can help it, son."

"My mom and dad couldn't stop it," I say as a lead weight lands firmly on my chest.

"I know," he mumbles. "But with the recent information and the FBI coming for you, we now have a bargaining chip. They won't speak to you until I have it in writing from the judge that Black-hole's parental rights have been revoked. You may need to put your wishes in writing or speak to the judge with me, but I don't think they will ignore your request this time. Just leave everything to me, Loki. I've got you."

Over the next two hours, Clinton Westbrook does as he promised. He takes the signed letter acknowledging all parental rights belong to him and Mrs. Westbrook, and the letter that releases Black-hole from any obligation to me, and locks them in his safe with the rest of my documents. Then we sit down and wait for the agents to come in. Surrounded by my best friend's parents, I learn what my government wants from me. I was right, though. This one moment in time changes the trajectory of my entire life.

CHAPTER 1

SLOANE

Present Day

Following Seth down the long corridor, I want to slap myself for being so careless. *Again*. It's stupid shit like this that causes my sister, who raised me, to question my ability to adult.

"I don't do this stuff on purpose, you know?" I try to reason with Seth, who glares daggers at me while also scanning our surroundings. A real-life super spy, his instincts are always on. "The least you could do is slow down, geez. You're almost twice my size. How do you expect me to keep up with you?"

A low growl emits from his body, and if I wasn't ninety-nine percent sure he had someone waiting for him at home, I would have found the sound excruciatingly sexy. Oh, who am I kidding? Single or not, the man is delectable! Seth is a big man—a big man with big secrets, *that* I'm sure of.

What are you hiding, Seth? I'll figure it out. I always do.

We were just upstairs at my sister's condo with her new husband, the once infamous playboy Preston Westbrook. *Crazy!* He's a billionaire, and I still don't know how to handle that sometimes. It's their first Christmas together, and Preston went a little overboard to welcome us all into his life.

Of course, I would be the one to do something stupid and leave my front door unlatched while everyone else in my new brother-in-law's family is on a manhunt to find one of their best friends.

"Sloane!" Seth hisses. "Did you hear me?"

I glare at him, about to fib my way out of another daydream, when I notice the latch on my apartment door is ajar. Not only is it open, but covered with what looks like blood. Suddenly, all I can hear is my heart beating in my ears.

"Ah, no. No, I didn't hear you," I whisper yell, slightly hysterical.

Straightening his shoulders, Seth repeats himself. "You. Stay. Here." He says it as if talking to a toddler. I'm about to roll my eyes when he continues, "If anyone, and I mean anyone, enters this hallway, you scream as loud as you can. Wake up this entire damn building. Got it?"

Wait, he's leaving me out here? Alone? Is he in-fucking-sane? I can't even sleep alone, and he thinks I can stand out here while he checks out my apartment? Before I realize I'm lost in my head, Seth has slipped out of his coat. As it drops to my feet, he draws a gun he had stashed in his backside.

Nice ass.

Focus Sloane, Jesus. I've never seen a gun up close before, though. *Will he let me hold it later?* That would be fantastic research! Maybe my next villain could be a gun-toting mobster? *Hmm, that would probably be insensitive considering my new in-laws' current situation with their friend?* But maybe down the road ...

Oh, shit. Seth's gone. Jerking my head left then right, my hair slashes across my face, and I almost scream. *Why do you get so lost in your stories, Sloane? Geez!* Hearing a clanking of pipes, I jump, and it's the last push I need to rush through the door.

What if someone is stealing my computer?

I can't write without it, and I can't support myself without writing. I really think about the stupidest shit when I'm scared. Without even realizing I've moved, I find myself at the entrance to my bedroom, and still no Seth. *Crap.*

His stern voice stops me just as I'm about to step inside. "I told you to stay put. Goddamn it. Can't you follow one simple direction?"

I'm so sick of everyone treating me like an imbecile, so I elbow him in the gut and slam my hand against the wall to turn on the light.

"Sloane, I haven't cleared that room," he hisses.

Glancing over my shoulder, I whisper back, "Then why are you out here yelling at me, superspy?"

I march into the room like I own it and stop dead in my tracks. Facedown on the bed is a large, bloodied body, and I scream. The body doesn't move, but Seth barrels into the room behind me. I'm already moving toward the bed.

Loki.

"Stop, Sloane, stop," Seth yells, unable to see Loki's face from where he's standing.

I drop to the bed beside him. I may not be the doctor in the family, but I know how to check for a pulse.

"Go, Seth. Get my sister. Get Emory, now. It's—It's Loki," I choke out. I've seen enough pictures I could tell his handsome face from a mile away. Even behind layers of dirt, blood, and God only knows what else, I can tell this is Preston's missing friend.

"Fuck." I hear Seth curse as he sprints down the hall.

I run to the bathroom and grab a bunch of towels and wet washcloths with lukewarm water. I could tell from one touch that Loki felt feverish, which probably isn't a good sign. Running back to his side, I drop it all on the bed.

Emory, hurry. Someone, I need someone to tell me what to do.

With great effort, I roll him onto his back before I climb

onto the bed. Kneeling beside him, I use the wet clothes to wash his face. I'm looking for the source of blood as I go, but so far, I've found none.

Leaning over him to grab a clean towel, I'm thrown back when his hand closes forcefully around my neck. His eyes are wild as he asks, "Who sent you?"

He's crushing my airway, and I can't make any sound.

"Who. Sent. You?"

His middle finger twitches just enough I'm able to choke out, "Preston. I'm— Preston sent me." His fingers relax a fraction as I read the confusion on his face.

"Loki! Jesus Christ, let her go," I hear Preston's voice but can't see anyone as my vision blurs. I barely catch the flash of my sister's hair as she runs past, plunging a syringe into Loki's side. I register shock before his eyes go glassy, and he falls back to the bed.

"That's only a mild sedative. If he's violent, it won't last long," Emory commands.

"I'm not violent. She's trespassing," Loki murmurs before his eyes close once more.

"We need to get him to the hospital now," Emory barks.

Dr. Emory Camden in control.

"No," Seth interrupts. "We can't risk taking him to a hospital. We don't have enough information. Our intel from SIA says no one is chasing him, but I know Loki. He wouldn't have gone through all these hoops, missed Trevor's wedding, or Preston almost dying if he didn't at least believe someone was after him."

Jesus, it was just a few short weeks ago Preston almost died from a genetic heart condition. It feels like a lifetime ago.

"I agree with Seth," Ashton says, interrupting my thoughts as he enters the room. "Emory? Can you check him out here if we get you the equipment?"

Ashton is Preston's youngest brother, and there's no mistaking the relation. Those Westbrook genes are strong.

"Ash, I ... he could have internal bleeding or broken bones. For all I know, he has a collapsed lung, or worse. He needs a proper examination in a hospital."

"If we get you basic equipment, can you rule out any life-threatening injuries?" Ashton asks again.

In Emory's silence, Preston asks, "Seth, do you think his life could be in danger if we bring him to the hospital?"

"I don't know," he answers, appearing defeated. Seth has been with Loki at SIA for years, so we all wait on his answer. "I just know Loki. He wouldn't have gone to all this trouble if he didn't have to. He crisscrossed the entire East Coast, leaving us clues. If he believes someone is after him, and it turns out there is, then yes, his life would most definitely be in jeopardy admitting him to a hospital."

All heads turn to Emory. My poor sister, who just got her medical license back, is being asked to do something that goes against all the ethics she swore to uphold.

Holding her elbows close to her body like her life depends on it, she finally agrees, "I'll do my best, but if I suspect anything I can't handle from this bed, he goes to the hospital. That's my deal, take it or leave it."

I almost laugh. Emory has always tried to play hardball. If these guys knew her at all, they'd call her bluff, but the only one smiling is her husband, Preston. Good man that he is keeps his mouth shut. He knows she would tend to Loki even if they didn't meet her demands, but I'm glad when they do.

"Okay, done," Seth says.

"What do you need?" Ashton asks.

"We still have Preston's ECG and a portable UltraSound machine in our closet upstairs. Let's start with those. Sloane, we need to get him undressed and cleaned up as best we can so I can do an exam."

As Ashton rushes past me with his orders, I realize Emory was also talking to me. I'm taken aback when she orders me to help. Most people ignore me and hope I'll just go away, but I should have known better. My sister raised me, she knows what I'm capable of, even before I do.

"Got it. I already tried his face, but that seemed to irritate him," I warn.

"The sedative will give us about twenty minutes. We'll have to see what Ashton can get for supplies. I can already tell Loki is severely dehydrated, which is why he's so disoriented, but I need to check for head injuries, too. Have you found where the blood is coming from?"

"My thigh," Loki croaks, causing both Emory and I to jump back, startled.

"Preston?" I yell. I don't mean to, but Loki's a little scary. "Come talk to your friend. Let him know we're with you, and we're just taking care of him."

"I can hear you, sugar," Loki groans as I lift his shoulder to remove his shirt.

"Yeah, well, you nearly strangled me to death the last time, so I'm going to let your buddy here do the talking for a bit."

His eyes widen in surprise at my words. His stare is intense and focused solely on me, and it sends a shiver down my spine. As if he can also feel it, the left side of his lip curls just before he nods off again.

"Hey, Loki. It's me, Preston. Where the hell have you been? I almost died and your ass was MIA. Now that you're home, we have to get you better so we can take turns kicking the shit out of you." Preston plays it off as a joke, but there's no mistaking the undertone of concern.

I hear a commotion in the hallway, and Emory turns just as the crowd from her apartment descends on us. Dexter and Sylvie are at the front of the line trying to enter, but Emory holds up her hand to stop them.

"I'm sorry. I can't have anyone else in this room. It's not a sterile environment, and I have no idea what I'm looking at in terms of his care. We'll keep you all updated, but I'm doing the best I can here. Please, everyone, go back upstairs."

"My earthly angel. You may have been sent to Preston, but in my heart of hearts, I know you're here to save another son, too." Sylvie nods toward Loki with tears in her eyes.

Jesus, talk about pressure! When has anyone other than my sister ever looked at me with such admiration, though? *Never, that's when.* I'm the family screwup, the black sheep. Black sheep don't get the expressions of love that Emory so rightly deserves.

"Mom? Let Dex take you home, okay? I'll call you with updates, but you don't need to sit vigil. You've been through a lot the last few months."

Sylvie's spine goes rigid, and her smile turns into a hard line. "Don't you dare try to send me away, Preston Westbrook! I'll be waiting upstairs for an update. I'll go home when I am good and ready, you hear me?"

"Oooh, someone's in trouuuble," Loki slurs.

"I thought you said this would knock him out?" I gape.

"It should have," Emory says, looking as confused as I've ever seen her.

"Excuse me, Mom. Ems, here you go?" Ash squeezes by Sylvie to enter the room. I can see the expression on Sylvie's face and know she's about to argue, but thankfully, Dexter guides her out of the room. "They have trained him for … well, let's just say he's been trained for everything. A horse tranquilizer wouldn't stop him."

"That's right, Ashy." Apparently, the sedative doesn't knock him out, it makes him playful?

"I'm going to need more information than that to treat him, Ashton," Emory scolds.

He hands her a chart and a bag of supplies.

After peering into the bag for a few moments, she looks up, ashen-faced. "Where did you get these medications, Ash?"

"The agency supplies them." He doesn't elaborate, and I can tell he won't.

Emory opens the folder and scans its contents.

"Holy shit," she whispers.

When I try to get a peek, she snaps it shut, shaking her head and mumbling about HIPAA laws. I want to argue that we're in my bedroom, but I notice her concerned face and stop.

"What do you want me to do, sis?"

"Let's finish getting him cleaned up so I can run some scans," she says distractedly while Preston and Ash exchange a muted conversation.

"On it." I go to the other side of the bed, then cut his shirt over his shoulder so I can slide it down his arm. His sleeve is folded tightly in the palm of his hand, so I try to pry it open. Running a hand over his corded forearm, his muscles finally relax. As I gently move down his arm, his fingers uncurl, and I realize he's holding onto something. Pulling it away, I unroll it to find the second half of a note Seth had received a few days ago.

"Ashton?"

He turns his head and stops speaking mid-sentence. Crossing the room, he takes the note from me. It's written in some sort of code I don't understand.

"Is it Julia's?" Preston asks.

"Yeah."

"It's good codes," Loki mumbles, apparently still aware of all that's around him.

"What does it say?" I can't keep the excitement from my voice.

Julia is a new friend of my sister... and now me, too, I guess. Her husband, Trevor, is part of Preston's pack. I don't know why I refer to these guys as a pack, but I do, and it suits them. Julia is a brainiac who created a high-level secret code that helped Loki bring down his family, a Boston area mob. *Gah, the story I could write about these guys!* Ash isn't as fast as Julia at deciphering the code I hand him, but he still solves it in record time.

The brainpower going on between those two could light up the entire city. I snort at the thought, causing everyone to turn their heads in my direction.

"It ... ah, it says, 'they're watching her. Four months. Red. Get Sawyer out,'" Ashton fumbles over the note.

As if we gave him a shot of adrenalin, Loki surges from the bed and turns in a circle. "They're coming for her."

Preston takes a tentative step forward with his hands raised, "Who, Loki? Who's coming, and who is she?"

He scans the room like a deer in headlights. "I-I don't know. I can't remember. I can't remember, but I know they're coming." Panic and fear cross his chiseled features. Staring straight at me as he says, "They want her."

We all watch in shock as he collapses to the ground like a ton of bricks.

"Shit, help me," I scream, trying to break his fall.

Preston and Seth are on him in an instant and pull him back to the bed.

"I'm going to have to sedate him. I can't do an exam with him wild like this, and if he can't remember, I need to prioritize a head injury check. Sloane, why don't you go upstairs with Seth? The fewer people we have in here the better until I can assess properly."

"No," Loki bellows, lunging at me once again. Grabbing me around the middle, he pulls me to him. "They're watching her. She stays with me at all times."

I stare at Emory, wide-eyed and more than a little scared. What the hell does he mean they're watching me? Did Jackson find me already? How would Loki even know that? I begin to tremble as Loki sways.

"Shh, Red. Don't worry. I'll protect you." He pulls me to

the bed, where he falls back, taking me with him and trapping me under his heavy arm.

I glance around the room in horror as everyone stares back. Finally, it's Emory who comes to her senses.

"Ash? You're sure this medication is labeled properly, and his medical charts are up to date?"

"Yes, ma'am," he says, gaping like a teenager about to get in trouble.

"Good. This will knock him out until we figure out what the fuck is going on." Emory takes a step forward and plunges another needle into Loki's arm.

CHAPTER 2

LOKI

I wake with a start, something I haven't done since I was a child, and I'm immediately on alert. When you work for the Select Intelligence Agency, you always, always know what's happening around you. Sleep is for the weak. Without moving a muscle, I scan the room. My room.

How the hell did I get here?

A rocking chair sits empty next to the bed. It's lined with more blankets than I would know what to do with. It appears I've had an audience while I've been out, and it makes my spine tingle. That's when I hear it—a soft, melodic voice trying damn hard to hold her ground.

"No, Seth. I mean it. You're not going in there again. He needs his rest, and since I'm taking care of him, the answer is no."

"Dammit, Sloane. I don't have time for this. If he wakes up, I need to be there to figure out what we're dealing with."

"I found him, and he's in my apartment. That makes him my responsibility. Emory checks on him four times a day, and she said to let him rest. So, until he wakes on his own, you're shit out of luck."

I hear the telltale sound of Seth's growl, but that only makes my mystery woman laugh.

"Listen, mister, I have dealt with every kind of man for my books. Your scary, growly façade isn't going to work on me."

"Façade?" Seth bellows, and I chuckle. Whoever this spitfire is, she isn't backing down.

"Yes, faç-aaade," she draws out. "Does your girlfriend know you're here creeping around a man that's been passed out for a week?"

"What ... how? What the fuck are you talking about?"

Holy shit! Does he have a girlfriend now? I've known Seth since the academy, so I know he generally keeps his home life private. *But a girlfriend?* That's news to me.

"I don't have a girlfriend, Sloane," he grumbles.

"A stripper friend, maybe?"

What the fuck?

"Sloane, I need to see Loki."

"I've got it. You're a dad. You have a little girl. All the glitter makes sense now," she says happily.

I can't hear Seth's reply, but I know she just knocked the wind out of him.

"Oh, relax, Seth. I watch people. I read people. I study them for my books. You're not hiding anything from me with your perpetual grumpy face."

I try to stand and put an end to his misery, but moving sends a jolt of pain throughout my body. I'm not nineteen anymore, that's for sure. I've been protective of Seth since the day I found him beyond the courtyard at the academy. Vic had gotten a jump on him, and he never stood a chance. Preying on the weak is a trigger for me, and when I found them, I made sure Vic never forgot me. He hasn't looked Seth's way since.

"Listen, I-I mean, you can't tell anyone, okay? I've worked hard to get to where I am, but there are people out there, in my world, who would love to take me down a notch by using my personal life against me."

"You mean Loki?" she seethes. The anger in her voice gets my attention. Whoever she is, I like that she's protective of Seth, even if she appears to annoy him.

"What? No. Jesus, Loki has always been in my corner. He's why I'm here now. But there are others …"

"What the hell, Seth? What decade are we living in? You mean to tell me someone would penalize you for being a single father?"

"Not while Loki was in charge, but now …"

Wait a minute. What is he talking about? I am still in charge, aren't I?

"Seth," I call gruffly, "get in here."

I hear a scuffle in the hall, and I'm curious who the guard is, but right now, I need to know why the fuck he said I'm not in charge. As the door opens, I see a shock of red hair first. When she glances up at me, my lungs collapse. There is a nagging sense in the back of my mind that I should know her, but my memory remains blank.

That's when I realize I can't remember a small chunk of time. Without taking my eyes off of Red, I bark orders at Seth.

"What do you mean *when* I was in charge? Why wouldn't I be in charge?"

Shit, did Red say I've been out for a week?

"Loki, I-I think we should call Ash in for this, too."

Finally, dragging my eyes off the bubbly ball of energy crossing the room to sit in the rocking chair, I look at Seth for the first time. He seems worried and nervous.

"Just spit it out, Seth," I command, but he's already typing away on his phone.

"Ash is on his way down. He's been staying at Preston's place. God, man, it is so good to see you." I see the relief wash over his face as he takes me in, and I feel guilty.

Why does he seem so worried about me?

"We've got work to do," I inform him. Attempting to sit up in bed, I feel a stabbing pain and try to fight through it. That's what I'm trained to do. However, before I can do anything else, Red is out of her chair and positioning me in a way that relieves the discomfort. I regard her uncomfortably.

"Who are you?" I finally ask.

With a smirk so sexy it sends blood rushing through my veins, she replies, "I'm Sloane. Emory's sister, the renter of this apartment, romance author extraordinaire, and now, your private nurse."

Emory. Emory. Emory? I have that niggling feeling again and smash my knuckles into my temples. *Why can't I remember?*

"Ah, Loki?" Her sweet voice fills the room. "Emory. Preston's doctor, remember?" Sloane murmurs just as Ashton enters the room.

"Jesus Christ, Loki. It's so good to see you awake. You scared the shit out of us," he says while wrapping me in one of those Westbrook hugs I learned to tolerate all those years ago. Okay, maybe tolerate is too harsh a word, but I can't focus on how good it is to be home right now.

"It's good to see you, too, Ash. We have work to do, though." Remembering we have an audience, I turn to Sloane. "Hey, Red? Would you mind giving us a few minutes?"

"Actually, I do."

Seth rolls his eyes, and Ashton chuckles.

What the hell?

"Listen, I see you've camped out here, and I appreciate you were taking care of me, but my work is confidential and could be a matter of life or death. Plus, this is my apartment, so I'm going to have to ask you to step out of the room."

"No."

Is this girl joking?

I look to the guys for backup and realize instantly that they have no intention of stepping in.

"What do you mean, no? This," I say, gesturing around the room, "is my apartment."

Her sparkling green eyes dance with mischief, and I know she's about to put me in my place.

"You may own it, but *I* am renting it. I have a signed lease, and I've checked; you cannot kick me out." She smiles as she rounds the bed, her wild, silky hair falling out of a ponytail that sits on top of her head. Before settling back into her chair, she opens a medicine bottle, then hands me two pills and a glass of water.

"Take those before the pain gets too bad. Doctor's orders, and you don't want to mess with my sister. One is an antibiotic, and one is just a mild pain pill. If Emory's sedatives didn't knock you out, you don't need to worry about those."

How the hell did she know I would worry about the pain pills knocking me out?

"Ah, boss? I've got some stuff to tell you, and it's okay to talk freely in front of Sloane."

Seth is acting dodgy, and I don't like it. Narrowing my eyes, I glare from him to Sloane, to Ashton before finally settling back on Seth.

"Well, what is it?" My irritation is bubbling over.

"Sloane, you have your notebook handy, right? You might as well take notes. I think we're going to need them to piece this together."

I watch in shock as she takes not one but two pens out of her ponytail and grabs the notebook on my nightstand.

"We're going to talk about this apartment thing. Soon," I say seriously.

"Can't wait, handsome." She winks. She actually freaking winks at me.

Ashton, the asshole, lets out a bark of laughter.

"What's the last thing you remember?" Seth begins.

"Why did you say I wasn't in charge anymore?" I counter.

"We'll get to that, but we have to figure out why you were running first. What is the last thing you remember?"

Rubbing my temples, I try to focus. "Talking to you. The last thing I remember is talking to you."

"Okay, good. Where were you? Do you remember what we were talking about? That will help us with the timeline," Ashton says, pulling a whiteboard into the room. He must have had it in the hallway, ready to go.

I close my eyes and will the memory to come. *Fuck*.

"I'm not sure," I admit. "I was sitting in a metal chair in a dingy room. The space was enormous, maybe a warehouse, and I feel like I was waiting for something, but I don't know what."

I open my eyes just in time to see everyone else exchange worried glances.

"What? What am I missing?"

"We're not sure," Seth confesses.

"I think it's safe to assume I spoke to you right before the explosion. We were talking about Preston. I told you about his heart and Emory. Do you remember any of that?"

A flash of a memory tries to form in my head, but it's gone before I can catch it. "She's a surgeon, right?"

"Yes," Sloane cheers. "Good job, Loki."

Is she a goddamn cheerleader, too?

Apparently used to Sloane's antics, Seth pulls up a chair next to her, trying to hide a smile. "Listen, we'll just have to lay everything out from our perspective and hope something jogs your memory. If not, we're going to have to start from scratch to clear your name."

"Why would I need to clear my name?" I ask through gritted teeth.

Ash and Seth stare at each other but say nothing.

"One of you tell me why the fuck I need to clear my name!" I yell.

"Vic listed you AWOL after you missed your second check-in," Seth admits.

"How the hell—"

"What is going on in here? Are you guys kidding me?"

Turning my head, I see an older version of Red. This must be Emory.

CHAPTER 3

LOKI

"Oh, no. You guys are in serious trouble," Sloane goads.

"Don't you, for one second, think I believe you're innocent in all this, Sloane."

This woman means business.

"I told every single one of you that you were not to start this, this … whatever this is until after I examined him. Don't any of you remember the lecture I gave you about traumatic brain injuries and how memory re-stabilization occurs?"

Peering around the room, I notice everyone has their head hung in shame. Whoever Emory is, she isn't someone they want to disappoint, which sets her apart in my book.

"Emory?" I ask hesitantly. "It's actually my fault. I heard my gatekeeper arguing with Seth in the hallway, and I ordered them both in."

Sloane snorts and mumbles something I don't catch.

"Hi, Loki." Emory's demeanor changes, and I notice the mask she's put in place.

Is that just for me, or does she do this with everyone?

Sloane places her hand on my forearm, and I stare at the foreign gesture.

"Don't worry, that's her Dr. Camden cloak. As soon as she's done examining you, she'll be back to herself, the heart of the family, as Sylvie calls her."

I see Emory roll her eyes, but that's quite the endorsement from Sylvie Westbrook. I let my puzzled gaze drift to Sloane. Once again, I wonder how she knew what I was thinking. I've spent years in training, learning how to be evasive and not let people in, and yet here she is, answering my unspoken questions.

"I study people," she states matter of factly, confusing me even more.

"Sloane, am I going to have to ask you to leave?" Emory scolds.

"Good luck. I already tried that, and look where it got me," I grumble.

Emory glances between Sloane and me before speaking. "He asked you to leave?"

"Yup," she says on a yawn.

"And you didn't leave?" Emory appears as confused as I feel.

"No."

"Why not?"

Staring straight at me, Sloane answers, "Well, he may own this apartment, but I'm renting it. That makes it mine, too, for now. Plus, I've stayed right by his side while making sure he's okay in between your check-ups. I knew if I left him, those two would come barging in here the second I walked away," she says, pointing to Seth and Ash in the corner.

She's probably not wrong, but how long has she been staying in that chair?

A prickling sensation forms in my chest, causing a quick intake of breath. The sound spurs Emory into motion. Placing a bag at the foot of my bed, she unloads all kinds of medical equipment, and I use the moment to observe.

While the two women look similar, their stature is

entirely different. Emory is of average height, too thin, and carries an air of seriousness with her. In contrast, Sloane, with her false bravado, has a tentativeness to her that's disarming. She's also one of the smallest women I've ever met, with curves in all the right places. No one would accuse her of being overweight, but she has hips and thighs that are perfect for holding onto while—

What the hell, Loki? I shift on the bed, attempting to hide the growing problem under the sheets.

One glance at Sloane, and I know she's caught me. Smirking, fucking smirking at me with a raised eyebrow, a knowing snicker escapes her full, pouty lips.

Great, Loki, you twatwaffle.

Emory clears her throat, and I realize I've been staring at Sloane for far too long. The thing is, Sloane never looks away. For all her bubbly, timid ways, she held eye contact, never once backing down. I wasn't trying to intimidate her, not really anyway, but my team says it comes naturally. Everyone looks away from my glare, eventually, and she didn't even flinch.

For Christ's sake, I didn't even realize she entranced me again. Tearing my gaze away, I find Emory searching my features with concern.

"Loki? Did you hear what I just said?"

"Huh? Ah, no, I'm sorry, I missed it."

Sloane giggles.

"Sloane, seriously? This is not a laughing matter. If Loki is missing pieces of conversations, that's vital information I need to know."

"Oh, Mis." The familiar sentiment seems to take the edge off Emory. "He didn't miss your question because of a head injury. I think he missed your question because of ahem, biology." Her grin is back, and she nods toward the bed, eyes dancing with mirth.

In slow motion, Emory and I look down and notice my boner at the same time.

"For fuck's sake," I bark, reaching behind me for a pillow to place over my lap.

What am I? Fifteen?

Now it's Ashton's turn to laugh, causing a rippling effect throughout the room. Except for me, I keep my scowl firmly in place.

"Aren't there privacy laws between a patient and doctor?" I ask pointedly, which flusters Emory.

"Yes, of course. Okay, guys, go wait in the family room."

Sloane lets out a huff of air, but Emory cuts her off before she can speak.

"Sloane, I know what you're going to say. We all appreciate how well you're taking care of Loki. Especially since he was so adamant that you not be out of his sight," she sends a pointed, distrusting glance my way, "but he's right. If he wants privacy during his exam, I have to honor that."

"Come on, Ramona," Ashton says while holding open the door. We all stare at him. "What? She reminds me of that character, Ramona Quimby. No?"

"No," Sloane answers, rolling her eyes.

"Okay, how about Nancy Drew?" I don't hear her response, but Ashton keeps going, "I've got it, Pippi Longstocking." The last is followed by a grunt, making me believe he just got elbowed in the gut. Somehow the thought makes me like that girl even more.

"Sorry," Emory begins, "my sister is a bit, ah, inquisitive, and it's putting all the guys on edge." I don't get to ask what she means because she rolls right into the exam. "We really should have you in a hospital, Loki. Head injuries like yours can be very serious."

My brain must still be foggy. "Why wasn't I brought to a hospital?"

Emory looks around uncomfortably. "Well, Seth and Ashton didn't think it would be safe. They're under the impression someone is after you, and if that is the case, they thought you would be in danger there."

"They're right," I mumble.

Who would be after me? I dismantled Black's organization, didn't I?

"Loki? I can see your brain working, but you can't force your memories to come back. In fact, forcing an issue like that can sometimes make it worse. You have a lot of injuries you need to recover from, and this may be your brain's way of protecting you."

"M-hmm. Right," I reply while my mind takes off. I need to piece this together before someone gets hurt.

"Loki, you need to listen to me. The more you force this, the harder it will be. Can you focus on me while we go over your injuries?" I turn my head to face her, and she continues, "I need you to understand that memories come back in different ways for different people, and sometimes," she looks away before continuing, "not at all. Something may trigger you, and everything will come rushing back. Or it could trigger you, and you'll have fuzzy recollections but cannot fit them together right away. After speaking with a colleague, and based on the tests I've been able to run from here, I believe you have retrograde amnesia. Since you have remained stable, it's reasonable to rule out any permanent brain damage. Do you understand that I could not run comprehensive exams on you to know any of this for sure?"

"Yes."

"Do you also understand that I'm a heart surgeon? This is so far out of my field of expertise I could lose my license for treating you? But given the circumstances, I'm doing everything in my power to give you the best care possible."

Swiping a hand over my face, I try to focus. This woman is doing an incredibly risky favor for a man she has never met before. The least I can do is follow orders for a while. Finding her eyes again, I say, "Yes, I do. Thank you, Dr. Camden."

"Okay, let's go through your list of injuries, then I will check on the wounds."

I say nothing in response, just give a slight nod of my head as I take an inventory of my body. It fucking hurts, and by the time she's done listing my injuries, it's no wonder.

"Obviously, the amnesia and laceration on your thigh were the most serious of injuries. Both will take time to heal properly. If you are unwilling or unable to go to the hospital, you must promise me you'll rest so that you can recover. If you're anything like your friends, I can only assume you're stubborn, but I'm serious about this, Loki. If I can't trust you to follow my orders, I cannot continue to care for you. My ass is on the line here, too. I have an oath to uphold, and this is dangerously close to a line I cannot cross."

The emotion in her tone has me refocusing my attention on her. "Yeah, I'm ... I'm sorry. Of course, I'll follow your orders the best I can. I need to work with my guys, though, to put together a timeline. If I can't figure this out, the people I love could be in danger. I've fought too long and too hard to let that happen."

Sighing, Emory takes a seat in the chair Sloane just vacated. With her eyes focused on me, she says, "Give me a few days, Loki. A week, tops, to observe you now that you're awake, and we will use that time to get you mobile again. If that all goes to plan, then the guys can take you to the Loki Locator."

"Loki Locator?"

Grinning, she shrugs her shoulders. "Preston gave up half our condo for the mission, so I figured it needed a name. Loki Locator just fit, and Sloane ran with it like wildfire." Pointing her finger in my direction, she levels me with a glare. "A few days, Loki. Sloane will be on watch, and no one is getting by her. I can promise you that."

I frown. "Watching me?"

"Yes. Since she was hellbent on taking care of you, and you weren't letting 'Red' out of your sight, it was the logical solution."

Red. That damn tingling sensation is back, and I know Red should mean something. *Why does she keep saying I wanted Sloane with me?* An image of my hands around Sloane's throat floods my vision, and I grimace just as Preston walks through the doorway. My grumbling little pixie-guard following closely behind.

"What is it, Loki?" Emory asks kindly while giving both our guests a scowl.

"When I got here, did I, I mean, did I hurt her?" I ask, nodding toward Red. My palms are suddenly sweaty at the thought of hurting Sloane. "I never would have harmed her intentionally. Perhaps she isn't the right one to stay with me?"

I hear Red scoff from the doorway, but I'm deadly serious about this. At least I have trained with Seth for combat, and he would stand a chance if I attacked him. I've never experienced PTSD, but I've seen it in enough of my men to know I'm not immune. My gaze shifts back to Red, and she narrows her eyes on me.

"Preston," Dr. Camden begins, "I'm going to tell you the same thing I told Ash and Sloane. Loki deserves his privacy during his check-ups. You need to wait in the family room. Now."

Preston, the ever-present asshole that he is, ignores her and strides confidently into the room. His gaze softens when it lands on Dr. Camden, then he leans in and grasps her face. That's when I notice the wedding band on his finger, and I'm hit with another thought. *Preston almost died, and he married his doctor.*

I glance away from the very graphic display to find Red staring at me with arms crossed and a tilt to her lip. *Can she read my mind?* Because I swear, she knows I just remembered something. Then she goes and does it again. She gives me the slightest nod, and I know it's true. Well, maybe not the mind-reading, but she is excellent at reading people. I'm brought back to the moment by Preston's cheerful voice.

"Nice try, Loki. Sloane is stronger than she realizes, and no, you didn't hurt her. Scared the shit out of her, maybe, but you didn't hurt her. Plus," he leans down and whispers, "when she's down here with you, she isn't cockblocking me upstairs."

"I do not cockblock you." Red glares from the doorway. Preston gives her an incredulous look, and she folds. "Fine, but I don't mean to," she says sullenly, and I know I have missed something in this conversation.

"Sloane doesn't like to sleep alone. Before you got home, she was finding her way up to our place more nights than not," Preston informs me, but not in the dickhead way I would have expected from him. His words are full of concern, and I'm reminded of just how much I have missed while I've been away.

"That's it. Everyone out. Now," Emory demands, taking control of the room.

Peering up at Preston, I find him staring at her adoringly. It's the way his dad used to look at his mom, and I clutch my chest. Knowing Red is taking in my every move, I quickly splay my hand and pretend to be brushing down my nonexistent shirt.

"I'm happy for you, Preston. Truly. I'm sorry I—"

Preston cuts me off, "We have plenty of time for that conversation later when everyone's here and you're feeling better. But mark my words, we will all be taking turns kicking your ass."

I don't have time to answer because Emory is ushering

everyone out. Once we are alone, she finishes her exam but leaves no doubt how serious she is about Sloane babysitting me.

And just like that, I'm twelve years old again with a crush on the hot as fuck nanny.

CHAPTER 4

SLOANE

It's been a week since Loki woke up. As he recovers, he's been able to stay awake longer during the day, but it's making him more restless. Stifling a yawn, I pace the kitchen, waiting for Emory to give me new instructions.

Every time she leaves, she hands me a new piece of paper with every last detail written down. God forbid she just tells me. But then again, I've never given my family any reason to trust that I'm capable of very much. I seem to live down to their expectations at every turn.

"Okay, he's all set. I removed the catheter, so he'll be able to move around more now."

Great, thanks, Emory. Now I'm picturing his junk.

"Is he big, like down there?"

"You did not just ask me if a patient's penis was big?" she scolds.

"No, of course not. I asked if our friend Loki had a big dick."

My sister is not a prude, but she still coughs to hide her embarrassment.

"I'll take that as a yes." I smirk.

"Listen, I have to get upstairs. Loki is doing really well, but he'll still need help getting around. His dizzy spells are better, but you should always walk next to him just to be safe. Otherwise, he should continue to rest for a bit longer, so keep bringing his meals to the bedroom." She pauses to take a long, unnerving look at me. "You know, you're a great nurse, Sloane. I'm proud of you."

"Because you didn't think I could take care of myself, let alone anyone else?" I sound bitter, then feel like shit. Emory is one of the few people in my life that believes in me. It's not fair to take my issues out on her.

Pausing at the door, she regards me cautiously. "The only one who has ever doubted you is you, Sloane."

Unable to make eye contact, I hold up her instructions for Loki. "I'll call if he needs anything."

She's on me before my next breath. We're not a family of overtly affectionate people, but Emory's time with Preston and his family has rubbed off on her. She wraps me up tightly in her arms. "I love you, Sloane."

Damn emotions. Blinking four billion times to ward off tears, I finally choke out, "Luvs."

Pulling back, she smiles. "This crazy family has its claws in you already, huh?"

Shrugging like a surly teenager, I let a grin slip past. "Lanie is one hard bitch to hate. Her luvs are contagious."

Lanie is the wife of Loki and Preston's other friend, Dexter. She's probably the sweetest person I've ever met.

"She is." Emory stands there, holding onto my upper arms, observing me like a proud mama bear. She stares for too long, and it makes me fidget. Thumb, finger, tap-tap-slide. "Are you still sleeping in the chair next to Loki?"

"Ah, not every night," I lie. Now that he's not taking the pain pills, it's harder to sneak in and out.

She narrows her eyes but doesn't question me. "I'll call you later."

"Bye, Mis."

Scanning her instructions, I'm relieved to see all I'm supposed to do is feed him, make sure he gets his meds on time, and help him to the bathroom. *Shit*! I was too on edge to ask Emory what that entailed.

Do I stay in the bathroom with him while he goes? I bet he's huge everywhere.

That's it. There is something officially wrong with me. All I have to do is go in there and say, "Hey, Loki. Need anything?" If he has to use the restroom, I just have to make sure he doesn't crack his head open on the floor. It's easy! Yet, here I am, pacing the small space of the kitchen like a scared, little girl.

"You'll never be anything but a scared, little girl, always waiting for someone else to take care of you." The memory of my father comes and goes so quickly I have whiplash. Well, screw him. I can do this. I can take care of myself and someone else. Watch me. I'm going any minute now.

Ugh! An exasperated sigh leaves my lungs with a wheezing sound.

It was so much easier to take care of Loki when he was asleep. I couldn't screw anything up. Now that he's awake and intimidating as hell, I'm nervous about going back into the bedroom. Not that I would mind checking out what was going on under that sheet. *Geez, he's*—

I'm interrupted by a loud crash that has me busting out of my fantasy and rounding the family room in only a couple of strides. Entering the bedroom, I find the bed empty. *Fuck*. I run to the bathroom door, yank it open, and mentally prepare to find Loki sprawled out on the floor, blood gushing from his head.

What I'm not prepared for is Loki standing in a pair of tight-fitting, gray boxer briefs while he gapes at my makeup rolling around the bathroom floor.

"What the hell are you doing?" I ask.

At the same time he says, "What the hell is all this?"

"Loki, what are you doing out of bed? You're supposed to ask me for help. Doctor's orders, remember?"

"All this shit wasn't here the last time I was home. Seriously, what the hell do you even do with this?" He holds up a thin handled makeup brush with wire spindles at the end.

Grabbing it from his hands, I tell him, "I use that to separate my eyelashes when my mascara gets clumpy."

"And this?" he asks, holding up three different bottles of concealer.

Ripping them from his grasp, I say, "I have fair skin. Sometimes, depending on the weather, I have to mix shades to get the right tone."

"Jesus, I just wanted to take a piss." He's pinching the bridge of his nose, and from here, I realize our vast size difference. Taking a step back, I look up, and up, and up. Compared to my five-foot-two frame, Loki is a damn Viking with the pecs and abs to match.

Jutting out my hip, I can't help the sarcasm that seeps from me. "And what? You thought it would be fun to play fifty-two pickup with my makeup bag?"

"What?" His incandescent caramel eyes fly to mine. "No, I … fuck. I got dizzy, okay? I went to grab for the sink, and everything went flying."

I was only teasing, but getting caught in his gaze, I realize he's off. *Shit*. "Okay, big guy. Let's get you back to bed." Wrapping an arm around his waist is almost comical. "Are you going to make it back to the bed?"

"I'm good, Red. I just need a minute to catch my bearings, and what I really need is a shower."

With my hand on his bare abs, my fingers flex at the image of him getting naked, and I misstep.

"Maybe the question should be, will *you* make it back to the bed?" He smirks.

Barely composing myself, I glance up. "I'll be fine, but

maybe you should hold off on your shower until I call Emory." I take a step forward, attempting to usher him with me, but he holds his ground.

"I desperately need to shower, shortcake. I don't remember the last time I took one, but I can promise you, we're moving into official caveman territory here."

"Oh, I do love a good caveman." I grin before realizing what I said. "Ah, so ... yup." Changing tactics, I position him so he is at least leaning against the sink. "We've given you sponge baths, so hygienically speaking, you're fine. But if you want to shower, we should still consult Emory first since you have that gaping hole in your leg." I try not to look down. Blood and gore are not my things, but what keeps my eyes firmly on his face is the bulge I noticed when I walked in.

"Who gave me a sponge bath?" he asks, crossing his arms like we will be here for a while.

Good Lord, I wish it were me!

"Ah, well, I did your upper body," I say evasively.

A slow, treacherous grin glides across Loki's perfectly symmetrical face. His dark hair hangs low on his forehead while days' old scruff glistens in the bad lighting. He has a dimple on his right cheek, and I imagine licking it.

"And what about my lower body, Red? Who sponged that?" His voice is low and sexy as hell.

The pads of my middle fingers and thumbs start tapping against each other as I look everywhere but at him. My body is itchy as the flush of a true Irish woman races across my skin. I pull the ends of my ponytail, tugging it tighter against my skull and buying some time as he lounges lazily against the vanity. His dizziness seems to have left the room, along with all the air.

Placing my hands on my hips, I narrow my eyes before answering. Loki thinks this is embarrassing for me, but he has no idea I'm about to flip his house of cards.

"Well, Ems and I started, but you kept mumbling about Red, and your lower half kept, er, waking up."

Now it's his turn to flush. Straightening his body, he responds, "As you said, it's biology."

"Yup, biology." I mimic his stance. "That's why we had to call in Preston."

"That ... Wait, are you saying Preston gave me a sponge bath?" His face distorts as he reconciles what he thought I was going to say and what really happened.

Crossing my arms and rocking back on my heels, I laugh. "Yup. I can't say he was any happier about it than you look right now."

"Preston washed my junk."

"Dexter too."

"What?"

I'm laughing so hard now tears are threatening. I know Loki has been friends with Dex, Trevor, and Preston since they were boys, but this goes above and beyond.

"Preston only agreed because Emory threatened to withhold sex. Then he told all the guys they would have to take turns. Dex drew the short straw the second time. Literally, they all drew straws. Ashton was up next, but then you woke up."

"I don't know what to say to that."

Leaning in, I can't help the insane urge to tease him. "Want to know if you got a boner with them?"

"Jesus Christ. No. No, I don't," he growls, and I swear, my clit responds.

Pushing away from the vanity, he turns to the door.

"No shower?" I laugh.

"Let's not talk for a few minutes, okay?"

"Sure." Falling into step, I wrap my arms around him in a U shape.

"Do you seriously think you'll be able to catch me if I fall?" he asks, eyeing my arms skeptically.

"Listen, buddy. Before you hauled me into bed with you last week, I broke your fall, so yes, I think I can catch you. Or, at the very least, keep you from busting up your handsome face."

"Handsome, huh?"

"I always call it as I see it, Loki."

"Good to know, Red. Really good to know." His smile is genuine, but he regards me cautiously. He's calculated in a way I've never encountered, and it makes me nervous. Tapping my middle finger to my thumb, I wait until he's settled in bed before stepping back.

"Why are you nervous, Red?"

"Who said I'm nervous?"

Holding up his hand, he models my nervous habit, tapping his middle finger's pad with the tip of his thumb. *His huge fucking thumb.* Immediately, I tuck my thumbs into my fists. I don't answer him; I just stare. Not the shifty, eye to eye kind of stare. The straight ahead, no hesitation, I can see right into your soul kind.

"Okie dokie," I say, clasping my hands in front of myself. "Are you hungry? I'm not going to lie, I'm a terrible cook, but I order take out like a Michelin star chef."

Cocking his head to the right, he continues to study me until I fidget and glance over my shoulder. "Is that a yes?"

"You can't wait to get out of this room." It's not a question. It's like he knows I'm a runner.

"You're funny, but I've got some writing to do, and one of my jobs is to feed you, so I'm going to go do that now," I tell him, pointing over my shoulder with my thumb.

He makes a show of moving his attention between my hands and my eyes. "Sure, Red. I could eat."

"Great. Any requests?"

"Something sticky." His voice is low, dangerous, and so freaking sexy I choke on my own spit.

"St-Sticky?" I stutter.

His mouth forms a devilish grin, but it's his eyes that tell the story. "I can't have you running just yet, Red. Who will bathe me?"

"Who said I was running?" *Holy shit, who told him I'm a runner?* I mean, yes, that is my modus operandi, but what the fuck? Bathe him? *Holy hell, yes, please!*

"I read people, too, Sloane." The wink he sends my way tickles my entire body like butterfly kisses, and I shiver.

"Sticky. I'll get sticky and call Emory about your shower. I mean, I'll get your shower sticky. No. Geez." I'm so flustered I actually stomp my foot while shaking out my hands like I can remove the heat his words have caused throughout my body. "I'll get you something sticky for dinner and call Emory about your shower." I don't wait for a response. I bolt out the door, his laughter following me down the short hallway.

CHAPTER 5

LOKI

Loki: Please tell me Sloane is joking. You assholes did not give me a sponge bath.

Preston: Don't worry, Lok. I was gentle.

Dexter: The worst five minutes of my life.

Ashton: Thank fuck you woke up.

Trevor: Well, dipshit, if you didn't have a thing for your babysitter, they wouldn't have had to do it.

Loki: I wasn't coherent.

Preston: Even drugged out of your mind, you seem to have a thing for my little sister.

Loki: Sister-in-law.

Dexter: Fuck, yes! MSL!

Loki: You had better be referring to the Mean Sea Level, Dex. Seriously, I need to talk to you all. Bring Seth. I have to figure out what the hell is going on.

Preston: Has Emory given you clearance yet?

Dexter: I'm not pissing off, Emory.

Ashton: I'm with Dex.

Dexter: MSL Ash? Yes! We've got this.

Ashton: Not Make Sloane Loki's, Dex. Seriously, Prince Charming, you need to chill. I'm talking about pissing off

Emory. She's been through enough. I will not be the one to fuck this up.

Ashton: Seth and I are working around the clock. Trust us.

Trevor: Sorry, Loki. I'm with them. Just try to rest and don't let Sloane ask you ANY questions.

Dexter: NO QUESTIONS.

Ashton: No innuendo either. That leads to questions.

Preston: You guys are such pussies.

Loki: wtf?

Dexter: She writes romance novels that make women lose their shit.

Trevor: My dick is going to fall off if Julia reads one more of her books.

Loki: ...

Preston: Pussies.

Loki: Fuck you all. I'll text Seth.

(Ashton added Seth at 7:33 p.m.)

Ashton: Hey, Seth. Tell Loki to chill out.

Dexter: And warn him about Sloane.

Seth: Jesus.

Loki: Seth, get your ass over here with my computer and all your files.

Seth: Sorry, man. You promised Emory, and no one goes against Ems. Plus, you've got the inquisitor standing guard. No one is getting past her.

Dexter: WARN HIM.

Trevor: Tell him not to answer any sexual questions.

Seth: You guys are fucked up. Sloane's a great girl. She's a romance writer who asks a lot of questions. I'll leave it at that. Dexter and Trevor, go find your balls. Preston, I heard she is working on your story next. (Laughing emoji)

Preston: Fuck.

Loki: Screw you all.

Ashton: That's what she said.

Closing my eyes, I take a few cleansing breaths and smile. *Why the hell are my friends scared of sexy little Red?*

"Ugh, I'm really not *that* bad."

At the sound of her voice, I mime a karate chop while jumping out of bed. The sound of breaking dishes and metal hitting the floor moments later has my pulse in overdrive even as my brain catalogs everything around us. *Goddamnit.*

In the span of two seconds, I've gone from prone to the offensive. My target once again, it seems, is Red, who is standing inches from me, white as a ghost.

"Are you okay?" I ask as I place my hands on her upper arms. When she flinches, I quickly hold my hands up, palms out in surrender. "Sloane? Are you okay? Did I hurt you?"

Biting her bottom lip that I can see is trembling, she shakes her head no before answering verbally, "I'm fine."

A quick nod of my head and I turn in place. "Fuck."

"It's okay, really. Just, why don't you … Ah, get back in bed. You don't have any shoes on, and there's glass everywhere."

Glancing at the floor, I realize I'm still in my boxer briefs and nothing else. *Isn't this my house? Don't I own some damn clothes?* "Red—"

"Come on, let's get you back in bed before you cut your feet."

Before I can argue, Sloane is tiptoeing through the room and guiding me back to the bed like a toddler. *What the hell happened? Did I fall asleep?*

"Emory said you'll likely be in and out of sleep for a while as your body catches up," Red informs me, once again answering my silent questions. "It's okay. I'm sorry, I shouldn't have startled you like that."

"This isn't your fault, Red."

A broken smile hits her face and sucks all the air from my lungs. "Oh, Loki. It's always my fault." She says it in jest, but I can feel the weight of her words. "Come on, hop in, and I'll go grab you more dinner. Super sticky, just for you." She winks, but her eyes aren't smiling.

I'm not sure what to say to that. I don't know her, but her words sit heavy in my gut, regardless. While I'm contemplating my next move, she slips from the room, and I'm sucked back in time.

"We'd like you to consider entering the Nightingales."

I flip-flop between Mr. W and Special Agent Anderson.

"He's fifteen years old," Mrs. W interrupts.

"We understand, but surely you know his IQ puts him well above his peers," the female agent asserts.

"Maybe intellectually, but he is still a fifteen-year-old boy," Mrs. W says with all the authority she can muster.

"Sylvie," Mr. W sighs gently, "let's just hear them out, okay?"

"Clint. He's just a child," she repeats, her lip trembling.

"A child that will have adult decisions to make. Decisions we need to be equipped to help him make." Turning to me, Mr. W places a hand on my shoulder. "Loki, this is just information. We'll decide what to do with it together, okay? Nothing needs to be decided tonight, or tomorrow, or even next year. These are just options. One option out of the millions you have ahead of you."

I'm interrupted from the odd memory by the sound of the doorbell. Everything in my body wants to scream at Sloane not to answer, but rationally, I know we're safe here. I made sure I locked this building down when I bought the place. Security went into overdrive when I left for my last mission. *My reactions aren't in line with reality.* That realization has me scared in a way I haven't been since I was fifteen. Unfocused minds lead to unstable situations.

I sit up in bed and hear whispers of a conversation coming from the entryway, but I can't make out words or recognize voices.

"Just give me a minute to make sure he's awake, okay?" I hear Sloane say as she enters the room with a broom and dustpan.

"Who's here?"

"Sylvie."

"I thought I was on lockdown?" I grin. I know very well no one says no to Sylvie Westbrook.

"Well, it's Sylvie Westbrook. Are you going to tell her no?"

"Fuck no."

"Loki Kane," Sylvie admonishes from the depths of the apartment.

"How the hell did she hear that?" Red whispers.

"She raised a barn full of boys. She hears it all. What are you doing?"

"I have to get this glass cleaned up before she comes in here." She's still whispering like she's trying to protect me, and it does something funny to my insides.

Glancing around the room, I see the mess I made only moments earlier. "I feel like I'm in a time warp."

Sloane glances up and smiles. "Emory said things would be fuzzy for a while. Don't worry about it."

"I'm sorry you have to keep cleaning up after me," I say, feeling ashamed. Then I notice the bandage on her toe.

"What the fuck, Red? Did you step on the glass?"

"Loki," Sylvie admonishes, popping her head into the room. "Oh, dear. Everyone stop. Right now, stop."

Red slowly stands and meets my gaze while Sylvie takes over.

"It's quite the mess in here, Loki." Sylvie levels me with a hard stare. "That makes me think you're not following the doctor's orders, and I have to tell you, I'm really very fond of your doctor."

I swear Red rolls her eyes, but I can't be sure.

"And you," Sylvie points right at Red, "you're going to have to be much more assertive if you're going to keep this pain in the ass in line."

Sloane laughs. "I can be tough when I need to be, Mrs. Westbrook."

"Tsk, tsk, Sloane. I've already told you. Sylvie is just fine." She crosses the room to stand in front of Sloane. "You're doing a great job, dear. I know it's not easy taking care of these big, growly men. Now, what is going on in here?"

"Well, first I heard a loud crash—"

"That isn't my fault," I argue. "The last time I was home, my bathroom wasn't full of all that shit."

"Our bathroom," Sloane interrupts.

I go to argue, but Sylvie laughs. "I can't believe it."

"Believe what?" Red and I ask in unison.

"GG was right again."

"What?"

"Who?"

"Oh, it doesn't matter right now," Sylvie says evasively. "Okay, then what happened in here?" she asks, sweeping her hand around the bedroom.

"The red ninja snuck up on me," I answer without thinking.

This time Sloane definitely rolls her eyes. "I brought his dinner, but he'd fallen asleep. When I set his food down, sticky as he requested," she shares freshly, "I saw my name on his text message chain. Dexter and Trevor seriously need to chill out. I only asked a few questions."

Sylvie bursts into a belly laugh I'm not sure I've ever heard from her before, and we both turn to face her.

"Sorry, sorry." She waves her hands. "I've heard about your questions, dear, and good for you. I just finished reading *The Story Of Us*, by the way. Such an epic love story those two had."

Red's entire body flames, and I watch in fascination as she swallows hard.

"You read that?" she finally forces out.

"Woo-we did I ever." Sylvie pretends to fan herself. "I have my book club reading it next week. I can't wait to see those old biddies heating up their Kindles."

"What is it you write?" I ask, beyond curious at this point.

"Love stories," Sylvie says automatically.

"Ah, yeah. Love stories," Red repeats. "Sylvie, did you read the whole thing?"

"I did. I'm old, not dead."

"Okay. Yup. Well, you two have a nice visit. I'm going to grab Loki more food and get a bag for all this glass."

"Sit," I order.

Red whips around and glares at me.

"Please, sit. Let's call your sister and have her look at your foot."

"And ask her about your shower?" Sloane shoots back.

Laughing, Sylvie shakes her head. "I don't know how GG does it, but that woman should buy a lottery ticket."

CHAPTER 6

SLOANE

*E*mory was not impressed with the two stitches she had to put into my big toe, but seriously, it wasn't that big of a deal.

"Don't let her ask any questions, Loki. Stay away from her, Loki. She's the devil, Lok—"

"I'm pretty sure no one ever said you were the devil," Loki's voice glides through the air.

"Jesus," I scream, jumping back from my standing desk. "What the hell are you doing out here?" I demand. "You're supposed to stay in bed—" All the fight leaves my body when I turn to find Loki leaning against the door frame in a fresh pair of red boxer briefs.

"Do you always wear boxer briefs?"

"Is this how the inappropriate questions start?"

"Ugh, whatever. I ask questions, so sue me."

"Yes, I always wear boxer briefs. They … ah, keep everything secure."

"Like a bra."

"Um, yeah, I suppose."

"Do you own any clothes?"

Loki taps his middle finger with his thumb's tip, causing

me to look at my own hands. Sure enough, mine are moving with his, so I place both hands in my back pockets.

He smiles at me, and my heart beats in time with the song playing on the lone Airpod still in my ear.

"Preston is bringing me some clothes. I guess mine are all in storage."

"That's too bad."

Loki tilts his head while he observes me like an animal at the zoo. "It's too bad that Preston is bringing me clothes?" He grins, and if I were sitting, I'd definitely be squeezing my thighs together.

"Uh-huh." Apparently, I speak stupid in the presence of hotter than sin. "No, I mean, it's good. It's good that he's bringing you some clothes. We can't both walk around here naked."

"You walk around naked, too?"

"N-Normally, but not r-right now, obviously," I stammer.

He narrows his eyes like he is trying to figure out if I'm telling the truth. "You know, we still have to figure out this living situation," he states casually.

"Yup. Any idea where you'll go when Emory gives you the all-clear?"

"Red, I own this place."

"And I have an ironclad lease, but I'm willing to let you stay until you get back on your feet." Stepping to my computer, I almost miss his next words.

"I don't know if I can even stay here without endangering you all, but I guess I appreciate the offer." He frowns, and it causes a small line to form between his eyebrows. It takes every ounce of willpower I possess not to reach over and smooth it out. "Once I sort through my situation, we can work on a long-term solution for the apartment."

It's cute how he says it like I'll be going anywhere. Smiling as sweetly as I can, I adjust my ponytail. "I have another eleven months on my lease."

Taking a seat on the chair next to my desk, Loki glares at me. Not an angry glare, more of a 'what the fuck' glare.

"Let's just say my 'situation' gets resolved next week, then what?"

"Well, I guess you'll have to find a new place, but you're welcome to stay here as long as you need."

"How hospitable of you." Loki is trying really, really hard not to smile. He isn't sure he likes me, but I'm a freaking fun girl, so I'll win him over.

"I think so." I grin.

"What if I don't want to find a new place?"

"You can stay here, but it's not like Preston's palace upstairs. It's pretty small. I'll probably get on your nerves," I tell him from experience.

"And it's only one bedroom."

I shrug my shoulders. "I've had roommates before. We can share."

"What if I want to hook up?" He's testing me, and I like his unexpected, playful side.

"Then you go to her house," I say as casually as possible.

"What if you want to hook up?"

Deciding to mess with him a little, I say, "I always want to hook up," and watch as he swallows his tongue.

"I'm not listening from the couch while you fuck some douche bag," he growls.

Smiling ear to ear, I feel lighter than I have in a very long time. "Then I guess we'll have to stay celibate. Or sleep with each other." I add the last part to elicit a reaction because I have no self-control.

A growl escapes Loki's throat, and he is standing a second later. We're only six feet apart, and I'm not sure what his next move will be, but I'm excited, anxious, and so fucking turned on.

We both hear the lock engage and turn to the door. With a questioning glance, he mumbles, "You're dangerous."

"I'm sure the same has been said about you."

"Hey, guys," Preston says happily as he waltzes into the room. "Loki, man, it's so good to see you standing up." He leans in for a hug and jumps back about ten feet. "Jesus Christ. Did she get to you, too?" Preston looks from me to Loki's groin and back again. "What did you ask him, sis? Please tell me you embarrassed this fucker."

"Ugh, I didn't ask him anything. I'll let you guys hang out. I'm going to shower. I don't want to bother Loki while he's sleeping."

~

IT'S BEEN three hours since Preston dropped off clothes for Loki. *Such a shame. Gawd, that man is sexy.* It's been one hour since I last checked on him. He assured me he didn't need anything, so I told him I would sleep on the couch, and I'm trying. I *am* trying. I wrote for a couple of hours, but my hero keeps growling like Loki, causing me to overheat every damn time.

Come on, Sloane. I have to get over this, eventually. Kicking the blankets off in an angry fit, I sit up. I can't have roommates forever. I haven't always been like this, but I definitely have some issues now, thanks to Jackson. It doesn't take a genius to figure that out.

It's too quiet, and I know I'm not going to get any sleep out here. Chewing on my bottom lip, I check the time. 11:09 p.m. *Loki must be asleep by now, right?*

I can get a few hours of sleep in the chair if I go in right now. Nope. Forget it. I'm not going there. Grabbing my noise-canceling headphones, I switch them on, and The Notorious B.I.G.'s "Hypnotize" blasts in my ears, blissfully erasing all other thoughts.

Standing at my desk, I grip the edges as the music washes over me. Slowly, my body slides back and forth in time to the beat. As the song picks up, my movements get bigger. By the time the chorus hits, my hands have found the keyboard. While I whisper sing the words, I read the last few paragraphs of Marco and Lucy, the main characters in my latest novel.

"All right, guys, what have you got for me tonight?" I whisper.

[finish sex scene]

Well, fuck. The one time I put a place marker in my manuscript had to be with Loki in the next room.

Okay, I can do this. Peering over my shoulder as I hit delete a few times, I'm relieved to see no light or movement coming from the hall to Loki's room.

Rereading the last paragraph a few times, I dig in. Well, I try to anyway. One thousand words later, I have to erase three-quarters of it because my tall, dark, and sexy Marco somehow morphed into my tall, sexy Viking. I freaking wrote Loki's name at least ten times.

The music takes over my body as I shake my ass. Coming to my senses, I scrutinize my currently unfinished book. When nothing else comes, I shake out my arms and check the time. 12:50 a.m.? *Seriously, that's it?*

Slamming the cover of my laptop, I roll my neck. How the hell am I going to get anything done on no sleep? Turning in a circle, I exhale loudly. I know I have two options. Head back up to Emory's and risk the eternal humiliation, or sneak into the bedroom and get a few hours of sleep in the rocking chair that has been my respite as of late.

Oh, Sloane. Like there was ever any question. Here's to praying Loki's medicine made him sleepy tonight. Popping my mouth guard into place, I tiptoe down the hallway.

CHAPTER 7

LOKI

*S*tomp, stomp, slide.

What the fuck is she doing out there? It's after midnight, and I can hear her bare feet pitter-pattering across the hardwood floors. Every time I think it's about to end, it kicks up again with vigor.

This is ridiculous. It's my goddamn house, no matter what she says. Thinking about her argument over the lease has me smiling, though, and I'm not a smiler.

What the hell have you had to smile about over the last ten years, asshole?

Crawling out of bed, I'm careful not to move too fast. The last thing I need is to have a dizzy spell while I'm attempting to spy on Red. *I need to stop calling her Red.* She has a name. "Sloane. Sloane. Sloane," I chant silently on my way down the hall. As the room opens up, her name dies on my lips.

What. The. Fuck. Is. She. Doing?

Her fingers are gliding across her keyboard smoothly, but her shoulders move in contrast to her hips that sway to a song I can't hear. Then they stop, and I suck in a breath only to watch them fall in unison with each other. Left hip, left shoulder. Right hip, right shoulder. And her fucking ass is shimming as her head bobs up and down, then left to right. I can almost see the music through her movements.

I don't know how long I watch, but my body aches for her, and it scares the shit out of me. I know this isn't a good sign. I don't have room for love or lust in my life. My goddamn family rarely sees me as it is. Just as I'm about to turn and head back to bed, she drops it like it's hot. Seriously, drops her ass to the ground and slowly rolls up, shimmying tits I can't see from behind.

Motherfucker.

Suddenly, as if she senses me watching, she straightens and slams her laptop closed. Faster than I should, I slide back into the shadows and beeline it for my room. Laying back, I pull the covers up to my chin like a child and listen.

Minutes later, with my senses heightened, I hear her creeping down the hall toward me. *What the hell is she doing now? Did she catch me being a creeper? What if she's a loony tunes nutbag?* With my eyes open a sliver, I watch as she stands in the doorway. She's warring with herself over something, but what?

Hesitantly, she sucks in a deep breath and moves into the room. Since she didn't kill me while I was unconscious, I'm mostly sure she's not out to hurt me. Still, I'm a little concerned when she stands at my feet, looking everywhere but the bed. In the cover of darkness, she bites her lip while her thumbs tap the pad of her middle fingers. *Such an odd habit.*

What are you up to, Red?

Finally, she heads to the corner of the room and attempts to manhandle the rocking chair. I should say something, but I'm too damn curious to see what she'll do.

It takes her a full three minutes to wrestle the chair, albeit quietly, into place next to my bed. Then she floats silently around the room, piling blanket after blanket onto the old chair before finally climbing in as if she plans to sleep there.

"Red, what the hell are you doing?"

"Gah-ack," she screams, and I watch in dismay as the rocking chair rolls to the back so far she almost tips over. Catching it with my toe, I lean forward to pull her upright before she tumbles to the ground.

When she's steady and facing me, she shouts, "You scared the shit out of me, you asshole."

"Me? I'm not the one creeping around bedrooms at midnight." *What she doesn't know won't hurt her.* "What the hell are you doing in that chair?" Preston's words about not sleeping alone crash into me as I scan her face. Even in the dark, her green eyes sparkle.

"I thought I heard you, ah, make a noise, so I thought I'd sleep in here in case you had a seizure or something." Rubbing her eyes, I can tell they've adjusted to the dark, but they dart around the room, anyway.

"And you plan to sleep sitting up in that chair?" I ask skeptically.

"Of course. Where do you think I've slept for the last couple of weeks?" She sounds a little pissed off, and I guess I would too if I had spent weeks sleeping in a chair.

"Red— What? You slept there every night?"

"Well, most nights," she says into her blankets.

"Where else did you sleep?"

"Um..."

"Where, Red?" Her hesitancy has me smiling, and for the life of me, I can't figure out why I like her so much.

"The first two nights, you wouldn't stay calm unless I was right next to you. Preston and Ash had to slide in to take my place when I had to pee." Warily, she glances up through her lashes as if nervous about my response.

The memory of vanilla enters my conscious, and I vaguely remember pulling her into my side.

"What do you remember?" she asks, crossing her legs in the chair and leaning forward, waiting for my secret.

"What makes you think I remembered something?"

In slow motion, she closes the distance between us. Using the tip of her finger, she smooths the space between my eyebrows.

"You get the tiniest line, right here," she whispers, her breath tickling the scruff that's grown along my jaw. "Your face is otherwise neutral, but this one line appears when something doesn't sit right with you. I saw it the first night when you didn't know who I was. As soon as I mentioned Preston's name, it formed. I saw it again when you were with Emory. You remembered something, right?"

As if realizing she is still cradling my face in a dark room while I lie in bed, she pulls back suddenly. The movement pushes a wave of vanilla my way.

She smells like vanilla and summer rain.

"Yeah, but nothing useful," I admit. Running a hand through my hair roughly, I slide to the other side of the bed and pull open the blankets. "Come on, you're not sleeping in that chair, and I'm sure as hell not sleeping on the couch. We can be adults about this."

"Adults, huh? I've never been accused of that before." Cheekily, she smiles but jumps into bed and adjusts the blankets. With her back to me, I almost miss the whispered, "Thanks, Loki."

~

I LASTED twenty-four hours before I had to go behind Emory's back. I've spent too many years with life or death as my only constants. I don't have time to wait until I *feel* better. If there's a threat, I'm figuring it out. Now.

"She's going to kill you. You know that, right? And I'll be next," Red mutters as we exit the elevator into the penthouse where Preston and Emory live.

"I'm not worried, Red," I say with a grin that falters when I see Emory marching straight for me.

"I told you," Sloane whispers before spinning in place and taking off toward the kitchen.

"Loki Kane. What did I tell you? Wait, is something wrong?" Emory is at my side and already preparing to examine me.

"No, sorry. Everything's fine. I'm fine. I have to talk with Ash and Seth. I'm sorry, this can't wait, not with my job and what I do."

"Loki—"

"Ems, he won't give in on this, and he's right. If he's in danger, just sitting here could put us all in danger," Ashton says, coming up behind me.

Throwing her head back, she stares at the ceiling for a long time before speaking. I chance a sideways glance at Ash, and he just shrugs. Apparently, neither of us dare to talk until she's made some sort of move.

"Fine, you know what? I only went to medical school, don't listen to me. I'm leaving in one hour to check on some patients at the hospital, though, and you will let me examine you before I go. Got it?"

"Yes, ma'am." We stand frozen as she stomps down the hallway. When she's out of earshot, I turn to Ash.

"I need a timeline, man. I'm missing something here, and we both know what that means."

"Yeah, I know. Come with me." He nods to the right, and we head that way. "Seth will be here in an hour. They called him into the office today."

"Why?" I bark.

"Not sure. Vic is in charge, though, so …"

"Fuck that guy."

"Are you ever going to tell me what happened between you two?" It's not the first time Ashton has asked since we started working together. Vic and I have butted heads since the academy, mainly because he's an asshole, but the real reason isn't my story to share.

"Not my story."

"Yeah, yeah. Okay, well, this is where we've set up." Ash pushes open the door to what had been a guest room the last time I was home. Lining the four walls are spreadsheets, maps, photographs, and notes taped haphazardly.

"You guys went a little CSI, didn't you?"

Ashton chuckles and points behind me. Above the doorframe is a full-size cutout of my head, with Loki on one side and Locator HQ on the other.

"Who the fuck did that?" I ask, laughing with him.

"I did," comes a voice my body is having a Pavlovian response to. I take a step back to regard her without gawking like a pervert. Today she is wearing blue camo leggings with gold zippers at the pockets and an off-the-shoulder, navy sweatshirt. Her hair is in her signature ponytail that sways behind her with each step.

I'm noticing for the first time that she's barefoot. Why that matters is beyond my mental capacity at the moment. I can't tear my eyes away, though, as she flexes her toes. I try not to let my gaze rake over her body as I raise my line of sight to her face, but fuck me. My eyes have minds of their own, and they take their time in their perusal of her form.

"How about if we don't eye fuck my little sister, huh?" Preston chuckles as he enters the room, causing Sloane to shrink a bit. The rosiness covering her cheeks makes a slow crawl down her neck.

"She's your sister-in-law. If she marries Loki, then he would finally officially be family, though," Ashton says while pulling down a projector screen.

"Whoa, I'm just helping a guy out. No marriage here," Red blurts, and everyone in the room turns to her. "What? I write the happily ever afters. That doesn't mean I'm looking for one."

What the fuck is going on?

"I think I forgot what a shitshow it can be when we are all together," I mumble and rub my temples.

"Are you okay?"

Somehow, Red heard me and pulled out a chair before I even realized I needed to sit down.

"Remember, Emory said to take it easy. You still need to hydrate, and head injuries are no joke. I had a concussion once, and it took months for me to get back to normal," she says while staring into my eyes. It's like she's talking to herself, and we're along for the ride.

My throat is suddenly so dry it's hard to speak. "I'm fine." It comes out through razor blades. Red studies me from mere inches away for a long minute, and then with a parting glance, she walks away. The second she is out of the room, my focus returns.

"Walk me through what we know," I order.

"Maybe we should wait for Seth?"

"Listen, Ash. We don't have the luxury of time. If someone is after me, I could be leading them all to you just by being here. I need something to jog my brain. I have a feeling... I don't know, but it's right there." I rub my temples again. "I just can't fucking remember."

Placing a bottle of water in front of me, Red murmurs, "Don't force it."

I hadn't even heard her come in. Putting my head in my hands, I realize I'm off my game. This is when mistakes happen, and lives are lost.

CHAPTER 8

SLOANE

"Coming up here was a mistake, Loki. You're not ready."

"I don't have a fucking choice," he bellows, causing me to step back. "This is not a game, Red. I don't have a normal job. I'm not a nine-to-five kind of guy. I hunt people. That is what I do, and if I'm not hunting, then I am the hunted."

"Hey! What the hell did I tell you?" Emory storms into the war room. "First, this is too soon," she says, gesturing around the room. "Second, don't you dare speak to my sister like that, ever. She's the one who figured out your stupid five points west clue. She is the reason you have any idea what's going on right now."

When Loki was missing, he had been able to get some messages to Seth and Ashton. They were spinning circles until I looked at their world from a different angle. I didn't really solve the mystery, but maybe I did nudge them in the right direction.

"Emory," I mutter, "It's fine. You don't have to stick up for me. I'm an adult and can do it myself."

"I'm sorry, Red. I didn't mean to lash out—"

"Honestly, Loki. It's fine. I shouldn't have interrupted. It's my fault."

"What? No—"

"Loki? Emory's right. You should also know that everyone is up to speed—all the Westbrooks and everyone in this room. When Vic cut off support by listing you AWOL, Seth had no choice but to bring us in. He needed all our resources. That should put you at ease with what you say around the girls." Preston's tone is neutral, but his body language is protective as he takes multiple steps closer to Emory.

I stare at Loki. I know he hears the words Preston says, but it doesn't seem like they are computing.

"All of you," he says, pointing around the room. "You all sat here, trying to find me?" Spinning in his chair, he levels me with a stony glare. "You didn't even know me."

Tapping my middle finger, I raise my eyebrows in challenge. "It was good research. Maybe I'll write a story about you someday."

He fights it, but I see the hitch in his lip as something electrifies the air between us.

"You can't handle my story, Red."

"I don't have to. I write my own endings."

"Ah, guys?" Ashton interrupts our staring contest.

"What?" Loki barks.

Taking a few steps forward, I silently take the seat next to him while he glares at me. Sweat is beading on his forehead, and I look to Emory for guidance. She nods to the water, so I slowly uncap it and hand it to him.

"I don't know what's happening," he finally admits. "I just have a feeling something is coming, and it won't be good."

Emory takes the seat opposite him. "Loki, you've had a traumatic head injury that we don't fully know the extent of because of this shitshow. I have been researching and asking colleagues about you. I genuinely trust you will be fine, but you have to give this time. I understand time is not a luxury, so whatever you're about to do, go into it knowing you're not functioning at full capacity. All of this combined can trigger symptoms of PTSD, and you need to be conscious of it. That is not something I can help you with."

Emory turns her attention to me as she stands, and I hate the sympathy, the pity I see there.

"I'm leaving for the hospital. Are you okay?"

Rising from my seat, I meet her at the door. "I'm fine, thanks. I'll see you tonight." I give her a hug with a pit in my stomach. She has spent her entire life taking care of me. She doesn't deserve my baggage weighing her down, too.

Silently, I make my way back to the table and sit next to Loki. I notice his shoulders relax as I pull in my chair. Clasping my hands in front of me, I stare straight ahead. Ashton is explaining something about the map on the wall, but I'm only half listening.

I need to get my shit together.

My life is a mess. I'm a wanderer, a runner, a free spirit chained by insecurity. Why am I even sitting in here? Loki isn't my responsibility, and no one asked for my opinion.

"Hey." Loki leans into me, invading my space and dragging me from my thoughts. "Are you okay? I'm sorry I yelled at you."

Shooing him away with my right hand, I say, "No worries. It's fine." Glancing around the room, I notice everyone is staring at me. "What?" I look behind us, but no one's there.

"Nothing, Sloane. We were just telling Loki how you figured out his clue about five points west. I don't think we ever thanked you," Preston says with a furrowed brow, as if it were some colossal transgression.

It's unsettling, so I try to ease the tension that has filled the room.

With the brightest smile I can muster, I say, "You can all thank me by answering all of my questions from now on."

"Fuck that," Seth says, entering the room. And just like that, the heaviness of the moment dissipates.

"What happened?" Loki and Ash ask at the same time.

"Vic is up to something, but I don't have any idea what. If SIA has anything on what you're running from, Loki, he's escalated it above my clearance," Seth tells the room.

"Okay. Start at the beginning. Run through it all, and let's hope something jars my memory."

"Here's what we know." Ashton moves to the front of the room where a pinboard is hanging. "I spoke to you on October 23rd around 3 p.m. At that point, you had captured, or …" his gaze drifts between Loki and me before continuing, "or eliminated targets B, D, and E."

"My half-siblings," Loki says flatly.

"Yes," Ash agrees contritely. "Target C was on his way to a safe house in East Boston, but you hadn't made your move yet."

"There was a missing piece I needed to find before I made my move on Luca," Loki says, as if remembering a movie clip from years ago.

"Right," Seth takes over. "Then we didn't hear from you for almost a month. Our next correspondence came shortly before Trevor's wedding."

"I was planning to be here for that. I was intercepting Luca, Target C …"

Loki drifts off, and no one speaks while he works things over in his mind.

"I apprehended him at the warehouse, but he was there for something. He was waiting for something. When I got there, he went mental."

I'm having a hard time listening to Loki as he struggles to get his memories in order, especially knowing he is talking about his own brother. As if he hears my internal scuffle, he turns.

"We were blood, Red, but not family. Hunt or be hunted, remember? Only one of us was getting out of that warehouse."

I have to swallow a few times before I can speak. "Loki, you don't owe me any explanations."

With a nod, he returns his attention to Ashton. "Agent Jason Carter took him in with Anton, but I waited at the warehouse."

"You can't remember what you were waiting for, though?" Seth asks more gently than I thought he could manage.

"No." Loki digs his knuckles into his temples again, as if he can push the memories to the surface. "That's where the explosion was, though, I'm sure of it. I can see the building in East Boston. I can see the alley I entered through, the riverbank I hid myself in, but I don't know what I was waiting for. Why the fuck can't I remember?"

Loki cradles his head in his hands, and I look to Preston for help but can't grab his attention. All eyes are focused on the man struggling before us.

"Seth, did SIA find anything at the site?" he asks hopefully.

"Seth," I warn. I know what they found. I may not know Loki well, but I know no man can take all this at once in his condition.

My warning has him raising his head in time to see everyone glancing at one another.

"What?" he asks calmly. Too calmly.

Attempting to pause this conversation, Preston says, "Hey, let's take a break, Loki. Dex and Trevor are coming over for dinner. You'll get to see Lanie and Julia again. I think they both have a bone to pick with you about your meddling."

"What did they find in the warehouse, Preston?" Loki asks again.

The atmosphere in this room is palpable, and I know I have no business being here, but I can find no way to escape. I want to run. When Loki was missing, I could eavesdrop on all this information because it wasn't personal. He was just a face. *Good research*, I'd thought. *God, I really am too naïve for my own good.*

"What did they find?" Loki screams.

"Human remains," Ashton says carefully. "SIA wasn't able to identify the body, but Jason was in charge of the crime scene. He believes someone placed them there, after the explosion, as a diversion."

Instinctively, my hand reaches out to touch Loki's shoulder in support. His forehead crinkles, but he doesn't otherwise respond. We sit in silence for nearly twenty minutes while he works through whatever memories he has —or doesn't have.

"I woke up in the mud, about thirty yards from the site, and inched my way into an alcove on the Charles River. I don't know how long I was there, but two men came looking for me. That's when I sent the first signal and the first memory I have since handing Target C to Jason."

Ashton appears to know what that means and begins rearranging papers all over the walls. I keep my eyes on Loki. At least for now, it seems his memories are lost to us.

"Loki, Vic is gunning for you. He made it clear. He'll bring charges on anyone found helping you."

"Placing an unidentifiable body at the explosion site makes it a lot easier for him to convince people I'm AWOL, though," Loki comments with no emotion.

I suck in a breath. I don't know what it all means exactly, but that doesn't sound good. Will Loki have to figure this out on his own?

Seth glances at me and smiles. "I've never been good at

following the rules, Sloane. Don't worry. We don't leave anyone behind." Turning to Loki, I see he's smiling, too. With his hand in the air, he fist bumps Seth, then Preston, and Ash.

"Welcome to the chaos," Preston says.

They all repeat it like a toast.

"It's something my dad used to say to us," Preston informs me. "It's a battle cry of sorts."

"You're preparing for battle?"

Loki angles his body toward me, his massive thigh pressing against mine, causing a flurry of activity low in my belly. Tilting his head, he observes me. The heat through his jeans is making me dizzy. "I always prepare, Red." His voice rasps as he speaks.

"How will you know when to lay your weapons down?" I ask, though I'm not sure if I'm talking about his situation anymore ... or mine.

Leaning in, so we're inches apart, he levels me with his gaze. "When I win." He doesn't look away, and he doesn't give me space.

We are too close for polite company, and Preston finally clears his throat. In my peripheral vision, I see his sly grin right before giving the goofiest thumbs-up I've ever seen.

"What's that for?"

He doesn't answer, just walks out of the room. Sometimes I wonder if that man ever grew up. A minute later, he comes back with a giant Nike shoebox and places it in front of Loki.

"What's this?" he asks.

I've rarely seen this playful, boyish side of Preston, but I've been told it exists. Whatever the thumbs-up was about is going to cause me nothing but trouble. I can see it in his face.

He looks under the table at Loki's combat boots before answering. "GG said you were going to need these."

"Lanie's grandmother? I've never even met her. Why the hell would she leave me these?"

"We don't question anything that woman does, but she hasn't been wrong yet," Ashton says, smiling like a madman.

We all watch as Loki opens the box. On top of a pair of running shoes is a note scribbled in the chicken scratch of an eighty-year-old woman.

Dear Chaser,

You're gonna need these to get her back. Life's a marathon, not a sprint.

GG

CHAPTER 9

LOKI

"So, I'm going to go ... um, see if I can help with dinner. You said Sylvie is coming soon?" Red asks Preston, already halfway out the door like her ass is on fire.

"She should be here any minute," Preston replies with a stupid smirk on his face.

"Okay. See ya."

Before I can say anything, she's gone. "What the hell was that about? And what am I supposed to do with these?" Holding up the running sneakers, I inspect them. Size fourteen. "How did she know my shoe size?" I wear a thirteen in everything but running shoes. I'm sure even Preston doesn't know that.

Every guy in the room just shrugs. Finally, Ashton laughs. "GG must have read it in her cards."

"Don't go talking bad about GG," Trevor says from the doorway. "That woman can probably put a curse on us from her mountaintop in Vermont."

I stand quickly, happiness filling my chest at the sound of my friend's voice. He's had a shitty few years. His father had been an unwilling partner in my sperm donor's illegal activities. When Trevor found out, he used all his energy to take down his father. Our stories, while different, parallel each other in ways I wish I could have prevented. Allowing the bitterness to take over Trevor's life for so long will always be one of my biggest regrets.

I couldn't have succeeded in my objective without his help, though. Trevor and his software played an integral role in taking down the most dangerous crime family of our lifetime. My family.

"You," comes a feisty voice I've only heard a few times before. *Julia*. "How are you feeling?" she asks through narrowed eyes.

"I'm good. We're just trying to piece a few things together," I say evasively.

"Good." She marches straight for me but stops three feet away. With her hands on her hips, she stares at me for a long time. Then the floodgates open wide.

"Thank you, Loki. Thank you for bringing Trevor back to Charlie and me. Thank you for not listening to his stubborn ass. Thank you for putting your nose into everyone else's business. Thank you for never giving up, for always watching our backs, even when we were too dumb to know. Thank you for playing God and for manipulating so much. I want to know how you orchestrated everything, but that can wait. Right?" She looks up at Trevor, who smiles at her with love.

"Yeah, I think a lot of this can wait," he says, coming to her side just before she launches herself at me. For such a petite woman, she sure can squeeze the hell out of a hug.

"How, how did you know everything? How did you know Lanie would be perfect for Dex or that I needed Trevor?"

"Jules, you just threw a lot at him," Dexter says from the hallway. "It's looking a little crowded in there. How about if we all meet in the family room, and we can let Loki have some space before the inquisition?"

"Holy ship, are you kidding me?" Lanie has squeezed her body between Dex and the doorframe to get a peek into the room. "Loki! I don't know if I should be angry at you or hug you and never let you go."

Peering around the room, I suddenly wish Red were here. Somehow, I know she would get everyone to back off and give me room to breathe. It's true that I helped bring these four together, but it wasn't entirely altruistic. I needed Trevor whole; I needed his help, and when he lost Julia, he was never the same. Bringing them back together was the only way for me to move forward. Plus, I fucking hated seeing him so miserable.

Releasing me from the hug, Julia finally takes a step to the side and laughs. She picks up GG's note, then holds it up for Lanie.

"GG found her next victim," she says through a fit of giggles. I haven't heard someone giggle in years. It's an odd sound. Do all civilian women giggle? I'm used to operatives, and they most definitely are not gigglers.

Pinching the bridge of my nose, I turn to Dex. "Yeah, I have no clue what that note means or why the fuck she would buy me sneakers."

Entering the overly crowded room, he claps me on the back before pulling me in for a man hug. "You will. It seems you've got a runner on your hands."

"A runner?"

"Yup," Preston says cheerily. "And not of the athletic variety. You may have played the merry fucking fairy in our lives all these years, but GG is the Godmother of Greatness. If she's pulling your cards now, I'd say you're up next for the nuptials."

I glance around the room, and every goddamn person in here smiles and nods as if that is just a fact of life.

"I don't know how to tell you all this, but I'm in hiding. We don't know who is after me. I live by a *here today gone tomorrow* mantra. There are no wedding bells in my future. I don't even know a woman, let alone one that would be a runner, as GG called her."

Don't forget about Red, a voice in the back of my mind tries to scream, but I shut it down before it can go any further. I'm a master of compartmentalizing. In my line of work, you have to, or you die.

With annoying confidence, Preston hands me Red's water bottle and asks, "You sure about that, man?"

I stare at the bottle for a moment, and then as if I conjured her, I hear Red's voice behind Lanie.

"Oh, hey, Lanie. You're early, Emory said you wouldn't be here for an hour, but I'm glad. I may have just started a small fire in the kitchen."

With all the chaos of a sitcom, we stumble over each other to get to the kitchen.

When I finally make it into the hallway, Red appears confused.

"Why the hell is everyone running?" she asks, my gaze locked on hers.

"Red, you just said there was a fire in the kitchen," I repeat her words while letting my senses feel for danger. I don't smell smoke, and I don't feel any heat. Either it's a small fire, or we overreacted.

"Jesus, Sloane," Preston bellows. "The next time you say there's a fire in the kitchen, make sure you mean flames and not a pissed-off French chef."

I stare down at her, unaware that I had once again closed the space between us. We are less than a foot away, and I tower over her short frame, but I can't take my eyes off her. When I'm this close, I can see the light smattering of freckles that cover her nose.

"Your eyes are smiling again. They sparkle when they're like this."

"It's those Irish genes," she whispers.

"Smiling eyes have been known to steal hearts away."

"Only in folk songs, Loki. Sometimes, smiling eyes are

just a way to get through the day." She nods her head and slips passed me down the hall.

I swallow, trying to compose myself. My heart races, and I feel lightheaded. The fucked up thing is, I don't think it's from my injuries. I think Red causes this reaction, and I don't know how I feel about that.

Clearing his throat, Seth steps into the hall. "If I were a betting man, I'd say you found your runner." Before I can pull my head from my ass to correct him, he continues, "I'm going to see what kind of information I can pull from SIA using Ashton's network."

"You will do no such thing. Not right now, anyway. We're having family dinner in one hour, which means all family, including you, Seth. You may not like it, but you're one of us now. Drinks and appetizers are on their way out," Sylvie says as she gracefully floats down the long hall.

When she reaches us, she gives Seth a big hug before shooing him to join the others. Turning her attention to me, the tears in her eyes make me uncomfortable. This woman took me in during my darkest days, and for the last ten years, I've avoided all meaningful communication with her. If something happened to me, I didn't want her to suffer the same fate she had when my parents, then her husband, died.

Reaching up, Sylvie cradles my face in her hands. "It's nice to have you home, Loki. My heart's been missing a piece without you here. Dinner will be ready at seven. Do you have a few minutes for an old lady?"

"You're not old, Sylvie, and I always have time for you," I tell her, wishing that were the truth.

"Hopefully, one day, that will be true, son. Come on. Let's sit in here." Sylvie walks into the war room and spins in place, taking in everything on the walls.

This must be painful for her. She thinks of me as one of her own children.

What would my mom have done in this situation?

"We don't have to stay in here, Sylvie. Why don't we use Preston's office?" I plead, not wanting to see her upset.

On a sigh, she pulls out a chair and points. I know that's my cue to sit. "I feel like I'm being put in time-out again."

Sylvie laughs. "When you boys were little, I rarely had to put you in time-out. It was usually Preston or Colt."

God, I miss those days.

"But, you're never too old for a heart to heart," she says gently.

Every muscle in my body tenses as she takes a seat.

"We've missed you, Loki. How are you?"

Unsure of what she knows, I keep it vague. "I'm good, Sylvie. I've missed being home."

"Is it over?"

Is it over?

"Don't bother sugar-coating anything with me, Loki. I've sat here every day since Preston returned from the hospital. I've listened in on all the briefings, I've written checks to people that should probably be in jail, but I did it to find you, and I'd do it again, too."

My ears prickle.

"I know you've kept your distance to protect us. We all know that, but every step away you take, the harder my heart holds on. That's what mothers do, Loki. We hang onto every scrap of hope, so I want you to be honest with me when I ask you this question. Is it over?"

Hanging my head, I debate how to answer and realize for the first time just how tired I am. Not physically, my body will heal. I'm tired of this life, of living in the shadows.

"I'm not sure, Sylvie. I can't remember, but I know something or someone is coming."

"So you'll leave again?" she asks sadly.

Glancing up, her tears gut me. "I don't know. My agency has appointed someone to my position, and nothing is making sense. I don't have any resources out here on my own."

Laying her hand over mine, she squeezes. "How quickly my pups forget. Loki, look at me."

It takes every ounce of courage I have, but I meet her gaze.

"You've always been a part of this pack. Even if you lose your way, they'll help guide you home." As if on cue, a howl erupts from the family room. "Sounds like the rest of the Westbrooks just arrived." She smiles. "You've never been alone, Loki. You've always had your pack. Perhaps it's time you found your way back and let them protect you for the rest of this journey I know you never asked for."

"But I've trained—"

"Yes, I know," she cuts me off. "You've trained for this. But did you ever ask yourself why? Or what you're going to do when this threat you've lived with your entire life no longer exists? This life wasn't your dream, Loki. This life became a mission you felt an obligation to fulfill. I was here the day Seth got word that you had handed over the last of your cocksuckers."

She said it with such a straight face I almost missed it. The hint of a smile forms and lets me know I heard her correctly.

"Here's the thing, Loki. Clint and I never had any secrets from each other. If you hadn't been just a child when all this happened, I would have called them cocksuckers, too."

"Ah, okay. Can you not say that word again? I'm not sure how to handle it," I admit. Part of me wants to bust open with laughter, but a bigger piece that still sees this woman as my adopted mother has me flushing a deeper shade of red than even Sloane. The thought of Sloane has me shifting uncomfortably in my chair.

"Oh dear, if you're spending time with Sloane, you'll have to get used to much dirtier words than that." She smirks.

What the fuck is that girl writing?

"Can I ask you a question?" Her voice is soothing.

"Of course." I'm not sure what she wants to ask, but I owe this woman my life.

"You went home. Why now?"

I had gone to my childhood home for the first time since my parents died when I left clues for Seth, but I don't remember much about being there.

"I'm not sure," I admit.

"It's been years, Loki. Why hadn't you gone back?"

"It doesn't belong to me," I blurt, causing Sylvie to gasp.

"Of course it does. Who do you think it belongs to?" she asks quietly.

"I know it belongs to me legally, but I'm sure that was an oversight."

"Your parents left everything to you. I'm sure Clint and I went over all that with you before you left for college." Sylvie's voice is full of concern, and I can see her second-guessing herself.

"You did," I assure her. "You both did. What I mean is, they left me money because they had to. They didn't have any other children."

"I'm confused, Loki. Your parents left everything to you because they loved you."

"But they didn't trust me," I yell, and immediately have to rein myself in. I've never told anyone my biggest fear. The reason I joined SIA, the reason I've stepped away from those I love.

From the corner of my eye, I see Ashton standing in the doorway, but Sylvie waves him off.

With the gentleness of a mother speaking to a scared child, she asks, "Why do you say that, Loki?"

Do I really want to get into this right now?

Standing, Sylvie crosses the room and shuts the door.

"We're not leaving this room until we discuss this, Loki.

Somewhere along the way, Clinton and I failed your parents, and I will not stand for that. Tell me why you feel they didn't trust you so I can finally set the record straight."

My eyes sting as I stare at the table. Contemplating my next words, I speak in a voice so low, I wonder if she can even hear me. "Dad worked his entire life building Kane & Co into what it was. When I was little, we talked about how I would work beside him one day, and he'd change the name to Kane & Son. I saw the will, Sylvie. When things got bad with Black, he and Mom changed the terms. They didn't trust me with his namesake, his legacy. They made sure if they passed, they would sell the company, piece by piece. I never had a chance to take it because I was only fifteen, but I know they thought I would sell out and become like Black. They didn't want his dirty hands on the company they spent a lifetime building."

I feel, not so much see, Sylvie sit back in her chair with a heavy sigh. My body is shaking with rage, hurt, and overwhelming sadness. Too many emotions are rolling through my veins that I don't dare utter another word.

CHAPTER 10

SLOANE

"They've been in there a long time," Preston observes.

One of his brothers, Colton, I think, whines, "I'm fucking starving. What the hell can they be talking about?"

Definitely Colton. Colton's the goofball. Ashton, the brain, works with Loki. Easton is in Vermont, and Preston has one other brother ... Glancing around the room, I find him in the corner. The lone wolf, Halton. He's a grumpy son of a bitch.

"Maybe someone should go check on them? They probably just lost track of time," Dex suggests from the other side of the room. I'm busy watching Halton in the corner, so I don't notice the childish game going on around me until it's too late.

With the slightest hint of a smile, Halton raises his pointer finger and places it to the side of his nose. It's such a strange thing to do, but he's staring right at me, raising his eyebrow and nodding to the side. Following his line of sight, I glance around the room. Every damn person in here has a finger pressed to the side of their noses.

What the hell?

"Not it," they all say in unison now that I'm aware of their ridiculous ritual.

"Not it? What are we, twelve?" I cross my arms, only to realize I sound like a sullen teenager. "Ugh, fine. I'll go get them."

Every man in the room—the Westbrooks, Dex, and Trevor—all stare at me with wide eyes. "What do you think they're going to do? I'll just knock on the door and tell them dinner is ready."

"But, Mom shut the door," Ashton stage whispers.

"Oh shit," Dex grumbles.

Making eye contact with Lanie, the only one incapable of lying to me, I silently plead for some direction. Biting her lip, she seems nervous, which causes my heart rate to spike. Finally, she shrugs like she doesn't know the right answer.

Freaking perfect.

"Jesus," I grumble, marching toward the hall.

"Don't curse," I hear a chorus of male voices say behind me.

Inhaling a deep breath, I take tentative steps once I'm out of view of the peanut gallery. Reaching the room, I pause. Unnaturally nervous, I raise my hand to knock just as Sylvie's stoic voice filters out from beneath the door.

"Loki, you're an idiot."

"What?" he asks, sounding shocked.

Good, me too. I've never heard Sylvie speak like that to anyone.

"Let me rephrase. You're a goddamn idiot."

"She's pissed," Ashton whispers beside me, and I almost scream. "You better give them a few minutes before interrupting." He moves passed me to enter the restroom.

"You want me to just stand here, eavesdropping?" I hiss.

"It wouldn't be the first time, right?" He smirks.

Asshole.

Okay, so what? Maybe I'll just wait for a break in conversation?

"Why am I an idiot?" Loki's words have me pressing my ear to the door.

"How old were you when your father changed his last name to match you and your mother's?"

His stepdad changed his name? What did he do? Take Loki's mother's name?

"I was five. He wanted to do it before I started school but had some pushback from his family."

"Not just pushback, Loki. His family disowned him."

"I never understood why he did it," Loki mumbles so quietly I almost don't hear him.

"You never understood?" Sylvie screeches, so unlike her customarily composed self. "Loki, he did it because the only thing that mattered was that the three of you were a family. He never wanted you to have to explain why you had a different name than your parents. He never wanted you to feel forced to discuss Black-hole until you were ready. He did it because he loved you and your mother more than anything else in this world."

"He gave up his family name, his family money, everything he worked for."

"Mostly," Sylvie agrees. "But, Loki, did you grow up poor?"

"What? No, you know that. I had a great life."

"Your father gave up a lot, but he left with his trust fund intact. He chose to use that to support you guys while he built his own empire, and I know for a fact, he would have done it a hundred times over. You, Loki, and your mom were all that mattered to that man."

"I know he loved me, Sylvie. That was never the issue. He didn't trust me to run his company. He was so sure I would cave to Antonio Black that he sold his company before either of us could get our hands on it. That was my legacy. He told me it was. We were supposed to run it together," Loki roars.

"Do you know that your father hated his family company?

He hated working there. He hated what the company stood for and how his family ran it. He worked there because it was what they expected of him."

Loki is silent, so Sylvie continues.

"I remember the day your parents went to change the terms of their will because they went back and forth about it for months, wanting to do the right thing. They came to our house first and dropped you off to play with the boys. You were about eleven at the time, and they were still wondering if they were making the right choice. Do you remember what you were doing when you were eleven, Loki?"

"Probably getting into trouble with Preston or one of the other boys," Loki grumbles.

"Sometimes, yes." Sylvie laughs. "But when you were eleven, you decided you were going to be a surgeon. Do you remember that? You would spend hours in my library with Ashton. You read every medical journal I could get into your hands while Ash plugged away building computers out of random pieces."

Picturing Loki, as a pre-teen tucked away in a library, makes my chest warm.

I bet he was a cute nerd.

"We spent hours in there," Ashton whispers, scaring the shit out of me again. "What did I miss?"

"Shh," I hiss. *Great, he made me miss Loki's response.*

"You told your parents that you were going to be a doctor. By the time you were thirteen, you had read more medical journals than most students during their residencies. John believed in you, Loki. He didn't want anything to keep you from your dreams, not even him. They didn't sell their company because they didn't trust you ... they sold their company because they had trust *in* you. They believed in you so much that if something happened to them, they wanted you to be free to choose your own path."

"They wouldn't have approved of the path I chose," Loki says so quietly I barely make it out through the door.

"Oh, Loki. I can't say what they would or wouldn't have approved of. But your mother was my best friend, and she knew you would face tough choices because of her actions. She never once regretted having you. You were the love of her life, but she did regret the life she brought you into. I believe she and John would have understood. I also know they would be proud of you. But I have to ask, Loki, what now? How long can you live like this?"

"I-I don't know."

"I think now is the time for you to make some hard choices, and when you do, for once, put yourself first."

"I don't think this is over, Sylvie. I can't shake the feeling that someone is coming for me, or for something, but I don't know what. I've survived on instinct because my instincts have never been wrong. I don't know where I'll be after this is over, but that's the thing. It's not over. It's my job to protect you all because it's my fault you were ever in danger."

"Bullshit," Sylvie spits.

Ashton gasps beside me. "I'm not sure I've ever heard my mother swear before," he says in awe.

"It's true," Loki screams. "If it weren't for me, Trevor could have had a normal childhood. Black would never have met his father if he hadn't been coming here for me. My parents would still be alive if I hadn't begged to come home early that summer, and none of the Westbrooks would be living with security that rivals the president if it weren't for me."

"Sit down, Loki." Sylvie just went from pissed to enraged. "For all intents and purposes, I am the only parent you have left, so you listen, and you listen good. My family has always had security because that's what happens when you have the kind of money Clinton was born with. Trevor's father had every opportunity to research his business partner, but he made a mistake. He took the easy way out."

I hear the scraping of a chair and feet shuffling. For a moment, I panic they will catch us eavesdropping, but then Sylvie speaks again, more gently this time. "Your parents are gone, there is no making up for that, but it isn't your responsibility to try."

"I don't know what to do if I'm not fighting for them," Loki admits, his voice sounding strangled.

"You'll find your way, Loki. But it's time to let your family back in. That's how we have always worked. You need us, and we've missed you so much. I understand that you still have work to do, but I think you need to clean up your loose ends and join the real world again. Every time you leave on a mission, you steal ten years from my life. I'm ready to have you home."

"I'm not sure I know how to live in the real world," he says with a humorless laugh.

"GG told me you might say that."

"Please tell me you're joking?"

"I wish I were, but that crazy old lady hasn't been wrong yet, and she had a lot to say about you during her last visit."

"What the hell could she have said about me? She's never met me before!"

The door suddenly opens, causing Ashton and me to barrel through. With his weight pressing into me, I stumble quickly toward the floor.

Shit, this is going to hurt.

With speed I didn't see coming, Loki wraps his arm around my shoulders, effectively hauling me one-handed from the hardwood floor just before my face hit. No one saved Ashton, and he tumbled to the ground beside us with a painful sounding grunt.

"I think you just took your first step in catching your runner," Sylvie says cryptically.

Turning me in his arms, Loki inspects me. "Are you okay?"

"Ah, yeah, I'm fine."

"Yeah, me too, buddy. Thanks for the help." Ashton's words drip with sarcasm.

"What do you mean? What runner?" Loki asks Sylvie's retreating form.

"You'll see," she calls over her shoulder.

Loki stands, holding me in close proximity, searching my eyes. "Are you a runner?"

"Come on, guys, I'm fucking starving," Colton interrupts from the doorway. "Dude, why the hell are you on the floor?" Crossing to Ashton, he reaches down and helps him up. "You guys ready to eat? I'm dying over here. Let's go."

Shaking free from Loki's grasp and his gaze, I turn to the door. "Yeah, I'm ready. Dinner smells amazing." Daring one last peek over my shoulder, I find Loki staring at me, unmoving.

"Ah, are you coming?" I ask him.

He nods but doesn't say anything.

"Okay, we'll see you out there then."

I try to calm my breathing in the hallway, then rush to follow the sounds of laughter and love pouring from my sister's dining room. Glancing around, I see an empty seat between Ashton and Seth. It will force Loki to sit at the other end of the table. *Thank God*. I need a little space. Our encounters are getting more and more intense—I don't do intense!

Am I a runner? Damn right I am. I often think of myself as a con-artist, except I don't steal anything. I may use men for experiences in my stories, but I take nothing from them. I don't even take the gifts they give me when I leave. And I always leave. That's the thing. I have a meet-cute, the *get to know you*, the *big breakup,* and I'm on my way. I've always been ridiculously good at making up the happily ever after.

I've had to be. Until Emory met Preston, happily ever after only existed for us in fairytales.

"Sloane?" Seth asks, leaning in closer so he can lower his voice. "Are you okay?"

"Huh? Yeah, why?"

Using his napkin to cover his mouth, he whispers, "Sylvie looks like the cat that got the cream, and the glare Loki has focused in our direction could start a fire."

My head whips up. I don't even pretend to search because I can feel him from across the room. When our eyes meet, my body goes up in flames.

Using my napkin, I glance down and whisper, "Is he pissed I was eavesdropping?"

This time, it's Ashton that grabs his napkin and leans into me. "That's not the look of a pissed-off man."

"Jesus Christ, put down the napkins," Loki barks across the table.

Giving Seth and Ashton the side-eye, I notice we are all sitting holding red cloth napkins over our mouths. We couldn't be more obvious if we tried.

"Language, Loki," Sylvie admonishes, but laughter laces her tone.

While sitting at the opposite end of the table, Dexter makes a big production of looking between Loki and me.

"Did you guys have sex?" Julia asks, pointing at me, then Loki with a fork.

"What? No, of course not," I screech.

"Don't sound so disgusted by it," Loki grumbles.

What the hell is happening here?

"Loki, you've been unconscious for most of the time I've known you." I sound hysterical, and I can't control it.

"Consent is sexy, you know," Julia chimes in because she can't help herself. "But you want to, right?" she adds, leaning in conspiratorially.

"Oh, he definitely wants to," Dexter laughs.

"I can't swear at the table, but these guys can talk about a sex life that has nothing to do with them?" Loki pleads his case to Sylvie.

Her placating smile gets him nowhere, and he sinks back into his chair, sulking.

"Je—ez," Colton corrects his language with practiced skill. "You guys are dropping like flies! I gotta say, though, Dex, you've got to chill out with the grand gestures a little. Not that you don't deserve an amazingly grand gesture, Sloane," he informs me before returning to the rest of the table, "but come on, dude! How are us little guys supposed to live up to those?"

"What?" My head is spinning, and I'm seriously trying to figure out how many steps it'll take me to get to the front door.

"Who said anything about a grand gesture?" Loki asks. "Seriously, what the hel—heck is going on here?"

"I think you've been away so long that you forgot what it's like when all you boys get together." Sylvie laughs. "And, our family keeps growing. Now we have Julia to add her special brand of fun to the mix, too."

"Thank you, Sylvie." Julia nods her head as you would to royalty.

I think I'm going to be sick.

CHAPTER 11

LOKI

Sloane is literally turning green as I volley between one asinine comment to the next.

"Sloane, if MSL lands in one of your books, do I get an acknowledgment?" Dexter, the dickwad, asks.

"Ah, MSL? I ... er—"

"Doesn't Loki have to screwup big time before the grand gesture?" Colton asks.

"Well, according to Sloane's books, yes, but I've been doing research. There doesn't always have to be a big fallout in romance novels. I do think they make for better reading, though," Julia explains.

"Why can't the girl be the fuck up?" Halton asks.

"Halt, language," Sylvie reprimands before conceding. "But good point."

"I totally think the girl could be the screwup. Geez, I almost ruined things with Dex because I couldn't get out of my own way." Leaning across the table, Lanie asks, "You won't make me seem like a total moron when you write our story, will you?"

"Ah, it won't really be your story. I was just asking for

ideas. I write fiction. It will all be fiction," Sloane replies on autopilot.

"Our story will be your bestseller," Preston boasts.

"No way. Our story has love, heartbreak, even the freaking mob. There is no way your story can top ours," Trevor challenges.

"Neither of you would have stories if I didn't help you get your girls," Dexter points out. "So, by default, I think that makes Lanie and I the top story."

"You're delusional."

"Get out of here."

"I'm not going to lie, Loki has some pretty big shoes to fill," Colton adds to the fray.

I glance around the table. Sylvie is thoroughly enjoying herself while everyone else is arguing about who had the best fucking love story. *How the hell does anyone survive in this chaos daily?* Glancing at Halton's sour face, I realize he's onto something because no one bothers him. On his other side is Seth, who shockingly looks comfortable and at ease here.

That's when I notice Sloane. Her thumbs are tapping her middle fingers at a frantic pace, and it makes me antsy for her.

Noticing my agitated state, Sylvie places a hand on mine, requiring me to look away from Sloane and make eye contact with her.

"She's not used to the chaos that comes with this big family, but if there was ever a person that needed the love of a large group, it's her." Sylvie nods her head in Sloane's direction, and I notice she's adjusting her ponytail again. That's the third time in less than five minutes. "It's okay," Sylvie encourages. "This is a lot for her. She was fine at Christmas, but I think that's because all the attention was on Emory. Go ahead."

Not that I needed Sylvie's blessing to leave dinner, but it sure makes the guilt a little less heavy. I stand so abruptly I nearly knock over my chair, causing everyone to turn in my direction.

"Loki, are you okay?" Emory asks, standing immediately.

"Yeah, I think I just need to lie down for a while. Sloane, think you can, ah ..." *Fuck, what the hell can I ask her to help with and not sound like a dick?*

"Yup, coming." As if rescued from the electric chair, Red jumps to her feet, saving me from having to come up with an excuse to get her out of here.

"Oh, hey, Sloane? Hold on a minute," Julia says while reaching behind her. "GG said to give you these."

I watch in shock as Julia tosses a giant box of condoms across the dinner table. Red stands frozen in place, so I snatch them from the air and shoot Julia a nasty look.

Taking Red by the arm, I guide her to the elevator. Once we're alone in the car, I let out a sigh of relief. Leaning against the wall, I pinch the bridge of my nose. From the corner of my eye, I watch Red. She's in shock, and I guess I would be too if I weren't used to those guys.

Taking a step forward, I bend my knees to get a good look at her. "You okay? I know they're crazy, but they mean well."

Red nods and attempts a smile, but I know it's bullshit.

"I forgot how intense it is when we're all together. Usually, Easton and Halton balance out the crazy, but with East up north, I guess Halt just wanted to stay in his own lane."

"I guess."

The elevator chimes, and I hold the door for her to exit first. As we walk down the hall, I keep my eye on her. I'm not sure why or what the hell I'm supposed to do now. I just knew she needed to get out of the pressure cooker, and I did, too. Halfway to our apartment, I hear a loud crash.

"Th-That came from your apartment."

She's right. No one else lives this far down.

The noise has Red freezing in place, so I grab her hand

and pull her back the way we came. Pressing the button while keeping myself between her and our apartment, I pray it comes quickly. The stairs are too risky since we would have to pass our door to get to them, and we can still hear chaos coming from the end of the hall. Thankfully, the elevator pings almost instantly.

Thank fuck.

Shoving Red inside, I want to press the button and make a run for our apartment, but I have no weapons on me. The smart thing is to get to Preston's and grab Seth. Hopefully, whoever is in there will still be around in three minutes.

The second the door opens, I drag Red into Preston's foyer.

"Seth," I yell.

He comes barreling out of the dining room, followed by Ash.

"Someone is in our apartment. Ash, take Red. Seth, are you armed?"

"Always."

"Good, let's go," I order, already standing in the elevator car.

The gruffness of my voice seems to wake up Red.

"Wait, no, Loki, wait," she says just as the doors slide closed.

"Loki?" Seth barks. "Focus, okay?"

Realizing I'm still staring at the doors, I shake Red's panicked expression from my mind.

"Who's in the apartment?"

"I didn't see anyone, just heard a crash. I'm not armed, and I had Red. I know how that sounds, Seth. I just meant I couldn't leave her in the elevator alone."

"Mhm."

I give him the stink-eye as he pulls a gun from the holster at his side. Handing it to me, he leans down and takes a smaller one from beneath his pant leg. The elevator chimes, and Seth exits first, hugging the left side of the wall. I follow behind on the right.

He reaches my front door first and motions for me to go ahead. Rushing past him in near silence, I stand on the other side of the door as he slowly pushes it open. I can see from here that someone trashed the place, but it's quiet now. I enter first. With Seth at my back, we watch the blindsides. The kitchen and family room are clear, as is the front hall closet. That only leaves the half bath and master suite. Creeping toward that end of the apartment, we find the half bath empty, but the bedroom door closed.

Silently, Seth motions me ahead. I slowly turn the knob with a racing heart as Seth rushes through the door to the left, and I cover his right. I push forward, checking the attached bathroom, and find it empty, too.

Lowering my gun, I see Seth standing at the foot of the bed staring at the wall. Turning, my stomach roils. *She's mine, and I'm coming for her.* It's sprawled out across the room in red paint like graffiti.

"Why the fuck didn't the alarm go off?" Seth asks, already in motion. He knows the drill and what needs to be done.

I'm frozen to my spot. They're coming for Red, and I'm ill-equipped to handle that information. *I'm too close to her already, is that it? Is that why I feel as if I might be sick?* This is exactly why I have been single all these years and why Seth keeps his daughter a secret. Wives and children are considered a weakness in this world.

"Loki," Seth barks, "snap out of it." He moves around me, engaging transponders to short circuit any listening devices that may have been placed in here while we were upstairs. When they're all turned on, he speaks again. "This is not on you. I don't know what the fuck is going on or who is coming for you and Sloane, but we will figure it out. First things first, we need to get the two of you to the safe house."

"No, let's get Sloane to the safe house. I'm staying and hunting this fucker."

"Listen to me, Loki. As your friend and as your colleague. We don't know who is after you or how Sloane fits into any of this. What we do know is that Vic is gunning for you, and now we are without SIA's help. Think of this rationally, please. Your best bet is to head to the house with Sloane and let Ashton and I figure this out. Plus, I've gotten to know Sloane. She won't last in a safe house alone. She needs you there." His demeanor changes as he talks about her.

His words hit me like a punch to the gut. *"She needs you there."*

"You want me to go into hiding while that asshole tries to discredit me and all the work I've done?" I'm talking about Vic, and Seth knows it.

"We don't know for sure that's what he's doing—"

"For fuck's sake, Seth. Someone placed a body at the explosion site, my explosion site after the fact. Only someone with insider knowledge would have been able to pull that off. I know we haven't gone over every detail yet, but that is the only logical explanation." My body seethes with anger.

"I know, but why is he bringing Sloane into it? It doesn't make any sense."

"I don't know," I admit. "But the note I was carrying said 'get Sawyer out' and 'they know she's with me,' right? I must have meant Sloane, not Sawyer, or maybe I transcribed the name wrong. Sloane has to be what they want. I just don't know why." My voice breaks a little on the last part.

"Hey," Seth says with vehemence, "we will figure this out. You need to remember that you're still healing, Loki. For so many reasons, let Ashton and I handle this."

"If Vic so much as catches wind that you've seen me, let alone are helping me, he'll fire you. Or worse, arrest you for aiding and abetting."

"Loki, that dingle dick may have fucked with my family

and me once, but I won't let him do it again. I'm fishing in the SIA pond this week," he says with a grin. "Then, if he wants to fire me, let him. Ash will have access to everything we need."

"This is asking a lot of you, Seth. You have an obligation at home you have to consider," I remind him. "You're all Sadie has."

His eyes soften as he lets down his guard. Sadie is and has always been his weakness.

"Loki, when Vic first listed you as AWOL, Ash and I laid everything on the line. Your family has taken me into their lives, their homes as one of their own. He and Sylvie have already made it clear that they are on my side no matter what happens. Sylvie even took Sadie overnight so I could be here helping Ash."

That grabs my attention. "She did? How did she know? I thought you kept Sadie separate from everything."

"I do, but those Westbrooks have a way of getting what they want," he says warmly. "What they wanted was to make sure I had all the tools necessary to help bring you home. Along the way, Sylvie found a soft spot for me, I guess." His eyes are downcast as if that news embarrasses him.

"She has a way of doing that," I agree. "But how does no one else know?"

"Ash said he understood why I kept her a secret. It's all about safety. Until I walk away from SIA, I'll protect that secret with my life if it means keeping her alive." He grins. "And Sylvie said it wasn't her story to tell."

*Freaking Sylv*ie. "She might just be the true mastermind of this fucked-up family."

"For sure, that woman has eyes and ears everywhere."

"You know, our time at SIA might be coming to an abrupt halt sooner than either of us anticipated?" I don't know what the future holds, but for me, for the first time in ten years, I'm feeling okay with walking away.

"I know, man. I've been thinking the same thing. I've stayed this long because of you. I owe everything I have to you, but when you're done, I'm out. I don't know what I'll do, but the time is coming."

I hate that he's stuck with this wretched life because of me. I'm also eternally grateful.

"I wouldn't be alive without you, man. I have a feeling Ash might have something up his sleeve for us when this mission is over. He's hinted at it before. I think he's just been waiting for us to be ready."

Choking on a laugh, Seth says, "That man is one scary fucker dressed in a million-dollar suit."

I grin because Seth has no idea. Ashton has been my secret weapon since I was fifteen, and I know that someday, the three of us will do great things. But first, I need to put the past behind me, once and for all.

"Let's get Ash down here. We're going to need him to wipe every piece of technology we own, maybe replace some. Then we'll gather whatever troops we have at our disposal to vacate the premises."

"The only troops we have right now are your family, Loki."

"Apparently, they're our family now." I give him a stern look. "Once Sylvie adopts you, she never let's go. The family is big enough now that they'll work as a diversion, and Preston has enough cars in the garage to pull it off."

"Yeah, but explaining this to them is going to take some work. Sloane and Emory are going to freak the fuck out. And Sylvie? She's just getting used to you being home. This will break her heart."

Swallowing razor blades before I speak, I say, "I know that, Seth. But what choice do we have? You, Ashton, and I will have to make them understand. There is no other way right now."

CHAPTER 12

SLOANE

"Ash went down there over an hour ago. What the fuck could they be doing? And why aren't they giving us any updates?" Preston grumbles.

Sylvie is across the room but shockingly says nothing about his cursing. *I guess she's probably more worried than all of us. Those are her boys.*

"Hey, luv. Are you doing okay? I can't imagine how scary this is for you," Lanie asks softly.

"Yeah, I mean, I didn't see anything, so I don't know any more than the rest of you. I guess I'm just scared for Loki."

The elevator chimes and everybody turns toward the sound. Seconds later, Loki walks in, flanked by Seth and Ashton. Loki's demeanor is stern, determined, and laser-focused solely on me. My body heats under his scrutiny, but he stops halfway into the room.

"Someone gained access to our apartment," Loki tells the room. With his gaze on me, the rest of our audience fades into the background. "They trashed the place, and … and they left a message."

"What kind of message? How the fuck did they get past security?" Preston demands.

"I watched the footage. They had a bypass code and entered through the fire escape," Ashton says while moving about the room. "I'm not sure how that's possible, but I'll figure it out."

Loki's gaze hasn't left mine. My eyes sting with dryness from not blinking. "Wh-What was the message? What did they want?" My voice is soft but unnaturally steady.

Loki and Seth share a warring glance before Loki's face softens. "You, Red. They want you."

I don't know if it's my own gasp or Emory's, but she is at my side as I feel my knees buckle.

"Why would anyone be after Sloane? That makes no sense. She hadn't even met you until recently," Emory inquires with the tone of a mother bear.

"None of it makes sense, Ems. Not one goddamn piece of it," Ashton says before barging into Loki Locater HQ.

In a calmer voice, Seth tries to diffuse the situation. "Ash is right, we don't have any answers right now, but they left no room for doubt what they were coming for." He says it gently, but it still knocks the wind out of me.

"Me? They ... they're coming for me?"

I don't even know who fuck 'they' are.

"Well, what do we do? Preston, how do we keep her safe?" Emory's voice shakes, and her bottom lip quivers.

"I ... Loki? What do we do?" Preston defers.

"We have to leave tonight. We'll need you all to act as a diversion, then Red and I will head to a safe house while Ashton and Seth sort this out," Loki replies. His eyes have yet to leave mine.

My body feels too heavy for my legs, and I silently sink into the nearest chair.

"For how long?" Emory screeches. "How will I know she's okay?"

Preston places a hand on her shoulder but looks to Loki for answers, too. Everyone in this room is making plans for me. I get no say. No one asks how I feel about it.

How do I feel about it?

"I don't have a timeframe, Emory. But I can promise you that nothing will happen to Sloane while she's with me."

The sound in the room fades to the Charlie Brown teacher. I hear bits and pieces, but most of it is just white noise in my head. Someone asks about new phones. Another says they'll get our clothing packed. I hear something about the mountains but no address. It's like a fast-paced thriller movie, and I'm standing still in the center of it, unseen.

"Sloane?"

Glancing up, I recognize Seth, but he isn't in focus. "I think she's in shock," he says to someone on my left.

Turning my head, I see Sylvie crouching down beside me.

"It's okay, dear. Everything will be okay. Can you come downstairs with us? We need to get you packed up, and I'd like to make sure you have everything you'll need."

Somewhere in the house, I can hear Emory crying, "Why can't we keep her here, Preston? We'll hire someone to stand guard at all times."

"Ems, we have to trust Loki and Seth on this. They'll keep her safe, I promise."

Shaking my head, I try to drown out the rest of their conversation. Standing, I walk to the elevator in silence.

What the hell would anyone want with me? Unless ...

"Hey, Seth?"

"Yeah?" Placing his hand at the crook of my elbow, he keeps me steady. "Are you okay?"

"Mhm. Are you sure this is something to do with Loki? Not some random psycho?"

Seth studies me for a minute, before a gentle smile crosses his face. "Do you think this is an ex-boyfriend or something?" He's making fun of me, but I don't tend to end relationships on the best of terms.

Without making eye contact, I shrug.

"Sloane, while I would love to hear about the enemies you make while writing your books, this one isn't on you. This was a professional, coordinated attack. A random ex wouldn't be able to get past our security systems. Whoever did this was highly trained and had inside help."

"Did what exactly?" I ask as we enter the apartment that's been gutted. "Holy shit," I say with a gasp. Placing a hand over my mouth, I look around in fear. There are holes in the walls as if someone took a sledgehammer looking for buried treasure. Broken glass litters the floors, and they have turned every drawer inside out.

"Grab just the necessities. Clothes, if there are any left intact, personal items, things like that."

"What about my computer?" I ask frantically. "I can't write without it, and I have a deadline coming up. I can't afford to miss a deadline."

Seth stares at me like I'm losing my mind. And, okay, in the scheme of shit going on, a deadline is probably not a priority. But it's mine. It's something I've done on my own, and that's where my brain is right now. Maybe it's less scary to think about a deadline than whoever was just in my home.

"Ah, I don't think there's much left, Sloane. Plus, you can't take any electronics with you. Ashton is working on replacements for you. Phone, laptop, etc. Ones that can't be traced."

"But ... but what about my book? It's on—" The words die on my lips as Ashton rounds the corner holding the pieces of my laptop. Someone has carved the word "mine" into the screen, and I feel lightheaded.

"Shit," Ashton utters, attempting to hide the pieces behind his back.

"Can you fix it?" I ask.

Sighing, he shows me the pieces. "I doubt it, Sloane. But, I'll have a replacement for you in about an hour."

"What about the work I had saved on it?"

"Sloane, this really isn't a priority right now," Seth says, his usual edge back.

"It is to me," I yell. "That," I say, pointing to the shattered laptop, "is mine. It's all I've ever done on my own. It is a priority for me."

Loki steps out of the kitchen. "It's okay, Red. I get it. Ash, do you think you can pull any files from there?"

Ashton glares at him like he just asked him to rob a bank. "Ah, probably. Eventually. But, we've got some other things—"

"We don't know how long we're going to be away, Ash. She needs this. Can you try? Please?"

Ashton closes his eyes and takes a long breath. "Yeah, I'll see what I can do."

"Thank you," I whisper.

"What else do you need?" Seth asks.

"Ah, my notebook and pens are upstairs. I have a trunk in the bathroom. It's kind of ... ah, big and heavy." I feel my face flame.

"And you need to take that with you?"

"If it's still there, then yes. It has, um ... some writing props and tools in it."

Gawd, if they only knew what kinds of props.

"Okay, I'll look for it," Seth offers. Glancing around, he tells Loki, "The closet is pretty shredded. You guys are going to need some clothes."

I hear glass crunching underfoot and turn to find Preston entering the apartment. "I'll have clothing sent over for the both of you within the hour. What else do you need?" he asks, glancing around in dismay.

"We're going to be in the mountains, so make sure she has the proper clothing and some boots," Loki says while staring at me with concern.

"I'm going to head upstairs and get your electronics set up." Irritably, Ashton heads for the door.

"We need to get you suited up and armed, Loki. The house will have everything you need, but I'd carry at all times," Seth says seriously.

"Yeah, just give me a minute, okay?"

I stare with blurred vision as Loki crosses the room. Standing inches in front of me, he lowers his voice. "It's going to be okay, Red. I promise. No one will hurt you."

"What if they hurt you, though?"

A sly grin lifts the right side of his mouth as he speaks. "Worried about me, are you, Red?"

"It seems like a good time to worry."

Placing his hands on my shoulders, he gives me a squeeze, and my entire body trembles from the contact.

"The only thing you have to worry about is being able to handle me for the foreseeable future. I'll take care of everything else."

His words are innocent, but they cover my body like a weighted blanket.

"Okay," I whisper as he takes a step back.

"Can you go upstairs with Preston while I get everything set up? We need to leave by nightfall."

"Come on, sis. Let's go calm Ems down before she has an aneurism."

Fuck. Emory is going to go mental.

"Ugh, she won't take this well."

"No, she won't," Preston agrees.

"Jesus Christ, Sloane. What the hell is in this trunk?" Seth asks, attempting to haul it down the hallway.

"Ah, my writing stuff," I reply evasively. "Is it still locked?"

"Looks like it. What the hell kind of writing stuff do you have to lock up?"

"The good kind," I say with a wink. "There are wheels on one side if you want to drag it once you get it out of this dumpster fire."

"Gee, thanks for the tip." He sets it down with a thud.

Preston, Seth, and Loki all stare at me. I can see the questions forming in their minds, but they aren't ready to know my secrets, so I turn and walk out.

CHAPTER 13

LOKI

Sitting in Preston's penthouse, I take a last look around at everyone here. Dexter and Lanie sit together in an oversized chair, his armed wrapped protectively around her. Trevor and Julia sit across from them, holding hands but not saying much. Pacing the room is Ashton, with Seth glaring at him every few minutes. Preston has been quiet in the corner with Emory and Sloane. I'm sure he's trying to keep them both calm. Halton holds court in the corner while their younger brother, Colton, tries and fails to keep the mood light. In the center of it all is Sylvie Westbrook, and she is staring right at me.

"We have quite a full house now, don't we?" she says with a sad smile.

"If Easton were here, you'd have all your boys together again."

"Someday soon, Loki. It'll happen soon. I'm counting on it. GG says he has his hands full with Lexi right now, though." Laughing, Sylvie draws the attention of everyone in the room.

Again with GG?

"What, are you telling me she has magical powers or

something?"

"Or something," Dex, Trevor, and Preston all agree.

"She's three for three, dude. I'm staying out of her crosshairs for sure," Colton promises. "I'm not looking to settle down, and that crazy old lady has a way of making it happen."

Rolling her eyes, Julia corrects him. "Ugh, she just reads cards, Colt."

"Same thing! I'm not getting mixed up in that, but it seems like Easton and Loki are on her radar. I can't wait to see what kind of plan Dex has for them."

"I hate to burst your bubble, but Dex isn't doing anything. No offense, Sloane, but I'm not taking advice from a woman who guessed my shoe size and cusses more than Julia."

Clearing his throat, Ashton takes control of the room. This kid has grown up so much in the last ten years. When we first started working together, he was a gangly teenager. Granted, I wasn't much older, but seeing him now causes an odd pang in my chest.

"We need to get moving," Ashton informs the room. "While Loki and Sloane are away, they'll have limited access to the outside world. That's for their safety and ours. Whoever is looking for them will keep tabs on us all. Therefore, it's imperative that you only use the burner phones I'll provide, and, even then, we should try to limit communication. Does anyone have any questions?"

Choking back tears, Emory asks, "Who will know where they are?"

"Ashton is the only one with direct access to us, but there are safety measures in place. Someone will always be able to contact us." I don't tell her we have contingency plans if something happens to each of us. There's no need to scare them any more than they already are.

"Okay, we need to get moving. Girls, I need you all to put these on," Ashton says, handing them matching hoodies, masks, and gloves. The rest of us have similar outfits. "From the time we step into the elevator until we are in the cars, it's important to keep still. No fidgeting or other mannerisms that make you easily identifiable. The SUVs are exactly alike and already cleared for tracking and other devices by EnVision securities. Each car has GPS, and we have programmed a route into the system for you. Once you are on the road, follow that route exactly. If you suspect something is off, you notify me immediately. Does everyone understand?"

Solemnly, everyone nods their head.

Following Ashton's instructions, he, Dexter, Lanie, Sylvie, Seth, and Halton leave two by two toward the elevator. They'll wait in four cars until the rest of us arrive in the garage.

"God, it's hotter than a whore in church in here," Preston grumbles.

"Your southern is showing." I wink, trying to calm him. "Everything is going to be okay, Pres."

"I know. I'm just ready for this shit to be over." Pulling me in for a hug, he whispers, "Take care of yourself. And keep your hands off my new sister." He can't even say it without laughing. "Or, maybe I had better tell you to guard your jewels. According to Dexter, those books get pretty wild."

Shaking my head, I shove him toward his car. Between us all, seven black SUVs are preparing to leave the garage. Climbing into ours, I hesitate and wonder if little Red can handle this beast, but I put my trust in her and shut the door.

"You really can't see anything with the windows tinted. I have no idea what car anyone is in," Red comments as she starts the ignition. After a lengthy fight with Emory, I agreed to let Sloane drive since I still had dizzy spells occasionally.

"That's the point, sweetheart."

"Soundcheck," Ashton's voice comes to life through the speakers.

One by one, everyone checks in.

"Let's do this," I announce and watch as the first car pulls out, followed by two more before Red pulls into the line. To an outsider, you'd think the president was pulling out on to Waverley Road as our motorcade hits the street. Three merge left while the other four turn right. We drive for a few miles with one car in front of us and two behind. One by one, they all take different turns while Red and I head north.

"All clear," I say into the car's smart system.

"Noted. Everyone, keep to your routes. The drive should take about two hours total and will run you in circles in some places. This is intentional, and I set your GPS to return you home when it's time. Keep an eye out for anyone following you. If there is anything suspicious, notify me, then detour immediately to the closest police station."

A chorus of acknowledgments comes through the speakers.

"I'm disconnecting Loki and Sloane now," Ashton warns.

"Be safe," Emory screeches before the car goes silent.

I'm good with silence, it's been my only companion for so many years, but something tells me Red shouldn't get too lost in that pretty head of hers. Unfortunately, my small talk game is shit.

"Red?"

If her seatbelt weren't holding her down, the damn girl would have flown out of her seat. As it is, her arm flails wildly, hitting the window before she screams, "Jesus Christ."

Thank fuck she kept the car on the road. *Note to self, don't startle the driver.*

"Sorry, Red. I didn't mean to scare you. I was just going to tell you it's okay to take your mask off now."

"Oh, right," she says, but I can feel her heart racing from my side of the car. Out of the corner of my eye, I see her remove her hood and then the mask. Her red hair that's usually pulled high on her head falls free in loose waves over her shoulders.

Why the fuck am I noticing how her hair falls?

With my eyes forcibly on the road, I try not to notice her sigh as she runs her fingers through that mane of hair.

"You know everything will be okay, right? I promise I'll take care of you. I know this must be some scary shit, but I'm the best at what I do. With Seth and Ashton on our side, we'll get this figured out."

"I know." She sighs again. "I have no doubt you'll take care of me. That's what everyone does."

She says it so melancholically that I wonder if she meant to utter it aloud. "What do you mean?" I finally ask.

"Nothing, never mind. How long of a drive do we have?"

I glance in her direction a couple of times, but she keeps her focus on the road. Monitoring the rearview mirror, I'm relieved we're not being followed. Either they weren't expecting us to run tonight, or our decoys worked.

"We should be there in a couple of hours."

I expect her to ask another question, but she sits in silence. I thought all those dipshits were afraid of her because she asks so many. *Why hasn't she asked me any?* How bad can they be? Maybe it'll loosen her up a little.

"Can I ask you something?"

Finally, she relaxes in her seat. Angling her body toward me ever so slightly, she smiles, and my stomach flips.

For fuck's sake, don't tell me I'm going to get the shits right now. I don't even think there are rest stops along this stretch of highway.

"Shoot, but fair warning, I'm an expert questioner." Her grin is the stuff that dreams and heartache are made of, and it gives me the same thrill I get right before ambushing a target. *Danger, danger, danger,* rings in my head.

"So I've heard." She may not notice my smile, but I can hear it in my voice. "That's what I wanted to know. What did you ask the guys that have them hiding every time you enter the room?"

"Oh my God." She smacks the steering wheel. "They are such children. Seriously, if you can't answer a simple question about sex, you shouldn't be having it," she scoffs.

"Very true. But you didn't answer me," I say, nudging her elbow playfully.

I'm relieved to see her smile. This situation isn't ideal, but I was truthful when I said I would protect her. She's safer with me than she would be walking down a random city street.

It has nothing to do with the asinine, innate need I have to keep her close.

"Fine, I guess it started with Dex. Lanie mentioned that he probably had blue balls when he was in London, so I asked him."

"You asked him if he had blue balls? That's it? I mean, it's personal, but it shouldn't have him running like a pansy."

"No," she laughs. "I asked him to explain what blue balls feel like … in detail."

"I …" The laugh that bursts from my belly echoes in the cabin of the enclosed space. Turning in my seat, I give her my full attention and notice a crooked grin peeking out from the corner of her lips. "That's a very specific question."

Red shrugs her shoulders. "I write romance novels from the female and male perspective. I want to make sure I get everything right. Would you want to read a book that said a woman's vag felt like a warm, wet sandbox?"

"Fuck no." But watching the words wet and warm leave those pouty lips has me wanting to find out how wet and warm she is.

Jesus, man. Get your shit together.

"See," taking her eyes off the road momentarily, she gives me a *'so what?'* look. "Most of my readers are female, but I do have a great male fanbase, too. I don't want to alienate them by saying 'he was so anxious to get inside of her tight, warm heat, his balls felt like bean bags' if what they really feel like are tight—"

"Okay," I interrupt. "Got it." If she keeps painting a picture, there will be no hiding my *biological reaction* to her, even in the dark.

"So?"

"So what?" I ask, suddenly feeling hot.

"Are you going to tell me what blue balls feel like?"

"No."

"What about when you go down on a—"

"No."

"Please don't tell me you're going to be childish like Dex and Trevor? If we are going to be isolated and I can't talk to anyone, you're going to have to answer some things for me, you know? Ooh, you know what I haven't written yet?"

She's all over the place now that she's talking.

"You know when you get on a roll, you make no sense, right? I can't believe I'm going to ask this, but what haven't you written?"

"Forced proximity. That's a big one. Readers love a good forced proximity romance. What kind of house are we going to? Is it a big mountain cabin? Will you have to chop wood? Would you chop wood shirtless? That would give me a great visual for a hero. Oh my God. Military mountain man who's grumpy and ..." Glancing over, I see that she looks embarrassed. "Sorry, once my head gets going on a story, it spirals sometimes."

I watch her with mixed emotions. "I've never met anyone quite like you, Red."

"Yeah, I get that a lot. It's why I don't have many friends. People get tired of pulling me from my stories."

"You spend a lot of time getting lost in them?"

"Stories can't hurt me." It's a knee-jerk response, and by her clenched jaw and white knuckles, I can tell she regrets it.

"Neither will I, Red. Neither will I."

CHAPTER 14

SLOANE

"*Neither will I.*" *Ugh.* What the hell was I thinking? Of course that's his response.

"So, tell me about this safe house?" I ask, changing the subject.

"I don't think it will be quite what you're expecting," Loki says evasively.

"Well, that's where you're at an advantage. I don't have any expectations."

My body prickles, and I know he's watching me.

"It's a cabin I bought shortly after college."

"Wait, if you own it, won't that be one of the first places they look for us?"

"Oh, sweetheart. Give me more credit than that. I always have a backup plan. My backup plan, Jacob Kelly, owns this cabin."

"You have a fake identity?"

"A backup plan," I repeat.

"And it's a camp you use for hunting?"

"It's a hunting camp in every sense of the word, but I haven't had much time to use it. There are no frills. It's a one-room cabin, but it has a pullout couch, too. The bathroom will be about our only privacy for a while."

"Ah, one room?"

"I told you, it's rustic."

"So, it won't be like … glamping?" I'm not sure how I feel about camping.

"What the fuck is glamping?"

"You know, like upscale camping?"

"Sweetheart, there's camping, and then there's a fucking spa. There's no in-between."

"Wanna bet?"

A quick glance to my right, and I see he's sizing me up. "Come on, Loki, wanna bet?"

"What are the terms?" His voice is growly and low, and my core clenches in response.

"If I win, you have to answer my question about blue balls."

"And when I win?" he asks.

"What do you want?"

"That's a pretty loaded question there, Red." The flirtation in his deep voice sends shivers down my neck.

"I'm an open book—"

"In three hundred yards, turn left." The Australian voice echoes in the small space of the car.

Pressing on the brake, I slow to a stop but am hesitant to turn. "There?" I ask, pointing at an overgrown path.

"Yeah, just …" Loki unbuckles and leans over me to turn a dial next to my door.

"What's that?"

"Four-wheel drive. It's been a while since I've been here."

Slowly, I make my way onto the makeshift driveway, and we immediately bounce around like we're at a trampoline park.

"Just take it slow, Red." Loki's soothing voice calms me, and we inch forward. "We're going to climb for about a mile.

Don't worry about the brush. Just keep the tires in the ruts of the road."

I want to give him a 'what the fuck' look, but don't dare to take my eyes off the road. True to his word, we climb the side of the mountain and finally come to a clearing. Set back against the forest is a traditional log cabin, each log notched and nestled into the next. Pulling up in front, I park and look to Loki for guidance.

"Welcome home. It's going to be cold as fuck in there. Why don't you take what you can inside while I go around back and get some wood for the fireplace?" He reaches into his pocket, and pulls out a set of keys.

Taking them, I notice he has attached them to a tiny candy cane. Holding it up to the moonlight, I can see it sparkles, and I look to him for an explanation.

He shrugs his shoulders. "I forgot it was on there. It was my mom's. Here …" After handing me a flashlight, he walks around the house.

I've been to the mountains before, but in the summer, so I'm not expecting it to be so damn cold. The floorboards creak beneath me as I rush up the front steps. Fumbling with the keys, I finally insert them into the lock. My fingers have frozen stiff in the few minutes the've been exposed to the frigid mountain air.

Jiggling the key, I finally get the lock to engage, and then take the flashlight out of my pocket. Shining it ahead of me, I open the door, and I'm startled to see four glowing, round eyes staring back at me.

"Aghh," I scream as two furry beasts dart toward me. I try to turn and run, but my feet get tangled, and I trip down the stairs just as two raccoons come barreling out of the cabin. Thinking they are attacking, I scream again.

Loki has rounded the corner before I even hit the ground, running for me at full speed. I see the confusion cross his face as he spots me. Turning my flashlight toward the stairs, I illuminate our houseguests who stand there glaring at me as if I'm the intruder.

"What the hell happened?" Loki asks, not at all affected by the mangy beasts now scurrying up the steps. Pulling me from the ground, he wraps me in his warmth, still searching for danger.

"Right there," I screech. "You have tenants. Dick and Harry over there were in the house."

"Dick and ... what?"

"The raccoons. They were in the house."

"Fuck. Okay, get back in the truck while I evict them."

"Dick and Harry."

"Sloane, it's almost midnight, and I need to get some very smart, very dangerous animals out of the cabin so we can go to sleep. Are you seriously going to argue with me about their names?"

"Nope. If you would like to name one of them, then by all means."

"I—"

"Okay, Dick and Harry it is. Let me know if you need any help."

"Just get in the damn truck. Please."

Smiling, I do as he asks. I know it killed him to add the word please to his demand, and it makes me laugh. Turning on the ignition, I blast the heat and then angle myself to watch the show.

Every few minutes, I see Loki dart across the open doorway, but so far, Dick and Harry are still inside. After twenty minutes, I take out the phone Ashton gave me.

"You can do everything you would normally do with this, but keep conversations short and infrequent. We will route all of your data through our office in Tokyo, so anything you send will appear as if you're in Japan."

"Social media is a huge part of my business. Can I still Google, post, Snap, Tok—"

"Sloane," he interrupts. "If you must post something, send it to me, and I'll post it for you, but yes, you can Google."

"I don't need a freaking babysitter, Ashton."

"It's not for content, Sloane. It's so I can make sure nothing inadvertently shows up in the background that can lead people to you."

"Oh ..."

"Yeah, oh. This is serious, Sloane. I know you need to work, but put everything you do into perspective for the time being, okay? It's all about safety."

Jesus, that was a sobering conversation. But, knowing I have permission to Google, I look up raccoons and what I learn is fascinating. It's also likely to piss Loki off. Ten more minutes pass, and he still hasn't come out, so I turn off the car and make my way inside.

"Don't move, Red. They have babies or something over there, and they get pissed if you get too close."

"They're kits," I tell him.

"Please. Please don't tell me you've named them, too."

"No, I mean raccoon babies are called kits. I looked them up in the car to see if there were any suggestions for removing them."

"Yeah? What did you find out?" he asks from across the room.

"Ah, the MSPCA basically says to let them have your house until the kits are old—"

"That will not happen," he interrupts.

"Yeah, I figured. Then we have to annoy them."

"You want me to piss off two protective raccoons?"

"The website says to play music and shine lights on them. The adults should leave. If they don't take the kits, we have to relocate them and make sure the parents know where they are. Then you have to find their entry point." Glancing around, I see the fireplace. "It's most likely the fireplace."

"Okay, leave the door open and slowly make your way to

me. Hopefully, we can harass them enough they leave without attacking us."

I do as he asks, and when I reach him, he steps in front of me. Glancing over his shoulder, he asks, "What now?"

"We play music," I tell him. Removing the phone from my pocket, I pull up my playlist. I'm glad Ashton thought to transfer that. I need my playlists for writing. After scrolling until I find what I'm looking for, I turn the volume up full blast and hit play.

"Milkshake" by Kelis comes on, and Loki glances at me over his shoulder. His expression is priceless.

"This is what you choose to irritate a couple of raccoons?"

"Hey, if a milkshake can bring the boys to the yard, it can get Dick and Harry to the mountain, too."

As if on cue, Dick and Harry start to move toward the door. Harry paces back and forth a few times, obviously not wanting to leave his babies.

"It's okay, buddy. We won't hurt them," I coo.

"Are you insane?" Loki hisses.

"Probably. Keep shining the light on him, though. They don't like it. Once they're outside, we can move the couch out there."

He glares at me but does as I ask.

"Go ahead, Harry. It's okay."

"Stop talking to him."

"Jealous?"

"Yes, Red. I've waited my entire life to have you coddle me like a child."

"Ha," I yell, making Loki jump. "See, it worked!" Harry finally makes his way outside, and Loki rushes the door.

Cautiously, I make my way toward the couch. There, in the center of the shredded cushions, are five babies. "Oh, Loki. They're new. Like really new babies. Their eyes aren't even open."

Coming up behind me, he peers over my shoulder. "They're fucking loud, though."

Hearing a scratching noise on the roof, we both glance up.

"Dick and Harry are trying to get back in. We'd better hurry. Let's bring the couch outside so they can find a new home for them."

"What? You want me to put my couch outside in the middle of winter?"

"Well, it's already ruined. Was that a garage I saw in the back when we pulled up?"

"Yeah, it's detached. More like an old barn than anything."

"That's perfect. Let's put them there, so they don't freeze."

"They're wild animals."

"Yeah, I know, but they still need shelter, and we can't touch the babies. They could have diseases, so our best option is to carry the couch out."

Pinching the bridge of his nose with one hand, Loki places his other on his hip. It's an exasperated stance, but he still looks hot as fuck.

"I can't believe I'm agreeing to this," he grumbles.

"Well, do you have a better idea? It's not like we're going to sit on this thing once they're gone, anyway. It smells like piss, and who knows what else is on there."

"Lovely. Let's get this over with. From what I remember, it isn't too heavy. Will you be able to lift an end?" I feel his gaze on me, silently assessing my ability to move furniture.

Realizing that we are still standing in the dark, I ask, "Is there electricity in here?"

"Of course there—" He breaks off, heads to the door, then hits the switch a few times with no results. "Mother fucker."

Scratch. Scratch.

"Ah, let's get these guys outside, and then we can worry about the power," I suggest. "It's probably just one of those fuse switchy things. You know, the things that are usually in a gray metal box?"

Loki stares at me for a second like he's confused, and I worry that maybe he's having some sort of memory issue. Then he shakes his head and chuckles.

"Yeah, Red. I know what the fuse box is. Come on, let's get these guys outside before Dick and Harry come looking for them."

Internally, I grin. I got Loki to say Dick and Harry.

CHAPTER 15

LOKI

It takes almost an hour to convince Red that the kits were fine in the barn. Once we had the babies settled, she left a trail of crackers—Hansel and Grettel style—for Dick and Harry. If I hadn't seen it with my own eyes, I wouldn't have believed it. But, sure enough, they followed behind and have now taken up residency in the barn with their babies.

Turning on the flashlight, I notice her entire body is shivering. "Jesus, Red. Your lips are blue. Let's get you inside and start the fire."

"You're sure they'll be okay out here?" Her teeth clatter as she talks.

"They're wild fucking animals, Sloane. They'll be fine. I promise."

I can see her fingers do their dance in the moonlight, and they are bright red from the cold.

"Okay, yeah. It's freaking freezing up here."

"Once I get the fire going, I'll bring in the clothes Preston sent. We'll need to get you dressed in something warmer."

With a smirk, she teases, "We'll need to get me dressed? Is that so?"

"Ah, no. I mean ..." This goddamn girl flusters me. No one has ever thrown me off my game.

"Well, what is it, Loki? Dressed or undressed?" Sloane teases. "Come on. I really am freezing." She's laughing, but I'm thankful it's so fucking dark because her words went straight to my dick.

Get your shit together, Loki. You have a job to do. She is not an option.

"I wish my mind and body would get on the same damn page," I grumble with my head down as I stomp back to the house.

⁓

WITH RED CURLED up in front of the fire, I go to work on the fuse box. Even with a flashlight, I can barely see the damn thing. Attempting to get a better look, I fold my body to fit into the compact closet so I don't hear Red approach.

"Hey, Loki?" she calls through a yawn.

Leaning away from the door, I come face to face with her, but all I can see are her lips. I try to focus on her eyes, but her damn mouth keeps drawing me in.

"Yeah?" I finally choke out. *Real smooth dipshit.*

"You struck out?"

Struck out? *I haven't even hit on her yet.*

A naughty grin takes over her face in slow motion. Leaning in, she whispers, "With the fuse box, Loki. You struck out, with the fuse box?" Her Irish eyes dance as she peers behind me into the darkness.

With my back against the doorframe, there isn't anywhere I can go but farther into her space, so I take advantage of our proximity.

"I never strike out, Red. But it's too damn dark to fix the fuse tonight," I whisper, my breath causing her hair to fan across her face, and I take pleasure watching her body shiver in response.

"So, what are we going to do?" Her words come out in a breathy whisper.

"I'm going to grab a few more things from the car, and then we'll go to bed. The fireplace will keep this place warm enough, but there isn't anything I can do about the power until morning." Our bodies are so close I can feel the heat that seeped into her clothing from the fire. But that isn't what's setting my body alight.

"I hope you like to snuggle," she quips.

Do I? I have no fucking idea. I've never been with anyone long enough to find out.

"Ah, I usually sleep alone. Why?"

Taking a step back, she motions toward the bed. "Well, with the couch gone, that leaves this."

Scanning the room, I see why she's asked. The bed is barely bigger than a twin. *Fuck*. I didn't think about the bed because I've never been here with anyone else. Pinching the bridge of my nose, I try to come up with a solution.

"We'll have to be adults, right?" She laughs, throwing the words back at me.

Swallowing thickly, I nod. "Right, think you can keep your hands to yourself?"

"Nope."

"Me either." It comes out as a growl without thinking.

Taking half a step closer, she whispers, "Maybe I don't want you to."

"You need me to, Sloane."

She narrows her eyes but says nothing. Balling my hands into fists, I fight the instinct to reach for her.

"What I need, Loki, is for people to let me make my own decisions." There's an edge to her voice that's new, and I wonder how much truth is in those words.

"Fair enough. But I'm not a decision you want to make. Trust me on this."

As much as my body craves her, we won't be going there. Not only could it put her in danger if Vic found us, but my sexual appetite wars with my need for control. I respect her wanting to make her own choices, but I require complete control with sex. It's just how I'm wired. For that, and so many reasons, I need to keep my distance.

"We'll see. I'm going to brush my teeth and get ready for bed."

I stand, contemplating my thoughts, as she closes the door. Once she's out of sight, I adjust myself. *Calm down, asshat. You're not coming out to play.* Needing to cool off, I head outside to grab our stuff as the first flakes of snow begin to fall.

It takes three trips, but I finally empty the car. The last load is Red's flipping trunk. *What the hell does she have in this thing?* It weighs a fucking ton. After wrestling it up the steps, I finally reach the door just as she steps out of the bathroom. I'm carrying the flashlight in my mouth because I needed both hands for this monstrosity. The second I see her, the flashlight falls from my lips, and the chest slips from my hands, landing with a thud.

Sloane stands before me in barely there panties and something resembling a tank top.

"Oh my God," she screeches, rushing toward me.

Please stop running.

I try to close my eyes, but it's too late. I have branded her bouncing tits to memory for life. I'm in such a daze—okay, possibly a fantasy—as she drops to her knees before me, that I'm frozen in place. It isn't until I see an extra arm that my mind catches up with the display before me.

"What the fuck is that?"

"It's ... well—"

"You have a fucking body in there, Sloane!"

What the hell is going on? Is she not who we thought she was? Is she working with Vic? Reaching for her, illuminated only by firelight, I grab the first arm I come in contact with and almost scream. It's frozen and … rubbery? I drop it, reach for the flashlight, and shine it on the shitshow before me.

In my stupor, her trunk has fallen open, spilling its contents all over the floor. Dildos, vibrators, and toys I don't want to know about have scattered everywhere. But it's the two lifelike dolls she is attempting to shove back inside of the trunk that have my attention. They're so realistic that I reach out to grab one just to make sure my brain isn't playing tricks on me.

In the span of three seconds, I've gone from having a hard-on for this girl to thinking she's a murderer right back to sporting a semi. The laugh that spills from my lips is maniacal, even to my own ears.

Placing my hands on my head, I laugh while gaping at the chaos. "What the hell is happening here?"

Red grumbles something under her breath, and it makes me laugh harder.

When is the last time I laughed so much?

"Red, look at me," I finally manage.

On her knees, she lifts her gaze to mine, and the floor drops out from under me. I was ready for angry. I was prepared for sass. I could have even handled a bit of both, but her tears gut me.

"Hey." After slamming the door shut behind me, I drop to the floor next to her.

"It's, it's not what you think. J-Just go to bed and let me clean this up," she pleads.

"Sweetheart? I don't give a fuck what it is. But, I need you to understand what just went through my mind, okay? I went from having a raging hard-on to thinking you were a murderer in the same breath. I'm so confused. I don't know what's going on, but look around. Tell me this isn't funny."

Without making eye contact, she surveys the room. Illuminated by firelight, it looks like we just knocked over a sex shop.

"I know everyone thinks I write my stories based on experience, but that's not entirely true." Her voice is so quiet, I have to strain to hear her. "Yes, the emotions come from life experience. Well, mostly, but I don't sleep with all of them. I use these dolls to make sure my sex scenes are as realistic as possible. I'm not a virgin, but I don't exactly have a ton of experience. And my stories? Well, they paint a pretty vivid picture for my readers."

There are so many places to go in her explanation. I'm not sure where to start, and I tell her so. "That's a lot of information, and I will most definitely have questions. But, let's start with the obvious. You're saying you use these guys," I pick up an arm and toss it back into the bin, "to help you write sex scenes?"

Covering her face with her hands, she mumbles, "Yes."

I reach over, remove one hand from her face, and force her to look at me. "You realize that is a lot easier to swallow than thinking you're a killer?"

I'm rewarded with a crooked smile that isn't quite sure which way it wants to go.

"I know this is weird."

"A little." I laugh.

This time, she joins me. Clutching her stomach, she laughs so hard tears spill from the corners of her eyes. Happy tears I can handle.

"I'm never going to live this down, am I?"

"Never. Come on." Offering my hand, I help pull her to standing. "It's late, and if I think about this too long, I'll have too many questions to sleep. Let's clean up, and we can revisit this shit tomorrow."

"Ugh. Can we not?" she asks hopefully.

"Not a chance, Red. Things just got a lot more interesting

around here." Grabbing the suitcase Preston sent, I hand it to her. "I think your clothes are in here. Why don't you get dressed, and I'll take care of this, er, stuff?"

"What do you mean? I'm going to bed. What do you want me to get dressed for?"

"You're not sleeping in that."

Her posture stiffens, and I know I said the wrong thing.

With her finger and thumb tapping, she purses her lips. "Are you sleeping in your boxers?"

Fuck.

"It's all I have."

"Me too," she fires back.

"I'm sure Preston sent something. Sloane, listen to me. We are already squeezing into that miniature-sized bed. Please, cut me some slack here."

She lets out an exasperated sigh but gives in. "Fine. If Preston sent some pajamas, then I'll wear them. But this is not over, mister."

"Fuck. Don't call me mister, Red." My voice is sounding hoarse.

Her eyes smolder as she glances over her shoulder. The firelight reflects off every inch of her delicious body. "Do you like to be in control, Mr. Kane?"

"I don't like it, Red. I require it."

"Good to know. Maybe you'll teach me a few things after all, Loki. It's about time I started taking control, too."

I don't have time to ask what she means because as she turns, all coherent thought leaves my brain. Her panties hug the curve of each cheek as she walks away. Her round, heart-shaped ass on full display. The ruching of her panties draws my eye right to her seam.

Can't go there, Loki. Cannot go there.

CHAPTER 16

SLOANE

*O*h. My. God. How the fuck did that just happen? Not only did Loki meet Jack and Jill, but he is out there picking up every goddamn vibrator that I own. *Hmm, I wonder if he knows how to use all those toys?* I bet he does.

Placing the flashlight on the counter, I open the professionally packed suitcase. I'm not used to the money my sister married into, and this is another example. I don't remember the last time I had new clothes, and I've never had anything designer. I'm almost afraid to touch anything.

After a little digging, I finally pull out a cotton satchel. Assuming this is underwear, I empty its contents into the suitcase and almost laugh. Knowing Preston, he specifically had someone buy these to mess with Loki. The only pajamas, if you want to call them that, are some of the sexiest lingerie I've ever seen in my life.

Choosing a set, I slip on the softest black silk I've ever felt. The cheeky panties and matching babydoll camisole feel like heaven. Inspecting myself in the mirror, I try really hard to like what I see.

"Do you like to be in control, Mr. Kane?"

"I don't like it, Red. I require it."

Jesus, I need to write that line into a book. As soon as the words left his mouth, my center melted. It shouldn't turn me on as much as it does. I'm fighting for my own control here, but his words have me ready to throw in the towel and say, "Yes, sir."

"You need to take control, Sloane. Not hand it over to another man that will leave you."

Knock. Knock

"Red? Did you say something?"

"Ah, no. I was just, um, singing?"

Singing, Sloane? Really?

Sliding the suitcase to the corner of the room, I open the door.

Loki stands in the doorway with his arms raised, hanging onto the frame, and his mouth falls open as he takes in my appearance. While tugging at the collar of his shirt, his eyes rake over my curves.

My body flames from within, and I try desperately not to fidget. The intensity of his gaze has me wanting to fan myself. We stand inches apart, but neither of us speak for what feels like an eternity.

"That's ..." I watch as Loki works to swallow before trying again. "That's what Preston sent for pajamas?"

Allowing my smile to form ear to ear, I nod.

"Well, at least his text message makes sense now."

Confused, I peer up at him. "What text message?"

"He sent a message in our group chat," he grumbles.

"What did it say?" I'm grinning wildly now because I have seen the exchanges that happen between these guys.

"He said, 'Good luck sleeping tonight. You're welcome.'"

Leaning in so our bodies almost touch, I mouth, 'Goodnight, Loki,' and slip past him. Climbing into the bed, I feel his gaze on me but refrain from checking. Eventually, I hear the bathroom door shut.

As soon as I lie down, my body surrenders to exhaustion.

∼

Gasping for air, I fly out of bed but can't catch my breath. Turning in circles, I look for something to grab hold of.

"Red? Shit, did I scare you?"

His voice startles me more, and I blink wildly, trying to locate the source. Loki steps out from the closet with his hands raised. "Hey, sorry. You're okay. I just dropped a wrench."

"What?" My voice cracks as I speak, and I place a hand on my stomach to calm my nerves. I've never been a morning person, but I can't seem to comprehend what the hell is going on. Peering around the room as my heart rate steadies, the events of the last twenty-four hours come rushing back.

"Sloane?"

Drawing my head back quickly, I rub my eyes and force my brain to focus.

"I-I'm fine, Loki. Sorry. I'm not a morning person. I just had a hard time figuring out where the hell I was. That's all."

He stares at me with concern. "Are you sure? You look like you've seen a ghost."

Taking a long breath in through my nose, I slowly exhale. "Yeah, I'm fine," I lie.

With tentative steps, he inches closer. "You seem to be 'fine' a lot," he states.

In the daylight, I'm finally able to take in our surroundings, so I ignore his comment. The place is even smaller than I first thought. I'm not a math person, but if I had to guess, I'd say the entire place is less than a thousand square feet. To my left is the kitchen with a fridge in one corner and cabinets taking up the rest of the wall. A small utility sink stands in the center under a square window. To the right of the sink is a two-burner stovetop with a slim oven door underneath.

Everything in here is miniature, and compared to Loki's vast size, it makes me laugh.

"I haven't been here in a long time," he says from behind. "It seems a lot smaller with two of us here." Sounding strangled, he clears his throat. "Ah, Red?"

Turning, I lift my gaze, and we make eye contact that sends a rush of warmth to my belly. He's so close, I could touch him if I only reached out. His breathing is erratic and loud. The control he holds close to his vest is slipping in his slow perusal of my body.

His movements are gentle but intentional as he places his fingers over my thumb and middle finger, halting my nervous habit.

"Do I make you nervous, Sloane?"

"No," I lie again.

He leans in even closer, the faint scent of aftershave hitting my senses. It's a woodsy, clean smell I'm not used to. Most of the guys I've dated douse themselves in cologne.

"You smell good," I blurt.

Geez, Sloane. Take it down a notch ... or fifty!

He shoots me a crooked grin. "I smell like you since you're a bed hog and were all up in my business last night."

"I was not." *Was I?* "Okay, it's possible," I concede. Realizing he is still holding my fingers, I tug my hand and pull away. Taking a couple of steps toward the sink, I look for a coffee pot but halt at his next words.

"If we're sleeping in that bed together every night, you need to sleep in something else—anything else. Just not that."

Glancing down, I take in my near nakedness. Strangely, I'm not self-conscious around him. I've always been okay with my body, and technically, I am covered, even if it's sexy, but I rarely have this much confidence.

"Do my pajamas bother you, Loki?" Gah, flirting with him shouldn't be so easy.

"Bother isn't the right word, Red. But if you keep wearing

shit like that, you're likely to end up impaled on my dick without our knowledge. You tend to, um, squirm in your sleep. If I hadn't woken up this morning, wandering hands could have led us down a very naughty path."

I suck in a gulp of air so suddenly I choke.

Gawd, Sloane. So sexy.

It takes half a beat before he is patting my back with a suppressed grin. "Easy there, killer."

"What time is it, anyway?" Glancing around, I can't tell if the power is on or not because the sun is shining off the snow so brightly I'm nearly blind.

"Ten thirty," he says gruffly.

"Oh, that early?"

"Early? How late do you usually sleep?" Moving past me, he grabs a coffee maker from the top shelf and plugs it in.

I guess he fixed the electrical issue.

Loki moves with graceful ease in the tight space but still gives me a wide berth.

"Well, I write at night until three or four, so I guess I normally get up around noon."

He opens the fridge and pulls out my favorite peppermint mocha coffee creamer. I notice someone has also stocked the shelves with the basics.

"Where did you get all this stuff?" Opening a cabinet, I see canned and packaged food stacked in neat rows.

"I pay someone to look after the place most of the time. Whenever I visit, his wife comes out and gets the place ready. That's why I was so surprised about the damn raccoons," he grumbles. "They couldn't have been inside long, or Marianne would have seen them."

"Oh, the babies. Do you think they're doing all right out there? Maybe I should bring them more crackers."

"Do not feed them, Red, or we'll end up with bears next time."

"Bears? Seriously?"

"We're deep in the Blue Ridge Mountains. Wildlife is all around. Granted, the bears are probably hibernating, but let's not tempt them, okay?"

"Eesh. Yeah, okay. No feeding wildlife. Can I check on them?"

"I have no idea, but my inclination is to let them be. Raccoons are wild animals. They have this 'living off the forest' thing down."

Inching closer, I watch the muscles in Loki's back work with each movement he makes. When he turns to hand me my coffee, I almost end up wearing it. I'm standing closer than he was expecting. Our proximity and the way he is holding out my mug cause the back of his knuckles to brush against my nipple, which pebbles immediately. Holding eye contact, I physically restrain myself from thrusting my chest forward into his palms.

"Dangerous," he growls but doesn't back away or move his hand. The heat radiating from him and the coffee a mere millimeter from my skin ghost over my hardened peak. It causes an almost painful sensation, and I swallow the urge to moan.

My gaze travels to his lips before darting back to his. There's a storm brewing in his eyes, and I want to dance in it. "Mhm," I finally agree. He has me tongue-tied, so I clamp my jaw shut before I make a fool out of myself.

I take a step back just as he steps forward. Bending at the knees, so we're face to face, he scans my features. "Please, get dressed, and then we'll make ground rules for while we're here. No matter how much my body reacts to you, Red, you are a job."

Ouch.

"I need to keep it that way. You're too important to my family for me to fuck this up."

A humorless laugh falls from my lips. "I'm not important, Loki. I'm a complication. Thanks for the coffee."

Geez, that hurt the old ego.
"You are a job."

Feeling foolish standing in silk lingerie after that, my face flames as I make a hasty retreat. I don't get far before his grumbled apology fills the air.

CHAPTER 17

LOKI

Fuck. I can be such an asshole.

"Sloane, wait. That's not what I meant. It didn't—"

She missteps at the sound of my voice but doesn't stop. Without making eye contact, she nods. "No worries, Loki. I know what you meant." Her falsely cheerful tone grates on my nerves, but she's locked herself in the bathroom before I can comment.

Pulling out a chair, I sit and wait for her. I cradle my head in my hands, tugging at the ends of my hair. I'm so out of my element. It has been years since I've had no direction. I've lived my life by a strict military schedule. I don't know what to do with myself now that I have nowhere to be and nothing to do.

The sound of water running drags me from my thoughts and plunges them right into the gutter. I force my eyes to stay open because if I even blink, my mind will conjure images of Red stripping out of that fucking silk bralette. Water cascading down her collarbone and dripping from her perfectly hard nipples. Remembering how they reacted to my brief, accidental touch has my cock springing to life.

Glancing down, I do what I haven't done since I was a teenager. I talk to my fucking dick. "I will not get you off while she is in the next room, fuckwad, so get it together and go back into hiding." When that doesn't work, I forcefully adjust him and go in search of our phones. Fucking Preston is going to get an earful.

I stacked all our belongings near the entryway last night, so I start there. Dragging the bags down one by one, I locate the electronics and pull out two new phones—one for each of us—and flip them on. We'll change out the phones every couple of days to keep our signals intentionally crossed.

As the phones boot up, something pink and fluffy catches my eye. Crouching down, I let my fingers trace over the soft material sticking out of Sloane's kink kit.

We're going to have to talk about this, too.

Hearing the faint sounds of singing, I figure I have a few minutes and open the trunk. I know I'm invading her privacy, but I justify it by saying I needed to push this pink stuff back in.

Once it's open, I run my fingers over the fluffy fabric that turns out to be a blindfold.

"I'm not a virgin, but I don't exactly have a ton of experience."

Her words will forever haunt me. Gently, I lift a small toy I know how to use and stifle a groan. *Does she use this on herself?*

Boundaries. We need boundaries. Rules.

And you're no good for her, Loki. Despite what these toys would have anyone else believe, I know she's too innocent for me.

How fucking innocent, though?

Slamming the lid shut, I grab a phone and pull up Preston's number. I'm glad Ashton thought to load everyone's info onto these. He doesn't miss anything.

Loki: You're a dick.
Preston: What do you mean?

Loki: You know exactly what I mean. We're living in eight hundred square feet. There's only one goddamn bed, and you send her with fucking lingerie that could rival Pornhub.

Preston: Hey, I'll have you know it's all high-end stuff. Plus, the girls picked that shit out. It would be creepy for her brother to do it.

New Message-Girls

Preston: Loki's pissed off about Sloane's wardrobe.

Lanie: What? Nooooo. Everything is super cute.

Julia: And fucking sexy as hell.

Loki: I am here to protect her, not fuck her.

New Message-Fuckers

Preston: Loki says he's there to protect Sloane, not fuck her.

Trevor: Why can't it be both?

Dexter: Does she want to fuck him, though? That's the question.

Loki: Stop saying fuck. Preston, stop involving everyone in my shit.

New Message-West

Preston: Sorry, guys. Loki doesn't want group chats, so I can't add you.

Colton: Come on. Don't leave me hanging.

Easton: ...

Ashton: Limited. Messages. Limited.

Loki: Fuck off, all of you.

New Message

You have to be kidding me.

Ashton: We got a lead, but it's going to take time. It's more involved than we thought. Nothing wrong with having some fun while you're there.

Seth: Keep her safe and happy (eggplant emoji).

Loki: I'm not crossing any lines with her. What lead?

Ashton: Famous last words, bro. Let us handle things here. Just lay low.

Seth: I think Julia stuck a present for you in the side of your suitcase. (laughing emoji)

Ashton: More condoms?

Seth: We'll let Loki find out ...

Loki: Fuck off.

"Everything okay?"

Flinching, I glance up. I hadn't heard her come out of the shower.

"Yeah, everything's fine. Just checking in with the guys," I say distractedly. I'll need to erase those messages later.

"And you needed a blindfold for that?"

Sighing, I realize I still have it in my palm. Glancing up, I shrug guiltily. "Sorry. It was hanging out of the kink kit—"

"The what?"

I'm losing all my faculties. I should be more composed than this.

"Ah, your trunk." My palms are sweaty, so I wipe them on my jeans, and she notices.

With a wink, she takes it from my hand and walks over to the trunk. It opens with a click, and the air becomes thick as the knowledge of its contents washes over us. I sit wide-eyed as she lifts one of the dolls and places it in the chair next to me. Of course it's the goddamn male with his junk jutting straight out.

"Come on, Red. Don't you have some pants for him or something?"

She looks at me like I'm speaking Latin. "For who? Jack?"

"For fuck's sake. You named them, too?"

"Of course. That's Jack, and this is Jill."

"Sloane. You cannot name your sex dolls Jack and Jill. Jack and Jill were brother and sister. That's gross."

"Really? I didn't know that, but I didn't read many

nursery rhymes as a kid. Okay, we'll name her ..." Red flashes a wicked grin, and my skin tingles. "We'll name her Pearl."

Standing as a hot flash overcomes me, I point to her and the dolls. "You name them, Red. Not us. Not we. Now, explain them to me again, so I'll know what the fuck to expect around here." My tone is harsh, but she laughs, enjoying my discomfort.

"Well, I write romance novels. My characters have sex. Sometimes, a lot of it. And, it's not like I've ever watched myself having sex, but I need to explain it in great detail. So I have these guys. I use them to test out positions."

I swallow so loudly it sounds like a soda can opening. Watching her lips say sex and positions over and over again is frying my brain.

"What do you mean, you test out positions? Do you have sex with them?"

"What? No, of course not," she screeches.

I'm baffled. Honestly, speechless.

"Listen, I'm not great with feelings. I would have these, um, uncomplicated relationships with guys."

"What guys?" I bark.

"Okay, dad." Rolling her eyes, she continues. "Just guys I would date, but I didn't always want to sleep with them. I mean, I've put out like fifteen books in three years. Yuck. I need to write epic sex scenes, but I can't always visualize them. I mean, have you ever tried to have sex standing up? It's not as easy as authors make it seem, and I want my scenes to be realistic."

"I'm not following, Red." Feeling a headache coming on, I pinch the bunched muscles at the base of my neck.

"Ugh, okay. I've been somewhat of a serial dater while I learned about different romance heroes. There was the grumpy boss. The asshole. The broken heart. The guy next door. A fireman. A—"

"Jesus Christ, Sloane. I don't want a rundown of every twat wad you've slept with."

"See, that's what's wrong with you guys. You all assume I've slept with them, and newsflash, I didn't. Most of them, anyway. And the last one wasn't even my choice..."

The words are out of her mouth before her brain catches up. But I heard every word.

"What the fuck happened?" My voice is deadly.

"I didn't sleep with them. That's why I have the dolls."

That's not what I'm asking, and she knows it.

"Sloane..."

"Loki, it's not your business. Just drop it. I write at night, but I'll try to adjust my schedule so I don't disturb you. What's your daily routine like?"

She's so cold and distant as she speaks. I take a moment to switch gears. My brain is still murderous, and my body is out for blood. A rage I've never known is bubbling just beneath the surface, and I need to get the fuck out of here. I don't know how to handle these feelings, but I know they're not in line with how I should feel about a job. That is what Red... that's what Sloane has to be. A job.

"We'll figure out a schedule later. I need to go."

"What? Where?" The fear in her voice rips my soul from my body.

"No." I inhale deeply, willing the oxygen to cleanse my temper. "I mean, I need to get out of the cabin. We're almost out of wood for the fireplace. I'll just be out back chopping it."

Sloane stands in the same spot as I put on my boots and coat. I hate seeing her fold in on herself like this. My bubbly inquisitor is a shell, grasping her elbows tightly at her sides, and there is nothing I can do. I feel volatile, and I need air.

"Sloane?"

She lifts her gaze slowly. Empty, hollow eyes meet mine. My nostrils flare as I grind my teeth. With hands balled into fists, my entire body is a hairsbreadth away from exploding with a fit of anger that has an invisible target.

"I'll be just outside."

She nods but still doesn't move. I'm an asshole for not knowing what to do. I'm an asshole for not consoling her, for not pushing her for information. I'm an asshole with the social skills of a caveman, and I'm the caveman that will kill the motherfucker that laid his hands on her.

I hit the woodpile at a sprint with shaking limbs. My movements are violent as I split, chop, and stack log after log. I don't know how long I force my body to comply with this manic rate, but by the time my brain has calmed, my knuckles are bloody, and the sun is attempting its early winter descent.

The feelings and emotions Sloane drags from me are uncomfortable. I haven't known her long enough to have this strong of a reaction. My mother always taught me love is a choice, not some lightning strike. *Love?* What the fuck is wrong with me? I don't even know what love is. Lust, it has to be lust that's clouding my judgment. *Lust.*

How long has it been since I've gotten laid?

The fact that I can't remember is depressing. I don't even think it's from memory loss, but maybe it explains my reaction to Sloane. Either way, someone hurt her, and I can't let it go.

Dragging a log from the pile, I set it on its side and take a seat. My brain is calmer, but the rage is still burning, so I take out my phone to call Seth. He picks up on the first ring.

"Hey, Boss. Seriously, you need to let us handle this—"

"Someone hurt her," I interrupt.

"Loki?"

"Do you know anything?"

He lets out a long breath. "Not really. She freaked out about the apartment's graffiti and asked me if I was sure it was someone after you and not a crazy ex-boyfriend, though.

I didn't realize she had a legitimate concern, so I downplayed it."

"Find. Him."

"Loki—"

"Do it, Seth. Find him. Ask Emory for any information she has about where Red has been for the last year. I'm betting it was recent, and then get me every fucking detail."

"Did she ask for this? You need to be very clear that this is something she wants, Loki. Do you remember how Rebecca was after her attack?"

Seth rarely speaks of his late wife, and he never mentions that day. It's something he will always consider his biggest failure, even though there was nothing he could have done. I know he's bringing Rebecca up for a reason, but I saw the fear in Sloane's eyes, and it makes the decision for me.

"Get the information." I hang up before he can reply. Snow is falling all around me in thick, wet sheets. Grabbing the wheelbarrow, I'm about to push another load of wood to the house when I hear a smoke detector go off.

Dropping the handles, I run.

CHAPTER 18

SLOANE

Come on! The Food Network said this recipe was foolproof.

The windows in this place have an old metal latch that isn't lining up correctly and keeps me from opening it. I grab the kitchen towel and start fanning the smoke detector just as the back door crashes open.

Loki moves around me like a controlled tornado. With precision, he evaluates the situation and eliminates the dangers. First, he removes my ruined coffee cake from the counter and puts the smoking pile of shit out in a snowbank. Then, he opens the front door, allowing for air to circulate front to back in the small space, all while pressing the reset button on the blaring alarm.

In the silence, the smoke slowly clears out. I count to ten and prepare for the lecture, but it never comes. Realizing I've kept my eyes shut, I crack one open and find Loki six feet away watching me. Scrunching up my nose, I finally open the other eye.

He must think I'm a freaking lunatic.

"What happened?"

My eyes widen in alarm. I had hoped he would let this go.

"Here, Red. What happened in here? We'll get to the rest later," he growls.

Slapping a hand over my forehead, I admit, "I can't cook. Like, I wouldn't even make it past the first round of The Worst Cooks In America."

"Oh-kay. So, you wanted to prove it?"

"Ha, ha. No, I keep trying. I don't expect you to understand. I'm sorry you had to ... handle my mess."

"That's what I'm here for, Sloane. I handle everyone's messes," he says gently.

"Not mine." My voice is icy, but how else do I make him understand?

"It's not a bad idea to have someone in your corner, Red." He moves toward the sink, and I notice his hands.

"Oh my God, Loki. What the hell happened to your hands?" I rush to the bathroom and grab a first aid kit I found earlier. When I reach him, I grasp his arm and drag him to the table, where I make him sit down. "What did you do?" I repeat.

As gently as I can, I tend to his hands.

"They just got scraped up chopping wood, Red. They're fine."

Lifting my eyes, I'm painfully aware that I'm on my knees between his legs. My heart rate speeds up as he studies me. Loki clears his throat, and the term *'chest heaving'* comes to mind.

"Red?"

"Ah, right." *Control your breathing, Sloane. Jesus, you sound like an animal in heat.* "Um, I'm sorry."

"Don't." His voice is a command and has me stilling my movements. "Don't apologize for things that aren't your fault. You do that with everyone. Don't." He takes a deep breath. "Please don't do it with me." Loki's voice doesn't leave room for negotiation, but it's taken on a softness I wasn't expecting.

"We need to wash out the cuts. I think you have wood chips and probably some splinters in them." Loki closes his fingers around mine, and I gasp. The innocent touch short circuits my brain.

"I said they're fine. What were you trying to make?"

My throat is suddenly too dry to speak, so I lick my lips and watch his gaze follow the movement of my tongue. "C-Coffee cake," I squeak.

He raises an eyebrow, and a grin follows. "You were making a coffee cake at dinnertime?"

"I told you I'm not very good at this adulting thing," I say. Shrugging my shoulders, I avert my eyes.

My body goes still as I feel him lean into me. With his mouth at my ear, he whispers, "No one is good at adulting, Red. Some are just better at hiding it. We all need a little help from our friends."

Turning my cheek a fraction, I stare into his eyes. "Is that what we are, Loki? Friends?"

Our faces are so close I feel the air swish around us as he inhales.

"Yeah, Red. We're friends," he replies hoarsely. The vein in his neck the only indication he isn't as calm as his body portrays. "And I take care of my friends. All of them, in every way."

"Every way?" I repeat.

He doesn't reply with words, only a slight nod of his head next to my face, and my lips part. If this were one of my stories, this is where the hero would lean in, capturing the heroine's mouth with his. But this isn't a romance novel, and I'm no one's heroine.

He sits back suddenly, and I'm left bereft. My body is flush with need, but sitting on my knees before him, embarrassment from his rejection has me blinking back moisture from my eyes. "You help your friends," I repeat, trying to find my words. Any words at this point would do. After opening the alcohol, I saturate a cotton round.

"Yes."

Way to give me something to work with here, Loki.

"Can I ask you a question?"

"Always," he whispers.

"How did you know Lanie and Dex would fall for each other?" I ask as a distraction while I apply the rubbing alcohol.

He hisses but doesn't complain. I've heard Lanie's love story, and Julia told me about her and Trevor. What always shocks me is how their happiness is a direct result of Loki's meddling.

"I didn't. Well, at least, not at first. After their first meeting, I was pretty sure Dex had met his match, though." He smiles at the memory. "My goal in getting Lanie to North Carolina was twofold. Dexter desperately needed a nanny ... a good one, and Trevor needed Julia. After everything went down with Trevor in Boston, I kept tabs on Jules. I know it was wrong, but I also did it to keep her safe. Then, I knew getting Lanie to take that job would eventually lead Julia back to Trevor. The first time I met Jules, I knew she was perfect for Trevor. Lanie and Dex were a happy by-product."

"But how did you do it?" I ask while pulling out a splinter with a pair of tweezers.

"Ah, looking for all my secrets, are you?"

When I tug a little harder than needed at another tiny piece of wood, he yelps.

"I'm teasing, Red. I had help, but we basically took over their computers remotely and made sure she only saw Dexter's ad from the nanny agency. Then, we flooded their inboxes with information about Waverley-Cay."

"Sneaky."

"Sometimes, you have to be," he admits.

"Did you ever worry they'd be pissed?"

"Life is all about choices, Red. I made choices based on the information I had at the time. Second-guessing myself wouldn't benefit anyone."

"Okay, I think I got most of the pieces out. You should wash up. Then we can put some Neosporin on the cuts."

"They'll be fine. Can I ask you something now?"

My body tenses at his words, and I drop my gaze to the floor. Hooking his index finger under my chin, he raises my face to his.

"Why coffee cake?"

I blink slowly.

"Wh-What?" This man makes me stupid. Words escape me when he's this close.

"Why coffee cake? You said you keep trying, so you've attempted to make it before?"

"Coffee cake?"

He grins but lets go of my face. I can still feel his finger on my skin, but at least the brain cells are functioning again.

"It's, um ..." I bite my lip. *Do I want to share this with him?* My sisters don't even know I do this. "Well, Emory told me once that my mom used to make a coffee cake every week. She would have it ready for the girls when they got home from school. I-I was too young to remember. Honestly, I was too young to remember anything about her. I've tried every recipe at least twice. I'm just a disaster in the kitchen ... in life, too, if I'm being honest."

Loki moves so quickly that I don't have time to register our movements. In one swift motion, he has stood and lifted me from the ground at the same time. Holding onto my biceps, he lowers his head, so we are nose to nose.

"First," he growls, "I'm done listening to you talk badly about yourself."

"Talk— What? I don't talk badly about myself."

"Second, I'm going to shower, and then we will make you

a damn coffee cake." He lingers so close our noses nearly touch, and I can't breathe.

"You bake?" I breathe, barely a whisper.

"I'm a man of many talents, Red." He leans in and rubs his nose against mine.

It isn't a kiss, and probably not meant to be sexual, but my core aches at the touch. The mewl that escapes my throat is an unfamiliar sound.

"So fucking, dangerous," he growls before releasing me.

I nod like a bobblehead as he stomps to the bathroom. When the door closes, I release all the air I've stored in my lungs in a whoosh.

What the hell just happened?

CHAPTER 19

LOKI

After peeling off my shirt, I turn the shower on as cold as it will go. I know it's fucking cliché, but I don't even think a cold shower will tame the steel rod between my legs. I release my belt buckle, then let my pants fall to the floor. Thanks to asshole Preston, I don't have any underwear. The dickhead sent lingerie for Sloane and no underwear at all for me.

I step into the spray, willing the icy waters to freeze my body and mind. Closing my eyes as the frigid temperatures do nothing to chill my body, I force my brain to make things right. *She's a job. She's too innocent for me. She's too young. She's trying to find her way, and I'm still lost. You can't go there with her, Loki.* As I recite this mantra, my hand has found its way to my cock of its own accord.

Visions of Red flood my mind, overtaking all conscious effort to keep her at bay as I slide my hand up and down my shaft. I can see her black lingerie hanging on the other side of the room, and it paints a fucking vivid picture. Sloane, on her knees before me, her lips parting on an exhale.

Fuck. Picking up speed, I rub my hand down my dick and roughly over the head. Faster and rougher. Her lips wrap around me while I fuck her face. I picture her on the bed with her toys spread out, and it's my undoing. Thick ropes of come splatter on the shower wall. I have to bite down on my cheek to keep from growling like a monster.

Goddamnit. The water goes from cold to scalding as I turn the nozzle. Placing both hands on the tile, I wait for my breathing to return to normal. Even as I clean up, I know I'm in trouble. Sloane Camden seems to be my kryptonite.

Shaking out my hands like a nervous teenager, I finally feel calm enough to face her. As I open the door, I find her standing in the kitchen with a hand on her hip.

"Hey, you look better," she says with a fake smile plastered to her beautiful face. It's still gorgeous, but not sincere. Her eyes aren't smiling, and her tone is back to bubbly and placating. I fucking hate it.

"Don't do that," I grumble as I stalk toward her.

Her smile falters but doesn't fade. "What do you mean? Do what?"

"Don't pretend to be okay to make it easier for me. You do that a lot. You hide your feelings to make everyone forget you're there. I won't forget, Red."

"No, you're mistaken."

"Am I?"

"Yes, you are. You know nothing about me." Her voice is soft, but her eyes shoot daggers.

"I'm not trying to fight with you, Sloane."

"It just comes naturally?" she bites out. Moving past me, she grabs a box of cereal from the cabinet.

"What are you doing?"

She looks from me to the box of Resee's cereal.

"Ah, I was going to have something to eat. How did your friend know this is my favorite?" she asks, holding up the box.

"I had Emory give me a list. That," I say, pointing to the

box of sugar, "is not dinner. That's a cavity waiting to happen. We can do better than that. Put it away."

Her body bristles at my command, and I know I've screwed up. Again. A tear-filled glare roots me to my spot. Tap-tap-slide. Her nervous habit gives away the emotion she's trying to bottle up.

She takes a step forward, then another until we are inches apart. Squaring her shoulders, her jaw sets in a tight line.

Come on, Red, let it out. I can see the words forming behind her eyes—She wants to lay into me for ordering her around.

Rightly so. I need to work on my fucking manners. It's been way too long since I've had to mind myself.

Without a word, I see the moment she gives up. Her shoulders slump, and she walks the cereal back to the counter. I can't reconcile this girl with the one who stood guard outside of my room.

"Why can you stand up for everyone but yourself?"

Her body tenses at my question, and I watch the tap-tap-slide of her left hand as she returns the cereal to the counter with her right. "What do you mean?" she whispers without turning around.

With cautious steps, I move until I'm standing right behind her. When she inhales, our bodies touch, and the scent of vanilla invades my nostrils.

"You had no problem yelling at Seth when I was unconscious. You hold your own with my idiot friends when you want answers. Yet, you back down every time something bothers you. You apologize for things you have no business apologizing for. I see all this, and I've only known you a short time. I'm willing to bet there's a lot more no one else sees, too."

She bows her head but says nothing. With her hands gripping the countertop, I can see her knuckles turning white. My body aches to touch her, to soothe her, but I realize there are some things she needs to learn to do for herself.

"I'm sorry, Sloane. I shouldn't be barking orders at you like I've done today..."

She turns suddenly and lifts her head to meet my eyes. "You're only trying to help—"

"Stop, this is what I am talking about, Sloane. You don't need to make excuses for my shitty behavior. I pissed you off. Why didn't you yell at me? At the very least, tell me to mind my own damn business?"

Lowering her gaze, she shrugs her shoulders.

"Maybe I'm just a natural submissive." Her words come out in a breathy whisper. Peering up at me through her long auburn lashes, she grins.

Fuck. Me.

"You use your novel writing and research as an avoidance tactic." Leaning in, I lower my voice, allowing the tone's gravel-like nature to take over as I speak into her ear. "You may have some submissive tendencies in the bedroom, but I see fire, too. It's okay to let that out once in a while. It's okay to stand up for yourself, even if it makes someone uncomfortable. You don't always have to come in last."

"Does your secret agency—"

"SIA, Select Intelligence Agency," I interrupt.

"Does SIA make you take psychology classes, too, Dr. Phil?" Her quip eases the tension in my shoulders, but I know I will help this girl find her voice.

Pulling my upper body back to give her a bit of space, I smirk. "You'd be surprised by the types of education I've had over the years. But that's not why I see you, Red. I see you because I've spent years deep in avoidance, too."

"What could you possibly be avoiding? You've faced your demons, Loki, and won."

"Did I, though? Yes, my family is safe now. Hundreds of people no longer have to live in fear, but what do I have to show for it? I've run on hatred and loathing for so long I don't even know how to fit back into the life I left all those years ago. Seeing Preston with Emory has really hit that home for me. Everyone moved on with their lives while I've been on the periphery. Watching from the outside, making sure they all stayed safe in their bubble."

"You haven't spent much time with them. It will all fall into place, Loki. They love you, and they're not about to let you slip away again."

Raking a hand through my hair, I sigh because I know she's right. I place my hand over Sloane's tapping fingers, and my body calms unfamiliarly. My life has always come with a certain level of anxiety. Standing in this eight hundred square foot cabin, holding her hand, I feel at home. I know I will regret this later, but for now, I allow us to relax into the comfort of silence.

Gently tugging her hand free, she lays it on my forearm, and it's like an electric shock right to my cock. "I'll help you adjust back into life. Being stuck here with me for God knows how long will be a crash course. If you can survive me, you'll adjust back in Waverley-Cay just fine." She smiles, and it almost reaches her eyes. There's a sadness there still, though, and it tugs at my heart.

"There isn't anyone I would rather be in hiding with, Red. I mean that." I wait until she glances up. Making eye contact, I say it again, "I'm happy to be here with you, Sloane. Who knows, maybe we'll be able to help each other."

"Yeah?" Her face transforms, and something inside of me changes. When her eyes smile at me like that, I forget the hatred and hurt I've built my life on. She makes me want more than I ever imagined, and I haven't even fucking kissed her yet.

No, Loki. Not yet. Not at all. You can't kiss her—

"So, I wasn't kidding about not being able to cook. It's one of the many skills I'm working on, but until recently, I never had a chance to try."

"Try cooking?"

"Try anything. My sisters worked their asses off, but they always took pity on me because I was the baby. I guess it started with Emory. She took the world on her shoulders, so the rest of us never missed out on anything. That trickled down to Eli and Tilly, but by the time I was old enough to help, they had a schedule. I just seemed to get in the way, so it was easier for everyone if I let them do it. The few times I tried to help with anything always ended in disaster."

"So you learned to blend in, not cause any problems, and do whatever you could to make life easier for those around you?"

She nods her head. "I guess."

"What about now? You're an adult, living on your own ..."

"And making a mess of my life at every turn." She smacks her palm to her forehead. "God, why does shit just fly out of my freaking mouth when I'm talking to you?"

My face beams, and I feel the happiness from my toes to my ears. "I guess I'm easy to talk to. Though, admittedly, you would be the first person in the world to ever say that."

I'm rewarded with a genuine laugh. When she places her fingertips on the side of my jaw, I forget how to breathe.

"You are shockingly easy to talk to, Loki. Thank you for listening."

"I feel like there is so much more I need to hear."

"Some secrets are better left unsaid."

"I disagree," I growl. She releases my face, and I miss the contact. "To recap, your issues are that you don't like to be alone. You put others first, even to your detriment. You don't stick up for yourself, and you pretend to be happy to make life easier for those around you."

"When you make a character map like that, I sound pretty fucked up. But, you forgot the biggest plot of all."

"Oh yeah, what's that?" I ask, unable to tear my gaze from her shining green eyes.

"I run."

Right, my runner.

"Baby, by the time I'm done with you, there will be nowhere you want to run to."

"Are you saying you're going to fix me, Loki Kane?" She smirks, but her eye contact is fleeting.

"No, Red. I'm not going to fix you. That would imply you're broken."

"Aren't I?"

"I don't think you're broken. I think you're lost, and we're all a little lost sometimes. You just need help finding your way home. I can't do it for you, but I can help if that's what you want."

"What about you? Can I help you?"

Fuck yes, you can help me by stripping down right here.

Jesus Christ, get a grip.

I like the way her body molds to mine when I lean into her space. Taking a deep inhale through my nose to calm my racing heart, the scent of her overwhelms me. "What are you going to help me do, Sloane?" I murmur.

Tilting her face, we are nose to nose as she works to swallow. The muscles in her exposed neck work hard, and I'm assaulted by visions of running my tongue down that silky skin.

"Live," she whispers. "I'm going to help you live. Teach you to have some fun. I'm going to help you adjust back to normal life."

"Civilian life," I mutter.

"It has a lot to offer." She grins.

Like you?

Fucking hell. What is going on with my thoughts lately? I have no self-control, and it's making me antsy. Moving a couple of steps to the left, I try to compose myself.

"Okay, so ... dinner?"

Crossing her arms over her rib cage, she leans against the sink. The action causes her tits to present themselves, and I feel light-headed.

"Hey, are you all right?" she asks, coming to my aid immediately.

"Yeah, I …" Blinking slowly, I try to get my shit together. I can't exactly tell Sloane that it's her fucking tits causing my brain to short circuit.

"Come on." She wraps her arm around my middle, and guides me to the bed. "You went from zero to a thousand when you woke up this morning, at 4:50 a.m., and you've been going non-stop since. You pushed too hard today, Loki. So dinner will be up to me." Her voice is upbeat, but I can see her fingers working. Tap-tap-slide.

"I'm fine. Honestly, I just need some food in me, and I'll be good to go."

"Get in bed, Loki. If you don't want cereal, I can manage a sandwich. That's about the extent of my cooking ability, though, so those are your choices."

"Sweetheart? You can order me to bed any damn day of the week, but this is what I'm talking about. See how strong you are when it's for someone else? This," I say, pointing to her body language, "says, *'Don't fuck with me.'* You need to apply the same standard when protecting yourself."

Sloane scowls but doesn't say anything.

"Okay, okay," I acquiesce. Turning, I let my pants fall to the ground. I pinch my shirt behind my neck, pull it over my body, and drop it to the floor as well. Climbing into the bed, I pull the sheet over me and smirk when I find Sloane drooling. "Did you like the show?"

"You're, you're not wearing underwear."

Oh shit.

"Oh, ah, Christ."

"Why, Mr. Kane, are you blushing?"

"Red, don't call me Mr. Kane while I'm lying naked in a bed." My voice is low as I fight for control.

The sharp intake of air tells me she gets my drift just fine.

"Listen, I-I'm sorry. Fucking Preston. He sent you all that, that stuff to sleep in, and the asshat couldn't even send a single pair of boxers. I completely forgot I was freeballing it when I just dropped my pants. I'm sorry."

Her face is flushed, and I swear, I caught her fanning herself. "No worries, it was a great show. Now I'll have inspiration for the scene I have to write tonight." Winking, she turns and heads to the other side of the room. There's no escaping each other here. We had both better get used to it.

I'm going to kill Preston. Grabbing my phone, I send a text to the first thread I find with his name.

Loki: You're an asshole.

Dexter: There's a lot of us on this thread, man. You'll have to be more specific.

Loki: Preston. Preston is a dingle dick.

Preston: How'd you sleep? (winky face emoji)

Loki: You're a grown man. Don't use the fucking winky face emoji.

Preston: (winky face emoji, winky face tongue emoji, winky face emoji.)

Ashton: Is this using technology sparingly? What did he do now?

Loki: He sent lingerie for Red, not fucking pajamas, and the asshole sent no goddamn underwear for me at all.

Trevor: No use in fighting it, Loki. GG is three for three. She's going for a grand slam.

"Sloane?" I mutter. "Have you spent any time with Lanie's grandmother, GG?"

"Not a ton. She's funny though, why?"

"Nothing, never mind."

Loki: I have never met this woman.

Dexter: Doesn't matter. She pulled your card. Batter up!

Loki: Just send some freaking underwear, please. And

maybe some flannel pajamas for Sloane. Big granny nightshirts in flannel would work, too, though.

Ashton: No packages.

Preston: Sorry, buddy. Good luck.

Loki: Fuck off.

Trevor: Luvs. Have you explained blue balls yet? (laughing face emoji)

They're the worst. They're also the best things to ever happen to me. I forgot how much I missed them. It's always been easier to push their memories away than to spend dark months knowing what I was missing.

I lift my gaze, and am mesmerized by Sloane's movements. Maybe this girl will bring me back to life after all.

CHAPTER 20

SLOANE

Loki was right. After some food, he was feeling much better, but now I'm the dizzy one. My new brother-in-law is a sneaky bastard. He may not have sent Loki any underwear, but he did make sure to send about ten pairs of gray sweatpants. Does he not know about the gray sweatpants movement that has been all over social media for years? Gah!

I have to sit here pretending not to notice the sizeable bulge in Loki's pants as he paces our small space. There's a storm rolling in, and he swears he can feel a draft. It's probably caused by his balls swinging every time he moves, but I don't mention that.

Attempting once again to focus, I turn my screen so Loki is only in my peripheral vision and open up my manuscript. I stare so long the words become blurry, but I cannot get my brain to cooperate. It's hyper-aware of every move my roommate makes. That's why when the phone rings, I nearly swipe the entire laptop to the ground with my wild reaction.

"Are you always this jumpy?" Loki asks, passing me on his way to retrieve the phone from the charger. It doesn't even matter whose phone is ringing because we talk to the same people, so I go back to my screen as he answers.

"Hey, Ash. What's up?" There's a long pause while Loki listens.

Glancing up, I notice he's frozen in place.

"I, is that normal?" Something in Loki's voice raises the hairs on my neck, so I turn to give him my full attention and find his penetrating gaze already on me.

"How many are there?"

Loki seems agitated, but it isn't causing my fight or flight to kick in.

What's going on, Mr. Kane?

"You want me to ask her? Seriously?"

Okay, now I'm nervous.

Loki sighs, visibly unhappy, but presses a button on the phone.

"Ashton is on your social media profiles."

The air I had been holding hostage slowly releases from my lungs in a huff.

"Hi, Ash! What? What's the matter?" I ask, searching Loki's eyes.

"You know what? Maybe you two had better have this conversation. Loki, call me back."

"Don't you dare wimp out on me," Loki bellows, but the screen turns black. Ashton already hung up.

"What's going on?" Oh, shit. *Did Jackson create another account?*

"So, he was going through your accounts and ... well, it's probably better if I just show you. Hand me your computer?"

"We aren't supposed to go on social from here," I tell him. My blood pressure is spiking, and my leg bounces rapidly under the table.

"I'll use a scrambler, and we won't be on long. He just wasn't sure how to respond."

"Did, did Jackson make a new account?"

His fingers pause on the keyboard, and his eyes drift closed as he sucks in air.

"Who is Jackson, Sloane?"

Damnnit. I guess not.

"It's not important. You're scaring me, Loki. What the hell is going on?"

Reaching across the table, he places a hand over my tapping fingers and squeezes. Then he rests our joined hands on my bouncing knee, and both fidgeting behaviors cease.

"You never have to be afraid when I'm here, Red. Never. I will protect you, I promise. You'll need to tell me about Jackson at some point." Turning the computer screen toward me, I'm assaulted by a barrage of dick pics.

"Ugh, seriously? You need to prepare me for that shit." Leaning in, I realize he has opened the messages app of my Facebook author page. "If you think this is bad, you should see the Twitter account."

"What?"

"Yeah. Is this what he didn't know how to handle? A bunch of dicks?"

"You're saying this is normal?"

"Well, no. It's not normal in real life, but for my public persona, it is. It's nothing to worry about. Most of the time, I just report and delete them."

Ping.

"What the hell is that?"

I shrug and open the box to the full screen. "Oh, it's just a message request."

"From who?" he asks, bewildered.

"How am I supposed to know?" Opening the dialogue box, I see his name.

Dom: Hello, Dear. You are a very beautiful woman.

"His name is Dom? Are you fucking kidding me?" Loki grabs the computer and starts typing.

"Hey? What are you doing? You can't respond to these

guys. This isn't a joke. Just ignore them and report it to Facebook. What are you writing?"

Loki doesn't answer. He just continues to type, erase, and retype over my questions.

"Loki? Honestly, this is my livelihood. You have to be careful with how you respond to this stuff."

His hardened gaze lifts to mine.

Shit. Now he looks pissed. Circling the table, I stand behind him to see what he is typing.

Dom: Hello. You are a very beautiful woman.
Sloane: Thank you. My husband thinks so.
Dom: Ah, you're married?
Sloane: Yes.
Dom: ...

"Seriously, Loki. Just end the chat."

Dom: Are you happily married?

"Happily married? What the fuck kind of question is that? Is he kidding me right now?" Loki barks. Hunching over the laptop, he types and erases a response.

"They're scum bags, Loki. This is why you can't interact with them."

Sloane: Yes.
Dom: I bet I could change your mind.

"That slimy piece of shit."

Sloane: Thank you, but I'm very happily married.

"You have to be kidding me? Loki, what are you doing? Do you realize that you're rage typing to a crazy man you've never even met?"

Loki glances up. "I'm not rage typing."

"Yeah, you kinda are," I giggle.

He ignores me and goes back into my profile. Once he finds the settings, he changes my status to married.

"Hey? You can't just make me a married woman."

"I just did."

"The most romantic proposal in the history of marriage,"

I say, rolling my eyes.

Ping.

Going back into the messages app, Loki growls. "That motherfucker."

Peering over his shoulder, I see Dom has sent a picture of himself masturbating.

"Blah. See? This is why you don't respond to this shit," I lecture.

"Can I kiss you?"

My head whips to Loki so fast I'm lightheaded. Surely, I heard him wrong.

"What?"

"Can. I. Kiss. You?"

He's struck me dumb ... again. Bobblehead Sloane, reporting for duty.

A growl rumbles deep in his chest as he lunges and drags me into his lap. With his hands on either side of my face, he watches my eyes.

"I'm going to kiss you, and I want to take a picture of it. Is that okay with you?"

Bobblehead Sloane replies for me. Luckily, that's enough of an answer for him because Loki closes his mouth on mine. His lips are firm but soft as he rubs them gently back and forth over my skin. When his hands tangle in my hair, my head falls back, causing me to gasp, and he pounces. He takes my bottom lip into his mouth with his teeth, and I moan. His tongue runs along the outside of my lip as if he's tasting me.

Adjusting my leg, I straddle him in the chair. My core comes into contact with his growing erection, and my hips swivel, begging for the friction. His tongue darts into my mouth, and I swear to freaking God, I might hear angels sing.

Shamelessly grinding on him, I'm lost. Loki never gives up control of the kiss, but I feel his body tensing beneath my fingers. He releases my lip with a pop and places his hands on my hips. He follows the gyrating movements for a few rotations and then holds me in place as he slowly pulls his head away.

"Red." The rawness in his voice worries me, but I already know he's going to put an end to this. Swallowing the lump in my throat, I wait for him to continue. "We can't get carried away here. We can't …"

"Yeah. Yeah, no, of course. Right."

His gaze leaves mine, and I turn to see what he's looking at. On the computer is a picture of us. His hands are in my hair, and his lips are almost touching my jaw. He's staring at me so intently in this picture, but it's the expression on my face that has me blushing. It's the most intimate picture I've ever seen of myself. I look wanton. Sexy. And it was all for show.

Confused, I scramble off his lap. With practiced skill, I swallow my feelings and put on a smile.

"Well, you got a good picture. I'm going to take a quick shower before I start writing. I get my best thoughts in the shower, you know? Okay, well, um, don't do anything stupid with Dom. Just, I guess, just erase it. He'll go away, eventually."

Stumbling as I turn, I steady myself and speedwalk the ten steps to the bathroom door.

CHAPTER 21

LOKI

I know I just fucked up, big time. But I cannot tear my gaze away from the screen before me. Sloane, I can't take my eyes off of Sloane. Her red hair is falling around my hands that I forced into her ponytail, but it's the look in her eyes that has me immobile.

Through the cloud of lust this picture initially elicits, it's the trust I see that has me off balance. Red's eyes tell her story, and right now, they're telling me she trusts me implicitly. Knowing she doesn't trust easily, I have to wonder if I have just done irreparable damage to our relationship.

Ping.

This cocksucker is going down. Pulling up the screen, I'm tempted to send him our picture, but it's an invasion of Red's privacy. Plus, I don't want that dirtbag seeing her like this. I don't want anyone seeing it. Caveman tendencies have me wanting to scream, *"She's mine!"* even though that can never be the case. Instead, I send it to my private emergency link, then erase it from her screen.

Turning back to Dom, I contemplate how to handle him for only a handful of minutes.

Sloane: Why would I want that limp dick when I have a real man at home?

Sloane: (image sent)

Sloane: Fuck off and don't bother me again.

Less than two minutes later, my phone rings, and I already know it's Ashton.

"Please tell me you did not just send a dick pic to a random stranger from your *safe* house?"

"I turned on the scrambler," I tell him, then close out all the screens and turn off the network.

"That was an irresponsible and stupid risk," he fires back.

"I know."

"What's really going on with you, Loki?"

"I-I don't know, dude. My head still isn't right. I can't remember something big, and it's killing me."

"I get that, man, I do. But that's not what I'm talking about. You just sent a fifty-year-old sleaze ball a picture of your dick. You responded emotionally."

"Retrograde amnesia?"

His bitter laughter echoes through the line. "That might work with some assholes, but not me. Sloane is making you feel things, and you're not fighting it. Six months ago, you would have been a robot. You wouldn't have called Seth and told him to find a man sounding like you'd happily cut anyone's throat that got in the way. You would have seen these messages from Dom and quietly blocked him."

He's not wrong. But what he doesn't know is that I would still have found the asshole who hurt Sloane. I just would have done it on my own, and I would have taken care of douche dingle Dom in a similar fashion. It's what I do. I take care of shit behind the scenes.

"I don't know, Ash."

"Want to know what I think?" He doesn't wait for me to reply. "I think you already know you're done with SIA, and you're struggling because you don't know where that leaves you. You haven't been without a plan since you were fifteen, and it's scaring the shit out of you."

"I'm not done with SIA until I can walk away a free man," I tell him.

"I would expect nothing less. Seth and I are working on it. Maybe you should use this time with Sloane to figure out what you want from life now? I'm not one to push things like this, but GG is rarely wrong. Maybe that's something you should explore while you have the time to do it, distraction-free."

"Explore Sloane?" I say, more to myself than to him.

Chuckling, Ashton replies, "Well, that's a dirty way to put it, but yeah. Figure out where you want to go from here, Loki. I have some ideas for you professionally, but you need to have your shit together before we go down that road."

"You've been waiting for this day."

"Waiting and planning. Ryan is retiring, and he is looking to sell EnVision Securities," Ashton explains. "I was prepared to take over until you and Seth got out. Now that your timeline seems to be escalating, we can look into a partnership if that's something you're interested in?"

I'm taken aback. I've always known Ashton would have a plan, but that he has built his plans around me in the best possible way is humbling.

"O-Of course I'm interested," I choke out. "We make a fucking awesome team."

"We do. I haven't talked to Seth yet, but I'd like him to be an equal partner. I know he won't have the capital to invest initially, so I figured we could spot him, and work it into the terms. I think it would be good for him, too."

Ashton is a Westbrook to his core. This family looks out for their own, and they really have taken both Seth and me in. Uncomfortable emotion threatens the back of my chest, and I'm thankful he can't see me.

"Yeah, me too," I agree.

"Okay, we can talk to Seth once we get Vic and his shit sorted. We have a plan for your future, Loki. Now, it's up to you to decide what it's going to look like."

"Right." Glancing up at the closed bathroom door, I have to wonder if my future is on the other side.

"I'll call soon with an update."

"Sounds good. Thanks, Ash."

"You got it."

Ending our call, I glance around the cabin. When did this place start feeling like home? Closing Red's computer, I stand to search again for the draft when I hear it—a muted buzzing sound. Checking her computer and the phones, I realize it's coming from the bathroom.

I knock twice. "Sloane?"

Nothing.

"Sloane?" I knock again, louder this time. Pressing my ear to the door, I hear nothing but the spray of the shower. *I'm losing my goddamn mind.* Resting my forehead against the door, I finally compose myself enough to pull away when her anguished scream makes my blood run cold.

Rushing through the door as images of someone pulling her through the bathroom window run through my mind, I'm disoriented by what I find.

Red is sitting on the shower bench with one leg dangling. The other is bent, propped against the shower wall. Her head is hanging back, and her eyes are closed. Her mouth is open and panting. One hand caresses her left breast, rolling a nipple between her thumb and forefinger, and the other is on the toy between her thighs. I should say something, interrupt her, but I can barely breathe, let alone think.

I can just see the edge of the toy from here. It's small. It must fit in the palm of her hand, but by the looks of things, it packs a punch. Her hand adjusts as her back arches. Tiny moans of pleasure squeak out from her lips.

With a hand still on the door, I catch my breath and know

I need to get out of here. I take a step to go but cannot take my eyes off her. Sloane's body quivers, and I force myself to take another step.

"Loki," she murmurs, cementing me in place just before her body convulses in the most erotic scene I've ever witnessed.

I'm still standing in shock with a painful erection when her eyes suddenly open wide as she gasps for air in the aftermath of her orgasm. I watch in rapture as her body comes down from the highest of highs, and then reality sets in.

Peering into the glass enclosure of the shower, I don't move. I don't even blink as she stares at me with dewy eyes.

Dropping her gaze to the floor, she removes her Airpods, then wraps her fingers around the edge of the bench. Her back rises and falls with each breath.

Snap out of it, Loki, and say something for Christ's sake.

When Red pushes to her feet suddenly, I'm filled with an awareness I don't know what to do with. Every inch of my body and soul needs to claim this woman. My hands itch to touch her, and I still cannot form a coherent word.

Standing bare before me, she opens the glass door and steps out onto the mat. Her gaze never leaves mine as she crosses the small space in three quick steps. When she's only inches from me, I find my voice.

Staring down into her emerald eyes, I try to form an apology. "Red, I-I'm so sorry. I thought I heard something, and, well? I knocked. You didn't answer."

She nods without breaking eye contact. *What the fuck is she thinking right now?* Unconsciously, she bites her bottom lip. Beyond her eyes, I can see the nervous movements of her fingers and want to soothe her, but she speaks before I can react.

"You require control."

Swallowing gravel, I nod.

"This is one area of my life where I don't need it."

Reaching up, she takes my hand in hers. Turning it over, so my palm faces the ceiling, she gently drops a soft, warm piece of pink, rubberized material into it. That tightly wound control I've been fighting to hold on to breaks. I close my fist tightly around the toy, and it begins to vibrate.

Without breaking eye contact, I take a step to the side and place it on the counter. Red's shoulders droop immediately, and I realize she misunderstands. Using quick movements, I circle her.

When her back is to my front, I lean down to whisper in her ear, "Toys won't be necessary our first time, Red. All your pleasure will come from me and only me. My fingers," I growl, running my index finger down her spine to the crack of her ass. "My tongue." Walking to face her again, I lean in to lick a line across her collarbone. "My hands." Moving to her side, I circle her once more and place my hand over her mound.

"Ahh," she gasps at the contact.

Circling my palm on her clit, I tease her opening with my middle finger as I pull her body into mine. When her back slams into my cock, I groan.

"Loki," she pleads.

"Yeah, baby?"

CHAPTER 22

SLOANE

"I — Oh, God." He cannot expect me to form sentences when he moves against me like that. *Can he?* Good Lord.

"Are you giving me control, Red?" His voice sounds low and dangerous next to my ear, and my core clenches. "You like my voice." It isn't a question. He just felt my body react to him from the inside.

Painfully slowly, he removes his fingers from my pussy and turns me around. Staring up into his eyes, I'm awkwardly aware that he is fully clothed while I am buck-ass naked. I fight the urge to fidget, but my fingers move in time with my thoughts. Middle finger-middle finger-thumb. Tap-tap-slide. Over and over again, until Loki reaches down and takes them in his grasp.

My heart pounds as he raises them to his lips. Taking my middle finger into his mouth, he sucks hard, then bites down on the pad of my finger, and I yelp.

"Is there anything you don't like, sweetheart?"

Ah, yeah, there's a lot I don't like. Asparagus comes to mind.

Holy shit, Sloane. Focus.

"A-Are you going to give me a safe word or something?" My voice wobbles while his eyes darken.

He releases my finger from his mouth, guides it to my clit, and holds it there. Lowering his mouth to mine, he speaks over my lips, "No, Red. I don't do safe words—"

"Gah!" My awkward gasp cuts him off, and he smirks.

"I don't do safe words because I am not a dom, and you're not a submissive. This isn't some fucked up shade of gray. This is us, and all you need is your voice. The second you don't like something, you speak up. You say no, and everything stops. I may require control, Sloane, but I need your trust more. Do you trust me?"

"With my life." There was no hesitation. I responded on instinct. In my heart, I know I can trust Loki with all that I am.

"Good. Don't move. I'll be right back."

"What?" I screech.

He smiles as he walks out of the bathroom, and I nearly come apart. Peering down at myself, I cannot believe I had a full conversation with that man-candy while completely naked.

The longer I stand in silence, the more I second guess myself, though. My body shivers as droplets of water from my shower slowly dry. Tap-tap-slide.

"Face the mirror," Loki commands from the doorway.

Keeping my eyes trained on him, I do as he asks—a look of appreciation covering his chiseled face.

"Eyes forward, Red."

Facing the mirror, I stare as he moves from the doorframe toward me with deliberate ease. He stops behind me and places his hands on my shoulders before leaning down to whisper.

"Look at how fucking sexy you are," he growls. Until now, I haven't allowed my gaze to leave his. Hearing his words, I glance up to see him watching my reflection before us.

My face is flushed, and my body is tingling with anticipation. My eyes linger momentarily on the extra pounds around my middle, and I self-consciously suck in my stomach.

Loki removes his right hand from my shoulder. Tracing a line down my spine, across my back, and over my hip, he squeezes the area just above my hip bone. Opening his mouth, he groans, "You're so fucking sexy, Sloane ... all of you."

His hand moves lower, his palm sliding across my belly.

"Stay in the moment with me, Red."

I inhale sharply as he pulls my pink blindfold from his back pocket. He holds it out before me in silent question.

With my heart in my throat, I nod my agreement. The last thing I see before I'm cloaked in darkness is Loki's appreciative but hungry gaze. Licking my lips, I wait.

Dear Lord, what the hell am I doing? Trying desperately not to fidget, I lose the battle when my toes start tapping out a nervous beat. I know Loki's watching me, I can feel the heat of him behind me, but I hear no sounds of movement.

"Trust me, sweetheart," he rasps, closer than I expected him to be.

"I-I do."

He releases a hot breath near my shoulder blade, and my knees buckle. *How the hell am I going to make it through this if a simple breath can knock me off my feet?* Loki places open-mouthed, wet kisses crisscrossing my back. Lower and lower he goes until I feel his tongue at the dimple of my ass.

Holy shit.

"Loki, I-I've never ..."

"Shh, Red." Palming my ass, he squeezes one cheek, then the other.

Do we do anal, Sloane? Gawd, now I'm talking to myself. But, is that something I ...

"Relax, baby. I'm not after your ass. Tonight, anyway." I

feel him grin against my body as his tongue dips lower down my crease.

Loki stands suddenly, my senses going into overdrive so fast I feel dizzy. Without sight, my ears strain to compensate. I'm panting in anticipation of his touch, and fight to drown out the blood rushing through my ears.

The clanking of metal has me tilting my head to the right. I hear a swishing sound, then the whoosh of his pants hitting the floor, and my body floods with warmth.

"Ahh," I purr as something soft floats down the side of my body. I get a whiff of Loki and assume he's teasing me with his shirt. Over and over again, it ghosts my body. Down one side, across my hips, then up to my center, it travels.

With firm pressure, Loki presses my back forward, leaning into me. I feel his naked form and gulp. Pressing his body into mine from behind, he guides my arms forward. He places them on the countertop, and continues to push my back down until I'm bent at a ninety-degree angle.

"Open your legs," he rumbles at my ear.

"Oh, God."

"Not God, sweetheart. Just Loki."

I don't get a chance to reply because he drops to his knees. With hands holding firmly onto my hips, he pulls them back, thrusting my body into his face. Widening my stance, Loki moves in closer. His tongue, gentle at first, laps at my opening while a hand snakes around my front, searching for a bundle of nerves. When his finger lands on my clit, he moves in slow, torturous circles. I'm overcome with sensation. While his middle finger plays my clit like the chord of an electric guitar, I see stars.

My core pulsates around him, and he growls, "Yes, Red. Fucking, yes."

I feel him grasping the end of the blindfold, and light floods my senses. Clamping my eyes shut, I try to revel in the moment.

"Open your eyes, Sloane. Look."

Hearing his voice, I open them immediately. Raising my head, I find his reflection in the mirror.

"Watch. I want you to see what you look like when you come."

I open my mouth to speak, but his fingers work their magic, and within seconds I'm spiraling higher than I ever knew possible.

"Watch, Sloane. See how beautiful you are," Loki grinds out.

I'm a panting, whimpering mess. My body is seeking release, and he knows it. Pushing back into his hand, he stiffens his tongue and makes a curling motion. My body thrashes violently against him, but he holds me steady.

"Come, Red. Come now."

As if he'd written the book of Sloane, my body responds. My legs tremble beneath me, and fireworks go off inside of my body—wave after wave of pleasure crash through me as he continues his ministrations.

Gasping, I plead, "Loki, p-please. I can't."

He releases me so quickly I have to straighten my arms to catch myself. With a hand on my bicep, he spins me. When I'm facing him, he lifts me onto the counter and stands between my legs. My brain struggles to follow along with our movements as I stare into his caramel-colored eyes.

Placing a hand on each side of my face, he lowers his mouth to mine. "You can, Sloane. You can, and you will. Can't is no longer part of your vocabulary. You can do anything you set your fucking mind to, do you hear me?"

I try to break free from his grasp as emotions overwhelm me, but he holds steady. We're not talking about orgasms here, and it's too much. Refusing to let me go, I blink back tears as I'm forced to see the honesty in his words.

He gives me a second longer to adjust to the emotions of his statement, and then his lips descend on mine once more.

When he releases me, my head falls back against the mirror, and I'm able to take him in. Standing before me, in all his manly glory, is Loki Kane. His mouth trails down my neck, and I crane it to the left to give him better access.

As if my brain is coming out of a fog, my hands wrap around his back. I'm desperate to touch any part of him I can reach. Trying to draw him in, I wrap my legs around his waist. I'm manic in my attempts to get him closer, but Loki is composed, and he slows my movements.

Pulling back, he lowers his gaze to my chest, and his cock bobs angrily between us. My eyes dart back and forth between his face and his dick while I wait for his next move. Somehow, I know he needs to be the one to make it. I want him to make it. When he leans down and blows warm air on my nipple, it hardens to a painful peak that he quickly takes into his mouth and soothes with his flattened tongue.

Jesus, this man knows how to use his tongue.

He trails a finger down my center, and I whimper, "Loki, please."

"Are you ready for me, sweetheart?"

"Fuck, yes."

A slow, Cheshire-like smile glides across his face as he wraps a fist around his engorged length.

God, it's huge. I nod, even though I'm not sure if he asked a question. Licking my lips, I tentatively reach out. My fingertip runs over the velvety head, and he hisses his approval. Bringing my hand to my mouth, I lick from palm to fingertip and watch his eyes darken.

Sliding my moistened hand back to his shaft, I give it a gentle tug and see Loki's jaw tick. Giving head has never been something I've wanted before, but with him, I crave it. I want this man's dick in my mouth like I want my last meal, and he knows it.

Placing a hand over mine, he guides me in the motion he prefers. It's firm and uncompromising. I have an insight into how he will fuck. Fast and hard. My pussy clamps down at the thought.

Wiggling, I attempt to slide off the counter. I need him in my mouth. Loki takes a step back, but doesn't let me fall to my knees as I'd planned.

"Not today. If you put that dirty mouth on my cock right now, it'll be over before we even start."

Start? Jesus, I thought we were in the final round.

Correctly reading my confusion, Loki chuckles. "Oh, sweetheart, trust me. This is just the beginning."

"Gulp."

Did I really just say gulp?

Loki reaches past me and opens a drawer where he pulls out a box of condoms.

"Apparently, we can thank GG for these," he grumbles while tearing the box open.

"That woman should be a spokeswoman for Trojan." I smirk. The smile vanishes as Loki rolls the condom over the weeping head of his shaft.

He steps forward, so my chest is flush with his rib cage, and I have to tilt my head to make eye contact.

"Are you ready for me, Red?"

"Yes."

"Do you want me to fuck you?"

"I told you I did."

"I need you to say it. Consent is sexy. It was drilled into all of us at an early age." He grins.

"Fuck me, Loki. Please."

He hooks an arm under my left knee and pulls my leg up the side of his body.

"What was it you said about sex standing up being impossible?"

"I-ah, oh shit."

He grins wickedly as he dips low, bringing his cock to my entrance. Standing to his full height, he slowly enters me.

The blood rushing to every part of my body whooshes loudly in my ears.

He dips again, but this time when he stands, he thrusts his hips up and forward.

"Ahh."

"What other positions do we need to demystify for you, Sloane?"

I shake my head because I can't speak.

"You're so fucking tight, baby. Do you feel how your body grips me when I pull out? Feel how you cling to me when I slam back in?"

Holy shit, maybe Loki should be the romance writer.

Gripping my hair at the scalp, he tilts my head back and then turns my face toward the mirror. I watch our reflection as he moves in and out of me. He leans down and bites the tender skin on my neck while speaking.

"Is this how you write your characters, Red? Tits bouncing with each thrust? Look at us," he commands. "You're so fucking wet, sweetheart. My cock is dripping with you."

"M-My stories have never been like this," I admit as he picks up the pace of his thrusts.

"Like, what?" He plunges harder into me.

"This, hot," I pant.

"I'm going to show you how fucking hot you are, Sloane." He slows the pace, steadily rocking in and out of me. The leg I'm standing on begins to shake. "I'm going to teach you how fucking valuable you are. Look at me."

I tear my gaze away from our reflection and am met with the most genuine expression of desire and admiration I've ever seen. It makes my throat tight, and I fight the urge to run.

"I mean it," he purrs.

Unable to speak, I nod a few times. Finally, he releases my gaze, and I gasp for breath.

Leaning down, he growls, "Wrap your arms around my neck, and hang on."

I barely have time to register his words before he leans down, hitches my other leg under his arm, and hauls me up his body. With his hands on my ass and both legs hooked over his forearms, he glides my body up and down his cock at a frantic pace.

Glancing over Loki's shoulder, I see my body bouncing on his in the mirror. The reflection that's staring back at me is unrecognizable. The girl in the mirror is confident, sexy, and ... and whole. I've never seen myself that way before. It threatens to pull me from the moment.

Sensing a change, Loki turns us. With my back to the reflection, my mind falls to Loki.

"Stay here, with me. In this moment, Red," he grunts.

I'm not sure how much longer my body can take this pace.

"I'm, I'm going to come. I-I can't—"

"You can," he roars on a powerful thrust. Holding me to him, he's seated in me as far as he can go, and I've never felt so full. Using my hips, he grinds me against his pubic bone, and I come undone. I'm vibrating with sensitivity. Every inch of me has an electric current running through it as wave after wave of pleasure engulfs me.

He's spiraling fast as my orgasm thunders through my entire body. With a deafening roar, Loki screams out as his orgasm takes over. My pussy is still quivering while the last twitches of his release escape him.

My head falls forward onto his chest as we both pant and wheeze.

"Loki," I manage, though I'm not sure what I want to say. My brain isn't fully functioning yet, so I just stare as my body falls back to earth.

"Shh." He kisses my forehead and carries me, with his cock still buried deep inside of my channel, to the bed.

He pulls the sheets back and gently lays us down, then slowly pulls out of me, and I gasp. The emptiness I feel from the sudden disconnect is unfamiliar, but Loki leans down to kiss me softly.

"I'll be right back. I have to deal with the condom."

"Okay," I mumble, blinking slowly. *Holy fuck*, is my last thought before I wake with a start to a darkened room and a sleeping Loki draped over my naked body.

CHAPTER 23

LOKI

Returning from the bathroom, I find Sloane passed out, and I stand awkwardly for a few moments just watching her. *What the fuck did I just do? What do I do now? What are we going to do now?* All the questions run frantically through my head, but as I watch her, I can't bring myself to care.

Crossing the room, I lock the doors and engage the alarm system before climbing into bed carefully so I don't disturb her. Sloane rolls over and curls herself into my side.

She fits here, next to me, with me. What's more shocking is how much I like it. I've never been a cuddler, but I've also never had a normal relationship. There's not anything normal about this situation either, but Red is nothing like my usual fuck buddies.

Using the term fuck-buddy with Sloane makes me cringe, and I loathe myself for even comparing the two. *Why though? What's different with her?* It's not like we discussed the future, so it's reasonable to think of this as a casual fling. My mind rages at that thought, so I pull her closer to my chest. Cradling her against my side, I focus on the here and now.

With her warm, pliable body tangled up with mine, I eventually drift to sleep.

"Siiiiip."

The sound of someone sucking in air wakes me with a start. Years of training have taught me not to react physically, but every sense is on high alert. The bed shifts, and it takes half a second to realize where I am and that Sloane is gasping next to me.

Opening one eye, I'm relieved to see we're alone.

"Are you okay?" I ask as she gingerly climbs off the bed.

"Gah. Geez, you scared me. Yeah, I'm fine. Just, um, going to the bathroom."

I watch as she hurries out of sight. That's the second time she has woken up in a panic. *How often does that happen?* More importantly, why does it happen? Folding my arm behind my head, I wait for her to come back. My dick stirs, remembering her body. When I hear the shower, I know round two isn't happening.

My stomach grumbles as I search for my phone. It's the middle of the night, but we never had dinner. Standing at the bathroom door, I hesitate. Do I knock? Walk in? What's the protocol now?

Deciding manners always win, I knock, and the door swings open on impact. Unsure of what to do next, I'm flooded with déjà vu in the best ways as Sloane turns to me and smiles.

"You know, most people consider a shower to be a private affair."

Laughing, I realize I'm relieved to see she's okay.

"Yeah, sorry. I was only planning to knock. I guess the latch didn't catch."

I stare at her for far too long as she turns her face into the spray—tiny rivers of water cascade down her body. *Ask me to join you, Red.* I adjust my stance to make room for my growing erection.

"Did you need something, Loki?" she finally asks.

Fuck, that wasn't an invitation. Discreetly, I attempt to adjust myself. Sloane's laughter proves I can't hide anything from her.

"Yeah." I swallow the feelings attempting to bloom in my chest. "I was going to make something for dinner. Are you allergic to anything?"

Her smile sets off painful sparks in my chest. I press a hand to the spot in a misguided attempt to alleviate the feeling.

"Loki? Are you okay?"

"Huh?" Lowering my hand, I flex my fists to rein in feelings I don't know how to handle. "Yeah, I'm fine. Sorry, I was just thinking. So, allergies?"

She gives a questioning glance but finally shakes her head. "Just shellfish. I'm good with everything else."

"Shellfish, got it." Backtracking out of the bathroom, I shut the door behind me.

What the fuck is wrong with me? I'm not some horny fifteen-year-old boy. I shouldn't have such visceral reactions to her.

Shaking my head and swinging my arms back and forth, I try to shake out all these feelings. Deciding pasta bolognese will have to do for tonight, I grab some hamburger. While the meat browns, I text Ashton.

Loki: Any hits?

Ashton: WTF are you doing up?

Loki: Cooking. Anything?

Ashton: Dude. It's 2 a.m. Why are you cooking at 2 a.m.?

(Ashton added Seth at 2:03 a.m.)

Loki: Sloane got in the shower and woke me up. We haven't had dinner yet. Do you have anything for me?

Seth: Why is she showering at 2 in the morning?

Loki: Jesus, why the inquisition? Just tell me if you've gotten anywhere.

Ashton: We're working on it. We told you it would take time. You might as well settle in there.

Seth: I'm estimating the timeline to be a month, at least.

Ashton: Is everything okay with Sloane?

Loki: Fine.

Seth: Fine? Have you answered her questions yet?

Loki: She hasn't asked any.

Why the fuck isn't she asking me any?

Seth: What do you think of her tattoo?

Loki: What fucking tattoo? Sloane doesn't have a tattoo.

Ashton: ...

Seth: ...

(Ashton added Dexter at 2:08 a.m.)

Loki: For Christ's sake. Stop waking up the entire damn family. Do you have a lead or not?

Dexter: What's up, guys? I have a shitload of kids that will be up in less than four hours. This had better be good.

Ashton: Loki slept with Sloane.

Dexter: No shit? Already? Jesus, GG is fucking psychic.

Loki: WTF? I never said I slept with her.

Seth: How did you know she doesn't have a tattoo?

Dexter: Don't worry, dude. I'll start planning the MSL plan.

Loki: Fuck off.

(Dexter added Preston and Trevor at 2:27 a.m.)

Loki: Just get me some intel as soon as fucking possible.

I turn the goddamn phone off before the other assholes can put their two cents in and return to my sauce. By the time the water boils, Sloane has emerged from the bathroom.

"That smells good," she sighs as her stomach grumbles in

protest. "Sorry." She shrugs sheepishly. "I didn't realize how hungry I was."

Sloane stands awkwardly on the opposite side of the room. I hate the hesitancy I see in her posture. When her fingers start their special dance, I growl. I don't mean to, but it fucking pisses me off. Her eyes widen in surprise as I stalk toward her.

"Listen to me. We both know there's a lot we don't understand right now. A lot is going on that we can't control, but your needs come first while we're together. You come first. Do I make myself clear?"

"While we're together?" she mimics absentmindedly.

"While we're together," I confirm.

"Are we together?" she asks warily. "I don't do relationships." She says it as if I poisoned her.

Tap-tap-slide. I watch as she scratches various places on her arms. She won't make eye contact with me, and it makes me irrationally angry. She's flushed and starts fanning her face as her eyes dart from the door to the window like she's plotting her escape.

With her attention occupied, she doesn't see me reach out, so when my palm closes over her twitchy fingers, she nearly jumps out of her skin. *This is bullshit.* Taking a step forward, I encroach on her personal space.

"You can't run from me, Red. If this is too much, we can go back to thinking of this as a job," I mutter.

Please don't be what you want. I'm not sure that's a possibility for me anymore.

She rears back as if I struck her.

"What do you want, sweetheart?"

"I, I make up happily ever afters."

"I'm confused. Does that mean you don't get one in real life?"

Is that what I want? Do I want to try for a happily ever after with this girl? Fuck me. The longer I stare at her, the more I think it's a possibility.

She bites her bottom lip, and I notice her body tremble. Placing my hands on her shoulders, I force her to look at me.

"Hey?" I try to steady my voice, but I feel out of control for the first time in my life. "What's going on in that head of yours?"

"I ... Loki, I ..." Her voice wavers, and I can't stand the space between us anymore.

Pulling her into a hug, I hold on tight. I ignore the sinking feeling that if I don't keep her close, she'll run eventually.

We stand in silence, but after a minute or two, she mumbles into my bare chest. Her breath tickles my chest hair as she exhales.

"I don't do relationships with anyone that matters."

Pulling away, I peer down into her eyes. She has no idea.

"Are you saying I matter?" I ask cockily.

"You're part of my sister's family, Loki. I can't run from you when things go bad."

She's more jaded than Trevor was.

"And things will go bad?" I'm fighting a smirk, but she sees it.

"I'm trying to be serious," she mumbles.

Kissing the top of her head, I release her and walk to the stove to stir the meat.

"I know," I call over my shoulder. "I'm listening."

"I, I just don't do real."

"Okay. Well, this isn't exactly real life, right? Us, here? Locked away in the cabin?"

Peering over my shoulder, I see her frown. "No, it's not, but I don't see your point."

I don't get yours either, sweetheart, but give me time.

"So," clearing my throat, I fight to sound casual, "we'll take it one day at a time while we're here. We'll just see how things go."

"We'll be friends with benefits?"

Internally I cringe. It's better than fuck buddies, I guess.

Focusing my attention on the sauce in front of me, I shrug my shoulders. "If that's what you want to call it." When she doesn't reply, I glance up to find her watching me.

"What?" Peering down, I make sure my cock hasn't fallen out of the sweatpants.

Fucking Preston and the underwear.

"Friends with benefits doesn't fit the version of you I've built up in my head," she admits.

I swallow hard. How the hell do I answer that?

"Well, how about if we leave all preconceived notions at the door? I've been alone for a long time because I've had to be. But I haven't been celibate if that answers any questions for you."

"How many people have you slept with?" she asks. Coming closer, she sits on the counter next to me.

"Eight."

"Huh."

"Huh, good or huh, gross?" I'm not sure why it matters, but suddenly, I want to know how she feels about it.

"Just huh? Not as many as I would have thought."

"Well, I was a late bloomer. And, as an adult, I haven't had much free time. What about you? How many people have you slept with?"

"Two."

I'm stirring the sauce and pause at her response. "Was I the second or third?"

"No, I've slept with two people total, so you're the second."

I turn the burner off but don't move away from it. Exhaling slowly until I'm sure my voice can remain calm, I turn to her.

"The man who hurt you—"

"Did not rape me," she whispers. "A-A neighbor stopped

him."

The wooden spoon I'm holding snaps in my hand.

Hopping off the counter, Sloane places a hand on my arm. "It didn't happen. I'm okay."

"That's why you wake up scared every night."

"Yes." She doesn't elaborate, and I'm not sure I want her to. "Listen, I just have a lot of baggage. My mother abandoned us. My father is or was a violent alcoholic. My sisters gave up their lives to care for me. I've always been in the way. I'm not good for anyone, Loki. That's why I keep relationships at arm's length."

Bull shit.

"I doubt anyone else sees things that way, Red."

"You're probably right, but I'm done living my life with rose-colored glasses. So, friends with benefits, huh?" She flashes a mischievous grin.

"Sounds good to me," I lie. Staring into Sloane's emerald eyes, I know I want forever with this girl. I don't know what that entails or what I'll have to do to convince her, but I've never been a quitter. We'll start as friends with benefits if that makes her feel better. But I also know with absolute certainty, I'm going to demolish her walls and then help her rebuild.

Tap-tap-slide.

"What's on your mind, Sloane?"

"How long do we have until the food is ready?"

Removing the pan from the heat, I'm ready to haul her to bed when her stomach growls again. "Food first, then bed."

"Yes, sir."

The low groan that escapes me echoes through the cabin.

"Fuck it. I'll feed you in bed."

Clutching her around the middle, I lift her easily and toss her onto the bed. Then, I rush to the bathroom, and grab a handful of condoms. I've never been so fucking happy to have a meddling GG in my life.

CHAPTER 24

SLOANE

"Bake at 350 for thirty-five to forty minutes?"

"Yup. You've got this. Just sit there watching it," Lexi instructs over FaceTime.

"Tell her to take it out when the edges are brown, not black. Brown," GG's voice calls from somewhere behind Lexi.

In the three weeks we've been at the cabin, Loki tried to teach me to cook, and it ended with a fire in the oven. Sylvie tried, and I may have given Loki food poisoning. Julia's mother tried to help three times, and we ended up with some bricks to line the fireplace with.

After speaking to Lanie, she suggested I try GG. Supposedly, she's the queen of coffee cake. Go figure.

"Let me have that phone, Lex. You go find your Grumpy-Growler and tell him to get his ass in here for dinner."

"Fucking hell, GG. He's not my anything," she yells back.

"So, Easton's still there?" I ask.

"Like a bad rash," Lexi grumbles.

"Oh, shush. He's doing us a favor. A little sunshine from you won't hurt if ya know what I mean," GG says, waggling what's left of her eyebrows.

"You want me to pimp myself out to Easton?" Lexi counters.

"Get out of here, ya sassy little shit."

"Love you, GG. Bye Sloane. Good luck with the cake. I'll talk to you tomorrow," she calls while walking out of the frame.

"Right, talk to you tomorrow," I grumble. I've spoken to GG every day for the last week because I keep burning the shit out of this *no-fail* cake.

"Don't go feeling sorry for yaself. That will get us nowhere," GG scolds when we're alone again.

"I'm not."

"Ya are. I wasn't born yesterday, Runner." She also refuses to call me Sloane. I'm Runner, and Loki is Chaser.

"Where is Chaser today, anyway?" she asks.

"He's down the hill waiting for Marianne to bring our supplies."

We've been here longer than he expected and needed someone to replenish our groceries.

"All right. How're things goin' then?"

"They're okay. Loki's getting antsy. The updates aren't coming as quickly as he would like, but we've fallen into a routine."

It's true. The first week was hard. Loki sprang to life every goddamn morning at 4:50 a.m., and I was still writing until three or four most mornings, so our schedules were in severe conflict.

"So, he's stayin' up later, and you're goin' to bed earlier? You've compromised and found ways to work in each other's lives?"

I bite my tongue. I learned early on with GG to watch what you say. She can turn the most innocent of comments into a marriage proposal.

"We're adjusting for the situation," I say evasively.

"Ah, huh. How's the sex?" She brings the phone close to

her face to inspect me, and I can see straight up her nose.

"Jesus, GG. That's none of ..." *Well, shit*. She just got me to out myself.

"Just as I thought. Now, you listen to me, Runner. Don't go sprintin' away from those feelings just 'cause they're scary. Most things worth a pig's ear are."

"I think you have the wrong idea, GG. Loki and I are just friends with ..." I swallow the rest of that sentence.

"Yeah, yeah. I've heard it all before, child. I learned all about those one-night standards with Julia. I swear ya girls keep me on my toes, but ya also keep me young. Things get harder before they get better. Just remember, life is a marathon, not a sprint. Marathons take training, practice, and hard work, but the reward is always worth the pain. Oh, Lord. I gotta go. Betty Anne will be here to get me soon. We have reservations at the diner. Tommy is working tonight, and we like to get our seats early, so we have the best view." With a wink, she hangs up.

GG is a perverted old bat, but she loves hard, and my broken soul secretly worships her for it.

I stare at the phone long after she's hung up. Every day this week, she's given me the same speech in one form or another. I hate to be the one to break her perfect matchmaking record, but marriage isn't in my cards, and certainly not with someone like Loki. He deserves the perfection I write about, and I'm no princess.

The front door bursts open with a gust of wind whipping through the air. I rush to close it just as Loki steps through.

"Argh," I scream. "I thought the wind blew the door open."
"Ah, sweetheart?"
"What?" I ask, grabbing a couple of bags from his hand.
"Are you, um, baking again?"
"Oh shit." I run to the oven, and rip open the door as black clouds of smoke fill the air. "No, no, no," I scream. "GG

walked me through every step. This isn't supposed to be ready for another five minutes."

Loki sidesteps me. Grabbing the oven mitts, he removes my burned coffee cake and sets it on the counter.

Burying my face in my hands, I want to cry.

"Hey," Loki coos, slamming the door shut behind him. "This one wasn't so bad. I think the smoke is from the one that overflowed yesterday. Don't cry."

"Don't cry."

Oh, Loki. If you only knew. I haven't cried in years. Removing my hands, I peer up to see his concerned face.

"I'm fine," I mutter.

"I know. Come here." Opening his arms, he engulfs me in an embrace.

I may not cry, but I am growing accustomed to these giant hugs of his.

"Another one bites the dust." Bitterness laces my voice.

"You'll get it, baby. I know you will."

As the days have turned into weeks, Loki and I have grown closer, but his easy affection still makes me squeamish.

"Any word from Ash?" I ask to change the subject.

"I know what you're doing," he murmurs in my ear before pulling away. "But, no. I spoke to him and Seth, but they're still stuck in limbo."

I hand him a roll of tinfoil from the bag, and he freezes.

"Loki? Are, are you okay?"

His eyes are glassy and unfocused.

"Loki?" I whisper.

He's staring, but it's not me he sees. Reaching out, I touch his arm, and his body jolts back.

"I, I …"

"You remember something?" He hasn't remembered anything in our time here, and it's slowly killing him.

"Yeah, but it doesn't make any sense. I need to call Ash."

"Okay, I've got the groceries. Are you sure you're all right?"

Loki's eyes soften as they regain focus.

"Yes, I'm good, Red. I'm going to call him now."

I nod as he moves to the bed and takes a seat. While I take care of the groceries and supplies, I listen in.

"We need to get in touch with Luca."

My head whips to him. I know that Luca is the brother he met at the warehouse in Boston, but I don't know anything else about him.

"I don't know," Loki barks. "I just know he's the missing piece. I can't explain it, but I have a feeling he holds the answers."

There's silence in the cabin as Loki listens to whatever Ashton is saying on the phone.

"It'll be difficult, yes. He must be in maximum security. Check the records, see if there's anyone on the inside we can use."

More silence.

"Keep me posted."

I try not to stare as Loki hangs up the phone. He stands without a word or a glance in my direction and heads to the bathroom. When the door closes, I inhale deeply. Loki hasn't shut that door in weeks. He's shutting me out on purpose.

I try not to let it hurt, but I'd be lying if I said it didn't sting. It's a good reminder that we are playing pretend. None of this exists outside of these four walls. I finish taking care of the supplies, then return to my computer. I'm behind on my next draft, so I put on my noise-canceling headphones and open my laptop.

The air shifts as Loki emerges from the bathroom, freshly showered, but I keep my head down. Each step he takes toward me sends a blast of awareness throughout my body. When he stops directly in front of me, I'm forced to meet his eyes. He motions for me to remove my headphones, and I comply.

"I'm sorry." The honesty in his voice melts my frozen heart.

"For what?"

"For shutting you out. I needed a few minutes to think, but I know it must have felt personal."

"You think I'm so fragile that something like that would hurt my feelings?"

"I know you're tougher than even you believe, but yes, I do think I hurt your feelings, and I'm sorry."

"Loki, you don't owe me any explanations," I mutter. I'm about to replace my headphones when his hand lands on mine.

"Come with me."

Glancing around, I try to figure out where he wants to go. "With you where? We live in eight hundred square feet. You want me in the bathroom again?" Visions of our first time together flash before my eyes, and I flush. We have christened every surface in this cabin, but our first time is branded to memory for life.

"I know what you're thinking about, Red, and we will have to revisit that position for sure, but right now, I want you to get your snow gear on and come with me."

Peering out the window, I notice the sun is beginning to set.

"It's okay. We won't be gone long."

I'm getting better about some things, but the dark still triggers me.

Groaning, I save my Word document and move to put on my winter gear.

"What are you working on right now?" he asks.

"Ah, you don't want to know."

Grinning, he gives me his full attention. "Now, I definitely want to know."

"He's a spy, and she's a runaway."

He straightens like he's offended.

"But, I started writing this book way before I ever met you." It's true. I don't need to tell him that Marco has taken on a lot of his attributes, though.

"Why do you look so frustrated every time you work on it?"

Do I? I hadn't noticed, but I'm not surprised that Loki did. I've been his primary source of entertainment lately. Every time I glance up from my laptop, I find him staring. At first, it made me antsy, but now, it brings me comfort.

"I don't know. I'm just struggling with his job."

Loki scoffs. "Why the hell wouldn't you ask me, Red? I've been sitting right here twiddling my thumbs for weeks. The guys can't believe you haven't asked me a single question about sex yet. But, to sit there struggling to write a character that could very well be me and not ask is crazy. Why wouldn't you ask me?"

He sounds angry, and I'm not entirely sure why.

"Are you mad that I haven't asked you about blue balls or that I didn't ask you about secret spy codes?"

"I'm not mad," he sulks.

After pulling on a pair of gray Surrell winter boots, I stand and cross the room.

"You seem mad," I point out when I'm standing in front of him.

"I'm not mad, but it's okay to trust me, Sloane. I won't hurt you. Plus, I'm losing my goddamn mind with boredom here. Helping you with some research would at least keep my mind busy, and I want to help, okay?"

"Fine."

He grins. "So, what do you want to know?"

"Well, right now, I'm struggling to come up with a code word. I know it shouldn't be this difficult, but I have stared at that screen for days, and nothing makes sense. What do you use for code words?"

"It really depends on the situation." Loki reaches for my coffee cake and cuts a slice.

"Ah, you probably don't want to eat that until I've tried it first. I don't want to give you food poisoning again." I cringe.

"It looks good this time, Red. I have faith in you." He puts a slice onto a plate as I grab my jacket. "Code words can be anything, but I generally like to keep them simple. Something that can be used in everyday life but not something you would say accidentally."

"Like what?" I ask, just as Loki takes a bite of the coffee cake.

His face scrunches as his jaw works to chew.

"Oh, God. Is it bad? Spit it out, Loki. You don't have to eat it."

"Salt," he finally says.

"Salt?"

He hands me a piece of the cake, and I tentatively taste it.

"Yuck." After spitting the cake into the trash, I run a napkin over my tongue. "Salt."

"Did you, by chance, mix up the salt and sugar containers?" he asks.

I rush to the cabinet, pull out the Tupperware we store the ingredients in, remove the cover marked sugar, stick a finger in, and pull out a few grains. Licking it, my shoulders sag in frustration.

"I'm such a freaking idiot."

"It was an honest mistake, sweetheart. It could have happened to anyone."

But it didn't. It happened to me, again.

"If we ever need a code word, I'd choose salt," he says, winking. "It's something you wouldn't forget. It's something that could easily be added to a conversation but not used so frequently that you risk using it accidentally."

"Our code word is salt?"

"Yup, come on. We have about an hour before the sun goes down. Let's go have some fun."

CHAPTER 25

LOKI

"I don't think you and I have the same definition of fun," Red mutters beside me.

"Trust me?"

"Always."

"I love that answer, Red." My voice takes on a gritty edge whenever I'm close to her like this.

Standing side by side in the field behind the cabin, I set up a small portable table, then lay the firearms flat on top.

"Have you ever held a gun before?"

"Do I look like someone people would trust with a gun, Loki?"

These goddamn insecurities that invade her every waking moment are killing me.

Leveling her with my gaze, I let her know how serious I am. "Yes, Sloane. You do. You look like someone I would trust with just about anything."

She swallows, and I can see her fingers working inside of her mittens.

When I lift the Glock, she flinches.

"Trust me," I murmur.

Pressing the release of the spring loaded ammunition magazine, it opens.

"This is a Glock-19. This," I say, holding up the magazine, "is where the bullets go."

Her brow furrows in concentration, and she nods as I describe each piece.

"The thing to remember about the Glock is there's no safety on the side like you see in movies. On these guns, the safety is a tiny, little lever in the center of the trigger."

"That doesn't seem very safe," she mutters. Wrapping her arms around herself in a hug, she watches me.

"These are standard issue in SIA and a few other alphabet agencies. You always hold it pointing away from yourself and aimed at the ground."

"Common sense."

Chuckling, I agree, "Yes, common sense. You'd be surprised how many people lose it around guns. Anyway, this particular magazine can hold seventeen rounds."

"I thought guns were silver."

Staring at her, I try not to laugh. "Most Glocks are black."

"It looks like a toy."

"Yeah, well it's a lot heavier than it looks. You ready to hold it?"

"No."

"Okay, let's start by loading the bullets. Here," I say, handing her the magazine.

"Loki, I'm not sure this is the best idea."

"I just want you to shoot it once. If you don't like it after that, we're done, but there's something freeing about knowing how to use a gun safely. Try it, for me?"

Sloane rolls her eyes but removes her mittens and takes the magazine from my hand. I lay the gun down on the table and watch as she loads the bullets after a quick demonstration.

"Good." Picking up the gun, I turn it so she can hold the

grip. "Take it in your palm with your finger off the trigger and keep it pointed at the ground."

She does as I ask, and I notice her hands are shaking.

"You've got this, Sloane. You're good. I'm right here."

She nods but never takes her eyes off the weapon in her hand.

"What if it goes off by accident?" Red's voice wobbles and catches on her words. She's terrified.

"Take a deep breath, sweetheart." Placing my hand over the top of hers, I repeat myself, "Deep breaths. It won't go off because you haven't pulled the trigger yet. We'll take this one step at a time," I assure, but her little body is trembling under all those layers.

"Sweetheart? I'm going to stand behind you, okay? I'm going to help."

She nods aggressively.

Stepping in behind her, I wrap my arms around her body. My right hand cradles hers as it holds the gun. Tipping her hand, I expose the left side of the grip and show her the release.

"Good. Now, see this?" I say, pointing to the lever between the slide and the grip, "this is the slide stop, and this is the slide here," I say, pointing to the top of the gun.

"Yeah," she squeaks.

"You're going to pull the slide back until it you hear a click."

Tentatively, she pulls it back, and it locks in place.

"Perfect. Now you can see into the chamber." Tilting her hand, I show her what I mean. "This way you can see it hasn't been loaded yet." I turn her hand in the opposite direction so she can see what we've done.

Her breaths are as shallow as mine and tell me all I need to know about her frame of mind in this moment.

"Now, press the magazine into the bottom of the gun until you hear a click." My body tenses as I watch her follow my instructions. "Good, this button here is to release the slide. When you do that, the bullets will load and it's ready to go. Keep the gun pointing at the ground and release the slide."

"Okay," she gasps, jumping when it snaps into place.

"The gun is loaded now," I remind her. Taking her left hand, I guide it into place. "You want to keep the palm of your left hand cradling the knuckles of your right hand and wrap your fingers into place. This will help you keep a steady hand when you go to shoot."

"Mm-hm."

Raising her hands to eye level, I point to the three sights located on the top. "See how there are two notches at the back of the gun and one in the front?"

"Yes."

"You want those to line up with your target. That's how you aim."

"Got it."

"Look straight ahead, see the targets?" I placed paper bullseye targets over some hay bales earlier in the day.

"I see them."

"Okay. I'm going to step back. I want you to line up the sights. When you're ready to fire, put your finger on the trigger and recheck your sights. There will be some kickback when you fire. It's not a lot, but since you're not used to it, it'll be a shock. Take one shot, then point it at the ground while you get a feel for it. If you want to take another shot after, you can, but pause in between each one."

"I'm sure one will be plenty," she grumbles.

"You ready?"

"I think so."

Stepping to the side, I watch as she lines up her sights, raises her head, and starts over. It takes her six tries before her finger ever lands on the trigger. I don't push her. I let her go at her own pace, even though I'm getting anxious watching her.

POP.

The gun fires, and her arm kicks back. She immediately lowers the barrel to the ground. I am so fucking proud of her I want to pick her up and kiss her. If she didn't have a loaded weapon and a twitchy finger, I probably would.

"Holy shit," she hisses. "I just shot a gun. Did I hit the bullseye?"

I grin. I'm not expecting her to hit anything, but I love her enthusiasm.

"I'm not sure. Want to check?"

"Yes," she wheezes like she just sprinted a mile.

After securing and placing the Glock on the table, we walk in silence to the hay bale. I hope this doesn't discourage her from trying again. Maybe I should have suggested we check the target after she shot a few rounds and hoped that she hit something.

Sloane reaches it first and stands there wide-eyed. I look from her to the target and burst out laughing.

"Holy shit, Red. Dead center." Now I'm the one standing in disbelief. "Want to try it again?"

"I do." She grins. "I really do."

Scooping her up in a hug, I hold her for a moment before releasing her. "Then let's go shoot some rounds."

We stand out there for forty-five minutes while Red shoots and checks every shot. By the time it's too dark to see very far, she has hit the target thirty-two out of thirty-four times.

My girl could have been a sniper. *My girl?* Staring down into those green eyes that sparkle even in the lasts rays of daylight, I realize that's exactly what I want her to be—my girl.

LOKI: **Anything on Luca yet?**

Seth: Nothing. Something isn't right with this, man. Even Vic is searching for him.

LOKI: What do you mean searching for him? He's in custody. And why is Vic looking for him?

Ashton: Not on text.

My phone rings a second later.

"What do you mean Vic is looking for him? Where the fuck could he be?" I yell.

"I'm starting to think Luca wasn't who we thought he was," Ashton states calmly. "I'm following a trail that is deliberately complicated and misleading. The hoops I'm jumping through point to him being on our side, in some manner at least."

My vision goes hazy as I recall bits of a conversation but not enough to grab hold of.

"We think Vic is in bed with the Russians. That would explain his behavior, but we cannot find the common denominator," Seth spits.

"Whatever it is, we need Luca. I'm sure of it," I tell them. "If he has made a deal with someone on the inside, I want to know who. I want to know the terms, and I want to know now. That asshole cannot walk free, or I'll be right back where I was ten years ago." Even as I say the words, my gut tells me I might be wrong about my half-brother. I thought the same thing about Miles, my youngest half-brother, though, and that almost got Lexi killed. I'm not taking that chance again. "Let me know as soon as you find him."

I hang up the phone and pace. I'm going to wear a hole in this damn floor. Sloane is in the shower, and it's getting late. I know she has two chapters she needs to get written, so I pull out the ingredients to make tacos. Passing the fridge, I see the remnants of today's coffee cake disaster. The soupy mess has finally congealed, so I scrape it into the trash before she sees it. She tries this fucking recipe every day. *Maybe it's the recipe?* I make a mental note to pay closer attention tomorrow.

"I don't know how the heck I mess that up so badly every day." Her soft voice breezes through the room.

Chuckling, I show her the pan. "I'm not sure either, but you do it spectacularly."

"That's something, right? Any luck with Ash today?"

"They're looking for Luca," I confide.

"Did they lose him?"

"We're not sure what the hell is going on. He should be in Lanesboro, it's a maximum-security prison, but he isn't showing up in Ashton's searches."

"What does Ashton say about it?"

"What he always says, he's handling it."

"You guys are close, huh?"

"I couldn't have accomplished anything I've done without him. The guy is like a human computer. He's been one step ahead of me since he was fifteen."

"It must have been amazing growing up with them all."

"Growing up with ..."

"Don't you remember what it was like there, Loki? That life? I didn't want that for my family," Luca rumbles. *"I will not allow them to take her. That won't happen. I did this for a reason—I enlisted for a reason. Have I done shit I regret? Fuck yes. Did I have a choice? I didn't think so at the time. But now ... now we have a chance to fix this together. You and I can make all this go away, but you have to trust me."*

CHAPTER 26

SLOANE

"Loki? Are you okay?" I ask as gently as I can. He spaced out over a minute ago. *Should I call Emory?* His gaze finally drops to mine as I take a step forward. I see the moment he comes back to me.

"Red," he gasps, reaching for me and pulling me into an embrace.

Pressed against his chest, I can feel his heart raging.

"Hey, are you all right?" I ask again. I try to back away to see his eyes, but he holds me tight.

"Yeah, yeah, I'm fine," he grumbles.

Slowly, his heart rate returns to normal, and his grip loosens.

"What did you remember?"

"How do you do that? How do you know what's going on before I do?"

"I study people, remember? You'll probably be the star of my next book since all the people watching I've done this month is you."

This gets a chuckle out of him.

"As long as you get the important parts right," he says, thrusting his perpetual semi into my stomach.

"You'd be the first guy to be okay with me writing about him, that's for sure."

"Sweetheart, I don't want to think about what you have or have not done with other dudes, okay?"

"Fine, what did you remember?"

"Just part of a conversation I had with Luca."

"Do you need to call Ash back?"

"No, not yet. It's only a partial memory. It doesn't make any sense. I need to think on it and hope more comes."

I glare at him for a moment. Emory has told him repeatedly not to force it, but the longer we're here, the harder he pushes. Yesterday I caught him making a timeline and filling in everything he can remember.

"Hey, don't give me that look. My body has healed. I just need my brain to release my memory so we can figure shit out. I was going to make tacos for dinner. Why don't you get some work done while I get them started?"

"How am I going to survive on my own when we get out of here if you keep spoiling me like this?" I meant it as a joke, but Loki's features darken, and I try to ignore the stabbing sensation in my chest.

"I don't know. It doesn't seem like it'll be happening anytime soon, though, so you're stuck with me," he grumbles.

"Loki ... I, I didn't—"

"No worries, Red. It's *fine*."

Loki hates the word fine. I know that was a jab at me, but I don't know what to say, so I retreat to my computer and work. This time, since actually running isn't in my cards, I escape into my story.

Dinner is strained, but I can't tell if it's because of my comments or because of whatever revelation Loki had that has him preoccupied. Either way, I'm not looking for an argument, so after I help clean up dinner, I return to my corner and work on Marco and Lucy.

I stare blankly for a long time because nothing is coming

to me. Eventually, I force words onto the screen, hoping for inspiration. After an hour, I'm ready for a glass of wine, but I don't dare move from my spot. Loki has not been able to sit still for more than five minutes.

First, he reapplied plumbing tape to all the faucets. Then he unscrewed, sanded, and replaced the latches on all the windows. Now he is checking every floorboard, for what I'm not sure. The guy cannot sit still.

Finally, I snap.

"Loki."

His head jerks to attention.

"What's the matter?" he asks, concern written on his face.

"Nothing's wrong with me. What's wrong with you? You haven't stopped moving all night."

"Nothing," he sighs.

"Nothing? What, are you bored?"

"Red, I am so fucking bored I'm ready to shave my head just to count the hair."

I stare at him, dumbfounded. "You're bored."

"So fucking much."

"Huh." He looks so cute standing there like a lost, little boy. Well, a lost, little boy in the body of a sex king. "Do you read?"

"Of course I read, but I didn't bring any books. I wasn't exactly planning on a forced vacation."

"Right," I say, trying to contain my amusement. "How long have you been this bored?"

"I've been counting fucking nails in the floor for the last week."

My shoulders shake as a full-body laugh racks my body. Trying to compose myself, I bite the inside of my cheek before raising my gaze to meet Loki's, who is glowering at me from the corner.

"You've been counting nails on the floor?" I choke out.

"I'm so glad you find this funny, Red. I haven't been in

one place for more than a month in years. Even then, I've always traveled in between. I'm going nuts in captivity."

"Awe, my poor, wild animal," I coo.

"I'll show you wild," he growls, moving toward me like the caveman he is.

Holding up a hand, I stop him. "Not that I wouldn't love some wild, animalistic sex right now, but I have a deadline, so it'll have to wait a few hours."

Sighing, he turns in place. I think he really might have a nervous breakdown soon.

"I have a Kindle you're welcome to use. You can download any book you want."

"This whole time you've had a kindle and didn't tell me?" He has the nerve to look mad.

"I had no idea you were so bored. I thought you enjoyed playing handyman around here," I giggle.

"The only plumbing I want to fix from here on out is yours. Give me the damn Kindle."

I reach into my bag and grab it while he pouts. Opening it up, I show him how to access the Kindle store.

"I'm surprised you've never used a Kindle before."

"Red, I haven't had downtime since I graduated college."

I gape at him as he climbs into bed and situates himself against the backboard. We're seated facing each other with the cabin spaced out between us.

"What about vacations?" Surely, he's had some sort of downtime.

"The last vacation I took was spring break with the guys our freshman year. We went to Puerto Vallarta, and Trevor almost spent the night in a Mexican prison."

"For what?"

"He was dancing on the bar, and let's just say it wasn't as solid as Trevor was. He crashed through it, and they called the police. I was only seventeen at the time, so I had to bail and missed all the fun, but Dex said Trevor was so drunk he threatened to buy the entire city."

"Oh my God," I laugh.

"It's funny. I haven't thought about that trip in years." His voice is soft as he recalls the memory. "That was such a great week. Everything changed after that, though. Preston lost his dad, Trevor lost his mom, and Dex started getting serious with his ex."

"What about you?"

"Me?" he asks, lifting his gaze to mine. "Things stayed the same for another year. It wasn't until I turned eighteen that the Nightingales came calling."

"The what?"

"The Nightingales. It's part of an elite task force not many people know about. Seth and I were in the inaugural class."

"How did you end up the boss?" It comes out sultry, but I am genuinely curious.

"I'm the boss because I worked my ass off. The genius range IQ didn't hurt either." He smirks.

"What is it with you rich people? You can't be happy being gorgeous and wealthy? You have to take all the brains, too?" I tease.

"Gorgeous, huh? Red, you flatter me, but if you keep looking at me like that, you won't get any writing done tonight."

I gulp audibly, and he chuckles.

"I love that you can't hide your reactions from me, sweetheart. It makes playing your body so much more fun."

"Holy, geez." Fanning myself, I look from Loki to my screen and back again.

"Writing first, Red. Then I'm going to bury myself so deep inside of you, you'll never ask to see another toy as long as you live."

My pussy responds to his words, and I have to shift in my seat, but I know he's right. I have a deadline, and as much as I would love to toss my computer aside and jump him, I'm still too new an author. It's such a fickle industry. I can't afford to allow anyone to label me in a negative light. It's why, for the first time in my life, I stick to deadlines.

"Okay, give me three hours."

He grins like it's a challenge, and I start the clock.

Holy shit, this man is going to ruin me for life.

CHAPTER 27

ASHTON

"How long?" My voice is deadly calm, but the rage burning from within sets my skin on fire.

"From what I can tell, it's been a few years, at least," Ryan states in his signature monotone.

Ryan owns EnVision Securities—the company my family has used for as long as I can remember, and the company I plan to acquire now that he's retiring.

"Why the fuck weren't Loki or I informed?" Seth screams. "We've been out in the field every goddamn day. He put his life on the line every fucking day. No one thought it would be beneficial to let him know that his own brother was working for our side?"

"What if Loki had killed Luca in that warehouse?" I ask. "Who is running this operation?"

"Michael Anderson." Ryan's voice comes through the speaker like molasses, and I want to fucking throat punch the guy.

"Anderson? Why does that sound so familiar?" I ask. "Where do I know him from?"

"He's the agent that went to your house after Loki's parents were killed," Seth rumbles.

What the hell?

"What else do you know, Ryan?"

"Just that Luca wants to talk to Loki, and they're putting all available resources into making that happen," he states vaguely.

"Do they know where Loki is?" Seth asks, concerned.

"No, and it's pissing everyone off. Whatever you guys have done to hide him is better than anything any branch of our government can do. I'm impressed. The three of you will do well with EnVision. I'm sure of it now."

That little admission is as close to fatherly admiration I've had in years, and it irritates me that it affects me so much.

"Thank you, Ryan. Anything else?"

Seth paces the room like a caged lion.

"I can get you to Luca, but I can't guarantee they won't interrogate you. Whatever Luca needs Loki for, they're keeping it close to their chest."

"No," Seth barks. "Not happening. Loki will never forgive me, Ash. Get Luca to come to us, or we'll figure this shit out on our own."

"That's not really how these things work, Seth, and you know it," Ryan scolds.

"But, it's worth a shot," I say. "Let's see how desperate they are to talk to Loki. Can you do that?"

"I can," he sighs. "I'm glad this is my last fucking job, though, because this may burn some bridges you're going to have to work to repair when you take over."

"I'll cross that bridge when I get there."

Seth glances up, and we have an entire conversation without saying a word. Neither of us trusts Luca as far as we can throw him, but with no other leads, we'll see this one through. Loki has put his entire life on hold for us. It's time we do something to clear his path for the future, even if that means working with his enemy. I only pray he'll see we had no other choice.

CHAPTER 28

LOKI

I'm going insane. It's been two weeks since I recalled the conversation with Luca, and still nothing. Ashton is evasive about him whenever I call, and that's making me fucking nuts. *What am I missing?*

Red stirs beside me. Waking with her every morning has become second nature. And she hasn't woken in a panic since our first few days here. If I'm honest with myself, I'm more relaxed than I have been in years. I don't remember ever feeling this way as an adult. She brings a childlike innocence to my life that's been missing since I was a teenager.

She burrows into my side, attempting to block out the morning light. She knows what's coming, yet she fights it every time. Our first couple of weeks were … rough. She's a night owl, and I'm up with the sun. Slowly, without even realizing it, we've adapted to each other's lifestyles as if we've always been together.

Instead of rising with the sun, we get up at eight and get in some form of exercise. We've tried snowshoeing, HIIT classes, and our own version of Cross Fit, but she hates it all. She complains every day, but she never misses a workout with me.

At night, we've fallen into a routine, too. After dinner, Sloane writes until eleven or twelve while I read, then we go to bed together every night. I've never had so much sex in my life. And it's not just sex. It's fucking mind-blowing, life-altering sex, nearly every day—we cannot get enough of each other. I'm tempted to ask the guys if it stays like this or if we're in some weird safe-house fairyland right now, but don't dare. The second I open that can of worms, Dex will start making wedding plans.

Peering down at a naked Sloane, I allow myself that fantasy for the briefest of moments. *What would life be like with you forever, Red?*

Brushing the hair away from her face, I start the process of waking her up. With the snow beginning to melt, we're going to try a road run today. Then, we have a full day of research ahead of us. She needs to learn all about the town she's writing, and I need to do some dark web surfing for Luca.

"Come on, sweetheart, time to get up."

"No," she groans and tries to roll away, but I snatch her around the waist before she gets far.

"It'll be over before you know it," I whisper.

"We both know that's not true. I can still feel *it* from last night." She smirks while I hover over her.

"So freaking naughty, Sloane." I nip her neck, and she screeches. "I like marking you as mine," I say, playfully waggling my eyebrows at her.

"Such a caveman." She yawns before stretching her arms.

The sheet pools under her cleavage, and it's all I can do not to lean down and lick a nipple until she writhes beneath me.

"Ah, ah," she says. "No way. I know that look. I need at least twelve hours to recover before you come anywhere near me with that monster cock again."

I groan as she climbs out of bed. We gave up on the

lingerie weeks ago, and while she claims to have never slept naked before, I've made it my mission to make sure she keeps up the habit.

While she's in the bathroom getting ready, I put on the coffee and check messages. I'm not sure what I expect, but every morning I look for an update. A sign that we're moving in the right direction—anything—but it hasn't come yet.

Loki: Update.
Ashton: ...
Seth: We're working on it.
Loki: Did you get a lead?
Seth: ...
Loki: WTF is going on?
Ashton: We're working on it. Let us handle this. You have to trust me, Loki.

"Ready?" Sloane's chipper voice cuts through my rage.

"Yeah. Just checking in with Ash."

"Nothing yet?"

"No. Come o—" The words catch in my throat. Checking behind her, I look for the rest of her clothes.

"What's wrong?"

"That's what you're wearing? To run in? On the main road?"

She glances down at herself. "Yeah, what did you expect me to wear?"

She's dressed in head to toe spandex, with just a hint of her midriff showing, but with her perfect fucking curves, it leaves nothing to the imagination.

"A sweatshirt?" I offer, hopefully.

"Not happening. Why, Mr. Kane, are you jealous someone might see me bouncing around town?" She cups her tits and jumps in place, exaggerating their movement with her hands.

"Yes," I growl. "Don't do that." Pulling her hands away from her tits, I drag her toward the door. "Let's get this over with."

"Okie-dokie, Mr. Kane."

Spinning, I pin her to the door with my body.

"Keep it up with the Mr. Kane shit, and we'll be getting our workout in another way this morning."

Her breath hitches, but she smirks, too. She knows full well what she does to me. Running three miles with a hard-on is going to be a bitch. At least my one pair of underwear was clean today, so something's keeping that fucker in place.

Slipping past me, Red jogs to the logging road that leads us away from the property. Watching her ass in hot pink spandex is going to kill me. I might as well quit now. If I make it back without having jumped her on the side of the road, it'll be a miracle.

~

Lexi: **How'd Sloane do with the coffee cake today?**

Loki: (picture sent)

Lexi: **WTF is that? It looks like a mucus-filled hairball baked in a cake pan.**

Loki: Pretty much.

Lexi: **But she keeps trying?**

Loki: Every damn day.

Lexi: **Good. Don't let her give up. It's important...she'll get it.**

Loki: Why do I feel like you know something I don't?

Lexi: **Because I do. Women always do. Peace out.**

Loki: Give East our love. Later.

Lexi: **Easton can suck a bag of dicks.**

Since the day I saved Lexi from my half-brother, Miles, we've had a weird friendship. When I stop to think about how entwined our lives have become, it's overwhelming. Finding out she was Lanie's cousin was a shock but brought our fucked up family full-circle, I guess.

Lanie and Dexter. Julia and Trevor. Even Preston has

settled down with Emory. It's a scene I never thought I would live to see. I never allowed myself to picture the future. I had to live in the present and not get caught up in the what-ifs. But what if that's not my life anymore?

"What are you thinking about so hard over there?" Sloane's voice drifts through the cabin.

"Just thinking about how much everyone's lives have changed. Lexi texted a few minutes ago to check in. It sounds like she and Easton are still at each other's throats."

"That doesn't surprise me." She laughs. "Are you okay?"

"Me? Yeah, why?"

"You look a little melancholy over there."

Not ready to have this conversation with her, I grab the Kindle and shake it in the air.

"I'm good. Just contemplating what to read next."

"You're a terrible liar," she admonishes. "But you can tell me what's up whenever you're ready."

I'm not sure how to feel about the fact that she may know me better than I know myself. I make a show of scrolling her Kindle, and eventually, she grabs her headphones.

"You don't have to use those. The music won't bother me. I can block anything."

She smiles like she's embarrassed before saying, "Yeah, I kind of need them sometimes." I notice her fingers move, tap-tap-slide, and now she has my full attention.

"How come?" I smirk while I wait for her answer.

Sloane slaps a hand over her eyes and peeks out through her fingers. Now I'm really freaking curious.

"I need them."

"Okay, why?"

"I have to blast music when I write the sex scenes."

The Kindle falls to my lap, forgotten, and I'm pretty sure I just swallowed my tongue.

"You're writing a sex scene tonight?" My eyes dart to the kink kit. *Will she need supplies?*

"Yes, and this might be my dirtiest book yet."

Is that right?

"Are you going to need, ah, will you need your supplies?"

She looks up, surprise crossing her face before confusion settles in its place.

"Huh, you know what's so weird? I haven't needed them." She sounds perturbed by the revelation, but I am dancing the goddamn merengue in my head. My ego goes from solid to over-inflated in mere seconds, and I want to beat my chest like I'm king of the jungle.

"You don't have to look so proud of yourself over there," Red teases.

"Oh, I'm so fucking proud of myself," I gloat.

"Yeah? We'll see how you feel about that when this book comes out."

Oh shit.

"Yeah, that's right, buddy. If I'm not using my supplies, where do you think these stories are coming from? My imagination is good, but not that good," she says, pointing to the screen.

"Ah, are you writing our sex life in that book?"

"Honestly? I'm not sure. I didn't even realize it was happening. Every other book, I've had to drag out Jack and J — Pearl. Guess we'll find out when I do my read-through."

Panic sets in. *Do I want the guys reading about our sex life like personalized porn? Wait. How detailed are her books? Do they think she's done all the shit she writes?*

"If you frown any harder, you might hurt yourself," she calls before dragging her Bose headphones over her ears.

Fuck me.

Stabbing the library key on Sloane's kindle, I search the backlog until I find her books. After glancing up to make sure she's occupied, I open one. It'll be like watching a chick-flick, right? How bad could it be?

∽

Two hours later

Loki: Sloane doesn't sleep around.

Preston: I'd hope not.

Dexter: You read her books, didn't you?

Loki: This book, these characters are not her. You fuckers better not be picturing her when you read them.

Trevor: Fuck off, twatwaffle. We're thinking of our wives and running from them after they read a new one. Pro tip—let them cool off for at least two hours after reading one of Sloane's books before doing the dirty, or you might hurt yourself.

Preston: Sloane writes them, so what do you suggest for Loki?

Dexter: Holy shit. Is your dick still working?

Trevor: WTF dude? Now Julia will read the new book and know it's you.

Loki: She isn't writing about us.

Loki: At least, I don't think she is.

Loki: It's all made up. It's fiction, none of it's real.

Dexter: So the sneak peek that Lanie got last week about Marco railing Lucy standing up in the shower wasn't you? Because I gotta tell you, dude, if it was? Props to you. That's fucking hard. I almost fell through the glass door trying.

Loki: Fuck me.

Preston: (laughing crying emoji)

Trevor: Christ. Are you the reason Julia suddenly wants me to be "The Boss" in the bedroom? I think I'm going to be sick.

Dexter: What book are you reading?

Loki: The Story of Us.

Trevor: Good God, man. That's a tough one. When

Henry walks away from Stacey? I might have shed a tear. Your girl can write.

She really can. I won't admit it, but her writing has stirred some pretty uncomfortable feelings.

Dexter: Lanie sobbed for three days after that one. I may have had to take a break halfway through before I could finish it.

Preston: Are you guys out of your tits? First, you complain because you're having too much sex. No such thing, btw. Now you're saying you couldn't finish a book because it made you feel too much? Do you hear yourselves?

Trevor: Fuck off, Pres. Read the damn books and then talk to us.

Preston: Done. I'll check in tomorrow after I've finished and prove you're all a bunch of pussies.

Dexter: #Realmenreadromance. Deal with it, motherfucker!

Loki: I don't even know what to do with you guys anymore.

Preston: Luvs

Dexter: Luvs

Trevor: Glad to have you back. Luvs.

Luvs? Maybe Preston is right. I'm not sure how to handle these feelings-happy-emotionally-in-touch guys I used to call my friends.

∽

"Hey."

"Jesus," I bark, attempting to hide the Kindle but end up smacking my face on it.

"Whatcha doin'?" Sloane drawls.

"Na-nothing. You just startled me. I didn't hear you."

I didn't hear her. I was so lost in her book that I didn't even see her cross the room.

"You seemed pretty focused on your book. What are you reading?"

"Military."

Laughter erupts from her sweet mouth.

"Military? Is that what it's called?"

"Ah, Military History, or something like that. Are you already done for the night?"

That was fast. What the hell time is it?

"Already? Loki, it's after one in the morning. I got carried away in a scene and lost track of time."

"You got carried away in a scene?" I groan. Reaching for her, I drag her into my lap and whisper in her ear, "Tell me about it."

CHAPTER 29

SLOANE

"Tell me about it," he growls into my ear, and I swear to all that's holy, my panties are soaked from his voice alone.

Biting my lip, I glance up at him nervously. "Do you want me to read it to you?"

"No, I want you to tell me. Right here. Right now, while we act it out. Scene by scene."

"Oh my God," I whimper. I won't make it through one sentence before he renders me speechless.

Loki's hands glide under the hem of my shirt, teasing the skin as he slips it over my head. I turn in his lap so I'm straddling him, and his eyes go hazy as he takes in my cleavage. The expensive underwear that Preston sent does wonders for my full D-cups. They've never looked so voluptuous.

Running a finger along the lacy edge of the plum-colored bra, he groans, and I feel him grow to his full length beneath me. My gaze never leaves his as he leans in and blows warm, damp air over my nipple. When it responds, he plucks it between his thumb and forefinger while his other hand snakes around my back to undo the clasp.

"Jesus, Red. I'm never going to get enough of you," he sighs as my breasts spring free from their confines.

"Everyone does eventually, don't worry," I tease. Before I finish my sentence, he has us flipped with my arms pinned above my head. His face is intense. *Is he angry?*

"I'm a lot of things, Sloane. A liar isn't one of them," he rasps.

"I … Loki, I didn't mean—"

"I don't give a shit what you meant, Sloane." Using my given name drives home how pissed off he is. I long to hear him call me Red, and not just because he's angry. Something about him calling me Sloane seems off and leaves me feeling hollow. "I know you don't do feelings. But guess what? You're not the only one in this relationship."

My eyes snap to his. My throat is so dry my tongue sticks to the roof of my mouth. But it's my stomach that's on the verge of revolting that has me worried.

"Yes, sweetheart. I said relationship. However you want to categorize us, it's some kind of relationship. One, I'm committed to for as long as you'll have me." His head dips again, and he doesn't give me a chance to respond.

Firm lips close over mine as his tongue licks and pushes at my seam.

A relationship? Where the hell did that come from? He can't be serious? What about when we get home? Surely, he'll want someone more like Emory or Lanie. Even Julia is better equipped to handle relationships than I am.

"Stop thinking, Red. Let me in," he mutters.

I draw a breath, and he makes his move. His assault on my mouth is fast and fierce. He's laying claim to me, and I'd be a damn liar if I said it didn't turn me on.

Sliding down the bed, Loki drags my body with him until he has me positioned in the center. I watch in a lust-filled haze as he climbs over me. Settling with his knees straddling my thighs, he lowers his mouth to my sternum and licks a line straight down my middle.

When he reaches the waistband of my leggings, he runs a finger just under the elastic back and forth until I'm squirming beneath him. With a wicked grin, he hooks his thumbs into the sides and painfully slowly lowers them down my leg. When they reach my ankles, I kick frantically to set them free.

"Jesus, Red. You're so fucking perfect. I want to lick every inch of you."

"O-Okay," I stammer because my brain cells evaporate at the sight of him lowering his sweatpants. His cock springs free, and I'm almost certain I've lost the ability to speak.

Glancing up, he smirks before lowering himself so our bodies touch. When he whispers next to my ear, my eyes fall closed, and my body sensitizes to his touch. "Is this," he smacks his dick against my sex, "what you want?"

My gaze flickers open on impact. "Yes. Now, Loki, please."

"Do you know what hearing you beg does to me?" he growls.

"Please, Loki. Please."

With his hand holding tightly to the base of his erection, he guides the head along my seam. My hips buck in anticipation, but he holds me still with a hand on my stomach.

"Hold still, baby. I'm going to make you come like this."

"Like, like what?" I pant.

He guides his cock up my opening but doesn't enter, and I moan in frustration. Loki repeats the motion, running his thick head along my lips until he grazes my clit. An exquisite pleasure ripples through my body at the sensation. Sliding down again, he coats himself in my wetness.

"You're so fucking wet," he groans as he rubs his heavy shaft across my clit. He picks up the pace, and my hips buck in response.

"I'm going to make you come, just like this, Red. Before I

enter that hot, wet pussy, you will come for me." He releases his grasp, and his dick bobs angrily between us. Lowering onto his forearms, he holds himself above me in a plank position while he pistons his hips in a beautifully torturous rhythm.

"Loki," I gasp. "Loki, I—"

"I know, sweetheart." He lowers himself a fraction to get more friction with his body, and I don't know how much longer I can last. Using the thick vein on his shaft's underside, he maintains contact with my clit, then picks up speed.

"Oh, fuck." My body writhes and shudders with the sweet, painful desire only an orgasm can satisfy now.

Loki brings a hand to cup my right breast. His calloused palm rubs roughly against my nipple, sending sparks straight to my sex.

I moan incoherently as Loki grins down at me. When he rolls my nipple between his fingers, my body quivers with the first hint of release. Glancing down, I see his cock is glistening. I've covered him completely as he glides between my lips. It's the most erotic moment of my life.

"Someday, sweetheart, I'm going to fuck you bare."

I flinch at his words. I don't do that, not ever. I can't even take care of myself—there is no way in hell I'm bringing a child into the world.

He must see my panic because he clarifies a moment later. "Not today, Sloane." He holds the head of his length against my bundle of nerves and grinds into me.

"I'm going to come," I manage to mumble.

"I'm going to fuck you, baby, fast and hard until we're both raw."

His words send me over the edge, and I spiral with the sweet release of my orgasm. In my erotic, blissed-out state, I hear him open the foil wrapper. He's on me again before I've even relaxed my grip on the handful of sheets I've used to tether me to the bed.

In one swift move, he impales me. "Fuck me. I can still feel your body spasming around my cock."

I'm suddenly frantic to get him closer. Wrapping my legs around his thighs, I pull him in to meet his body thrust for thrust, but it's still not close enough. I wiggle my arms free from his hand, and reach up to place them on his muscular back.

My nipples drag against his chest hair on each downstroke, causing an ache deep within me. When he buries himself to the hilt and tilts his hips, I shatter around him. It happens so fast, I don't have time to prepare. My body erupts around him as I gasp for breath. He's chasing his own release, and I'm still spiraling.

Loki growls in appreciation. "There is nothing I love more than feeling you come undone when I'm deep inside of you. You're fucking perfection, Red. The way your walls cling to my cock when I pull out, then suck me back in when I ram into you. Nothing has ever felt this good, baby. Nothing."

His grunts and groans become louder, and my body shivers in response. I've barely come down from my second orgasm when he rolls me over and positions me onto my knees. "This is going to be fast, and hard. If it's too much, you have to tell me."

His open palm lands against my ass cheek with a loud snap when I don't answer, causing me to yelp.

"Agh! What the hell?" I peer over my shoulder and find Loki standing behind me, stroking his sheathed shaft. Okay, watching Loki jerk off is now the most erotic thing I've ever seen. *How the hell can he keep topping himself?*

His free hand returns to my ass, and massages the pink flesh. "Did you like that, Red? When I spanked you, did you like that?"

Did I?

"I-I don't know," I answer truthfully.

He steps closer. Leaning over my body, he plucks a dangling nipple and pinches it. "Do you want me to do it again?"

No! Yes! Geez, I don't know. Apparently, my body and mind are at war because I catch myself nodding yes. Sliding his left knee to the outside of mine, he keeps one hand manipulating my nipples as his other kneads the flesh of my ass.

My eyes close as the pleasure of his hands overwhelms me.

Thwack.

"Gah!" It comes out on a breathy moan, and I'm shocked to realize I liked it. "Again," I whisper.

"That's my girl," Loki growls just before his hand lands on my other cheek. Releasing my nipple, he moves behind me and uses both hands to knead my reddened ass. Lowering my face to the mattress, I get lost in the sensations.

Loki tilts my hips as his tongue does dirty things to the sensitive skin between my pussy and ass. Sensations I've never felt ricochet up my spine from the foreign invasion. His hands move to my hips as he stands, and a fraction of a second later, he plunges into my center. Pushing up onto my hands, I meet him thrust for thrust.

"You're perfection, Sloane. Jesus Christ, you feel like, you feel like home," he screams. He wasn't lying when he said this would be fast and hard. His thrusts come at a manic pace, and with one final push, I feel his dick twitch as he fills the condom with his seed. He doesn't pull out right away, so I stay awkwardly on my hands and knees.

"I, you're amazing, Sloane. I know our situation hasn't been ideal, but I'm, well," he pants, searching for words. "I'm just glad you're here with me. I want you to know this means something to me, okay?"

My throat closes, and I can't speak, so I nod and lean forward slightly, helping him disengage from my body. Falling back onto the bed, I gasp for air, but not because of the sex. My throat is tight from his words, and I don't know how to respond.

That was undoubtedly the most intense, electrifying, and holy fucking wow sex of my life. Sighing, Loki rolls to his side. I hear him tie off the condom and drop it to the floor before settling in at my back. Wrapping an arm around my middle, he pulls me into his front.

"Who knew you were such a spooner," I tease through a yawn. I'm exhausted and can't bring myself to think about all the words he's thrown at me today. *Relationship? More? Means something?* Does he have any idea how stabby those words make me?

"I had no idea. I've never been with anyone long enough to find out. But I want to be clear about this. I like it because it's you. I like you, Red. I want you."

For how long? A voice in my head screams. *How long until you leave me?* I know it's not a healthy dialogue, and I do my best to shut it down, but some demons are too ingrained to stay down for long.

"I want you for as long as you'll have me," Loki mumbles just before the soft gurgles of a snore escape his lips.

"I wish I could believe that," I whisper.

Hours later, I'm still lying next to him, wide awake.

He says he wants me for as long as he can have me. What does that mean? Rolling in his arms, I watch his beautiful face—peaceful and at ease in his sleep.

"How long do you want me for, Loki?" I whisper, barely more than a breath.

His brow furrows in his sleep, and he pulls me closer.

"I love you, Red," he mumbles.

Is he asleep?

My body stiffens, and my lungs scream with the air trapped there. *What the hell did he just say?* I watch his face for any sign of awareness, any indication that he knows what he just uttered, but his face remains passive and relaxed.

Loki loves me?

He can't love me. Loki deserves the fairytale, the happily ever after, and that's not me. I'm not even the fucked up heroines I write. I'm worse. He doesn't mean it, and he's sleeping. I can't hold him accountable for what he says when he's sleeping. Sleeping or drunk.

Right? Aren't those the rules?

CHAPTER 30

ASHTON

"Are you sure this is what you want to do?" Seth asks from the doorway. With his shoulders hunched up around his ears, I have a physical reminder of how he feels about my plan.

"We've been over this. I don't see another way. Ryan and I have spent two weeks combing through every piece of information we could find, and there isn't even an inkling that Anderson is dirty. We have to go into this meeting assuming Luca is legit, but prepare for the worst." Slumping into my office chair as the weight of what I'm about to do sinks in, I turn to Seth for guidance, but he cuts me off at the knees.

"How involved have you been in our missions over the years?" he asks flatly but enters the room and sits down across from me.

"What do you mean?"

"I'm not a fucking imbecile, Ash. I know how smart Loki is, but I also know he gets his intel from you more times than not. How many of his missions were you behind?"

Running a hand over my face, I stall for time.

"What does it matter?" I finally ask.

He sits quietly, observing me, and it's unnerving. When

he finally speaks, I come to understand why Loki trusts him so much.

"It doesn't. Not really, anyway. But, I'm always curious about the guys who prefer to hide in the shadows. It's a rare quality to be a silent hero. I'm willing to bet you knew about Julia before Loki did. I'm also willing to bet that somehow you managed to put that bug in his ear without him ever realizing it."

I shift in my chair uncomfortably.

"I'm not planning to blow your cover, Ash. Just help me understand why you work in the dark like this."

Sighing, I lay my cards bare. If we're going to be partners at EnVision he deserves to know my story or part of it at least.

"Mostly, it comes down to the fact that I'm a Westbrook. I have responsibilities that come with that name, so I couldn't just enlist in the Nightingales like you two did."

"They wanted you, though, didn't they?"

Nodding, I let out a long breath. "I made a stupid error on Loki's first mission. It wasn't long before Montgomery found me. He pushed me, and I was close to signing up, but then I saw the pressure Preston was under after my father died. He was just a kid himself trying to run a billion-dollar empire." I shrug my shoulders because there isn't much else to say. "Family will always come first. I had to choose my family."

I can't help the smile that forms as I finish my thought. "Luckily, Montgomery decided I was too valuable an asset to Loki, and he found a way to work the system so I could keep assisting him."

"You would have done it regardless, though," Seth states sagely.

"Of course. Once you're a part of our family, Seth, we don't let you go. Loki is my family, just as Preston and the other dick heads are. The same goes for you, too, you know."

He chuckles. "Yeah, I've heard Sylvie Westbrook has a habit of taking in the strays."

"Only the good ones. But in all seriousness, choosing to hear Luca out has been a difficult decision to make. At the same time, I hope you know I wouldn't be doing it if I felt we had any alternative."

"I know," he grumbles. "I just wish it didn't feel like we were betraying Loki."

"That makes two of us," I admit.

∾

"They'll be landing in three minutes," Seth's voice comes through my earpiece.

"Are Ryan's men in place?"

"Roger that. We have you covered from every angle, Ash. I'll meet them at the helipad, and then I'll be by your side for the rest of the meeting. Landing now."

"Got it. Be safe, everyone."

I didn't tell Seth this, but the primary reason I stay in the shadows is that I'm not cut out for this espionage bullshit. I'm a computer geek. I work with numbers, spreadsheets, and data mining. I'm the information finder, and I'm most definitely the weak link in the field.

Please, God, let me fake my way through this. Loki's life just might depend on it.

Less than two minutes later, Seth opens my office door and ushers two men inside. One, an older gentleman I recognize from all those years ago. The other, a spitting image of my friend.

Seth is more rigid than I've ever seen him. I can tell he's hanging onto the tightrope of his emotions where Luca is concerned. I can't say I'm fairing much better. Staring into the eyes of Loki's enemy, my innate need to safeguard him wars with the logical side that tells me to hear Luca out.

Mr. Anderson crosses the room with the self-assured confidence of a man in charge. I'm going to have to knock this asshole down a peg or two, but once again, Seth beats me to it.

"Stop," he bellows, causing Luca to cringe and Mr. Anderson to halt mid-stride. Moving toward us, Seth pulls out two chairs from a side table and places them six feet apart and facing me.

Turning to face our guests, he orders them to sit, then rounds the desk to stand at my side.

Relief rolls off my shoulders in waves.

"I've got you," he mutters under his breath.

Fuck. I must look nervous. Steeling myself, I focus my attention on the two men before me. With all the strength I can muster, I control the room for the rest of our meeting.

Pointing to Luca, I issue my command, "Speak."

He glances between Mr. Anderson and Seth. Mr. Anderson shrugs his shoulders in acquiescence and leans back into his chair. Crossing his right ankle over his knee, he's the picture of calm.

I could take some lessons from this asshole.

"What do you want to know?" Luca asks.

"Everything, asshole," Seth barks.

Mr. Anderson chuckles, but Luca furrows his brow as if contemplating where to start.

"How about you start at the beginning?" I already know the basics from my research, but I need to hear it straight from his mouth.

"Well, like Loki, I have a different mom than the other Blacks. The difference is, Loki's mom fought for him. My birth mother sold me the first chance she had."

"That's why you and Miles are only five months apart?"

"Yes," he bites out. "Miles is a mean fucking bastard."

"Yeah, we know. What else?"

"I never fit in with them because I was a bastard. The only

time our siblings ever accepted me was when Loki would visit. As soon as he arrived, the target was off my back. I'm not proud of using him as a scapegoat, but sometimes you do what you have to do to survive."

I don't answer because I can't imagine growing up like that. My brothers and I had our shit, but we've always had each other's backs. I nod to encourage him to continue.

"Shortly after Loki left our house the last time, there were rumblings of things to come. It was the first time I truly understood how sick and twisted my family was, especially my father. After my brothers told me what he planned to do to Loki's parents, they assumed Loki would have no alternative but to return to Boston. That's when they started making plans to come after all of you."

"They hadn't counted on my parents stepping in," I offer.

"No, and it sent my father into a tailspin. It's one of the few times I saw him make mistakes. But it was in his rage that I found an escape."

That has my attention. "How so?"

"Your father called Antonio Black the day Loki's parents were killed in the car accident. He let him know that Loki's mom had left custody to them, along with all the documentation she had saved on him over the years. Your father told Antonio under no circumstances would he ever get his hands on Loki, then he hung up," Mr. Anderson fills in.

"My father erupted into a fit of rage I'd never seen before. He made us pack our bags that night, and we touched down in Waverley-Cay shortly after. He didn't have a plan, just a lot of guns, and he was coming for you. Somehow, in the early morning hours, I talked him into letting me go alone to speak to Loki. He dropped me off on the other side of the bay, and I swam to your shore. I sat there for hours waiting for someone to come home."

My stomach rolls as I remember that day. "You met Colton on the beach," I say, remembering how Colt had come running inside shortly after Mr. Anderson arrived to say he had made a friend on the beach. We were both young at the time, and Colt had a habit of imaginary friends, so no one thought much of it. Knowing now that Luca could have shot him dead but didn't, does nothing to ease the unsettled feeling in my gut.

"Yes. He told me Agent Anderson was at your house, and I knew then that was my only chance. I waited at your gate for them to leave and then jumped in front of their car. I joined the FBI as soon as I turned eighteen."

"What the fuck?" Seth screams. Rounding the table, he lifts Mr. Anderson by the lapel of his jacket. "Why the fuck wouldn't you tell us? All this time, Loki has been living half a life, thinking he was doing this all alone, and you had his goddamn brother in the ranks this entire time. Why?" Seth's voice echoes in the confines of my office.

"Release me, Special Agent Foster."

Years of training have Seth following orders, and taking a step back. I watch Seth fight a war within himself.

"Why?" he bites out through gritted teeth.

Straightening his jacket, Mr. Anderson replies calmly, "We needed Loki, but we also needed a man on the inside. It's a good thing, too, because we wouldn't have known how complex Antonio's operation really was. If we hadn't had Luca on the inside, I fear Loki wouldn't have made it as far as he did."

"You don't know shit about Loki," Seth defends.

"Seth," I say, trying to rein in my own emotions, "let's hear them out."

For the next hour, we hear the back story of how Luca aided us in all our missions for the last eight years. It's an eye-opening, exhaustive breakdown, but it leaves no doubt in my mind that I need to bring him to Loki. If we have any hope of clearing his name, we'll have to rely on his half-brother.

CHAPTER 31

LOKI

Loki: Update?

I grab my phone and recheck it. It's been three hours since I sent that message, and I have no response from Ashton or Seth. The messages aren't even showing as read, so I have no fucking idea what's going on.

"You okay?" Sloane asks over the top of her computer.

No, I'm not okay, but I don't tell her that. Putting a voice to my concerns makes them real, and I'm not ready to go there yet.

"Yeah, I'm fine," I lie. "I'm just waiting for an update from the guys. What are you working on today?"

Sloane eyes me skeptically, and I know she doesn't believe me. When she looks at me like this, I see my future so clearly—running EnVision with Ash and Seth, living in a house that she's turned into a home. Her. I see my future clearly, and it consists of Sloane.

"Ugh, social media," she groans. "If I had known how many hats I would have to wear when I first started publishing, I may have chosen a different career. Social media is the worst, but it's a necessary evil if I want to sell books."

"What's so bad about it?"

Sighing, she reaches up and tightens her ponytail. "I'm forced to put myself out there daily. I have to open myself up to my readers, who, thankfully, are amazing. But, putting yourself out there also opens you up for judgment. People can be cruel when sitting safely behind their computer screens."

"How so?" The thought of anyone disrespecting her has my hands itching to fight.

"Oh, Loki. I could go on for hours about this. Basically, you'll always have the people you can never please. Unfortunately, most of the time, they're also the loudest. They like to let everyone know you're not perfect. They thrive off calling out every mistake you make and trying to cancel you. They enjoy ripping you apart personally. It's pretty rough on the ego," she admits.

"Then why do it?"

"Because for every douche canoe, there's a reader who emails to tell me my story got them through something or that they connected in a way that moved them to tears. Luckily, the assholes of the world are far and few between, but knowingly putting yourself on the chopping block for them is a hard pill to handle sometimes. Then, you get the dick pics."

My head whips to hers. "Have you gotten more?"

"Always. I get them weekly, if not daily. I try not to check it too often. Someday, I'll hire a personal assistant who will handle the deletions, but for now, that job falls to me."

By the time she's done speaking, I realize I'm pacing the cabin again. "At least Dom isn't bothering you anymore," I grumble.

"Ah, right," Red agrees, but her voice betrays her and has me pausing mid-stride.

"What? He hasn't written back to you, has he?"

Her eyes are dodgy, and I feel my blood pressure rise.

"Not just to me, no," she answers evasively.

"What the hell? Is he looking for a harem now?" I bark.

"Ooh, you know what I've heard is selling really well right now? Reverse harems. I would have to do a ton of research to write one, but the emotional suckage I could pull from those characters would be out of this world."

"Please don't," I groan. The idea of Red researching orgies has me wanting to punch something—namely, a faceless dipshit named Dom.

"Not your cup of tea, is it?" she teases.

"Not when I have to picture you researching it, no. What the hell is that asshat saying now?"

"Who?"

"Who? Dom! What the hell could he possibly have to say after I …"

"After you what, Loki? What did you do?" she asks, amused. I'm willing to bet she already checked that particular chat thread.

"I did what I needed to do to get rid of him."

"Well, it doesn't appear to have worked." She smirks.

I cross the room and am standing at her side within seconds. "What the hell did he say now?"

"Ah, you probably don't want to know. Honestly, Loki, I was only teasing you. This is, unfortunately, just part of the craziness that comes with the business of being a romance author."

"What. Did. He. Say?" I bite out.

"Ugh, all right, caveman. Have a look for yourself." Turning the computer screen toward me, my hands ball into fists as soon as I see his name.

Leaning forward, I read his words and have to work to contain my rage.

I want to invite you and your male companion to visit my school for submissive training. While your friend will not participate, he is welcome to observe. I can ensure we will exceed your needs. -Dom

"Is he fucking kidding me?" I yell.

Yanking the screen closer, I rage type.

She does not require your services, you crazy old fuck. If she wants help learning to be submissive, I'll do it. If she wants to test the waters in any area, I'll do it. Her wants and needs are not your concern, so get off her goddamn dm's and get a life, you worthless piece of shit. She's mine. Send.

"Loki! You can't do stuff like that," she screams. "This is my career. There are ways of handling this bullshit. What you just did is so unprofessional. I can't believe you would think so little of my career that you'd do something so careless."

Wait, what?

"Red—"

"Don't. Don't you Red me." I've never heard her voice so icy.

"I-I'm sorry. I didn't mean to undermine you or your career. But I also don't want fuck heads coming at you like that. I-I'm serious about you, Sloane. I need you in my bed, in my life, and my heart."

Where the hell did that come from? But it's the truth, isn't it? That's what I want. She's what I want.

She opens and closes her mouth multiple times like a fish. Just when I think she will finally speak, I hear the telltale whirring of helicopter blades.

My hand closes over hers, and I'm pulling her from the chair before she can blink. I've shoved her into boots and a jacket as her brain attempts to catch up. I count as the sound gets closer and estimate I have one and a half minutes before that bird touches the ground.

"I need you to listen to me. That," I say, pointing to the ceiling, "is not a good sign." I reach into the closet, pull out the gun she has been using for target practice, and hand it to her. Pulling open the door, I yank out the bag with the clips and ammo. "I need you to—"

The phone rings, interrupting me, and I run to grab it while continuing to throw shit into a bag for Sloane.

"What?"

"Don't shoot. It's us," Ashton says over speakerphone.

"What?" Sloane and I ask in unison.

"We're touching down, don't shoot us."

"Why …" I glance down at the phone in my hand and see he's disconnected the call.

"What's happening?" Sloane asks with a shaky voice.

"I don't know. I have a feeling I won't like it, though," I admit.

My girl stands there with a gun hanging limply in her unsteady hand.

"Baby, you've got this. If you had to, you could protect yourself. With this," I say, lifting her hand holding the gun, "and this." I point to her head. As I stare into her uncertain eyes, the door bursts open. Ashton stands in the doorway with Seth right behind him.

My jaw goes slack as they enter, leaving my half-brother, Luca, standing in the entryway.

"What the fuck are you doing bringing him here, Ashton?" Red's voice cuts through the haze of memories attempting to flood my head.

When Luca holds his hands up in surrender, I realize Sloane has taken a few steps forward with the gun aimed straight for Luca's head. She's become a damn good shot, and from this range, I have no doubt she could end him here and now, but I don't want that blood on her hands.

"Sweetheart," I whisper from behind, "stand down."

Even as I say the words, my hands have found their way to the weapon at my back. Just because I don't want the blood on her hands doesn't mean I'm letting this asshole walk out of here. As she lowers her arms, I raise mine.

"Loki, put the gun away. It would be best if you heard

what Luca has to say in person. That's why we're here," Ash mutters.

I'm so confused. I trust Ash and Seth with my life, but bringing an enemy to my doorstep has me rethinking everything I know to be true. Slowly, Luca lowers his arms.

"Do you remember Nadja?" He stands with his arms crossed at his chest. His posture and presence are so much like my own. *If our lives had been different, would we have been friends instead of enemies?* The thought is unsettling.

"Nadja?" I repeat as pressure builds in my head. My eyesight blurs, and I fight to remain standing as memories flood my brain.

"Shit. Loki, are you okay? Help me get him to the chair." Sloane's voice mixes with the rush of memories.

Strong hands grip my forearms, and I thrash against the constraints.

"Loki, it's just us," Seth states calmly on my left. "Emory said this might happen. We need to take this slow. Just sit down while your body and mind catch up."

Incapable of speaking at the moment, I nod. My head is on a swivel while I search for Red, and I'm pleased when I find her beside me, throwing Luca a death glare. My girl could make grown men crumble with that look, and I love her for it.

Holy fuck. I love her.

We make eye contact, and her features soften. Giving me a gentle nod, she returns her gaze to Luca. She's guarding my life again, and I've never seen anything so sexy in all my life.

"Loki, I'm sorry for crashing in on you like this. We were afraid if we told you in advance, you wouldn't meet with him," Seth admits.

"Of course he wouldn't, you asshole. What the fuck, Seth? Someone had better start speaking, now, or I will use this." She slowly raises the gun. "And I am a great freaking shot, so don't test me."

"Okay, GI Jane. Take it easy. Do you think I'd bring Luca here if I didn't know for certain we could trust him?" Ashton rationalizes.

Even in my haze, I can tell Sloane is making him nervous. *Good. Red might be the only one truly on my side right now.*

"Nadja," Luca repeats, crossing the room slowly and taking a seat across from me.

"I swear to Christ, if one of you doesn't start talking right fucking now, I will shoot someone," Sloane screeches.

My hearing fades in and out as blood rushes through my ears. Luca tells us what brought him here as memories fighting to take shape flash across my vision like a movie reel. I only hear bits and pieces. He was in Waverley-Cay after my parents died—he met Agent Anderson. He joined the FBI two years after I enlisted with SIA.

"If that's true, why the hell didn't Loki know about it?" Sloane demands.

I give her a half-smile through the migraine fog that has settled over me. My girl is asking all the right questions.

"The alphabet agencies don't like to share information," Seth growls. "Even when an agent's life is on the line, apparently."

"That's stupid." Sloane crosses her arms over her chest. With the gun in her right hand tucked under her arm, her left hand squeezes her right elbow. That's when I see it. Tap-tap-slide.

"Come here, Red." My voice sounds stronger than I feel, and she does as I ask. After removing the gun from her grasp, I set it on the table behind me then pull her down into my lap. Placing my palm over her tapping fingers, she relaxes.

I see the question in Seth and Ashton's eyes, but I don't linger on them. Instead, I use every ounce of energy I have to make sense of the rush of memories filling my conscious. Sloane closes her small hand around mine, and a sense of calm I've never known in these situations washes over me.

Is this how Trevor feels with Julia at his side?

"I almost killed you in that warehouse," I say, glaring at Luca.

"No shit," he fires back.

Visions of him screaming wildly as I aimed my gun at him come to me. *What was he yelling, though?*

"Do you remember everything, then?" Sloane whispers.

"No. It-It's coming, but it's like I can't process it all."

"Would it help if I recounted what happened in the warehouse?" Luca asks. He's more soft-spoken than I remembered.

Glaring at him, I have a hard time reconciling a lifetime's worth of hatred with the bits of memory I'm gathering.

"Loki?" Ashton steps forward. "Emory told us you could feel overwhelmed by information. She likened it to having a nasty hangover where bits of your memory come at different times."

That's exactly what it feels like, the worst fucking hangover of my life.

"But, the thing is," Ash continues, "Vic is closing in on Luca. He knows Luca isn't in Lanesboro, and that means our window to catch him is getting smaller."

"Do you know what Vic's done?" Sloane asks.

"Besides being the world's biggest fuckwad?" Seth barks.

"Watch it, Seth." My voice is deadly. I love Seth like a brother, but that doesn't mean I'll stand by while he speaks to Sloane like that. When he smirks at me, I know I've just outed myself where Red is concerned. Surprisingly, I'm okay with them knowing. In fact, I feel a shock of pride in them knowing how I feel about her.

I wait for Seth to continue, but keep a close eye on Luca. My gut says I can trust him, but I'll keep all my senses on high alert until I have all the information.

"Vic is cousins with Stanislav Mikhailov," Ashton interrupts.

My body goes rigid, and Sloane turns to look at me. I lift her off my lap, stand, and set her back in the chair while I pace.

"Wh-Who is Stan Mikalove?" Sloane mumbles.

"Stanislav Mikhailov is a very dangerous man. He's the head of the Russian mob family taking over the Boston territory now that my father is out of the picture," Luca confides.

"How the hell didn't we know this about Vic?" I try not to yell, but my voice still raises a few octaves.

"He had help concealing it, and he never had contact with his mother's family until after his father passed away while we were in the academy. I don't have proof yet, but I'm willing to bet it was Montgomery," Ashton vows.

"Montgomery? No way. He's been my biggest advocate. He's always been on my side," I point out.

"He has," Seth agrees, "but did you know his daughter is engaged to Vitali Solonik?"

"Since when? She's just a kid. Jesus, she can't be more than nineteen. We went to her sweet sixteen party a few years ago."

"She's eighteen. They met at boarding school. Something isn't sitting right with that relationship, but I haven't been able to turn up anything solid yet," Ashton informs us.

"So it's possible Montgomery has been connected to them this entire time?" I clarify.

"Yeah, and since Solonik is Mikhailov's brother-in-law, I'm guessing they targeted her early on. They must have found some information they could use, and now they have the entire Montgomery family under their thumb." Agitated, Seth pushes away from the wall he was leaning on.

"When did you figure this out?"

"I didn't. You did, right before the explosion in Boston," Luca chimes in.

"Fuck," I scream, slamming my fist into the wall.

Sloane screams, and I feel like an asshole.

CHAPTER 32

SLOANE

Loki slams his fist into the wall, and I scream involuntarily.

"Fuck. Sweetheart, I'm sorry. I'm sorry I scared you." Loki is at my feet before I close my mouth.

"Y-You just startled me. I'm fine," I assure. Truthfully, I've never seen Loki lose control like that, and it scared the shit out of me.

"Don't do that with me, Red. Fine doesn't cut it. I'm sorry, I will do better." Taking the seat beside me, Loki entwines our hands and places our joined fingers in his lap. Methodically, he rubs circles with the pad of his thumb over the delicate skin between my thumb and forefinger.

His movements ease my heart rate, even with the chaos lurking.

"Loki, I-I need to know if Nadja is all right. I'm dying here not knowing how the pregnancy is going." Luca's voice is filled with emotion, tears threatening the back of his eyes.

Loki's hand wraps tightly around mine, almost to the point of pain. Glancing at him, I can tell he's fighting with a memory. No one else in the room recognizes he needs a minute, but I do. I know him. It's like he is a part of me, I feel his pain deep in my chest, so I intervene.

"Why would Loki know where this girl is?"

"This girl," Luca rumbles, "is my fiancée. She's pregnant, and is Mikhailov's only daughter."

"You knocked up a mob princess?" I can't help myself. This is the stuff that makes romance novels so great.

"When I first met her, it was under the pretense of also being the son of a mobster. Things were never supposed to become real, but Nadja had a way of getting under my skin. We were spending every minute together so I could learn how Mikhailov operated, but the more time I spent with her, the more I realized she was just like me. We were both victims of our circumstances, and … well, things just happened. When we found out she was pregnant, I knew I had to get her out. I hadn't accounted for Loki being as good at his job as he is, though."

Loki's hand is clammy. A quick peek to my right, and I see beads of sweat forming on his brow line. I tighten my grasp on his hand, then watch as his self-awareness slowly returns.

"Nadja is safe. She's with Claire." Loki's voice crackles, like speaking physically pains him.

"She needs prenatal care, though," Luca pleads.

"Claire was my nanny as a child. When I moved in with the Westbrooks, she returned to school. She's an Ob-Gyn nurse-practitioner now. Nadja is in excellent hands, and I guarantee she is receiving all the prenatal care she requires." Loki's voice is eerily monotone.

Luca's shoulders slump as he gasps for air. "Thank fuck," he mumbles.

We sit in silence for a while. Everyone seems to understand that Loki needs time to place all this new information before making a plan.

"They were never after Red." His voice cuts through the cabin, making me jump.

"I don't think so, no," Ash confirms. "But that doesn't explain your note."

"Nadja is in Sutton, on Red Sawyer Way with Claire," Loki reveals.

"What about the four months' part?" I ask, remembering his note.

Four Points West-Sutton. They know she's with me. They're watching her. Four Months. Get Sawyer out.

"Nadja was four months along when Loki hid her," Luca explains.

Jesus. Things slowly fall into place as I glance around the room.

"I'm sorry we wasted your time for so long, Sloane." Loki won't make eye contact with me, and I feel sick to my stomach.

"You didn't waste my time, Loki. You—"

Luca speaks at the same time, cutting me off. "We're running out of time, man. It won't be long before Vic figures it out. He's already gunning for us. Once he learns about Nadja, he'll have no qualms about destroying everything in his way."

Loki reaches behind me for a laptop. Opening it up, he starts dragging file after file to the screen. "We need to make a timeline and make sure we haven't missed anything. Then, we make our plan of attack."

My loveable caveman has turned into a military machine right before my eyes, and I can't handle the change. Standing abruptly with no plan, I glance around the room until my eyes land on Seth.

"Want to come to watch my target practice? You won't believe how good I am." It's a little boastful, but I need the air of confidence so I don't crumble in front of everyone. I don't know what I expected the outcome to be with Loki, but having it end so abruptly isn't what I'm prepared for.

"Ah, right now?" Seth asks, his eyes darting between Loki and me.

"Go ahead, she's a really good shot." Loki throws a half-smile in my direction, and my stomach clenches painfully.

What the fuck is happening?

"Okay, Sloane. Let's see what you've got," Seth says, dragging me by my elbow as a big brother would.

"We'll be back in a bit," I tell no one in particular. Watching the table as I walk away, I realize no one was listening anyway.

～

"Holy shit, Sloane. You weren't kidding. You've hit bullseye nearly every time," Seth calls as he walks toward me with the paper target in hand.

Smiling at the praise, I let my grin speak for itself.

"How often are you practicing?"

"We come out every day."

"We?"

Shrugging my shoulders like it's no big deal, I turn away from him so he can't see me blush.

"Yeah, we kind of fell into a routine, I guess. We exercise together, eat together, do chores together, we even work together." I leave out the sexcapades that have replaced my research. There's no need to embarrass us both, but from his smirk, I have a feeling he knows.

"You know, there's nothing wrong with admitting you like each other," Seth points out while helping me clean up our mess.

Flustered, I blurt, "Oh, I don't do relationships, Seth."

"I know you say you don't, but what do you think a relationship entails, Sloane? Because to me, it means spending time with someone who encourages you to be better, to do better. It means spending time with someone because it's fun and learning to adapt to each other's lives because you like having them close. So, from where I'm standing, you've been in a relationship with Loki for months. You just never labeled it."

When he puts it that way, he may have a point.

Is that why I got so upset when Loki shut down on me?

Deciding to put it away until I talk to Loki, I turn toward the cabin. "Come on, big guy. It may be spring, but it's still freaking cold up here in the mountains. Let's go check on the other guys."

"Sounds good to me. I'm freezing my balls off out here." He chuckles.

"Such a baby. Oh shoot, do you have the empty magazines?"

Glancing down at his hands, I see they're empty.

"No worries. You head up to the house, I'll grab them and meet you there."

"Okay. Thanks, Seth."

"Anytime. But maybe you could make some coffee?"

"As long as you don't expect coffee cake with the coffee, I can do that."

"Nah, I've heard about your baking. I'll wait until you perfect it." He winks.

"Why is everyone so convinced I'll figure it out?" My insecurity is showing , but I really need this answer right now.

He stares at me for a moment, choosing his words carefully.

"Because we all see what you can't, Sloane. You're capable of so much more than you allow yourself to believe. Someday, you'll see yourself the way the rest of us do. Now, get inside before your toes freeze off."

Swallowing a lump the size of a basketball, I nod, then jog

up the steps. Before I open the door, I watch Seth round the cabin. Just as I'm about to turn the handle, Loki's voice cements me in place.

"This isn't a life for a family, Luca." Loki's voice has a sharp edge to it.

Is this what he's like as Special Agent Kane?

"Don't you think I know that?" Luca bellows back.

"What is it you want to do exactly?" Ashton interrupts, more calmly than the other two.

"I want to put Vic away. Then I want to get my girl as far away from her fucked up family as I can." The malice in Luca's voice is palpable.

"Then what?" Loki mocks. "Do you seriously think you can continue with the FBI? It doesn't work that way, little brother."

Is it just me, or were the words little brother dripping with contempt? Does Loki know something we don't?

"Why do you think I've spent my entire adult life alone? Never, not once letting anyone get close to me?"

I feel like he knocked the wind out of me.

No one? Not even me?

"I live a solitary life because having a relationship is a liability. I learned that the hard way with Trevor, Preston, and Dex. Are you willing to take that chance with Nadja? Is it worth the constant fear that someone could grab her? Because I sure as shit never found anyone worth that risk."

My stomach heaves, and I double over, trying to catch my breath.

How could I have been so stupid?

"Yes! Fuck, Loki. She's worth everything. I'll walk away from it all tomorrow if it guarantees we can live in peace together. She's my life. I'll do anything in my power to make sure she's safe."

Lucky girl.

"Hey, you okay?" Seth asks, climbing the steps behind me.

With my hands on my knees, I take a deep, cleansing breath before plastering a smile on my face and standing.

"Yeah, I'm fine. I just stubbed my toe. But, I, ah, I forgot I need to check on Dick and Harry, my raccoons. They're in the shed. I'll be right back. Help yourself to the coffeepot. Loki can tell you where everything is." By the time I've finished speaking, I'm already down the stairs and halfway around the cabin.

When I glance back, I see Seth standing stock still with his hands on his hips, shaking his head.

CHAPTER 33

LOKI

A burst of cold air accosts me, and I turn in my seat, expecting to see Red. When Seth shuts the door, an unexplained sense of dread washes over me.

"Where's Sloane?"

"She said she had to check on her raccoons, Dick and Harry? Is she messing with me?"

I can't help but laugh. "No, she really named those beasts Dick and Harry."

Why is she checking on them now? As far as I know, it's been weeks since she's been out there. All it took was a short video about rabies, and she lost interest fairly quickly.

"Was she okay?"

Seth shrugs his shoulders. "She was on the porch for a bit because she stubbed her toe, but I didn't see it happen. This is a lot to take in, though, man. Maybe she just needs a breather."

"Maybe," I mumble as the sickening feeling creeps higher into my chest like a lead weight.

"Listen," Luca picks up our interrupted conversation, "I don't care what it takes. All I care about is being with Nadja. Are you telling me you plan to stick with SIA for the rest of your life? Because I have to tell you, that sounds like a pretty fucking miserable existence. You deserve more, Loki. We both do." The conviction in his tone has me nodding in agreement.

"No," I finally admit. "Once we put Vic away and clear my name, I'm out."

"Me too," Seth informs Luca as he takes a seat at the table.

"So we need a plan to take him down," Luca states.

"It's not just Vic," Ashton makes a point of acknowledging Luca. "Not if Mikhailov is after you, too. We have to end this all, or you'll be running for the rest of your life."

I'm not sure how I feel about my half-brother right now. Our goals are aligned, and maybe they always have been, but it's hard to turn off a lifetime of hatred. Staring at him, though, I know deep in my soul I'll help him. He didn't deserve the life we've led anymore than I did, and he doesn't deserve to be hunted for the rest of his life because he fell in love.

What would I do if someone was after Sloane?

I'd go bat shit crazy. That's what would happen because I love her. I'm fucking in love with her.

A gust of cold air fills the room, and I know my girl is home. Turning in my seat, I'm floored by what I find. I'm out of my chair so fast I knock it over in my haste to get to her.

"What's the matter? What's wrong? What happened?" I'm already opening the door to search for whatever caused her to cry.

"N-Nothing," she hiccups. "I was just happy to see the raccoon babies doing so well." She's lying, and I fucking hate it.

"What really upset you, Red? I'll kill whoever upset you." I realize in that moment it's not an empty threat. I'm prepared to spend the rest of my life wiping her tears and shredding the ones who cause them.

Peering over her shoulder, I find Luca watching us with

the sadness of lost love. This is what they all feel. This is why all my friends have gone stupid—they're all drunk on love.

"You don't have to kill anyone, you idiot." She tries to sound playful, but I know better. I'm about to drag her outside and demand answers when Ashton's phone rings.

"What do you mean? How?" he yells.

The rest of us watch him nervously.

"How long do we have?"

Ashton marches to the door and yells to the pilot, "We need to be in the air in three minutes." Returning to his phone call, he says, "Done. Get the Kane compound set up."

Turning to us, he starts issuing commands.

"Vic is en route. Somehow, he followed us. Seth, Loki, and Luca, you need to get on the chopper now. If he finds you guys here, you're done."

He's right, but he's also out of his goddamn mind if he thinks I'm leaving Sloane behind.

"Loki, I know what you're going to say, but Sloane has to travel back in the car with me. If we get pulled over, it'll be easier to explain that I was picking up my sister-in-law from her writing retreat than anything else."

"They'll scope the place for fingerprints," Luca states.

"The building won't be standing by the time they get here," I bark. "Baby? Will you be okay with Ashton?"

I hate that she looks so fucking scared, so lost, and that I still have no clue why she's been crying, but Ashton is right.

She works to swallow, and her fingers begin their tap-tap-slide. "Yeah, I'll be fine with Ash. I'm fine, Loki. I'm not your responsibility. None of this had anything to do with me, right?"

"That's not what—"

"They're going to be here in less than ten minutes," Ash interrupts. "Loki, get in the air. Sloane, what do you have to take with you?"

"Ah, my, ah…"

"Sloane, I'll carry out your trunk. Grab your personal shit from the bathroom and your computer. We can replace everything else."

She nods in understanding and beelines for the bathroom.

"Seth, I'll meet you outside in one minute. Ashton, pack up her laptop," I instruct, then I follow her into the bathroom and shut the door.

"I'm okay, Loki. You need to go."

"Something is wrong, and I don't like leaving this way. As soon as it's safe, I'll meet you at home, and we can talk about everything, okay?"

"Home?" she squeaks.

"Yeah." I grin. "You've still got a few months left on that lease, and it turns out, I'm going to need a place to crash. We can pick up where we left off here."

She seems alarmed, but I'm running out of time. "Whatever is going on in that head of yours is not fine. But I promise you we'll sort through it all together. I promise." I drag her into a hug and only relax when her rigid body finally melts into mine.

"Loki, now." Ashton bangs on the door, and she peels herself away.

"Sloane, I lo—"

The door bursts open, and Ashton appears. "Now, Loki. You have to leave now. They're closing in fast."

We follow him out of the bathroom, but I grab the gun from the table and hand it to Sloane. "Keep this with you at all times, do you understand? You know how to use this. You're a natural shot. Keep it with you and use it if you have to."

"Are you sure about that, Loki?" Ashton asks nervously.

"She's a fucking good shot, Ash. If there's trouble, she's who you want on your side."

His eyebrows raise, but respect is written all over his face.

Turning back to Red, I say, "If you can't believe in yourself, then believe in the confidence I have in your ability to protect yourself." I lean in and place a chaste kiss on her lips. "I believe in you, sweetheart. I'll call you soon." The sadness that washes over her beautiful face kills me.

Ashton must sense I'm warring with leaving her because a second later, he is at my back pushing me toward the door. Grabbing Sloane's kink kit, I carry it out the door and place it in the trunk before climbing into the helicopter.

The last vision I have is Sloane standing on the porch of our cabin with a tear-stained face. I hate myself for not knowing how to fix this for her. Fuck, I don't even fully understand what upset her in the first place. But leaving her like that was like leaving an enormous piece of my soul behind.

"She's lost," Luca's voice comes over my headset.

I want to fucking punch him in the face, but he's right.

"She's been off since I found her on the porch," Seth adds.

"What the hell happened on the porch?"

Seth shrugs. "Did she hear something she shouldn't have? We all know she doesn't have a problem eavesdropping." He means it as a joke, but it makes me murderous in my defense of her.

"She only listened to my and Sylvie's conversation because you pricks were too chicken shit to come get us yourselves," I hiss.

"Holy shit," Seth mutters.

"He's committed." Luca laughs.

"What the hell are you talking about?"

"You love her. You're in love with Sloane." Seth turns in the bucket seat to stare at me. "I'm happy for you, man. It's about fucking time you lived your life for you, not your responsibilities."

"Oh, shit." Luca's stifled voice echoes in my ears while Seth's words run circles in my mind.

"What?" Seth asks.

"You were pretty adamant about never finding anyone worth the risk right before Seth walked in."

"Jesus, Loki. Is that what you said?"

"I wasn't necessarily talking about me. I was trying to feel Luca out to make sure it was worth the pile of shit it will take to get them out of this mess."

Fuck me. Red can't possibly think I'm not serious about her. Can she?

We hear the explosion from the air, and my chest constricts with a brutal, stabbing pain. The three of us turn to look over our shoulders at the smoke rising through the trees.

"That was too fast. That was too fast," I scream. Grabbing the door handle, I fight to control my reactions. Everything is closing in on me. I feel like I'm choking and cannot get enough air. The overwhelming sense of dread takes over my entire system as adrenaline rushes through my veins.

"Fuck," I hear someone yell right before they thrust a paper bag into my hand.

"Breathe, Loki. For Christ's sake, breathe."

"There's no answer," Luca yells.

"Keep calling until Ashton answers," Seth demands.

"No. No, that was too soon. Turn around," I scream at the pilot.

"Keep the course," Seth counters. "We cannot turn around, Loki. I'm sorry, but that will be a death sentence for us all."

I've unbuckled my harness and have my hands on Seth a second later. "Turn this fucking thing around now. I don't give a shit about anything, Seth. I have to make sure my girl is okay. That was too fucking soon. It went off too soon." My voice is desperate as my soul cries out in pain.

Seth moves quickly and disengages my hands from his

throat. "We can't do that, Loki, and you know it. Calm the fuck down. Give Ash a minute to respond."

"It's been a goddamn minute. Turn this thing around, or I'm jumping." I'm already reaching under my seat for the parachute.

"Luca, help me," Seth rumbles as he attempts to subdue me.

I have the backpack on and am buckling the last of the straps when Luca screams, "Text. We have a message."

Ripping the phone from of his hand, I pull up the message from Ash.

Ashton: We're out. Heading north. Get to Kane Lane and wait for instructions. Sloane and I will return to Waverley-Cay when we've lost our tail. Wipe all phones now.

Loki: Is Sloane okay? I need to talk to her.

Ashton: Yes. Not yet. Destroy the burners. I'll contact you when we have new phones. Wipe them now.

Loki: Fuck that, Ash. Let me talk to her first.

*Your message is undeliverable.

Loki: Ashton.

*Your message is undeliverable.

I throw the phone to the ground so hard it shatters. My heart raging is all I can hear in my ears.

"What did he say?" Seth's voice is calm, and it grates on my last nerve.

"They're headed north. We need to wipe all phones and head to my parents' house. He'll contact us when it's safe."

"What about Sloane?" Luca asks. I spin on him so fast I think I might kill him just for uttering her name. "Loki, I know what you're feeling right now. It's how I have been for the last six months, but you have to take a step back and realize this is what's best for her. I don't know Ashton as you do, but from what I can tell, he's been your right-hand man, your intel for years, right? We have to trust that he has a plan for this."

"And if he doesn't, you can bet your ass he'll have one before we touch down in Waverley-Cay," Seth adds.

What they're saying is reasonable. They're right, except I'm anything but rational when it comes to Sloane. The realization lights a fire under my ass. First, I'll end this bullshit once and for all, then I'm going to marry that girl.

"She thinks I'm not serious about her," I mumble.

"I hate to say this, but maybe that's not a bad thing right now," Luca says.

"Watch it," Seth grinds out.

Luca raises his hands, and Seth stands down. "I just mean, wouldn't it be easier to handle Vic if you knew she was safe? If he catches wind that she's connected to you, she becomes a liability. You said it yourself."

"Are you suggesting I let her suffer thinking I don't love her?"

"For the time being, yes."

"Fuck you. That's not going to happen. I'm getting my girl. I'm going to kill Vic, and then I'm moving on with my goddamn life."

So many questions flood my mind as I settle back into my seat. *Would she be safer if I let her go? How do I feel about Luca? I can't spend my life without Red. Red is my life.*

With new determination, I focus my energy on one task and one task only—Make Sloane Mine.

CHAPTER 34

SLOANE

Five days later, Ashton finally drops me off at Loki's apartment. It's been an intense few days. I've been jumpy ever since Ashton pressed the button that blew up our cabin in the woods. The fact that these men all know how to do this shit has my fingers doing their nervous dance. This crap shouldn't happen in real life.

"Are you going to be okay?" Ashton's voice, though gentle, scares the shit out of me.

Clutching my chest, I face him. "Yeah, why wouldn't I be?"

While we moved from hotel to hotel, sometimes two in one day, it's given me time to make a plan. I'm not giving Loki the chance to ruin me. It was close—I'll admit that. Another day with him, and I could have found myself uttering those three tragic words. *I love you.*

Ashton doesn't realize it, but he saved me from myself. Now I just need to set my plan in motion and get the fuck out of here before I crumble. Ash may have saved me from saying the words, but they weigh heavy on my heart, and I need to be alone for the breakdown that's looming.

"Loki will come by as soon as he can, I'm sure."

My chest constricts hearing his name.

"Oh, that's not necessary. I'm sure he's busy. I'll be out of his way in a couple of days at the most."

"Out of his way? Sloane, what are you ... he cares about you. You know that, right?" Ashton's concern makes me twitchy.

"I'm sure he does. He cares about us all. That's what he does, right? Cares for his family? Protects them? It'll be better if I'm out of his way so he can focus on his work. It sounds like Luca is going to need all the help he can get."

"That's not what he's doing with you—"

"Sloane? Where are you?" my sister's voice calls out from the entryway.

"We're in the kitchen, Mis." My old nickname for her, a mix of mom and sis, slips past my lips and makes me smile.

"Oh my God. Thank you, Jesus." Emory rushes me like a linebacker and has me in a death grip a second later.

Peering past her shoulder as it smothers me, I see my other two sisters, Tilly and Eli, standing in the doorway.

"Whampoosh," my words come out mumbled, and I have to push Emory back a little to get air so I can speak. "What are you two doing here? You must have finals right now?"

"You're whisked away by the secret service. Then we have minimal contact with you for months, and you seriously think we're not going to come running the second we find out you're home?" Tilly admonishes. "For such a smart girl, you sure have some stupid tendencies when it comes to our family dynamic."

Emory is clutching my hand so tightly my fingers go numb. I wiggle my hand, and she loosens her grip but doesn't let go.

"Sloane?" Ashton's voice cuts through the chatter of my sisters. "I've spoken to Loki. He doesn't just care for you—"

"It's fine, Ash. I'm fine with where things are. I am fine.

I'm actually planning to leave in the morning so he doesn't have to worry about me."

"What?"

"Where are you going?"

"You can't leave again." My sisters all yell their protest at the same time.

"I'll be back. But I need to finish this book. I was thinking I'd go visit Lexi in Vermont if she has room. I've never been, and it'll be a great setting to finish this story."

"Why, Sloane? What's going on?" Emory asks just as Eli turns on Ashton.

"What are you talking about? What's going on with Loki? Did something happen between them in that cabin?" Eli is a little scary sometimes, and Ashton senses it.

Taking a step back, he shakes his head. "It's not my story to tell. But, Sloane? I'm telling you, I've never seen Loki like this with anyone."

"And I heard what I heard, Ash. It's fine. He has plans—shit he has to take care of. I don't fit in that plan, and honestly, I'm not sure I want to."

"I'm not sure what the fuck you heard, but I'm telling you, Loki will lose his shit over this."

I roll my eyes and turn my attention back to my sisters.

"Do you think we could call Lexi and ask her? I want to hit the road first thing in the morning."

Emory wipes a tear from her eye, and I bite the inside of my cheek. I have to stay strong. I can't stay here, in Loki's space, and pretend to be okay. Not anymore, and not around him.

"Yeah, hun. We can call her," Emory chokes out. "Are you sure this is what you want to do?" She's asking me but staring at Ashton.

"Yup. It'll be a new adventure," I lie with as much fake happiness I can muster.

"This is fucked up, Sloane. I'm sure you're misreading this entire situation. I don't know what you heard, but I'll bet my life that you misinterpreted it. At least talk to him before you leave."

"Ash, you and I both know Loki. He's a man bound by honor. He has a job to do, and he does it very well. He doesn't have room for anything else in his life, and I'd be a fool to think otherwise."

"Jesus Christ, Sloane. I'm out. But I'm warning you, Loki will find you."

"It doesn't matter if he does. I'm not hiding from him, Ash. I just know where his priorities are. I won't stand in the way of something he has worked his entire life for."

He leans in for a quick hug but says nothing.

"Sloane?" Tilly asks after we hear the front door slam. "You know I love you, but you're not exactly a love expert."

"I have an Amazon author account that begs to differ with you on that." My sarcasm is cutting deep today.

"No, you're an expert at fake love. Fairytales. The stories you create. You fucking suck at real-life love," Eli mutters.

"Tell me what you really think, Eli. Jesus. Harsh much?"

"Oh, Sloane. She's not wrong, and you know it," Tilly points out.

"Okay, guys. Let's calm down," Emory comes to my rescue. "Sloane, are you sure you're okay, though? Ash seemed pretty insistent that something was going on between you and Loki."

"Something was ... sex. Amazing, mind-blowing sex. And now it's over. End of story. Can we call Lexi now?" I move away from the kitchen island and stand in front of the windows.

Please, just get me out of here.

"Sure," Emory sighs.

Less than an hour later, I tell my sisters I have a headache, and they head home. Sitting on the couch with my knees to my chest, I let the emotions wash over me. This time tomorrow, I'll be in Vermont. Not really on my own, but far enough away from Loki that I can start over.

I should have protected myself better. Why did I let him into my heart? I know better.

CHAPTER 35

LOKI

Ashton: Loki fucked up. Dex, I don't know what he did, but you better work your magic on some kind of rockstar plan.

Loki: WTF are you talking about?

Ashton: Sloane's leaving. What did you do?

Loki: What do you mean she's leaving? Where the fuck is she going? Why hasn't she called me?

Dexter: Okay, break it down for me. What did you do? I need to know the details so I know what kind of make-up scale we're looking at.

Loki: I didn't do anything.

Ashton: Well, you did something because she thinks she's in your way. She's leaving tomorrow, so she doesn't bother you.

Loki: Fuck. She really thinks I don't love her.

Trevor: You love her?

Preston: You motherfucker. Did you hurt my little sister? Emory is up here, bawling her eyes out. I am going to cut your dick off and shove it up your ass.

Loki: Fuck you.

Loki: I didn't do anything intentionally. She overheard

a conversation she shouldn't have. I didn't mean what I was saying; I was trying to get a read on Luca.

Trevor: Luca? Your brother? WTH, man. What's going on?

Ashton: I'll fill you in later. Right now, Loki needs to talk to Sloane.

Loki: We're going dark at 0700 hours.

Preston: She'll be gone by then, asshat.

Loki: Clear the garage. I'm coming over now.

Preston: Done.

Ashton: On it.

Dexter: Make Sloane Loki's is in motion.

Trevor: Let us know what you need from us.

These dipshits have gone soft, and this time, I'm thankful for it. I'm not sure what I'm walking into with Sloane, but losing her is no longer an option.

"Loki? Where are you? We have a problem," Seth yells up the stairs. I'm sitting in my childhood bedroom, and I feel at peace with my lot in life. It's an odd feeling, but I'm pretty sure I'll get used to it with Sloane by my side.

"Me too," I yell back. Standing, I make my way to the hall and down the stairs to find him and Luca leaning over a computer table.

Sighing, I enter the room. This doesn't look good.

"What's up? I have to get to Sloane before we leave."

Seth looks up, and my gut rolls.

"That's not a good idea, Boss."

"Why?" One word that carries enough venom to take out an army.

"Jason is on Vic's team. He also worked with Luca."

Turning to Luca, I expect him to fill in, but Seth continues talking while Luca stares at the ground.

"Jason just got a message to Luca. Vic is onto Sloane. He followed Ashton's car and lifted her prints from their last hotel."

"Why does she have prints on record?"

"Vic lifted them from her TSA pre-check status," Luca announces.

"Fuck." My insides coil so tightly I feel sick to my stomach. "He can't get his hands on her."

"Ash is dispensing a team to your place for her now. But, Loki? You have to keep your distance until this thing is over. Vic is counting on you going to her."

"I can't leave things the way they are. We're looking at a couple of months, at least, to collect enough evidence to put that fucker away. I-I can't let her go off to God knows where thinking I don't care about her."

"Call her," Luca suggests.

"This isn't something that can be done over the fucking phone."

"You might have to ask Ashton to talk to her for you then," Seth admits. "It's too risky to go yourself, and you know it."

Lunging forward, I send my fist through the sheetrock. Then do it again, and again before Seth wraps his arms around my biceps and pulls me away.

"Loki, calm down, man. This isn't forever, but you have to do the right thing here."

"Fuck you. Going to her is the right thing," I scream.

I know it deep down in my soul. Leaving things as they are, however temporary it may be, is a death sentence. Swallowing my pride, I choke out, "Please, Seth. I know how she thinks. Please help me get to her so she knows I'm not abandoning her. Everyone in her life has left." I gasp for air like it'll be my last as a surge of panic overtakes me.

"Jesus, Loki. Calm down." Seth releases me as Luca grabs water from the bar. Uncapping the bottle, he hands it to me, and we all notice my hands shaking.

"I'm losing my fucking mind," I mutter.

"Women will do that to you, brother." Luca chuckles. "Try

having one yell at you in Russian while hormonal and crying. It gets ugly, quick."

Staring at my half-brother, I see a man instead of an enemy and nod.

"You know you'll have to go into hiding?" I ask him. "Just because we put Vic away won't mean you're in the clear. It could take years to get to her father."

Luca pulls at the back of his neck angrily. It's something I often do, too. *Did our father do that?* I shake that thought away before it fully forms. Who gives a fuck what that piece of shit did.

"Yeah, I know. I've saved every cent I've ever made from the FBI. They froze all my other assets, and rightly so. I'm just glad I had to foresight to have my paycheck deposited into a legal account."

"Are you worried about money?" I'm shocked by the level of concern I have for him, a man that's been an enemy my entire life.

"No, Nadja and I won't need much. The agency should be able to set us up nicely enough."

I glance at Seth, and with a nod of my head, he knows I want him to look into that. Luca has lived the same life I have, but I have considerable means at my disposal, thanks to my parents. I'll make sure they have all they need to live comfortably.

"We'll make sure of it," I promise.

I place the water bottle on the table just as we hear the front door chime indicating someone is here. *Why the fuck didn't the alarms go off?* Seth has pulled his weapon and is already hugging the doorframe with Luca right behind him. *How am I the only one unarmed?*

"Loki? Where are you?" Ashton yells from the foyer.

"Jesus Christ, Ash. Warn us next time," Seth yells, walking into the hallway. "I could have shot you."

"Don't be so trigger-happy, you asshole. I locked this

place down. No one is getting in without the password and a biometric key," Ashton fires back.

Luca places his Glock back in its holster and walks to the couch, shaking his head. "You've got some pushy friends. You know that?"

I laugh because it's true. "Yeah, I know. But they'd take a bullet for me in a heartbeat."

Luca nods with an unreadable expression on his face. "I hope to find that someday," he mumbles.

Crossing the room, I place my hand on his shoulder. "You just did, Luca. We have your back."

"Thanks, Loki. That … it means a lot to me."

"You couldn't call and let us know you were coming?" The edge in Seth's voice is unmistakable.

"No, I couldn't," Ashton retorts. "I had to park at my mother's house and trudge through the woods, so no one would see me coming here. I have to assume Loki is losing his shit over Sloane, right? So, I'm here."

"What are you going to do?" I ask.

"Vic is watching this house. He can't get a read on it, even with heat detection because of the deflectors we have all over the perimeter, but he suspects you're all here. Seth and I are going to leave in separate cars to cause a distraction. They will automatically assume the cars are carrying you or Luca. You," he says, pointing to me, "are going over to Sylvie's house the way I came. Take one of the cars in her garage over to your building. Preston has it cleared out. Use his elevator to the penthouse and then take the stairs down to your floor. I wouldn't stay long, though. An hour tops. We have work to do before you guys hit the field in a few hours."

I stare at him, unable to speak. Ash may be the quietest of the bunch, but he doesn't miss a thing. "Th-Thank you, Ash. I-I—"

"Need to get going," he interrupts. "We don't have much time. Luca?"

"Yeah, what do you need?" Luca jumps to attention, and I have to appreciate his dedication. I still have a small kernel of doubt that I wish I could wipe from my memory, but I try to remind myself that it's just years of pent-up hatred trying to redirect itself. It's fucking hard, but I have to trust him.

"I need to know everything you have on Mikhailov and Solonik. Every single detail. Leave nothing out. Even if it seems irrelevant to you, I want to know. Getting you to Nadja depends on it." Ashton may stay behind the scenes, but he knows how people work. He's covering all the bases by throwing Nadja into the mix. I'm just glad he's on my side.

"Done," Luca speaks immediately. "How do you want it?"

Ashton hands him a burner phone. "I'll call you on this as soon as I'm in the clear. I want the rundown while I'm out driving aimlessly, but I want you putting it all into this encrypted software while we're gone."

"Got it."

"Loki? Get going." Ashton hands me a phone. This guy must have them stuffed into every possible crevice because he passes Seth another one. "I'll send you a signal when it's safe to leave Sylvie's. She has all the keys lined up in the garage and knows you're coming."

Standing abruptly, Luca sets up the computer and gets to task.

"Thank you. All of you, for understanding. I just can't leave Sloane this way."

Seth chuckles. "Love fucks everyone up at some point."

"Just make it quick, okay? We have a long road ahead of us," Ashton adds.

With a parting nod, I head out the back door into the cover of night. I have no idea what I'll say to Sloane, but she will be mine.

CHAPTER 36

SLOANE

I gave up trying to sleep an hour ago. It's strange. I had almost forgotten what my life was like before Loki. With him, I never once had trouble sleeping.

That's because he sexed you up so hard every damn night that you couldn't stay awake if you tried.

"Ugh, the sex," I mutter to an empty room. Wrapping my arms tightly around my knees, I try not to think about what life will be like now. I rest my head on my bent legs when I feel the anxiety rising from my belly to my throat.

Why does this hurt so much? It's not like we were together, not really anyway. I hate that he made me feel like I could do things, though. When I was with him, I honestly believed I was going to be okay—that I was worth something. And now that I'm alone again? The panic attacks and sleepless nights are worse than ever before.

"Why am I such a fuckup?" Glaring at the empty walls of Loki's apartment, anger takes over my sadness, and I jump to my feet. Okay, I can't sleep, but I can write. I don't need to sit here in this pity party for one.

After placing my headphones over my ears, I flip through

my playlist. I need something loud and angry. Really fucking angry, and …

My thumb lands on Eminem's "Darkness".

"Hello darkness." I press play and close my eyes as my head sways to the beat. "I don't want to be alone." My fingers rest on the keyboard, and I type, "I don't want to be alone." As the song ends, a heavy hand falls to my shoulder, and I scream.

Without thinking, I send my elbow flying backward as I jump to my left, searching the room for a weapon. I hear the grunt of a man, a sound I've heard before, and I fight to focus on the heap that's doubled over before me.

"Loki? Holy hell, what are you doing sneaking up on me like that?"

"I— Fuck, that hurt, Red. I called out, but you didn't hear me."

Tap-tap-slide.

What the heck is he doing here? *Protect yourself, Sloane. He said he's never met anyone worth sticking around for—that means you. Run before he can hurt you.*

"What are you doing here, Loki?" My body deflates faster than it should, but the adrenaline I had moments ago is now eating away at my heart.

"Ashton said you're leaving," he accuses.

"Tattletale," I whisper.

Loki attempts to close the distance between us, but I take a step back and use the table as a shield. Without paying attention to what I'm doing, I open my notebook with all my plans for Vermont. He glances down, and his face transforms into a scowl.

"Where are you going?" he growls.

"Not that it's any of your business, but since I'm in the clear, it's time to move onto my next story. I'm going to stay with Lexi for a while and finish my book."

"Who is Stephen?" he asks through gritted teeth.

Dropping my gaze, I realize what I've just shown him.

"Ah, he works at Lexi's lodge."

"Why do you have notes on him?" His voice rumbles through the room, making me wish I had run tonight.

Keep it together, Sloane. You don't owe him anything. He made his position very clear.

Shrugging my shoulders, I walk backward toward the kitchen. "He's single. Lexi thought he would be a good fit."

"A good fit for what?" he spits, barely containing his emotions as he stalks me.

"I don't know, to hang out in case I needed inspiration." I turn and take three quick steps, putting the island between us. I know Loki would never hurt me, but I'm beginning to feel like prey. I know him well enough to know that when he's hunting, he never loses.

He slams his palms on the counter with such force I feel the floor shake on impact. "Explain to me why you would go hang out with a random stranger without even speaking to me first."

"I didn't realize I needed your permission. I've never had a dad, Loki, and I don't need one now."

"I'm not trying to be your father, Red. We both know that's the furthest thing from my mind when it comes to you."

"Yeah, well, you don't have to be anything to me. You have a job to do, one that requires you to be commitment-free, and honestly? That's just fine with me. I don't do relationships. You know that, and I know that. I was a fun distraction, nothing more. I get it."

The flash of hurt that crosses his face makes my stomach leap into my throat. *Don't let him in, Sloane. You heard him. In his own words, he said you weren't worth it. I'm not worth it. He said I'm not worth it.* I repeat the words in my head, drowning out any shred of hope that tries to fight through.

I swallow hard as I look anywhere but at him. The pained

sound coming from him is almost my undoing, but I'm in self-preservation mode here, and I hold tight to my pain. *Everyone leaves you, Sloane. Everyone leaves in the end—that's why we always leave first.*

"Look at me," he hisses, sending shivers up my spine. When I don't respond, he yells it again, "Look at me, Sloane." Using my actual name is like a slap to the face, and I react as if he had.

When my gaze finds his, I'm shocked to see tears there.

"Look me in the eye and tell me you don't have feelings for me."

"Why? Why do you care? You have a job to do, so my feelings don't matter."

You've been here before, Sloane. Men always want what they can't have. You have firsthand, painful memories of this. Don't let him do it to you, too.

"You're a goddamn liar," he bellows.

"Why are you doing this?" My voice cracks as a single tear fights to be set free.

"Why do I care? Are you seriously that dense? Don't you get that I'm not like this with everyone? I've never had what I felt with you in that cabin. I told you already that was a relationship whether you wanted to believe it or not. I care about you, Sloane. I lo—"

"You're saying I'm worth it. When no one else in your life has ever been, you're saying I'm worth staying for?" The sob that escapes rips my throat raw.

"Yes. No, I mean, yes, of course, you're worth it, but I can't stay. I have to catch Vic and help Luca. You know that."

For how long, Loki? How long will I be worth it?

"Loki, don't do this. We both know it can't go anywhere. You deserve someone like Emory or Lanie. You deserve the heroine that's your equal in every way—a woman that's not as broken as I am. I don't even know if I want children, not that I think this would go that far. I-I'm just not what you need, can't you see that? I can barely take care of myself. I'm not equipped to care for someone else, too. I-I'm not what you need." It takes every ounce of strength I have to push those words past my lips, and I cough to cover another sob trying to force its way out.

An unfamiliar buzzing sound fills the room, and Loki grabs a phone from his back pocket.

"What?"

While someone speaks on the other end, I hug myself tightly. I'm not sure how much longer I can hold out from him. He's saying all the right words. He's here, saying he cares about me, and I want nothing more than to believe him.

"No, I need more time to—"

I back myself into a corner as I watch his demeanor change.

"I-I can't do that, Ash."

His gaze cuts me to the bone. Whatever Ash is saying is breaking Loki right before my eyes. He turns his back to me before hanging up. When Loki turns back, there's a darkness in his eyes I've never seen before. As he glares at me, a painful chill runs through every fiber of my being.

His jaw clenches so tightly I can see the veins bulging in his neck and forehead, and he's breathing heavily through his nose. I'm reminded of a dragon when he is like this. Whatever happens next will wreck me. I can tell by his eyes. He's preparing to break me.

Loki takes a step forward before catching himself and taking three steps back. He rubs a hand over his face, and when he looks at me again, his expression is stony and ice cold.

"You're right. I'm not the one for you because my job will always come first."

I suck in air so forcefully it hurts.

He's playing with me, just like the rest of them.

"You were a fun distraction, but you're a child afraid of your own shadow. You have childish fears that hold no weight in my world. I only came here as a courtesy to say good-bye and to let you know you don't have to worry about the remainder of your lease. It'll be nice to have my own space again."

I stare at him, unblinking. *This is what I wanted, right?* I'm vaguely aware that I'm bobble-heading him again, but I can't form words. My throat is so dry I can't swallow, and if I open my mouth, I might vomit.

"I have to get going. Ash is waiting for me. It was good to see you, though. I'm sure I'll see you around at family functions and such." His steady voice masks Loki's pained expression. If I hadn't been looking, I would have thought he was leaving here unscathed.

My head bobs in agreement. Before I know what's happening, Loki slams the door, and I crumble to the ground where I stood. Tears I once left unshed flow freely for the man who just crushed my soul without even trying.

Painful, devastating sobs wreak havoc on my body as I curl into the fetal position on the kitchen floor. I curse myself for catching feelings. I curse Loki for getting my hopes up, but mostly, I curse my inability to be loved by a man like him.

CHAPTER 37

LOKI

I sit just outside of the door, with my head pressed against it until Ashton comes to collect me. I couldn't bring myself to leave. I let her agonizing cries torture me for almost forty-five minutes because I deserve the pain.

"Loki, we have to go. I'll call Emory and have her come down to stay with Sloane. You did the right thing. Someday she'll see that."

"No," I choke out. "I just broke the most beautiful soul I've ever known. Not just broke it. I shattered her into a million pieces to keep her safe. I don't think the damage I caused her already fragile trust will ever recover." My words come out through mucus-filled sobs of agony. I've been through every kind of hell during my days in SIA. Not a single one of those has ever hurt like this.

"You didn't have a choice, man. Vic is too dangerous. If he's watching her as closely as our intel says, you know this was the only way to keep her safe."

"What did you find out?"

"Ryan sent it over just before I called you. Mikhailov put a hit out on Sloane unless we return Nadja to him within the week."

"He's pitting me against Luca."

"Yeah, my guess is he thinks you'll turn on Luca to save Sloane."

"Right, because as far as he knows, Luca and I are enemies. He obviously doesn't know Luca is FBI. What do I do, Ash?"

"You just completed the hardest part of this mission." He motions to Sloane's door, and my gut rolls. Fairly sure I'm going to vomit, I rise to my knees as dry heaves wreck my body.

When I'm able to speak, I ask, "What's the timeline? What do I need to do?"

"Now you have to decide if you trust Luca enough to work with him. I don't see any other way for this to happen if you aren't on the same page. As far as a timeline, we have to move fast. Getting evidence on Vic will be the easy part. Mikhailov and Solonik? Jesus, Loki. I don't know. Look how many years it took us to nab Black."

"That's not happening this time, Ashton. We're finishing this now."

"Can you work with Luca?"

That's the million-dollar question. *Can I?*

"I think so. I want to talk to Claire, though. She's been with Nadja for months. She has a sixth sense about people. If there's some bullshit happening, she'll have already seen it."

"We can do that from the car. We really have to get going now, though. You're too exposed here."

"Is Sloane's security team here?" I won't be able to leave until I know she's guarded and safe.

"Yes. One on the stairwell. One at the elevator. One in the alley by the fire escape, and one in an apartment next door watching all the cameras. They will switch out with another team every twelve hours. We have her covered, I promise. I handpicked all her guards myself."

"Call Emory." I sigh. "I'm not leaving until I know someone's with her." I slide back down the wall until I'm a heap on the floor and wait.

"What the fuck did you do, Loki?" Preston's angry voice carries from the end of the hall.

Emory rushes past me with barely a glance and enters the apartment in search of her sister.

Preston stops in front of me. When I lift my eyes to meet his angry gaze, his face falters. "Fuck, Loki. What the hell is going on?"

"I-I had to hurt her." Preston's face morphs to rage at my words, but I push on. "I had to lie to her. I had to."

"What did you do?" His question is staccato as he holds onto his temper.

"He didn't have a choice, Pres. Vic put a hit out on her. We got word an hour ago," Ashton attempts to calm him. "He had to make Sloane hate him, so she'll stay away until we fix this."

"I love her, Pres. More than I ever thought possible, but I had to hurt her so she would stay away." Unable to control my emotions any longer, a tear leaks from my eye, and I make no attempt to hide it. I've spent so long keeping feelings at bay, and now there's no stopping the tsunami that hits.

"Christ, Loki," Preston sighs as he slides down the wall beside me.

Sloane's cries only intensified after Emory entered, and each one slices deeper into my soul.

"Come on, Loki. Let's get you out of here. We're pushing it as it is, and listening to this isn't doing anything for your mental state right now," Ashton pleads.

"I deserve the pain, Ash. I did that to her."

"And you will fix it, just like you do everything else, but first, you must keep her safe."

"What do you need from me?" Preston asks. "I'll talk to Ryan about security. I won't—"

"I have a full team guarding her, but she doesn't know, and it's probably better that way for now," Ashton tells him. "It's best if you don't say anything to anyone. We can't have someone slip. She has to hate Loki for now."

"You want me to lie to my wife?" Preston growls.

"Look at it this way ... a little white lie of omission to keep her sister alive, or tell her and risk something happening to Sloane? I'm pretty sure she'll forgive you for this one," Ash announces, his annoyance barely hidden.

"What a fucking mess," Preston mutters under his breath.

"She ..." I struggle to get the next words out. "She's planning to go to Vermont to stay with Lexi tomorrow. Keep her away from fuckwad Stephen, whoever that is, but it will be a good distraction for her. Just make sure she gets there," I order. Hauling myself off the floor, I place my palms on the door one last time. As if I can feel her on the other side, my body shivers.

"I'll take care of her, Loki. I promise. End this shit, then come get your girl. In the meantime, I promise you we'll take good care of her." Preston stands and slams into me with a Westbrook special.

"You Westbrooks and these fucking hugs. If Sloane hadn't turned me soft, you fuckers would have."

He gives me a playful pat on the back, and I swallow the emotion threatening to drown me. With superhuman strength, I turn and walk to the elevator bank. Sloane's gut-wrenching sobs are branding my soul with each step.

I'm so sorry, Red. I'll make it up to you. I'm so sorry.

"Dexter is going to have his work cut out for him this time," Ash mutters next to me.

"What?"

"His plan won Lanie. His plan helped Trevor win Julia back, and then he did it again with Preston and Emory. He will have to go epic Prince Charming for you to fix this, though."

"Fuck you. That's not helpful, you know that, right?"

Chuckling, he steps into the elevator before me. "That girl was made for you, Loki. This whole family will burn the city to the ground before we let you lose her. Let's take care of business, and then we'll figure out how to make Sloane yours."

"We?" I ask over my shoulder.

"Yeah, we. We're a team, man. Professionally, and personally, you're stuck with me."

Sucking air deep into my lungs, I put on my game face. "Let's end this fucker."

Ashton nods and presses the parking garage button. As the doors slide closed, I'm forced to leave Sloane behind. For now.

～

Three days later

LOKI: **How is she?**

Ashton: **Her team said she drove north for an hour and turned around.**

Loki: **Where the fuck did she go? That was three days ago? Why didn't anyone tell me?**

Ashton: **I'm not giving you daily updates because you need to keep your head on straight. She's at her father's house in Camden Crossing. She hasn't left the house since she got there. Do your job and let me take care of Sloane.**

Asshole.

～

Loki: Did you know Sloane isn't in Vermont?
Preston: Yes.
Loki: Is she okay?
Preston: She isn't answering anyone's calls.
Loki: ...
Preston: Let us handle it.

~

Two weeks later

Two weeks with no contact, and I feel like my heart is ripping in two. How did I ever live without her in my life?

"You miss her." It isn't a question. Luca is making a statement. Turning to him, I see the same pain reflected in his face.

"How have you made it all these months without Nadja?"

"It's knowing that if she were with me, she might not be alive that keeps me from running away with her. Right now, she's safe, and I have an opportunity to make sure it stays that way."

"What will you do if this goes south?"

"I've given Ashton access to all my accounts. Everything. If I don't make it out this time, he promised to make sure Nadja will remain safe."

I should have known. Ashton has his hands in everything.

"It will get easier, Loki. It won't always be like this. I have to believe that. We were dragged to the underbelly of the world by a father that didn't deserve us. We will be what changes our destiny from now on. He no longer dictates our lives, and together, I know we can keep our girls safe."

Not wanting to get into too many details with him, I go for levity.

"Jesus, I hope it won't always be this way. Two weeks in a

goddamn car with your swampy ass is making me want to turn myself in just for the fresh air."

Luca chuckles, and I feel a shift between us. The possibility of a friendship with him doesn't seem so far off anymore.

Glaring at my phone, I read the latest message from Sloane's security team, and the tension in my jaw nearly cracks my teeth.

"Check in on her, Loki. You'll be useless on this mission if you can't see through the haze of hurt."

Flexing my hand a few times until I'm sure I can text without breaking the screen, I sink into my seat and text Preston.

Loki: Her team just told me she hasn't left the house. Not once in almost three weeks.

Preston: She turned her phone off too.

Loki: WTF? Preston, I'm worried about her. I can't focus. I need to know she's okay.

Preston: We're on it.

Loki: How?

Preston: Everyone is on their way here now. We're heading to Camden Crossing within the hour.

The knot in my chest unfurls slightly.

Loki: A Westbrook Rally?

Preston: You know it. We'll snap her out of it. Focus on your job, Loki. Let us take care of her. I promised you I would, now promise me you're ending this shit. I won't lie to you. She isn't in the best headspace—she needs you, man.

"Loki? Are you ready?" Seth's voice comes through the speaker.

"Yeah," I choke out. "Are you in place?"

"I am. This won't be like any mission we've ever been on, though. Technically, we're on the wrong side of the law here. If we don't get him, there's a good chance we'll all go to jail."

"We'll never make it that far. Vic will kill us first." I know that with certainty. "Are you okay? You have Sadie to think about."

"If I were with anyone else, it wouldn't even be a question. I would have walked already, but I've always put my trust in you. We've come too far not to finish this, Loki. Sadie has to be added incentive for us not to fuck this up."

"We all have something to fight for," I acknowledge. "I won't let you or Sadie down. But, just in case something goes wrong, you know Sadie will be taken care of, right? I know she will."

Seth clears his throat. The thought of leaving his daughter an orphan too much to contemplate. His voice is raw when he answers. "Yeah, Ashton promised to fight for her if something goes wrong."

Of course Ashton did. I know the guys joke that I've been a merry fucking fairy in their lives, but the truth is, it's always been Ash.

With all the sincerity I have, I say, "We're in this together. We'll come out of this together."

"Welcome to the chaos?"

Raising my fist to Luca's, I reply, "Hell yes. Welcome to the fucking chaos. Let's go." Together we'll face whatever the future has in store for us.

CHAPTER 38

SLOANE

My phone hasn't stopped ringing in three days. Eventually, I shut it off and stuck it in the freezer for good measure. After Loki left, I spent the night with Emory and Preston, and I gave up trying to mask my pain the second they walked in. It was all-consuming in a way I didn't know existed, and I'm pretty sure it would have killed me to try.

Not even Preston's threats of ripping Loki's balls off could ease the stabbing ache in my chest. *When had I fallen for him? Am I as bad as he is? Do I only want him because he doesn't want me?* A sinister laugh falls from my lips. That's the icing on the cake now, isn't it? Finally, wanting a man I can never have is my ultimate punishment.

When I was able to form a coherent thought, I knew I'd never make it to Vermont. The idea of seeing anyone sets off new waterfalls of inconsolable tears. For the first time in my life, I want to be alone. That's why I'd retreated to my childhood home in the first place.

I'm not sure how many days I've been here. My inability to sleep makes them all blend together. Admittedly, I rarely leave the couch, but that's okay, right? I'm allowed a few days of self-pity.

Bang. Bang. Bang.

Lying on the couch, I grab the nearest pillow and nearly suffocate myself trying to block out the noise.

"Sloane! Open this damn door right now," my sister Eli's angry voice yells through the door.

Rolling over, I make myself as small as possible. There's no way Eli can see me from the window anyway, so if I stay quiet, maybe she'll just go away.

"For fuck's sake, Sloane, we know you're in there. Open up."

Who the hell is that? Julia?

"Sloane, sweetie? We're all worried about you," Lanie's soft voice barely registers through the thick wood.

Ugh, please go away.

"I will happily break down this door if you don't open it right now." Preston's happy, playboy charm is slipping into something almost fatherly, and it makes me smile. He'll make a great dad someday.

When it sounds like a battering ram is hitting the door, I sigh and sit up. Knowing he might actually break the door down, I stand, stomping my foot like a spoiled teenager. Catching sight of my reflection in the window, I make a half-assed attempt at taming my hair before deciding I just don't give a shit.

After undoing the deadbolt, then the other three locks Preston had installed, I finally open the door to a rather large, concerned group. Emory rushes past everyone and engulfs me in a motherly hug. I watch from her embrace as Tilly, Eli, Julia, Lanie, Preston, Dex, and Trevor enter the house.

"Why do rich people travel like this?" I grumble.

"Oh, sweetheart, this isn't a rich thing. This," Dex sweeps his arm around the group, "is a family thing. We're a package deal, and you're stuck with us now." He smiles, taking a seat where I had just been.

"Jesus, you look like shit," Julia remarks, stepping forward for a hug but stopping short when she gets close. Instead of a hug, she grabs my arm. "Where's the bathroom?"

"Ah, upstairs," I reply uneasily.

Is she expecting me to escort her?

"Okay." She takes off her heels, then her jacket. While she's rolling up her sleeves, I get nervous. I know Julia is a little, ah, odd, but I've never experienced this level of crazy from her. *Is she preparing to fight me?* Dragging me behind her, she announces, "We'll be back in thirty minutes."

"We will?"

"Julia?" Lanie warns.

"I've got this. No worries. Sloane, show me where your bathroom is."

"Uh, okay. Come on." I lead her up the stairs and stop at the doorway. "Here you go."

"Nope, here you go." Before I can protest, she has shoved me into the small room and kept pushing until I was standing in the shower stall.

She wouldn't dare.

The bitch reaches around me and turns the water on full blast. *Fucking hell.* Icy water pummels my clothed body, and I scream.

"What the hell, Julia?"

"It's time for some tough love, and I'm just the woman for the job. Get cleaned up and meet us downstairs."

"You're insane," I yell.

"Insanity and genius often go hand in hand, or so I've heard. You've got ten minutes."

I watch as she leaves, and when I can finally compose myself, I peel the wet loungewear I've been wearing for a few days off and leave it in a pile on the shower floor.

Shower. Smile. Tell them you're fine. Smile. Get them to leave. I repeat that mantra until I believe I can do it.

Twenty minutes later, I've composed some version of myself that they'll believe is acceptable and head downstairs. My clothes hang loose, and I realize I must have lost some weight in the last few days. With a smile plastered in place, I steel myself for the firing squad.

All heads swivel to me as I enter the small family room.

Tap-tap-slide.

Everyone in the room shifts, and Emory pats the seat next to her.

"What is this? An intervention?"

"Yes," Julia blurts as everyone else in the room says, "No."

"Right. Okay, well, what's up?" I try to keep my tone cheerful.

"What's up?" Eli screeches. "Are you shitting me?"

I stare at her like she's lost her mind, but everyone in this room knows it's me. I'm the one losing my grip on life.

Tap-tap-slide.

"Sis," Tilly tries more gently than Eli, "when's the last time you ate?"

"Ah, I don't know. I had pizza not that long ago."

"This pizza?" Trevor asks, holding up the box and removing the receipt that's taped to the side. "Sloane, you ordered this over a week ago." I cringe when he opens the top and sees it's almost entirely intact.

"When's the last time you left this house?" Julia asks, looking around at my mess. Luckily, it isn't too bad because all I've done is sit on the couch and cry.

"Okay, everyone, give her a break," Preston comes to my rescue.

Emory pats the couch again, and I sandwich myself between her and Eli.

"Tell us what he did so I know what kind of plan I have to make." Dexter's deep, rumbly voice fills the room.

Glancing around, I realize he's talking to me. "What? What are you talking about?"

"Loki. What did he do? I know he's in the field, so I can't ask him, but it looks like I'm going to have to pull out the motherload of grand gestures for this one."

"N-Nothing. Loki didn't do anything. He just told the truth."

"Which was?" Julia asks, crossing her arms like she's preparing for war. For such a tiny human, she's quite scary. Trevor wraps an arm around her and whispers something in her ear. The sight causes my heart to splinter.

After pulling Julia into his lap, he turns to me, "Listen, Sloane. We've known Loki our entire lives. Whatever he did, we'll knock some sense into him."

Dear God. I don't think I can take much more of this.

Tap-tap-slide.

"Guys, honestly, I'm fine. Everything is fine. Loki has a job to do, and it's not something he can just leave. It's all he has ever known, and he made his choice. End of story. SIA needs him, and that kind of life isn't conducive to relationships."

Preston is pacing to my left, and it makes me so nervous I jump at the sound of Trevor's booming voice. "That's bullshit. He isn't staying with SIA. He and Ash are taking over EnVision as soon as this shit is over. Who told you he was staying with SIA?"

I gape at him. "Loki did." *Didn't he?*

"Well, he lied," Dex announces.

"Why the fuck would he do that?" Trevor mutters.

"I left my phone in the car. I'll be right back," Preston interrupts, but no one pays him much attention.

"Why would Loki lie? What did he say exactly?" Julia asks, taking my pad of paper and a pen from the coffee table.

I search one set of eyes after another, looking for answers no one has. "I don't remember, exactly. He said ... basically, he said we were just a fling, and it was fun while it lasted. He said I'm a child that needs to grow up and that I should have known this would never amount to any-anything." My voice catches on to the last word, and I hate myself for it.

"That asshole." Lanie's soft voice cuts through the silence, and we all stare at her in shock. One thing I learned quickly about Lanie is that she doesn't swear. Ever.

"Loki is in trouble now. He got Lanie to swear. He'd better watch his back," Trevor jokes.

"But that doesn't make any sense," Emory whispers. "I heard him talking to Preston. He ... none of that sounds true to me."

"Why would he say it then?" Eli asks. Her defenses are rising, and she can be a mega-bitch when she's in mama bear mode.

We all sit, wide-eyed with no answers.

After a while, Dex speaks up, "Guys, what do we know about Loki?"

"That he's a son of a bitch who's getting a foot up his ass when I get my hands on him," Eli promises.

Trevor and Dex chuckle while Julia jumps up to high five my sister. Julia and Eli are so alike it's scary.

"If this is true, we'll hold him down, but Loki has spent his life protecting us. How did he do that?" Trevor is staring at Dex, and a full conversation happens between their expressions.

"He did it on his own without letting us in," Trevor answers, and I swear I can almost see the lightbulb appear above his head.

"What are you saying? You think he hurt Sloane on purpose? That's even worse." I'm not positive, but I'm pretty sure Julia just growled.

"What?"

Tap-tap-slide.

"No, he didn't hurt me. We weren't like that." With seven

sets of eyes focused on me, I feel the second my walls break. One tear turns into two before a steady stream flows silently down my face. "It doesn't matter," I sob. "It doesn't matter because he would have left eventually. That's why I wanted to go to Vermont. I leave first. I always leave first so they can't hurt me." With an audience, I vomit the words I've never said out loud before.

Emory pulls my head into her chest as Eli lays her head on my back. Tilly crouches down in front of me, and everyone else sits silent, witness to my mental break.

"Sloane," Eli whispers. "Who? Who leaves?" She's treating me with kid gloves, and it makes me cry harder.

"Shh, it's okay, Sloane," Emory coos, and I snap.

Pulling away, I jump to my feet. "No, it's not okay, it's not. Your moms left. My mom left, and Dad was never here. Emory left for school, and you guys would have left me too if I hadn't gotten out of here first. Don't you see? That's what I know; that's what I do. I leave. I was supposed to go, not Loki. I'm supposed to walk away first."

"Holy shit. GG was right again," Trevor mutters. "You're a runner."

"I thought Lanie had some fucked up mommy issues, but Sloane might take the cake." For some reason, Julia's comment makes me laugh.

I'm in emotional overload, and my body doesn't know what to do next. I have to turn away from my sisters because their tears only encourage my own. Not knowing what else to do, I crumble to the floor and rest my head on my knees.

"Sloane?" Lanie's gentle voice whispers. Peeking above my knee, I see Lanie is on the floor, face to face with me. "You're scared. It's okay, I've been there. When Dex started chasing me, I ran home as fast as I could."

"Dex loved you, though," I choke out.

"Oh, honey. I won't pretend to know why Loki pushed

you away, but I know what a man in love looks like now. There is no doubt in my mind that man loves you."

"I-I don't d-do relationships," I stutter. I'm not sure why I am still fighting this—self-preservation, maybe? I just can't admit that I love him, too.

Lanie's smile is genuine, understanding, and full of sadness as she watches me. "I didn't either. Dex had to fight for me." She glances over my head, and her expression changes as she makes eye contact with her husband. When her gaze returns to mine, it's determined, and I can see the love written all over her face. "I spent my entire life believing I was unloveable. I convinced myself I was too much trouble, too much work, too damaged to accept his love. But he never gave up. He pushed, and he fought for me. I have to imagine, living the life Loki has, he's a little broken, too. Maybe, what you need to do is find a way to allow yourself love, and then go spread that knowledge all over him like the goddamn superstar you are."

An unexpected giggle escapes my throat, and the noose around my heart expands a little more.

"You know what being part of this crazy family has taught me, Sloane?"

I return my attention to Lanie and shake my head. "No, what?"

"That family truly is what you make it. Parents can be assholes, but when you open your mind to love, family in all forms will find you. You have three amazing sisters. You have us, and I'm willing to bet, if you fight a little for him, you'll have Loki, too."

"I-I'm scared," I whisper. "What if Loki meant what he said? What if I really can't do relationships? I'm pretty messed up, Lanie. What if he just doesn't want me?"

"Oh, chica. We're all a little messed up. I don't swear because of what some stupid jerk did to me when I was ten. I almost lost the best thing that ever happened to me because I was scared of love. The truth is, love isn't something to be scared of, though. Love is something you choose. On the days you feel lost, choose love again. Look around you, Sloane. Love is all around. None of us are going to let you fail."

Doing as she asks, I make eye contact with everyone. I don't see pity or embarrassment. What I see looks an awful lot like unconditional love.

"Where the hell do you people come from?" I ask as a joke, but seriously, if ever there was a family I would want to adopt me, it's this group of friends.

"Sloane, I'm so sorry you felt like we were all abandoning you," Tilly cries.

Shaking my head, I swallow hard three times before my words will come. "No, I … we don't. That's a Sloane issue. It's not anything you did. Please don't apologize."

"Sis, your issues are our issues, don't you see that?" Emory scolds.

"We're a package deal," Dex reiterates. "You're stuck with us. Now, let's talk about how we're going to make Loki yours." The smirk that covers his face causes me to blush. This man means business, and I have a feeling there is very little he can't accomplish when he puts his mind to it.

The front door swings open, and Preston walks in with bags of Chinese food. Something about the way he moves makes me wonder if he knows more than he's letting on, but I'm drained. Emotionally, I've been hung out to dry, and I'm suddenly too tired to question him.

Is love something you choose? Am I strong enough to make that choice? Those questions are at war in my head the rest of the night, but with practiced skill, I smile, nod, and make it through the rest of the evening, pretending to be okay.

CHAPTER 39

LOKI

Preston: I need updates. We found Sloane, and she's in rough shape. Whatever you said shattered her. The guys are inside putting her back together, but they know you, man. They know you pushed her away on purpose.

Loki: I need more time. Keep her away. We got Vic this morning, but she isn't safe until Mikhailov goes down, too.

Preston: How the fuck do you expect me to do that? Dexter's in there making plans for MSL or MLS or whatever the hell he's naming your love match. We can't let Sloane hurt like this either, Loki. She's a fucking toothpick. She's not eating, and by the dark circles under her eyes, it doesn't look like she's sleeping either.

I have a visceral reaction to Preston's last message. Knowing I've hurt Red to the point of physical pain shreds what's left of my heart.

Loki: I need a couple more weeks, Pres. Then I'll spend the rest of my life making up for the pain I've caused.

Preston: You better hope you have nine lives because I think you're going to need them for this.

"They're moving Vic again." Lifting my head, I see Luca drop into the chair opposite my desk. The guy looks like shit, and I feel a pang of guilt. "There was another attempt on his life this morning. Mikhailov doesn't like being backed into a corner, and he's clapping back hard."

My mind strays as I stare at Luca.

"Earth to Loki. Where'd you go?" He waves his hand in front of my face, and I'm pulled back to the present.

"Did you have anyone growing up?"

Luca cocks his head to the side and leans back in his chair. "What do you mean?"

"I had my parents, Claire, my friends. Did you have anyone?"

He turns his gaze to the window, lost in thought. It's a while before he speaks, and when he does, I hear the strain in his voice. "There was a cook who was nice to me for a long time. When I was eight or nine, she stopped coming to work. I never got the full story, but I was told the boys had found out and had her dealt with. When this is all over, that's one of the wrongs I need to right."

"That wasn't your fault."

"I know that, but I need to know what happened to her and then do what I can. She was the only one to show me kindness until I met Nadja. In school, I tried to make friends, but as soon as our brothers found out ... well, let's just say they made sure everyone stayed away from me."

"That's a lonely life." I'm not sure what I would have done without my friends.

"We're all handed different lots in life, Loki. That was mine. I won't let it dictate my future, though."

"I'm sorry I didn't know this sooner. I would have—"

"You would have what? Don't go feeling sorry for me. You may have had family and friends, but I know your life was no picnic. You've existed on the fringes of life to protect those you love. I'm willing to bet that's been lonely, too."

"I didn't realize it until Sloane, but yeah, my life has never really been my own."

"I think it's time we change that, for the both of us." The conviction in his voice breaks down the last of my walls I was holding onto with him. We're both trying to right the wrongs of our father, and we'll get there faster together.

"You don't look like you've been sleeping," I note.

Luca rubs a hand over his face with a sigh. "No, it's been a struggle. Nadja is due in four weeks. I'm a fucking mess knowing I'll miss the birth of my son."

"It's a boy?" I ask, surprised. I can't believe I never asked him this.

Lifting his head, I'm met with the beaming smile of a proud father to be. "Yeah, Nadja found out a couple of weeks ago. The little guy had been hiding at all the previous ultrasounds. Um, I-I don't think I ever thanked you, Loki, for getting her to Claire. She said Claire has been amazing, almost like a mother. It's something Nadja has never had, and it's made a stressful pregnancy so much easier."

"Claire is amazing," I admit. "She told me Nadja is a lovely person."

"Nadja is fucking amazing. The kindest, most loving woman I've ever met. How she came from such evil is beyond me."

"That can probably be said about us, too, you know?"

Luca's cynical laughter fills the air. "Touché, brother. Touché. Can I ask you something, though?"

"Shoot."

"Who is Claire, really? A nanny wouldn't know how to go into hiding on a second's notice. She also wouldn't have the knowledge or skill set to protect Nadja like she is."

I smirk because I've been waiting for this question. "I can't believe it's taken you this long to ask."

"In all fairness, I think we've both been walking on eggshells around each other. Trust doesn't come easy for either of us, so I didn't want to rock the boat. As hard as it was, I knew your track record. I've watched your career, and I had to trust that you'd do right by Nadja, even if you were unsure about me."

"Fair enough. Claire was my nanny growing up, but she was a Navy SEAL before that. My parents knew there was always a possibility that Black would come after me. They wanted me protected at all times, so they paid Claire well to make sure that happened. After they died, I kept her on the payroll. Living the way I have, I never knew if or when I'd need a backup plan. She had the skill set and a protective soft spot for me, so it just made sense."

"I knew it had to be something like that. You know, in all the times I looked you up, she never showed in any searches. Not even when I used FBI resources."

"You don't say," I smirk. "My father was an intelligent man. Coupled with my mother's worries and Claire's particular abilities, they taught me to ghost at an early age."

"You're lucky, Loki. I'm glad you had that support system."

"I'm sorry you didn't. You're not alone anymore, though. You know that, right?"

"I'm learning." He grins. "Ashton is a pushy fucker."

A chuckle escapes, and it's a nice departure from the anxiety that's taken residence in my neck and shoulders. "That he is, but he's a good man, and he knows his shit."

"I hope you're right. The sooner we end this, the sooner we can get to our girls."

Our girls. Never have two words sounded more right.

"Right. Are you ready for Mikhailov? I assume he's getting sloppy because Vic is talking?"

"Yeah." Luca stands and paces in front of my desk. "I'm afraid they're going to get to Vic before the trial, though.

Where is that going to leave us? You're technically a fugitive until Vic signs his confession. And, if Mikhailov kills him, how will we ever have a life? It took ten years to bring down our father."

Raising my hand, I stop him. "Antonio Black is not our father. He was a sperm donor, but never a father. John Kane was a father. Clinton Westbrook was a father. You will be a father, but let's be clear about Antonio. He doesn't deserve that distinction."

Luca seems taken aback by my vehemence, but eventually nods in understanding.

"I'm going to be a father." The awe in his voice makes me yearn for that feeling. Fatherhood was never on my radar before, but I can see my future so clearly with Sloane.

"Yes, you're going to be, and you'll be a damn good one, but first, we have work to do," Ashton states with authority as he enters the room. "We move in five days. My intel shows Mikhailov is meeting Solonik in Steel Creek on Friday. Seth is running surveillance now, but it looks like this might be our only shot at them together. Solonik has a private plane booked for Friday night under a pseudonym."

"Where the fuck is he going?" I seethe.

"There's no flight plan listed. They're flying out of Aero Plantation, so they don't have to file one," Ashton tells us while dumping a heap of files onto my desk. "As long as they aren't near a controlled airspace, they can fly without one."

"So, if we lose him on Friday, he's gone." Luca's anger shows in his clenched jaw.

"He'll never make it to Aero Plantation, Luca. We're going to make sure of it." I'm firm in my vow. "We have no option but to succeed."

"Done. Tell me what you need me to do."

"We have a shitload of intel to cover, but with Mikhailov getting restless, I don't feel comfortable bringing anyone else in. That means we'll have to rotate shifts on surveillance and intel."

"What are we looking for?"

Ash raises his gaze to meet mine. "Everything."

Clapping him on the back, I laugh. "Way to narrow it down for us there, buddy."

"I do what I can." He smirks, handing us each a stack of files.

Moving to different corners of the room, we set up shop. Raising my fist, I say, "Welcome to the chaos."

Ashton and Luca repeat it, and I realize our brotherhood of friends and family has just gained another member.

◦

"We're a day out; you feeling okay about all this?" Ashton asks as he enters my office.

"There's no other choice. I'll do whatever it takes to make this mission succeed."

"I know. But, you have more on the line than you've had before. I just want to make sure your head is on straight."

I swallow painfully before answering. "Her team said she went to the grocery store a few days ago." I can't say her name. It hurts too much.

"I know. I went by yesterday."

My head flies up to meet his eyes. "What?"

"I knew you'd need an update before we go in tomorrow, so I dropped by."

"H-How is she?" I croak.

"She's lost a lot of weight, but she was up and showered and..."

"What?" I bark.

"She was trying to bake. By the looks of it, she's been trying—a lot."

A smile forces its way out, even through my pain. "Coffee cake?"

"Ah, if you want to call it that." He chuckles.

"She's determined. That's a good sign."

A loud beeping interrupts us, and Ashton pulls out his phone.

"Fuck," he yells. "Luca isn't responding. Neither is Seth."

"What? Responding to what? They're on surveillance today," I say, rising from my seat.

"They have both missed the last two check-ins," Ashton barks as he rounds my desk. Shoving me out of the way, he opens the computer and pulls up our footage from the cameras on the construction van Seth and Luca are in.

Frozen to my spot, I somehow know Mikhailov has them. My family, my brothers, are in the hands of a murderer. Thoughts of Nadja and Sadie flood my memory until I feel dizzy.

"Fuck me," Ashton whispers.

Glancing down, I see the video feed. A large truck side-swiping the van, followed by eight armed men surrounding it. The cameras cut out when bullets pierce them. The last thing we see is someone dragging Seth from the van. It's impossible to tell if he is unconscious or dead.

Ashton drags the trash can out from under the desk and heaves. My stomach is in knots, too, but a burning rage fuels my desire for vengeance more. Every muscle in my body strains against my skin, and I have to forcefully control the tremors attempting to make their way through my body.

The buzzer to the security gate rings, and Ashton flips the cameras to my front entrance. A UPS worker stands tearfully at the gate.

What the fuck?

Pulling my gun from its holster, I bolt out of the house at a dead run.

With my gun aimed, I scream, "What do you want?"

"I-I ... Listen, I-I don't know what's going on. This is the second time I've had a gun pulled on me in the last twenty minutes. They threatened to kill my wife and kids if I didn't deliver this by 3:10. Please, man. Just, just take the damn thing. I'm running out of time."

Jesus Christ.

Taking tentative steps, I hear Ash running down the drive behind me.

The UPS worker throws the package at me. "What is your name?"

His eyes are shifty, and I think he's about to wet himself.

"Buddy, I'm a United States Select Intelligence Agent. Those men that pulled a gun on you are extremely dangerous. Give me your name so I can send someone to your home to keep your family safe." I reach into my pocket, and pull out my wallet that contains my badge. Stepping forward, I show it to him. "Ash? Get his name, address, and locations of all family members, and then have Ryan get someone on them."

The poor civilian is shaking and on the verge of passing out, but he listens and starts talking to Ash. I turn and head back to the house.

Opening the envelope, I steel myself for what's likely inside. A picture falls out first—Seth, bound to a chair with a gun to his head. He's been roughed up and has blood all over his face. The pounding in my ears intensifies as adrenaline courses through my veins.

My phone rings, and I know instinctively to press record before answering.

"You have thirty-six hours to get Nadja to me, or they both die," a thick Russian accent demands.

Ashton rushes into the room and starts typing wildly on the computer as he tries to trace the call.

"I need proof that my brother is alive."

A menacing laugh comes through the speaker, chilling me

to my core. "Your brother? Your brother, you stupid fool. He is no brother to you. Luca knows where to place his allegiance."

I hear muffled screaming followed by the distinct sound of metal hitting human flesh. The low groan confirms my suspicions.

"Let me speak to him," I grind out.

"Can't do that. Luca is on his way to Camden Crossing. Do you know anyone in Camden Crossing, Loki?" The harshness of his accent makes the words even more sinister. "Thirty-six hours. Time starts now." He hangs up, and Ashton sinks into the chair.

While Ash pulls himself together, I make all the necessary calls. This means war, but first, I need to make sure everyone else is safe.

"They're trying to make you doubt Luca," Ashton grinds out.

Turning my head, I nod. "I know."

"I used every resource I had to look into him, Loki. He's on our side, I'm sure of it." I hate that he doubts my trust in him.

"Ash, I know you did. I believe you, and I believe in him. Claire has spent every minute with Nadja for months now. The SEALS trained her to spot holes in stories, tear people down, and she believes in them, too. Now we have to get our shit together and get our boys back. Are you ready?"

"Welcome to the chaos." Ashton's determination shows in his face. He's out for blood, and these fuckers are going down.

CHAPTER 40

SLOANE

The damn smoke detector goes off for the second time in five minutes, and try as I might, I can't reach the freaking thing.

The doorbell rings, and I run in place for a solid minute, trying to decide what to do. Answer the door, or shoot the smoke detector with Loki's gun. Sighing, I know the responsible thing to do is answer the door.

Checking the peephole, I don't recognize the guys outside. "Can I help you?" I yell through the door.

"Sloane? We work for, ah, we work for your family. We got a signal that your smoke detector was going off. Is everything okay?" a deep male voice asks.

My family? What the fuck? Are they watching me now?

"Yes, I'm fine. I'm just ah, baking. No fire. It'll go off in a minute."

"Would you like us to take a look at it, ma'am?"

It would be easier if they took the fucking battery out, but I'm no dummy. I'm not letting a stranger into my home.

"No, thank you. I have it under control. Have a good day."

Running back to the kitchen, I open all the windows, then

swing a sheet pan back and forth wildly until the smoke clears and it stops beeping.

Jesus, I need to stop burning shit.

Staring at the mess I've made again, my shoulders slump. *Come on, Sloane. You can do this. Why the hell is this so hard?*

"Okay, I'll call my sister about the stalkers, and I'll try again." Spending so much time alone, I've taken to talking to myself. I've also been very convincing when I tell myself that is completely normal behavior. "Welcome to my shitshow, everyone."

Sloane: Why do I have babysitters outside?

Emory: ...

(Emory added Preston at 3:15 p.m.)

Preston: What's up, ladies?

Sloane: Why do I have babysitters outside?

(Preston added Ashton at 3:16 p.m.)

Ashton: I'm kind of busy right now. Is everything okay?

Sloane: Someone had better tell me why the fuck there are two men on my street that know my smoke alarm just went off.

Emory: Your smoke alarm? Are you all right? Did you call 911?

Sloane: There's no fire, now answer the damn question.

Ashton: It's for your protection. Don't dismiss them, and don't try to hide from them. They won't bother you, but they will keep you safe. Do not fucking argue with me about this. I have to go.

Sloane: ...

(Ashton left the conversation)

Emory: ...

Preston: Loki will explain when he can. Just do as Ash asks, please.

Sloane: Asks? You mean demanded? What the hell is going on?

Emory: Sloane, please. Just let them do their job.

Is she kidding me?

(Sloane left the conversation)

Sloane: Any idea why I'm being guarded like a criminal?

Julia: Because you write sex scenes so hot they're probably illegal in multiple countries?

I laugh even though I'm trying to be angry.

Sloane: Besides that.

Lanie: ...

Lexi: Because Loki is an asshat. Just go with it.

Lanie: What Lexi said.

Why do I get the impression that everyone in my life knows something I don't? Plopping down on the couch, I let my head fall back and take a deep breath.

Listen to Loki. Loki didn't mean what he said. Choose love.

Everyone's words from last week have been ringing in my ears all hours of the day and night. Choose love. They make it sound so easy. Choose love, like I can just decide one day that I'm over my issues. Just because I say screw it, I choose love, doesn't magically change everything.

"Love takes work, Sloane. Lots of work and choosing to be happy. Choose love." Lanie had said it with such conviction, such heart.

Is it that simple? Can I choose love and happiness? Staring into the kitchen, all I see is my mess everywhere. It's my mess, though. I can clean it up. That's the way it should be, right? You make a mess, and you clean it up.

What about the mess that is my life? *Who caused it?* Me, my parents, my ex. Walking into the kitchen, I pile the dishes into the dishwasher and run hot, soapy water to clean the pans as I contemplate my issues.

Why do I run? Because I don't want to get hurt. Is that normal behavior? No, I know it's not. Look at Emory and Lanie. They opened themselves up; they took a chance on love, and I've never seen happier people.

"You can't control other people. You can only control yourself and how you react to them." Emory's words from my childhood pop into my head, and it takes me a minute to realize why they're important.

I can't control what my parents did. I can't control what Jackson did. I can't even control what Loki will do when I go see him. *When I go see him?* It seems like my heart knows what I want. I just need my head to catch up.

Standing here, washing dishes, I realize those things that have hurt me are out of my control. But, I can decide how they affect me going forward. I don't have to give them the power. The power, the decisions, they're all mine to make.

"So, what do you want, Sloane?" I glance around the room as if an answer will suddenly appear. When my gaze drifts to the giant bag of flour on the table, I sigh. I know what I want. The question is, am I strong enough to go after him?

To buy more time, I make a deal with myself. I'll try this fucking coffee cake recipe one more time. When it fails, I'll sit down and make a pros and cons list. That seems very adult-like, right? Pros for all the reasons I should give love a chance. Cons for all the ways it could go wrong. It'll help, I'm sure it will. But first, I bake.

Taking out all the ingredients, I press play on my phone. Immediately, music blasts through the surround sound that Preston had installed. Geez, Emory really hit the jackpot with that man. Not because he's rich as fuck, but because he's thoughtful. Come to think of it? We're all lucky to have him.

The Chainsmokers come on, and I turn up the volume. It's a song I've never heard before, but the words suck me in. Checking my phone, I see it's called "Family".

How apt. My family. The song ends, and I scramble to

replay it. The song touches me so profoundly that tears mix into the coffee cake batter by my fourth listen. Finally, I have to pause to wipe my eyes because I can't see the recipe.

I want a lifeline, a family—I want what Emory has. What I need is Loki. The realization has a calming effect, and it freaks me out a little. When in my life have I ever known with such certainty what I wanted?

"Okay, Sloane. It's time to put on your big girl panties. If this cake comes out edible, I'll go to Loki, no questions asked. If it's a steaming pile of shit, I'll make my lists." I pat myself on the back for good luck and place the pan into the oven.

Thirty-five minutes later, I'm sitting at the table staring uneasily at a beautiful, perfectly baked coffee cake. Hesitantly, I taste it with a napkin in hand, ready to spit the offending sweet out.

"What the hell?" I mumble over another bite. I'm shoveling it into my mouth at an alarming rate. "This can't be right?" Crumbs fly from my mouth, but in my utter shock, I don't give a shit.

"Okay, this was a fluke. Obviously." The freaking cake is amazing. *What in the actual hell?*

I sit, staring at it for a long time. *Big girl panties, Sloane.* Right. Big girl panties, but I can't seriously base my potential relationship on a baked good, can I? No, that's ridiculous. One good cake is not an indication of anything; I need to make more.

Grabbing my mixing bowl, I start all over. I can't help eyeing the cake on the counter suspiciously. Like, what the fuck did you do?

Ugh, I'm losing my mind.

New deal. If this cake turns out like that last, I'll tell Loki I love him. Holy fuck. I love him. *Focus, Sloane.* If I can bake this cake again, I'll go to Loki. If it turns out like my other three hundred, I'll make my lists.

Oh my God. I did it. Sitting in front of me are five perfectly baked coffee cakes. Five! Loki knew I'd get it all along. I smile at my creations, and now I'm ready to get my man.

CHAPTER 41

SLOANE

The funny thing about my father's house is the garage. There are bay doors on both the front and the back of it. My sisters told me that when he could hold down a job, he would restore old cars in there, so having the easy in and out access was useful.

Thanks, dear old dad. Today, I'm counting on my babysitters not knowing that tidbit of information. The last thing I need is an audience. If Loki turns me down, I want to hide my face and cry, not face a bunch of strangers who know my shame. I've rarely left the house, and when I did, I walked, so hopefully, I can sneak out.

Loading all five of my coffee cakes into my father's ancient jalopy, I pray that it even starts. I have a plan to get myself to Waverley-Cay, but if the car doesn't run, I'm shit out of luck. With my foot on the brake, I turn the key in the ignition. The old Chevy spits and sputters a few times before turning over and finally catching.

"Yes." An unreasonable amount of pride escapes in a very unladylike display, but I have bigger things to worry about. After I press the receiver, the garage's back door slowly slides open with a creak and a squeal. *Jesus, doesn't this thing know I'm trying to run away?* A laugh escapes at my thoughts. For once, I'm not actually running away. I'm running full speed ahead and hoping Loki will catch me. That's a fucking terrifying thought, and I let off the gas for half a second.

"Nope, not today, Sloane. You're going after what you want, and nothing is going to stop you." Pep talk complete, I slide the boat of a car out of the garage and down the back drive that no one has used in years.

When I hit the pavement, I check my rearview mirror and am relieved to see nothing but darkness. With the giddiness of a teenager sneaking off to a bonfire party, I settle in for my three-hour drive.

With each passing mile, the anticipation turns to anxiety. My palms are sweaty, and the butterflies that started in my stomach have turned to a hive of angry bees fighting to find an exit. By the time I roll into Waverley-Cay, my knuckles are white from grasping the steering wheel, and my fingers went numb about a hundred miles ago.

The closer I get to Westbrook Bay, the waterfront community where all these guys grew up, the worse I feel. Sweat is pouring down my spine and settling uncomfortably in my ass crack. *Great. I'm going to tell the man I love that I love him with swamp ass. Super classy, Sloane.* The urge to plant my palm to my forehead is so strong I nearly do it until I pass the Westbrook sign. I don't know which house is Loki's, but I know it's next door to Preston's childhood home.

What do I do now? Slowing to a crawl, I creep through the neighborhood and realize all the security gates are heavy iron with ornate details. Almost all of them have an initial or a name. *Okay, look for Kane.* The sun is setting, making it difficult to see, but I pass one I recognize. It has a giant WB in the center. Westbrook. That means Loki's has to be on either side, except the Westbrooks are the end of the line.

There is no other house on their right side. Turning around, I backtrack to the next driveway. I had missed it on the way in because the gate is wide open.

That's strange? Why would he have this enormous security gate and leave it wide open?

I sit just outside of his driveway for a few minutes to calm my breathing. *I can do this!* It's just Loki, for crying out loud. Our time in the cabin was the best of my life, and I have to believe he felt something, too.

Ugh, the cabin seems like a lifetime ago. Pressing on the gas, I slowly pull into his driveway. Unlike the Westbrooks, this one has a steep incline. When I reach the top, I hesitate to put the car in park. There are so many vehicles I wonder if he's having a party.

I duck down to peer at the house through the passenger side window. The house is comparable to the Westbrooks' in size, but Loki's is Mediterranean in style. It's beautiful, but I don't see any signs of a party. He's rich. Maybe he just has a lot of cars?

No more excuses. Turning off the engine, I slip out of the car before I lose my nerve. I stack the coffee cakes on top of each other and march to the front door with as much confidence as I can muster. That confidence lasts until I hit the first step and realize I left the house in hot pink bunny slippers. Forehead meet palm.

Knowing there's nothing I can do about it now, I tug the cakes against my hip and press the doorbell with my free hand. I hear someone shout and then a bunch of noise I can't decipher, but no one comes to the door.

What the hell? I came all this way with damn cake. The least he can do is answer the door, so I ring the bell again. When that doesn't work, I bang on the door with all my might.

"Loki Kane," I scream. "I know you're in there. Open this

goddamn door. I made cake." Yes, I know I sound hysterical. It's warranted when your heart is on the line. Holding my gifts in one hand, I take a step forward to place my ear against the door just as it opens.

Loki stands on the threshold, and I'm so happy to see him I almost miss the hard line of his jaw. His eyes seem pained, and he's more disheveled than I've ever seen him.

Did I make a mistake coming here?

Unsure of what to say, I hold the cakes out in front of me like a peace offering.

"I did it." I don't disguise the pride in my voice even though it wobbles as I speak.

His gaze darts from me to the door and back again. I see the softness and pride in his eyes for the briefest of seconds, and then he glances behind the door again.

What the hell is going on?

"Five times," I say stupidly. "I made it perfectly five times."

Loki lurches forward as if someone shoved him, but I can't see past his large frame, to be sure.

"Here, I-I made them for you. I-I was hoping we could talk." I stumble over the words, but I get them out.

"Camden," Loki's voice is harsh, and I flinch. "I already told you there is nothing between you and me. You need to get that through your head. You were a distraction, nothing more. And I would rather have someone shove your clean romance trash up my ass than eat one more bite of your salty, shitty cake. I hate salt, Camden. I told you at the cabin how much I hate salt. You need to leave and don't come back." He slams the door in my face, and I stand there, wide-eyed, gaping like a blowfish.

Hurt and hate war for space in my heart. Hate is more comfortable, so I unwrap the cake and throw them by the handful at his front door.

"Fuck you, Kane. *Kane*, what the hell was that?" My

throws become more aggressive, and by the time I smear the last bits of the coffee cake on his front door, the hate dissolves back to hurt and anguish.

My shoulders slump as I make my way back to the car. After wiping my hands on my jeans, I climb in and stare at the mess I made. The tears don't take long to form, but these aren't like anything I've felt before. They burn my flesh as they travel the length of my face. A scorching reminder that I was just thrown away, again.

Resting my head on the steering wheel, I turn the key and start the ignition. I need to get out of here. He's probably watching and laughing at me from the window. Swiping angrily at my eyes with the back of my sleeve, I replay his vicious diatribe.

Camden? He's never once called me Camden. I had no idea he hated trying my cake so much. Did I ever even know him? He played my body like it was made for him. We did things I've never done with—

Salt. He called me Camden and said salt. Remembering our conversation in the cabin, I realize he was using our code word.

My gaze shoots back to the house. Loki's in trouble. With as much finesse as I possess, I quickly take pictures of the license plates I can see from my vantage point before speeding down his driveway at an alarming rate.

Think, Sloane. What do I do? What do I do?

Grabbing my phone, I yell, "Siri, call Ashton." His phone rings and rings before going to voicemail. "Siri, call Seth." Again, I get voicemail. I try them both three more times to no avail.

Sitting at the bottom of Loki's driveway, I peel out and head toward the Westbrook estate. At the gate, I press the buzzer repeatedly. Preston's mother, Sylvie, comes across the speaker at the same time the gates begin to open. I don't have time to wait, and I ram through them, trying not to worry about how much that will cost me to fix.

I pull up in front of the house and jump out of the car with it still running. I burst through her front door and start yelling.

"Sloane, dear, what's wrong?" Sylvie comes rushing into the foyer, looking alarmed.

"Do you own a gun?"

"Ah, are you all right, Sloane?"

"Do you own a gun?" I shout. "Loki safe worded me. Do you own a gun?"

"You mean like *Fifty Shades*? I don't think that requires a gun, Sl—"

"No," I interrupt. "You don't understand. I went to Loki's house to tell him I loved him. I made the cake. I didn't even burn it. He sneered and told me I was only a distraction, but then he used our code word. He called me Camden and said salt."

"Honey, you're not making any sense."

I feel like my world is crashing all around me, and I don't know what to do. "Sylvie, someone is in that house with him. Someone that shouldn't be there. He was trying to tell me he's in trouble. I've tried to call Ash and Seth multiple times, but no one's answering."

Understanding crosses her perfectly painted face. She grabs my arm and drags me through the house to an office in the back.

"Pull up a chair, Sloane. Let's see what's going on over there."

"Wh-What do you mean?"

Sylvie gives me a gentle smile. "Loki left that house empty for over ten years. I've been taking care of it until he was ready to return. Part of that was upgrading the alarm system. I had cameras installed all over the property so my security team could monitor it remotely. I turned them off when he went back a few weeks ago, but I should be able to reactivate them. Just give me a moment."

I stare at this woman with an admiration I've only ever had for Emory. Sylvie Westbrook may be the epitome of a lady, but she raised five boys and took in at least four others. She's no pushover, and she knows how to get shit done.

Grabbing a chair while she opens and closes multiple browsers, I slide in next to her and see the moment the feed comes to life. She starts clicking buttons, and the screen rolls from room to room. We both gasp when we come to the office.

They have Loki tied to a chair behind the desk. In one corner, we see Seth slumped over the restraints holding him up. In the center of the room, Luca is a bloodied mess. A man twists his arm in an unnatural way, and Sylvie cries out.

Thank God there is no sound.

Another man turns to Loki, and I see he's wielding a knife. His body hides the blade, but I see Loki's face, he's in pain. When the man steps back, we see blood gushing from Loki's open palm.

Holy fuck. This is really happening.

Sylvie is mute and unmoving. She's in shock.

"Sylvie," I yell, shaking her arms gently, "do you have a gun? Where's your security team? Can you scroll through to find how many men are in there?"

She comes to and bobs her head. "I— Yes, we have guns. What are you going to do? Do you know how to use them?"

"I have to do something, and I have to do it now. Loki taught me to use a Glock. My aim is good enough. Can you help me get into the house? Where is your security?" I ask again.

"Um, yeah. Yes. There's a service entrance. Most people don't know about it. It's an old house. There are secret passages in the walls, like this." She presses a button on the bookcase, and a hidden door pops open. "The layouts of our homes are different, but they were built at the same time."

"Does Loki's open to the office like this one?"

"Yes, but I can't remember which wall it's on."

"Where is your team, Sylvie?" I ask for a third time.

She glances away, and my heart sinks. "I sent them home. They watch remotely from their office most days. No one is after me. I-I didn't think it was necessary." Tears fall from her face. "I was so stupid."

"No, Sylvie. This is not normal, none of it. I need you to call your team. Then get me your guns and tell me how to get into that house. I'm going to scroll through the feed and find out how many people are in there." Just as I turn my attention to the screen, I see two men drag Ashton into the room. I slam the lid shut so she can't see. "Sylvie, you need to hurry."

Nodding, she runs from the room, and I open the screen again. *Oh my God. Please don't be dead, Ash. Please don't be dead.*

It takes less than five minutes to find out there are six men standing guard. Four are in the room with my guys, and two are roaming the house. Sylvie draws me a map, and her team is en route. They told us not to go anywhere near the house, but I saw the video. Her team is too far away, that leaves us.

"Sloane, I'm scared. Those are professional criminals. They captured three highly trained special agents. Loki will never forgive me if you get hurt."

"Sylvie, I know what I'm up against. I know I'm not trained for this. I've never fired a gun before I met Loki, but they will kill them if I don't go. All of them. I just have to be enough of a distraction to keep them alive until help arrives."

She embraces my upper arms and stares into my eyes. "You're a special young lady, do you know that? I know I praise your sister for all she has done, but never think that I haven't noticed your talents, your love, and your spirit as well. If you're going in, then so am I. Come with me."

Oh shit. Great, now I'm going to end up in hell when I die for dragging June Cleaver into the wreckage.

We stop in a mudroom. Bending down, Sylvie hands me a pair of tennis shoes. Holding them up, I see the distinct pattern of Louis Vuitton. *Jesus, I'm going to hell in a pair of Louis?* I slide my feet into them just as she hands me a heavy vest.

"What's this?"

"Kevlar." When she notices my shocked expression, she explains, "Sloane, I had five boys and three others that practically lived here. Clint would take them all shooting sometimes. If you think I'm letting eight boys and a man-child go into the woods with guns unprotected, you don't know me very well. These are child-sized, but they'll fit us just fine."

Slipping into my vest, I turn to her. "Sylvie, I can't let you go into that house. Too many people need you. Emory, she needs you."

"We need you, too, dear. Come on, let's go."

As she leads me to the side of the house, I formulate a plan. "Listen, I'll go in through the service entrance. You need to go to the front and cause some sort of distraction. Something loud enough that we can hear it from inside the house. That's how I'll know they're distracted for at least a second, and I'll make my move."

We stare at each other, knowing what we're about to do is incredibly stupid but necessary.

"Okay, honey. This is the path to Loki's house. It's a little overgrown, but it's paved under all the brush. Just follow it. At the clearing, turn right and go down the slope. You'll see the service entrance in the back, built into the hillside."

"Got it." My voice wobbles. Before I can say anything else, Sylvie's phone rings.

"Okay, give me five minutes. Then make as much noise as

you can." I squeeze her hand for support, then turn and start running.

"What team? What are you talking about? Sloane?" I hear Sylvie yell my name, but I'm already in motion. If I turn back now, I'm afraid I'll lose my nerve. "Sloane?" she yells again, but I'm too far gone.

Please, God. I'll never ask for another thing, just please don't take Loki. Please.

CHAPTER 42

LOKI

Six hours ago

Ashton is sitting behind my desk while I stand in the corner, going over everything I'll need to get my guys back.

"We have to move, Ash. Are you—"

The front door bursts open, and I draw my gun, but I'm too slow. Armed men swarm the foyer, dragging Seth behind them with a gun pointed at his unconscious skull.

"Drop your weapon, Mr. Kane," a heavily accented man demands as he steps over Seth's lifeless body.

Glancing over my shoulder, I see Ashton has pulled his gun, too. In a split second, I weigh my options.

"Don't even think about it, Mr. Westbrook. If you look out your window, you'll see my man has a weapon aimed straight for your brain."

I give Ash an imperceptible nod, and he lowers his gun.

How did I fuck this up?

"Your friend here was nice enough to share his handprint with us. You really should look into a retinal scan next time.

That would have made it more difficult for us to gain access. I expected more from you, Mr. Kane."

"Fuck you," I spit.

Retaliation is swift and fierce. The butt of a gun lands on the back of my head, and I drop to my knees. With blurry vision, I see them drag Seth into the office as two more men enter my home with Luca.

"I'd rather die," Luca chokes out as he slides past me on the floor.

I know what he's saying. He would rather die than give them Nadja. It's a pact we make when we sign up for jobs like this. We keep the innocents safe. I know the second they drag him by, they will torture us for information. Ashton will be first because he's a civilian. They believe he will be the weak link, and I almost heave at the thought. Ashton has only ever brought good into this world, and he's about to experience the devil himself because I brought it to his doorstep.

For the next five hours, they alternate between Ashton, Seth, and Luca. Leaving me unscathed is a tactic I know well. One of the first things SIA teaches you is to dissociate with your surroundings, so I do. Tied to the chair, I block out the brutalized screams of my friends.

The doorbell rings, and it breaks my trance-like state.

There's a flurry of Russian exchanges when the doorbell rings again. The man guarding me is watching his boss, waiting for orders.

A voice follows the pounding on the door, Sloane's voice, and she's pissed off, but I've never been more scared in all my life.

"Bring her in. Perhaps she will encourage Mr. Kane to talk."

My blood runs cold. Then I hear Ashton speak. His voice is low and almost inaudible. But he tries again. "She has a full security team with her. If you let her in this house, they will raid it within seconds. I gave them the orders. They are not to allow her in here at any time."

I catch sight of Ash as they pull him from the room. He just saved Sloane's life, I'm sure of it.

She bangs on the door again, and my guard cuts me free. Mikhailov yanks me to my feet. "Get rid of her." He shoves me forward, and I see another guard standing behind the door with a gun pointed at where she's standing on the other side. "You make one mistake, you give her one clue, and we'll shoot her where she stands. Do you understand me?"

My heart lurches in my chest when I open the door. Sloane stands there, presenting me with her coffee cake. Pride shooting from her every pore. It takes only a second and hard shove from behind to get to the task.

The hurt embedded in her gorgeous face when I'm through guts me, slamming the door in her face is the final nail through my heart. Nothing these assholes can do to me will be worse than that.

Mikhailov has his goon turn me around just in time to see a knife slice the side of Ashton's face. The blade enters near his right eye and slices downward past his lips and over his chin in slow motion.

"No," I scream, charging them. Three men tackle me to the ground and bind me to a chair while I kick and fight with everything I have. They call in another man to help hold me down, and it still takes them longer than they would like. When they have me subdued, Mikhailov steps forward and drives a knife into the palm of my hand.

Time passes slowly as I hear Ashton's grunts grow quieter. Eventually, silence blankets me, but it doesn't last long.

"Now, the fun begins, Mr. Kane. Have you ever seen your friends gutted like a pig before?"

I spit in his face, and he laughs. The sound is more demonic than anything I've ever heard before.

I'm fighting to regain the headspace that will allow me to survive what's coming next when Ashton is dragged to the center of the room by an ankle. He leaves a trail of blood in his wake, and I snap.

I fight and thrash against my restraints so much my heavy, wooden chair tips over. Mikhailov orders someone to sit me upright when we hear the explosion. I'm dropped to the ground again as all Mikhailov's men run to the foyer, shouting in Russian.

I hear a click behind me. I know that sound. Someone just opened the secret passage. I can't see behind me from my angle on the floor, so I have no idea if it's friend or foe. Since it hasn't been used since my childhood, I'm praying for a friend.

Lifting my head, I see one of the guards enter the room as a bullet buzzes overhead, hitting him dead center in the heart. He drops to the ground, and the haze of gunfire begins. Bound to my chair, the most I can do is try to take cover.

Amidst the blasts, one hits me in the chest, knocking me and my chair to my back. The last thing I see is a red ponytail falling to the floor. *Red. No, not my Red.*

CHAPTER 43

SLOANE

An explosion happens across my chest, and I'm thrown to my back. I can't breathe. I can't move. Terrified doesn't begin to describe the emotions coursing through my mind. *I think they shot me.* Bullets are still flying overhead, and I didn't save Loki. We're both going to die.

The house suddenly goes silent, and my panic kicks into overdrive. I can only manage short, shallow breaths, and it makes everything worse.

I hear sirens and yelling but can't make out any words. I feel like I'm drowning.

A man leans over me, and the tears spring free without any warning. *Is this really how I'm going to die? With this ugly fuck leaning over me?*

The man laughs. "Well, my wife seems to think I'm handsome. We can't all be as good looking as Kane."

Crap, did I say that out loud?

Wait. W-What the hell is going on? His hands are all over my body, and I'm not sure what he's doing. *Where's Loki?* Have they killed him already? The man asks me a question, but I can't hear him. His face is the last thing I see before my world goes black.

∽

Beep. Beep. Beep.

Fluorescent lights blind me when I open my eyes. Why the hell do people still use those lights? They flatter no one, ever. *Holy shit, everything hurts.* Groaning, I attempt to lift my head, but excruciating pain ripples from my neck to my toes.

"Hey, hold still. Don't try to move," a gentle voice I recognize instructs from my right. My gaze follows the sound, and I find Sylvie sitting there. It's then that I realize she's holding my hand.

Wait. Why is she here and not with Loki?

"Loki?" My voice cracks. It feels like I've been eating sand for a year.

"He's in surgery, but he is going to be just fine. They need to remove the bullet you put in his chest." She smiles.

"What? I shot him?"

"Not intentionally, but yes. When you were hit, your gun misfired. Emory is with him now, and she promised he would be okay. They also need to do a CAT scan because he was hit in the head again, but Emory is confident he'll make a full recovery."

I remember Ash lying on the floor, and I wish anyone else were with me because I'm scared to ask her.

She seems to sense my hesitation and continues speaking. "Seth has some broken bones but is otherwise okay. The girls are sitting with him now. Luca, h-he was in pretty rough shape. He came out of surgery almost an hour ago. The boys are with him."

What about Ash? I want to scream as she takes a moment to compose herself.

"Ashton will heal," she says evasively.

"But?"

"His face will carry a scar, but I fear the internal wounds will take longer to overcome. He's in his second surgery now.

We have a plastic surgeon flying in from California to start the cosmetic restructuring tomorrow."

"Oh my God."

"He will be okay, dear. He has us, and that's what families do. We will continue to pick him up until he can do it on his own again."

"I think I have a lot to learn about family," I mumble.

"We're very good teachers, dear. The good news is, this is all over now. I never realized how exhausting it was carrying around the weight of what-ifs. Because of you, all of my boys are safe. We don't have to live in fear, and we can all live our best lives because of you, Sloane. You've given me a gift I never thought I would see in my lifetime. You gave us all freedom."

I choke on the tears that try to suffocate me. "I-I didn't do that, though."

"We need to work on your ability to take a compliment, Sloane. You did do that. I'm telling you that you did. Don't argue with me."

It's the first time a mom has ever scolded me, and oddly, I find it comforting.

"Yes, ma'am. When can I see Loki?"

"Emory said she would take you to see him as soon as he's out of surgery."

Exhaustion takes over. "Okay, I-I'm just going to rest my eyes for a little while."

Sylvie leans over and kisses my forehead. "Sleep, sweet girl, rest. You'll need your strength to deal with Loki. He's a terrible patient, you know."

I smile but drift off to sleep before I can respond.

∼

"Sloane?" I hear my sister's voice, and my eyelids flutter, fighting to open. "Take your time. You've been through a lot."

I nod my head, but I'm so groggy my eyes refuse to cooperate.

"What's wrong with her?" Eli demands.

"Nothing is wrong with her. The doctor gave her a mild sedative to help calm her down. She went through acute trauma, and she needs rest to recover."

"I'm okay," I rasp while my eyes remain closed.

"You asshole. What were you thinking going in there like that? You're not Lara Croft, you know?"

"Eli," Emory scolds. "That can wait."

"Well, she better hurry up and get better so I can kill her stupid ass."

My lips curl into a smile before I drift off again.

∼

"She's still asleep?" Tilly whispers.

"Yeah, but I think she might be waking up. They weaned her off the sedatives this morning, and she's been moaning more," I hear Lanie say in a hushed tone.

"Is she in pain?" Tilly's voice wavers.

"I—"

"Yes," I croak. Slowly, I open my eyes. "I feel like I was hit by a truck."

"You kind of were," Lanie says gently. "Dex told me you took a hit at such close range it really was like getting hit by a car."

"Jesus," I mutter. "Can I see Loki now?"

I see the girls exchange a look and the monitor beeping with my heart rate speeds up.

"Yes, you can see him," Emory states, grabbing some hand sanitizer as she enters the room. "They're wheeling him back from his CAT scan now. I have to warn you, though, he's … well, he took another hit to the head. His memory is a little scattered right now."

I swallow the lump forming in my throat and force out my question. "Does ... does he remember me?"

Emory hugs her elbows tightly at her sides, a sure sign she is uncomfortable.

"Does he?" I demand.

"Yes, but I don't know how much he remembers, Sloane."

I absorb that information in silence. "Has he asked for me?"

Emory looks to Eli for help.

"Has he asked about me?"

"I'm not sure, hun. I'm not in charge of his care, so I haven't seen him awake for very long."

Forcing myself to sit, I cry out in pain. "Fuck."

Emory runs to my side. "Sloane, you can't move around like that. You have a bunch of broken ribs and a punctured lung."

"Christ, no wonder I can't breathe. I need to see him, Emory. Please, take me to see him."

"Are you sure you're ready?"

"Yes. Even ... even if he doesn't remember, I do. I remember what we were, and because of that, I need to see for myself that he's okay."

"Okay, let me get clearance from the nurse's station. I'll be right back."

Tilly follows her out the door, and though she whispers, I still hear her question.

"Can't you talk to the guys? His doctor? Anyone? Just make sure he remembers how he feels about her before we go wheeling her in there? Do you really think she can handle it if he doesn't?"

"Till, your whispering skills suck," Eli scoffs.

Tilly peeks her head around the corner, appearing guilty. "Sorry."

"It's okay. I know you're just looking out for me, but I need to see him, Till."

She nods, and we all sit in silence while we wait for Emory to return.

By the time the nurses have me unplugged and ready for transport, nerves have crept their way in, and I wish the doctor had left the sedative in place.

"Are you ready?" Tilly asks hesitantly.

"Yes."

"Okay, let's go. I'll take her down," Emory tells the orderly.

I'm surprised to see Preston, Dex, Lanie, Trevor, and Julia waiting for us in the hallway.

"What the hell? You guys seriously need to stop traveling in a pack. It's not normal."

"Neither are we, sweet cheeks. Haven't you learned by now? This is how family works."

"Yeah, families that don't actually have to work," Eli mutters.

Preston wraps a brotherly arm around her as Emory wheels me down the hallway. "You see, Eli. That's the beauty of being part of our family. We're richer than sin, and we take care of our own. Like it or not, you're one of us now, so when family calls, we drop everything. Got it?"

"Rich people are so weird."

I don't see it happen, but I hear her squeal.

"Did you seriously just give me a noogie?"

"Damn straight, I did. What are big brothers for?"

"I don't know. I've never had one," she barks.

"Well, maybe you should come intern for me this summer so you can get the full effect."

"Are you serious?" I hear the skepticism in Eli's voice, but I know Preston. He means everything he says.

"One hundred percent."

"But, Westbrook Enterprises has a waitlist for internships that are years in the making."

"Ah, nepotism at its finest," Dexter jokes. "We won't tell if you don't."

Listening to their conversation, I'm at ease. No matter what happens with Loki, I know I'm going to be okay—our family will be okay.

CHAPTER 44

LOKI

"I need to speak to Dr. Camden," I yell for the twentieth time. Why the fuck won't anyone get Emory for me? I need to find Sloane.

"Mr. Kane, I told you. She's with a patient. I've already paged her. You're her next stop. Please, try to calm down."

"Nepotism at its finest. We won't tell if you don't." Dexter's cheerful baritone echoes in the hall.

"Dexter," I shout. My voice is hoarse from the effort.

He ducks his head in the room a second later. "What the hell, man? Are you trying to wake the dead?"

"Where—"

"The yelling is not cool, Loki," Julia scolds.

Trevor enters right behind her, and the three of them start folding up the bed next to me.

"What are you doing? I—"

"Glad your lungs are working, dude, but some poor schlep out here just dropped a tray of piss because you startled him with your uncouth ways." Preston swaggers into the room, followed by Lanie.

"Where is—"

"Preston, help us get this out of here," Dex calls.

"On it."

"Guys. What the fuck? Guys!" I yell again, but everyone keeps moving about the room as if I'm not here. Sucking in as much air as my body will allow, I let my temper fly. "Stop moving. Where the fuck is Sloane? I ..." The words die on my lips as Emory backs into the room, dragging a bed behind her.

"I guess that answers the question of him remembering you," Sloane's sister, Eli, quips.

"What? Why wouldn't I remember her? Sloane?"

Emory wheels the bed into place next to me, and I see my Sloane, my Red. With a tear-stained face, she watches me. I see the fear and the hesitation in her eyes, and I lose it.

"Get me up. Emory, get these damn cords off of me before I rip them out."

"Loki, you, you can't. You need to stay still."

"Get me into her fucking bed right now, or I'll do it myself."

"He means it, Ems. Tell me what you need me to do, I'll help," Preston offers.

"But, the hospital has rules. I—"

"For crying out loud, Emory. Haven't you learned, sometimes, it's okay to let money make the rules. This, right here, is one of those times."

"I'll start making the calls," Dexter sighs. "This hospital board is probably ready to quit because of us, you know?"

"Whatever, we donated six million dollars to their new research facility to bend the rules when I almost died. If they want to keep the donations coming in, they will shut their faces."

"Preston, I work here," Emory hisses.

"And you're a damn good doc, honey. But, sometimes, you have to put away the doctor hat and just be Mrs. Westbrook. This, right here, is one of those times." Preston grins. I'm pretty sure he will be in the doghouse for that comment, but Emory sighs and steps in next to me anyway.

"Rich people problems." Eli smirks.

"Welcome to the chaos," we all say in unison.

A few moments later, I'm sliding into the bed next to Sloane. We are both hurting physically, but I won't allow her to hurt emotionally alone for another second.

"Can you guys give us a few minutes?" I ask the room.

"Yeah, I need to go make sure Dex gets approval for this," Emory waves her hand at our bed, "too."

I smile and settle in next to a silent Sloane. When the room empties, I turn her face to look at me, and her walls come crashing down.

"I-I thought you wouldn't remember me," she sobs.

"Oh, sweetheart. I'm sorry you thought that. I have a concussion, and things were a little fuzzy when I first woke up, but I never once forgot you. I plan to spend the rest of my life showing you how much I remember you."

"That's a long time," she whispers.

"Because of you, it is. What in God's name were you thinking, Sloane?" My voice catches as tears cascade down my cheek. I haven't wept openly in a long time, but now that she is safe, in my arms, the emotional toll of the last few months weighs heavy on my heart. "I could have lost you."

"I-I saw that man stab you. Then I saw them drag Ashton in by his foot, and I knew they were going to kill you. No one could get to you in time. Westbrook Bay was too far from town. Even if Sylvie had called the police, they wouldn't have gotten to you in time. We made the best decision we could."

"Knock, knock," Seth's tired voice precedes him. "Ah, I didn't mean to eavesdrop, but I'm heading home to get to Sadie. She's pretty upset, and the nanny has been on around the clock for days."

He walks closer to the bed and takes a seat next to Sloane. Taking her hand in his, he lays his head on the bed. His shoulders shake with emotion. When he raises his head, I see he's joined us in our tears.

"Thank you, Sloane. Thank you for stupidly risking your life like you did. M-My daughter, she isn't an orphan because of you …" The emotion is too much for him, and he fumbles over his words.

"Seth," Sloane's voice is muted and her eyes heavy.

"If Sylvie hadn't gotten through to Preston, though, this all could have ended very badly."

"What do you mean?"

"Sloane ran through the woods. Her security team had no idea what was going on."

"What?" It comes out harsher than I intended, but maybe some details I'm better off not knowing.

"I-I didn't know they were there. I thought I snuck away from them when I left Camden Crossing."

"That's another issue altogether," Seth says dryly. "Their plan was for Sylvie to create a distraction so Sloane could slip into the room. After that, I don't know what her plan was. Luckily, Preston called just as Sloane was taking off. He told Sylvie there was a security team at the front gate. They rushed to your house and set off a series of mini-explosions."

I gape at Seth, then turn my focus to Sloane. "That's when you snuck into the room and started shooting up the place?"

She shrugs and glances down at her chest. "I didn't mean to shoot you, though."

Her confession causes a burst of laughter from Seth and me. We both grab our chests—everything hurts.

"You didn't shoot him. I saw the report. Initially, they thought your gun had gone off when you fell because they found it so far from your body. But after forensics went through, they found it was a stray bullet that ricocheted from one of the undercover agents."

"Oh, thank God," Sloane murmurs. Her eyes are blinking

slower and slower. After a few moments, soft snoring fills the room.

"Have you seen the guys?" I ask.

Seth stands and comes to my side of the bed, so we don't have to talk over a sleeping Sloane.

"I have," he replies solemnly.

"How are they?"

"Luca took the brunt of it physically, but he's doing okay. He had just spoken to Nadja when I saw him. He's happy that Claire is bringing her home. He has a long recovery ahead of him, but he'll make it."

It's the words he isn't saying that make my stomach roil.

"And what about Ash?"

Seth swallows and rubs a hand over his face before speaking. "Ash is in a dark place, man. He wasn't prepared for this shit, and they went at him hard."

Guilt invades my soul. This is my fault.

"Did you speak to him?" I manage.

"Briefly. He told me his prognoses like it was a spreadsheet, then told me to get the fuck out."

My head whips to his.

"Yeah, I told you. He's in a dark place. I don't know what it will take to pull him out, but he won't even let Sylvie into the room."

"What the fuck did they do to him?"

"Besides disfiguring him? I'm not sure. It pisses me off a little that Sloane killed them all, though. I would love to have my shot at those motherfuckers."

"Is it bad? His scar?" I'm almost scared to hear the answer.

"I didn't see it. Sylvie has a specialist flying in from California. He seems convinced he can make it better, but he'll always have some sort of scar. It's not the physical scars I'm worried about, though, Loki. This is the kind of thing that changes a man."

"I know. We can't give up on him. No matter what it

takes, we'll get Ashton back from whatever hell they threw him into."

"You can count on me," Seth says with conviction.

"I know I can. Thanks, man."

"Thank you. And, thank her." He leans over me and kisses my girl on the forehead. "I'm going home. Call if you need anything."

"I will. Thanks, Seth."

He nods and walks out the door while I'm left contemplating how to handle Ashton. My brother, my friend who is living in purgatory, because of me.

~

A WEEK LATER, Sloane and I are ready to be discharged from the hospital. Truthfully, I could have gone home a few days ago, but if they think I'm ever letting that girl out of my sight again, they have another thing coming.

While I'm able to move around with minimal discomfort, Sloane is still mostly immobile. The first time I saw the bruising that covered her entire front, I felt sick to my stomach. But when I realized she bruised through her delicate body and it covered her whole back as well, I lost it. She has six broken ribs, a punctured lung, and internal bruising, but she's alive, and I'll take that.

"Emory?" She's sitting beside Sloane reading over her discharge papers with her. "I'm going to go see Ashton before we leave."

"Loki, he's still not allowing anyone in. Even his doctors are having a hard time getting him to talk." Emory's words are pained, and it's echoed in all of our expressions.

"I'm not leaving here without seeing him. I don't give a fuck what he wants at this point. I need to speak with him, and he will listen to me."

"Okay. I have no idea what you'll walk into. He denied

giving me access to his records. He's in rough shape, Loki."

"I-I know," I mumble.

And it's all my fault.

Leaning down, I kiss Sloane on the cheek. "I'll be back soon." Something in her discharge paperwork catches my eye. "Why does this have Preston's address on it?"

She stares at me with wide eyes.

"She'll still need care, Loki. She can't go back to my father's house. She'll need someone to help her with everything from getting dressed to feeding herself until some internal inflammation goes down." Emory looks at me, confused.

"I know." I ping pong between Emory and Sloane. "I'm going to take care of her. Unless ... is this what you want, Red? Do you want to stay with Emory?"

"I-I didn't know where else to go," she whispers.

"What do you mean? I want you with me, always. Is that not what you want, too?"

"I didn't get to make a grand gesture with you guys, so you've obviously missed a few steps," Dexter gloats as he enters the room.

Irritated at the situation, I snap, "What the hell are you talking about?"

"Well, if we had made a grand gesture, Sloane would have known how you felt. As it stands, you might have to spell it out for her."

"Yeah," Preston's brother, Colt, chimes in, entering the room. "Fuck grand gestures. Sloane here took care of that on her own. She shot up mobsters to save your stupid ass. I think she wins hands down in the grand gesture department."

"What the hell are you morons talking about?"

"Isn't it obvious?" Colt asks.

"Apparently not," I say through clenched teeth.

"Oh, bless your heart." Dexter laughs. "Sloane is going to

Preston's house because you haven't made your intentions known."

I gape at everyone in the room. "Is that true?" I ask, turning my attention on Sloane.

"I-I …" She glances at everyone, silently asking for help.

"Oh, hell no." I march to her bed and look her square in the eyes. "My intentions, Red, are forever." Dropping to one knee, she gasps. "I had hoped to do this with a ring, but since my intentions are in question, I'm going to tell you right now. I intend to marry you. I intend to spend the rest of my life with you. I intend to have a family with you, and I intend to spend the rest of my life making up for all the assholery I've put you through."

"That's a lot of intentions," she giggles.

"Don't mess with me right now, Red. I need to hear you say yes."

Cough. "Ah, you didn't actually ask a question," Dex interrupts.

What? Yes, I … Oh for fuck's sake.

"Sloane Marie Camden, this is a placeholder proposal. I'll do it right when we're not in the hospital, when you're not in pain, and when we don't have an audience …"

"Ah, that's not how we do things, Loki. Everyone witnessed mine and Lanie's. Same with Trevor and Julia. And we were all in on Emory's real one, so … ya know."

"Oh my God, Dex. Shut the hell up," I yell.

"Sloane, please say you'll marry me. We will redo this whole shitshow at a later date, but I want to be very clear, my intentions with you are forever."

Through a mix of laughter and tears, she nods her head yes.

"Thank Christ. Put Westbrook Bay down as our address. We'll have to renovate to make it our own—"

"And an exorcism," Colt interrupts.

Shaking my head, I take a deep breath so I don't kill

someone. "Okay, maybe that, too. But, baby, I had a great childhood there. I have amazing memories, and that is where you showed your badass self for the first time."

"We all saw the cake smashing video," Colt laughs. "That was fucking awesome."

Sloane hides her face in embarrassment.

"No, baby. You're not allowed to be embarrassed about that. Look what you accomplished that day. Seth, Luca, Ashton, and I are all alive because of you. Because of you, Sloane, but this is *our* future, not mine. If you can't go back to that house, we'll tear it down and build a new one, or start fresh anywhere you want. Just tell me what you want," I plead.

"Welcome to the world of rich husbands," Emory jokes.

"What do you want, Red?" I whisper, ignoring everyone else.

"I just want you, Loki. Just you, wherever you are, is where I need to be."

"As soon as you're healed, we're opening that kink kit of yours, and I'm going to fuck the fuck out of you."

"Ew. That's my baby sister, you asshole." Emory makes a gagging noise.

"What the hell is a kink kit, and how do I get one?" Colt asks excitedly.

"Please, don't tell Lanie. I don't think my junk can take anymore right now," Dex whines.

Leaning in, I kiss Sloane in the most impolite way I can manage without hurting her. "I have to talk to Ash. I'll be back soon, and we'll go home, okay?"

Her smile is like the sunshine that breaks through the fog. How the hell did I get so lucky?

"Home." It's one word that holds so much weight for both of us. She's spent her life running from home, and I've spent mine protecting it. Together, we're about to bury our ghosts and make a forever home.

CHAPTER 45

ASHTON

"I don't give a shit what his wishes are. I've waited a goddamn week to see him. His mother is crying every day because he won't let anyone in. You know what? I'm a US SIA Agent, and I am going to speak to him. If you don't like that, call the police and see what they have to say about impeding an investigation." Loki's voice is rising with each word.

I knew he'd come, and I knew he'd be the one to pull out all the stops to get in, but knowledge does nothing to ease my rage. Knowledge, or lack thereof, is what landed me here in this position.

My hospital door bursts open, and Loki stomps in.

"SIA is disbanding. You didn't have a leg to stand on out there. If they call the authorities, they can arrest you."

"I'll take my chances." I can hear the smirk in his voice even without making eye contact. "What the fuck is going on, Ash? Sylvie is a mess. Don't take your anger at me out on her."

"Anger at you? What the hell are you talking about? Why the fuck would I be angry at you? And, before you get on your high horse, have you ever stopped to consider that I'm not letting her in for her own benefit? What mother needs to see the monster her son has become?"

"You're here, like this, because of me, Ash. Who else would you be angry with?" he yells.

The door opens, and a nurse sticks her head in.

"We have some shit to work out. I will not hurt him, and he will not hurt me, but there will be yelling. Shut the door and get used to it," Loki grinds out.

Loki has been my best friend since I was eleven years old. If my face allowed a smile, I would have. When he's pissed off, he doesn't care who hears it.

"This is not your fault, Loki. Go home. Take care of Sloane. Thank her for saving you all for me, but leave me the fuck alone."

If only one of her bullets had taken me out, too.

"Bullshit, Ash. You were involved in this because of me. You were helping me. You were never part of SIA. I never prepared you for this shit, so this is all my fault."

"I relieve you of your misplaced guilt. Now go."

"Hey, dickhead. That's not how this works. That's not how our family works. Whatever dark place those fuckwads dragged you to? I will spend my life pulling you to the surface. You will not drown in their evil. Do you hear me? You're allowed to be upset. You're allowed to grieve or do whatever the fuck you need to do. What you're not allowed to do is shut us out. You can run, and you can hide, but we will never leave you alone. You're in a dark place now, Ash, I get that. I don't know what they did to you, but I swear on my life, we will stay in the trenches with you until the sun shines again."

"Noted. Now leave."

"Fucking dick. I'm not leaving. I'm not done. Sylvie has not left this hospital, did you know that? Emory sneaks her into empty rooms so she can sleep for the few hours her Xanax allows. She doesn't give a rat's ass what your body looks like. She just needs to see you, Ash. A little piece of her dies every time you deny her."

"I failed her, and you. I failed everyone." My tone is cold and emotionless. It's the only way I'll survive this guilt. "Just let me have that. Let me deal with the fallout in my own way."

A vase shatters against the cement wall, and I turn my head to face him.

"Glad I finally have your attention." The door creaks and Loki screams before it even fully opens, "Get the fuck out."

"Go home, Loki."

The overhead lights flicker to life, and before my eyes can adjust, Loki is standing over me.

"Explain it to me. Explain exactly how you failed us," he sneers.

"It was my intel. It was my information that caused you to let your guard down." My voice is at its breaking point. The kick to the throat I received early on ensures my voice will never be what it once was.

"Your intel told us exactly what it was supposed to. When they left my house, they were headed to that plane. Don't you dare let their moves discount how valuable your insight was. You can lay here and mope. I'll let you wallow in the what-ifs until you're stronger. But hear me now, none of this was your fault, and we will spend eternity bringing you back to life if that's what it takes. Sylvie is coming to see you in one hour, and you will let her in. If I find out you pulled any bullshit, we will take shifts ensuring you never have a moment to yourself again until you're out of this."

I know he means it, so I just nod.

"I'll be back in the morning, and Seth is coming in the afternoon. When the darkness comes, do what I do."

"What's that?" I ask because I need to know.

"Remember, there's always someone ready to welcome you to the chaos." Loki leans in and wraps me in a hug the

Westbrooks are known for. I don't have it in me to reciprocate, though. I lost my Westbrook mojo when I let those fuckers into our lives. "I'll be back in the morning. Don't fuck with Sylvie."

I nod because words hurt too much. As soon as I can escape this prison, I will run until no one can find me. At least then, my actions won't hurt anyone else.

CHAPTER 46

LOKI

"What do you think of the title?" Sloane asks.

Turning my body toward hers, I catch the smile she saves just for me. We're lying in bed in the condo that started it all, and she's finally finished the rough draft of our story. After reading it, we realized there was no use denying it. This book is the story of how we fell in love.

"One Little Heartbreak," I read aloud. "But we have a happily ever after?"

"True, but one little heartbreak is what gave me the kick in the ass to see through my shit. As much as it hurt, I'm stronger because of it."

Taking the laptop from her hands, I place it on the nightstand. "I am so fucking sorry, Red. A piece of me died that day. I don't think I'll ever recover from seeing the hurt in your eyes when I pushed you away."

"Loki, we've already talked about this. Can't we just forget it ever happened?"

"No."

"It's okay. I promise, and we're here now. That's all that matters," she tries again.

"No, that's not all that matters." I stare at her with such

conviction that her body reacts as if I've touched her. "I will spend the rest of my life making up for it, Sloane. I promise you now, I will never hurt you like that again. From this day forward, in sickness and in health, for richer or poorer, I will spend my days loving you."

"I think you're supposed to save those for your wedding day."

"Our wedding day, Red. Ours."

I can't take it. I pounce, and I'm straddling her a second later. Dragging her arms above her head, I lean in to nibble her neck. We've been home for a few weeks now, and her bruises are healing, but she's still tender in places, and I've memorized every single one of them.

Gently grazing her ribcage, I hover over her most tender spots. Placing butterfly soft kisses where she hurts the most, I revel in the whimpers I elicit.

"I want to marry you, Red. I want to love you for the rest of my days, and I want to be the one to chase away your fears. I want to protect you, learn from you, encourage you, and watch you fly. I want to be your partner, Sloane. In life, in love, and everything in between. I love you more than I ever thought possible."

Tears leak from the corner of her eyes as I stare at my future—a future that is full of love and family. It's not something I ever thought I would have, but as I sit over her now, I have no doubt in my mind. My happily ever after has just begun.

~

"How long do you have to wait to ask someone to marry you?"

Preston drops the box he was holding. "Ah, you've been home for less than a month, dude."

Glancing around the room, I'm reminded of all the

memories I had here as a child. I'm sad to let them go, but there is no other way forward. When Sloane and I left the hospital, we came straight to Kane Lane. The second we walked into this house, we knew it could never be a home. The memories of gunfire and bloodshed would always haunt us.

At first, I thought we could make it work, but then Sloane mentioned Ashton. My best friend for so many years.

"Do you think Ash will ever be comfortable coming back to this house?" Sloane asks with tears in her eyes.

"I-I don't know."

I round the corner to the office and see the stain where Ashton had lain, and my stomach revolts.

"Loki, I'm, ah, I'm not sure I can stay here."

Surveying the room, I know this can never be home.

"I wanted to ask Lanie the second I got back from London," Dex admits, "but she wasn't ready. That's something you have to consider, man. Lanie had been through a lot and had some shit to sort through. Sloane is the same way."

"So you think I should wait?"

"Did you already get a ring that's burning a hole in your pocket or what?" Trevor laughs.

Reaching into my front pocket, I pull out the ring.

"Jesus, Loki. Where's the damn box? You're going to end up losing it carrying it around like that," Trevor scolds.

"The box wouldn't fit in my jeans, and I like having it close like I'm holding onto a piece of her or something."

"Blah," Colt gags while sticking his finger in his mouth like a ten year old. "What the hell happens to your man card when you fall in love? Is that a requirement? You fall in love, and you become a pussy?"

Trevor throws a pillow at him from behind, knocking him off balance. "Watch it, Colt, or I'll sick GG on you."

"Holy shit, you wouldn't dare!"

"Want to bet?" Trevor pulls out his phone.

"Okay, okay." Colton mimes zipping his lips, and we all laugh.

With Easton still in Vermont, we're only missing Ashton, and that knowledge makes my chest ache.

"He'll come around, Loki. We'll make sure of it," Preston whispers beside me.

Unable to form words, I pat him on the back.

"The upstairs is done," Halton grumbles. "You know, we could have hired someone to do this shit?"

"And miss spending time with your grumpy ass? No way." I smirk.

"You sure you want to tear this place down?" Dex asks from across the room. "We had a lot of great memories here."

Searching the room, I agree. "We did. But the past has held onto me for too long. Building new will be a fresh start. Sloane and I can tear down what hurt us and build a stronger future because of it. It just seems like the right thing to do." I swallow multiple times. "And I think my parents would be proud of me. They only ever wanted me to be happy, and Sloane makes me feel fucking alive. I've never felt so free or loved as I do when I'm with her."

Preston tackles me from behind. "I'm so fucking happy to have you back."

Before I know it, Dex, Trevor, and Colt have all piled on, too.

"You guys are a bunch of idiots," Halton chides from the doorway.

I see the moment Halton realizes his mistake. As if someone just announced he was it, every full-grown man in this house charges him. Wrapping the grumpy bastard into a hug, they tumble to the ground.

"Pig pile," Colt screams.

With my body still sore, I watch from the sidelines. Happy and relieved to be part of the chaos again.

EPILOGUE

LOKI

Three months later

"Are you sure *this* is how you want to propose?" Dex asks for the third time in ten minutes.

"Trust me, she'll appreciate it."

"I don't know, Loki. There's nothing romantic about this. It just seems kind of … I don't know, icky?" Trevor groans.

"Listen, I didn't even ask you guys to be here. You're the ones insisting on being a part of it."

"Had I known you were coming up with your own plan, I may have given it a second thought," Seth mumbles. "Seriously, this is what you want your family and friends to see?"

"Sloane is going to love it."

"You guys are so messed up. I don't even want to know about the kink kit," Halton Westbrook grumbles, stomping down the path in his sweatpants.

"You don't know what you're missing, dude," I reply with a wink. "Okay, everyone, line up. Let's make sure your letters are all in line."

"Jesus Christ," Easton grumbles. "I can't believe Mom made me come home for this."

Staring at all my brothers lined up, I'm hit with immense sadness. Dexter, Trevor, Preston, Seth, Easton, Colton, Halton, and Luca all stand on the beach in matching gray sweatpants, but there's a gaping hole in my lineup. Ashton continues to shut us out. He lives in the darkness now, and I'm struggling to keep him close.

"He should have been here today, Loki. I'm sorry," Preston's voice pulls me from my thoughts.

"I think we've lost him," I admit. "I don't know what will bring him back."

"We will. We'll show up every day and open his blinds. When he retreats, we'll track him down. When he fights, we'll hand him the gloves. I think he has to go through stages before we get him back. We just have to be there for all of them."

"I'm scared for him, Pres. He's had my back since we were teenagers, and it's killing me that the Ashton I knew might be gone."

Preston elbows me. When I look up, he nods to my left.

Standing at the edge of the beach, leaning on a tree, is Ash.

"He's still in there, Loki. He wouldn't be here if he wasn't. We just have to be patient while he sorts through his shit."

"I'm going to go talk to him."

"Good luck. He may be here for you, but he still isn't talking much," Preston warns.

Making my way through the sand, an unease that has never existed between us before hangs heavy.

"I didn't think you'd come."

"I'm fucked up, Loki. We both know that. But you are and always have been my brother. I just can't stand up there in front of everyone. I'm sorry." His voice is hoarse and barely more than a whisper.

"I know. I'm glad you're here though."

Staring at the ground, he says the last thing I was expecting. "Jackson has been taken care of."

It's like the wind has been knocked out of my lungs.

"What?"

"Ryan took care of him. Called it his last act as the owner of EnVision." Ash swallows hard. He is still having so much trouble speaking. "He'll never hurt Sloane or anyone else again."

I have so many questions, but we're interrupted by a happy squeal.

"Uncle Ashton."

Turning, I see Seth's daughter, Sadie, charging us full speed.

"Fuck," Ash mutters under his breath.

Sadie runs and catapults herself into Ashton's arms. He's still not steady on his feet and hides under layers of clothes, even in the heat, but this sassy little six-year-old girl doesn't see any of that.

"Hi, Uncle Loki," she says from her perch in his arms. "See how good Uncle Ash is at catching me?"

"He is pretty good," I agree.

"You know why I love his booboo so much?" she asks so innocently, but both Ashton and I cringe. *From the mouths of babes.*

"Ah, why?"

"My mommy had booboos on her insides, and we couldn't kiss them better. Uncle Ash's are right here. I can kiss them better all day." I watch in shock as she leans in and plants a messy kiss right to his cheek.

He's stiff in his posture, but he doesn't pull her away. If anything, holding Sadie is the first time I've seen the light in his eyes since before his injury.

My phone beeps, and I look down. "The girls are on their way," I tell him.

"Guess you guys had better get into position then."

"Nah, I'm gonna stay right here with you, Uncle Ash."

I look from Sadie to Ashton and smile. No one can say no to that little girl.

"Great," he grumbles, but it lacks conviction. The Westbrooks are a family of huggers, and right now, what he needs is that tiny embrace, so I leave them and head to my spot.

∽

Sloane

"WELL, IT'S NOT MONO," Eli says sarcastically.

Gripping the sides of the sink, I stare down in disbelief.

"How did this happen?"

"Well, Sloane, when two people fall in love, the man sticks his penis in the woman's vagina and—"

"Shut up, you smart ass. I know how babies are made, but how did this baby get made?"

Staring around the room, I realize not everyone knew, and I feel like an ass.

"Ah, so, Preston had a vasectomy after he found out about his heart defect." Every head in the room turns to look at Emory. "He didn't want to take a chance of passing on the gene, so we used donor sperm."

The room erupts in a chorus of "Oh, my God" and "Congratulations, Emory."

My sister is going to have a baby of her own, and I couldn't be happier.

"It, ah, I didn't want to tell everyone today," she says uncomfortably, "but Sloane found the test in the bathroom and insisted I take it."

"True story." I grin. "I'm going to be an auntie."

All the girls crowd around Emory and give her all the love and attention she deserves. My phone buzzes, and I reach for it.

Preston: Are you guys on your way?

Sloane: We had a little setback, but I'll load everyone up now.

Preston has yet another surprise for Emory, and this time, I'm the only one in on it. It's my job to get her to Westbrook Bay on time, and so far, I'm failing.

"Hey, guys. We have to get going. Everyone's waiting on us."

"I'm so glad they are doing this for Sylvie. That poor woman has had a miserable time raising all these boys." Emory states, utterly oblivious to the real reason we're gathering today.

"Yeah, umm, okay, so everyone ready? Preston sent a car to pick us up. It's downstairs."

"Rich people," Eli mutters.

I'm with her. I'm still not used to everything that comes with being a part of this family.

Twenty minutes later, we pull into Sylvie's house, and everyone bolts from the car, leaving me sitting there wondering what the fuck just happened. A second later, Sylvie pops her head in.

"You ready, dear?"

"Me? For what? This is a surprise for Emory. What the hell?" Peering through all the car's windows, I see everyone has scattered.

"I know, come on," she encourages. Stepping out of the car, she leads me along the side of her house to a path I know leads to the beach. I only make it a step or two before realizing the trail is lined with bouquets of condoms.

"What the hell?" I turn around, but Sylvie stands at the end of the path, encouraging me onward. My heart rate spikes, and my breathing becomes shallow. Walking farther into the path, I come to some signs that hold my favorite quotes from the books I've written.

My heart is trying desperately to leap into my throat, but

I press on. I know the trail isn't long, and just as I start to see a break in the trees, something catches my eye. Off to the left, Ashton sits. Little Sadie is climbing his back like a jungle gym, and I pause to watch.

I clutch my chest at the sight. Ashton isn't the same man he once was, but seeing him with Sadie gives me hope for the future. As if he senses someone watching him, he lifts his head. When we make eye contact, he nods, mouthing, 'Thank you.' It's the longest conversation I've had with him since everything happened.

Tears fill my eyes, and he gestures for me to continue. Stealing a breath, I take the final steps, utterly unprepared for what I find in the clearing.

Standing at the water's edge in a line are Dexter, Trevor, Preston, Easton, Halton, Colton, and finally, Luca … all in grey sweatpants, no less. It's a scene straight out of a calendar—hottest billionaire version. I take a step forward when Loki's voice filters over the ocean air.

"Blue balls are a condition caused by excess blood trapped in the penis and/or testicles for an extended period of time without sexual release. Blue balls are not dangerous, so says Google, and generally easily remedied. But, my dear Red, I don't believe that is what your voracious mind has been asking all this time, now is it?"

Glancing around, I notice everyone I love standing off to the side, smirking.

"You, sweetheart, want to know what blue balls feel like, in detail, if I remember correctly."

Preston and Trevor separate in the line, and Loki steps out from behind them. In slow motion, he walks to me with a smirk I don't recognize. Standing before me, he takes my hand in his.

"You wanted to know what blue balls felt like, right? And I needed a grand gesture."

Unable to control my laughter, I jump and wrap him in a hug.

"What are you doing, Loki? This is crazy."

He holds me tightly. "I love you, Sloane, but let me finish," he whispers. "This is going to make Dexter and Trevor so uncomfortable. It'll be fun, watch."

He releases me, and I turn to see the guys once more.

"I conducted a survey to come up with the best description of blue balls."

"What?" I screech. "You did not," I say, swatting his chest.

"Okay, kids. Come with Nanna Sylvie. This next part is just for the big kids." She smiles and blows us all a kiss.

As if on cue, all the kids jump up and run toward the house. As soon as they are out of sight, each one of the guys holds up a piece of posterboard. Taking a step forward, I realize what's written on them—descriptions of blue balls.

"You see, Sloane. When you enter this family, it's not just me you're getting, but a whole family. You got a small taste of that when Emory married Preston, but now it's your turn to get the full effect."

Dexter steps forward, shakes his head, and mumbles, "Blue balls feel like when you stub your toe. It throbs and is painful, but you know if you can survive it, it will eventually end."

He falls back into line as Trevor steps forward. "Blue balls feel like pressure. Pressure without relief."

Preston is up next. "Blue balls feel like a dull, constant pain. Never enough to cause permanent damage, but enough to drive you insane."

Easton doesn't step forward but growls his displeasure. "I cannot believe I had to come from Vermont to fucking do this. Blue balls feel like having to sneeze but can't."

"That's oddly, a very accurate depiction," Loki murmurs next to my ear. He runs his finger up and down my spine as each of the guys reads their cards. I'm so lost in the sensations Loki is causing I miss the rest.

When Luca lowers his card, Loki turns me in his arms.

"I love you, Sloane. My Red, my runner. I want you with me always. I want to be the hero you write about. I want to show you for the rest of my life that you are the only heroine for me. I want the happily ever after with you."

He turns me in place just in time to see the guys rip their shirts over their heads. Each man has a letter on his chest, and it spells out, *will you*. Butterflies spasm in my stomach as sweat rolls down my back.

Holy shit.

I don't know if I should laugh or not. Then Loki counts to three, and all the guys spin in place. On their backs, they have letters that say *marry me?* Luca's back holds the question mark, and he wiggles in place, making it dance.

Tears form, and then I get the shock of a lifetime. The guys tug at the front of their pants, and they rip away from their bodies in one fell swoop. *Sloane!* Is printed on the asses of their boxer briefs. Laughter explodes from my body. I laugh so hard, my legs threaten to give out, and tears stream down my face. Glancing around, I see all my sisters and friends are snapping pictures and laughing, too.

"So, what do you say, Red? Is this proposal better than the one in the hospital bed?"

Turning, I see Loki down on one knee, holding the biggest ring I've ever seen. It sparkles in the sunlight, shooting rainbows onto his face.

"I think I told you recently what my intentions were, Sloane. I meant every word. I will spend the rest of my life proving that to you. You are my life, my love, my world. Please do me the honor of becoming my wife?"

A strangled sound escapes my throat, and we stare at each other in shock.

"Was that a yes?" he asks hesitantly.

I open my mouth, but only air comes out in an undignified wheeze. I see the flash of panic cross his face, and I do the only thing I can when he renders me stupid. I nod my head like a maniac and wave my hand in front of his face.

When he reaches for me, my heart calms, and I'm finally able to choke out a verbal, "Yes, Loki. Always, yes."

He lunges and draws me to his side. His lips devour me, and I know I'm home. It isn't long before our family and friends surround us. Their incessant chatter is interrupting our moment in the best possible way.

This is what a family should look like—family by blood and family by choice. All connected in the ways of the heart.

EXTENDED EPILOGUE

DEXTER

5 Years Later

"Tate, can you help me find your brother's shoes, please?

He rolls his eyes but turns to help. At thirteen, he's just hit a growth spurt that puts him at six feet tall. The kid might outgrow me by the time he can drive. I have mixed feelings about him growing up, but he's a good kid, thanks to Lanie.

"Any idea where they put them this time?" His voice croaks with signs of puberty.

"None. Liam usually takes them off by the door, but I only found one. Deacon's could be in the ocean for all I know. This is why I told your mother we should just buy them four of everything."

"That's wasteful, and besides, then we would be searching for eight shoes instead of four."

He may not be Lanie's by blood, but he is his mother's son in all the ways that matter.

"Dex? Everyone's going to be here soon. What's taking so long?" My gorgeous, sweet wife comes walking around the corner in a light blue sundress, and I have to widen my stance to allow for the expansion happening down there.

"Geez, Dad. Why are you so gross? Can you not stare at her like that? It creeps me out," Tate groans.

"Newsflash, buddy. Don't think I haven't noticed the way you've been staring at Sadie lately."

"What?" he scoffs. "Dad. She's been my best friend since I was eight. You—"

"All right, boys. Dex, stop teasing him. He'll realize in his own time."

Tate volleys between the two of us. "You're both insane. Dad, you're on your own. I'll make sure Sarah and Harper are ready."

He may be tired of his dad giving him shit, but he has a soft spot for his siblings and a protective streak that rivals my own.

"You have to stop teasing him about Sadie, Dex. He's just growing into these hormones. He doesn't understand them yet. But when he does, you better be on him about protection."

I can't help but laugh.

"It's not funny, Dex. I will not be a forty-year-old grandma." She leans down to unearth one of the twin's shoes from inside a backpack, and a growl erupts from deep in my belly.

"Jesus, Lanie. You're so damn sexy."

"Because I can find missing shoes?" Her delicate laughter can still stop my heart.

"Because you're mine." I stalk toward her, but she retreats.

"Oh no you don't. You're the one who insisted on having Sloane's book release party here. Everyone we love will be here soon, and I'm not walking around smelling like," she glances around in search of our mini-humans; when she finds the coast clear, she whispers, "sex."

"Then this might be the shortest book release party Sloane's ever had." Lunging, I grab her around the waist. Hauling in her for a kiss, I waste no time entering her delicious mouth.

"Oh my God, Dad. Seriously, you need to stop. We have company."

Glancing up, I see Tate cross the room with Sadie close behind.

"It's just Sadie. She's family, so she doesn't count. Hi, Sades." I've been calling her family more and more lately to get a rise out of him and today is no exception. His glare is so similar to mine. He will be a badass in a boardroom someday.

Tate will never correct me and say she's just a friend while she's standing there. He wouldn't want to hurt her feelings, but he never misses a chance to remind me that she's family adjacent when we're alone. Because there are no legal or blood ties to her, she's family by choice. I have a feeling that may change someday, though.

"Hi, Uncle Dex. My dad dropped me off. They're driving around for a little while because Stella just fell asleep."

I grin, knowing how much Tate hates it when she calls me Uncle, and Lanie elbows me in the gut.

"No problem. Can you guys help us get the littles outside? They're probably safer out there with GG anyway."

"Sure," Tate grumbles.

"Dex, you're such a pain in the ass, you know that?"

Lanie's mouth has gotten dirtier over the years, but she still only swears when she really means it.

"That's what dads are for, sweetheart. Now, come on. Let's get this party over with so we can have a party in my pants later."

"Oh my God. Dad jokes now, too? Who did I marry?"

"The love of your life?" I answer helpfully.

Her eyes soften. "Yes, the love of my life. I don't know where I'd be without you."

I don't ever contemplate where the kids and I would be if Loki hadn't led her to me. Our futures are bright because of her, and that's all that matters. My life has meaning, and my soul is at peace. All because of my amazing wife.

~

Trevor

"Jules? Come on, we're going to be late, and Preston will never let us live it down."

"I just don't understand why she has to bring forty-seven trucks. Liam and Deacon have a billion of them. Why does she need her own? She won't even play with them. I'll just end up schlepping all this shit into Lanie's house for nothing."

Charlie walks behind his mother, picking up his sister's toys that drop from his mother's hands. He might be my twin, but his personality is all Julia.

Cassie comes down the stairs in head-to-toe tulle. My little girl is the epitome of an oxymoron. She gets her style sense from her auntie, Lanie, much to Julia's chagrin, but she gets her negotiating skills from me.

"Mommy. I need my trucks because Deacon broke one of mine last time he was here. We are going to sit down like big kids and work out a trade. How can I make a trade if I don't see all my options?" At five years old, I can't tell if she's going to be a heartbreaker or a card shark. Either way, my girl has spunk.

"Trevor? Please talk to her." Julia turns to Charlie. "Thanks, buddy. Do you have everything you need?"

"Yup." He holds up his backpack. "I made a deal with Sarah and Harper, but Uncle Dex said he didn't think his girls like playing with army men anymore."

Julia places her hands on her hips. "Did he now? Well, you know what I say to that?"

"Jules," I warn. "Last time they played army men, Sarah

ended up crying because they cut all her dolls' hair off to use as rope."

"That was Harper's idea," Charlie blurts. "She said we had to tie up the prisoners."

"Good Lord. You three are going to be so much trouble," I grumble. "How about this, you can bring them, but if Sarah gets upset, you'll have to find something else to play?"

I can almost see the debate happen behind his little eyes. Finally, he agrees.

"Awesome. Charlie, take Cassie and help her find a bag for her trucks so we can get going."

"Roger that," he says, giving me a little salute on his way past.

Turning to Julia, I can finally appreciate her dress. It looks so familiar, though. Why—

"Jules? Is that the same dress you wore the night we met?"

Glancing down, she appears unconcerned. "Hmm, I'm not sure. Possibly, why? Is it too tight? It's too tight and too short, isn't it?"

"Oh, baby. That's definitely the dress. I will never forget that night as long as I live. I can't believe you still have it."

"Well, it's perfectly acceptable. Why would I get rid of it? That seems wasteful."

I've recently sold my latest start-up for an obscene amount of money, but Julia will always be frugal. The girl could have anything she wants, and I could count the number of times she has willingly gone shopping on one hand.

How the fuck did I get so lucky with this girl? Even after all this time, just the sight of her electrifies something in me.

Leaning in so my lips graze her ear, I ask, "Do I need to remind you how we took that dress off in Boston, sweetheart?"

Her little body shivers at my words.

"I fucking love the way you respond to me. Let's go to our room. Give me five minutes alone with you—"

"Daddy, we're ready. Come on, my boys are waiting for me to play." Cassie's sweet, little voice is like a bucket of ice straight to my groin.

"Grrr. Jules, this is going to be the shortest book release party we've ever been to."

"Trevor, it's the only book release party we've ever been to. Sloane hit the New York Times Best Seller List. You have to be on your best behavior."

I glance down at my trousers, then back up at my wife. "Two hours, Jules. That's it, or we will have to find a closet at Dexter's house. I cannot look at you in that dress all night. Two hours."

She plants a kiss on my cheek and whispers, "Does it help to know I'm not wearing any panties?"

My throat closes, and I choke on my tongue. "Kids, I have to talk to Mommy for a minute. Why don't you put on one of your shows for—"

Julia yelps and runs out of my grasp. "No way, Trevor. We're late as it is. We'll have to have our *talk* later." She winks and picks up the kids' bags.

I'm left following behind my family to the car while attempting to adjust the steel rod, promising to leave me uncomfortable for many hours to come.

∽

Preston

"We are never going to get out here," Emory complains as she runs room to room, collecting all the shit our children will need for three hours.

I had no fucking clue kids could require so much crap.

Multiply it by three, and we need a goddamn Uhaul to get anywhere.

When we decided to try IVF, we knew there was a chance of multiples, but Dr. Chasen still assured us implanting four embryos was the way to go. Almost eight months later, Katon—or Katie—Weston, and Benton were born. I had to stick with family tradition on the names, and luckily, Emory agreed.

"Daddy." Katie's high-pitched scream has me dropping everything and sprinting to her door only to find her sitting in a pile of dresses. I have a feeling she and Cassie are going to manage some painful dents in our credit cards when they're older.

"What's up, sweetpea?"

Tearful blue eyes stare up at me. "My jewels is gone," she cries dramatically. "Wesson and Benty took um."

Jesus. Those two are going to be the death of me. They're like my brother, Colton, but on crack.

"Are you sure they took them?"

"Yes, Daddy. I is so sure." She nods her head earnestly.

I doubt she's wrong. The boys have turned into clever little kleptomaniacs recently.

"Okay, sweetpea. What color are they? I'll go find them."

Katie stares at me like I have six heads. "They is all the colors, Daddy."

I feel like there should be a big "duh" at the end of her sentence, but thankfully, I have a few years before that. *I think.* I don't really know, to be honest. Emory is a whiz with them, and I'm learning as I go. Being a father, a good father is the hardest fucking job I've ever had. It makes me miss my dad every day.

"I'll be right back." Stepping out into the hall, I yell, "Wess? Benty? Where are you?"

Uncontrolled giggles float from under their door. I'm willing to bet my identical little maniacs are hiding under their beds again. Stomping like Bigfoot, I make my way to their door and knock.

"Where are my jewels?" I growl.

Emory passes me in the hallway, and I forget to breathe. Dr. Camden is gorgeous, Emory is beautifully sweet, but Mommy Westbrook makes my spine tingle with need. Every passing day, I find new ways to love my wife.

I'm often overwhelmed by emotion just looking at her. She saved me in so many ways, and a love I've never known existed grows stronger every day.

Banging on the boy's door again, I absentmindedly keep up the charade. "Where are my jewels?" I growl. The sounds of little boys scampering tell me I have a couple of minutes, so I chase down Emory in the family room.

Wrapping my arm around her waist, I breathe in deeply. Just the scent of her has my dick aching for release.

"Preston," she scolds as I grind myself against her ass. "You need to get the princess' jewels so we can get out of here. I will not be late for my sister's party."

"How about a quickie?" I ask, nibbling on her ear.

"We don't have ti— Oh, God. Preston, we—"

"Daddy, my jewels," Katie cries.

Tipping my head back, I let out a long breath.

"It's okay, hun. We really do have to get going," Emory coos.

"Right." Sucking in a breath, I stomp off to grab my troublemakers and load them into their car seats.

Forty-five minutes later, we are finally backing out of our driveway.

∽

Loki

"I'm pretty sure she wore that dress to fuck with me," I grumble.

"Fuck, fuck, fuck," my two-year-old, Luna, mimics.

Oh hell.

"Dadda, that potty talk." Hattie, our four-year-old, scowls.

"See, it's not so easy learning to watch your mouth, is it?" Preston teases.

"Hey, girls? I think Auntie Lexi has some candy for you. Why don't you go ask her? She's sitting with—"

I don't even finish my sentence before my girls are teetering across the lawn, searching for their target. They have a sweet tooth like their mother. My gaze drifts to Sloane again, and I groan. *What I wouldn't give to eat her for dinner tonight.*

Dex stomps over to us, looking pissed off.

"Who pissed in his Cheerios?" Preston whispers.

"My thoughts exactly," Trevor mumbles.

When Dex is within earshot, I ask him. "What's with the face?"

"What face?" he barks.

Preston and I exchange a look, and we all start laughing. Well, everyone but Dex.

"That face," Trevor says, pointing at Dex. "What's up?"

He sighs and scrubs a hand over his face. "Can I be honest with you guys? I mean, I've been a father the longest, right? So, I can drop some truths here?"

We all shift uncomfortably. The last time he dropped some truths was to tell us that our wives would likely shit herself during delivery and not to make a big deal about it unless we wanted to sleep alone for the next year.

I sneak a peek at Red and immediately have to think of the least sexy things I can manage before I sport wood here in my circle of friends. *Old lady tits. Sloane's tits. Jesus. Football, think football, Loki.*

"Loki? Are you listening to me? This is serious."

With my eyes closed, I answer, "Nope. I'm not listening. I'm trying to think of football, so I'll stop rocking a semi while four billion kids are running around."

Preston jumps back like I just exposed myself in public.

"That's what I'm talking about. We're outnumbered here. I haven't been able to get my wife alone in two weeks. Two fucking weeks, and look at her. No, scratch that, don't look at her, but look at her! What the hell am I supposed to do?"

"I can't help you there, man. My kids are two and three and still find their way into my bed most nights. The last time I had sex was during naptime, and I had to chase Sloane down in the laundry room, so we didn't wake up the girls."

"See? See?" Dex screeches. He's on the verge of hysterics, and if I weren't in the same boat, I might laugh.

"Thank God. So, it's not just me? I thought I was a terrible fucking father," Trevor gripes. "I was ready to go to therapy to make sure I didn't screw them both up."

"You guys have no idea what you're talking about. Try having three of them at the same exact stage," Preston whines.

"Don't start that shit with me, Pres. I had a six year old, two-year-old twins, and newborn twins at one point. Now that they're getting bigger, I'm a sinking ship."

Glancing around at my group of friends, I see the same pained expression on us all.

"What the hell has happened to us?" I ask. "We have the best lives, and we're sitting here complaining like a bunch of babies."

Seth joins our group just then and laughs. "What you guys need is an adults-only vacation. Parenting is fucking hard. It's hard on you and your relationships. Trust me on this, take a trip without your kids. You'll be better parents for doing it, and then maybe you'll be able to join family functions without giving off enough testosterone to light up the entire East Coast."

He walks away, and we all stare at each other in a daze.

"How did he get so smart?" Dex mutters.

"I think it has something to do with Aria. He was a grumpy prick before her," I explain. "But ..." I glance around at all the guys. Preston's brothers all sit on the opposite side of the lawn looking as miserable as we do. The only one without a scowl is Seth.

"He just got back from a trip, didn't he?" Preston's awed voice rings out. "And look at him."

"He was like us, but worse," I agree.

I'm still staring as he makes his way to Ash, and the familiar stab of guilt hits me when we make eye contact. Ashton has never held me responsible for his injuries, but I carry it as a black mark on my soul every day.

"Are you in? Earth to Loki. Are you in?"

Turning my attention back to the guys, I see they're all wielding their phones. I missed something.

"In for what?"

"Jesus, get some blood running north for Christ's sake. We're booking a trip—kid-free for all of us. Are you in?"

"Fuck yes." I don't care if it is tomorrow or next week. Some time alone with Sloane is exactly what I need.

A chorus of, "Daddy!" rings out, and we all turn in time to see all our children headed toward us at full speed. We drop our drinks, ready for the ambush as an entire team of kids charge.

All four of us speak at once, but it's Dexter's voice that comes out strong.

"You know, for all our complaining, this life is pretty fucking awesome, too."

We all grin, nodding in agreement. I wouldn't change this life for anything in the world. Tweak it so I can have some alone time with my wife? Absolutely? Change it? Not for the world.

Preston raises a fist and we all shout, "Welcome to the

chaos," then take off running to meet our little ones halfway. When we collide, we all take the fall, rolling around in the grass, letting them think they took us down, and in a way, they did.

Glancing to my left, I laugh with my friends. All four of us have been tamed and brought to our knees by our wives. Our children came along and gave us purpose. They gave us hope when sometimes it's hard to see the light.

Turning the other way, I find Ashton. A half grin is all he can manage, but it's there. Our kids bring us light, love, and happiness in a way none of us could have ever predicted. Our wives make us whole. As hard as it was for all of us to get to our happily ever after, I'd bet my life that none of us would ever change a thing.

GG'S COFFEE CAKE RECIPE

Hi Luvs!

This is my real life GG's coffee cake recipe. I hope you luv it!

Pre-heat the oven to 350 degrees
Ingredients:

- 1 8oz block of cream cheese
- 3/4 C of sugar
- 2 eggs
- 2 C flour
- 1/2 tsp baking soda
- 1/2 C butter (room temperature)
- 1/4 C whole milk
- 1 tsp vanilla
- 1 tsp baking powder
- 1/4 tsp salt
- 1/4 C brown sugar
- 3 C fresh berries (I like diced strawberries, blackberries and blueberries but any fresh berries will work)

1) Beat the cream cheese, butter and sugar until smooth.

2) Slowly add in the milk, eggs (one at a time) & vanilla.

3) Combine dry ingredients in a medium size bowl.

4) Add the dry ingredients into your butter mixture in 3 batches. Do not over mix.

5) Pour the batter into a greased 9x13 pan.

6) Pour berries evenly over the top of the batter.

7) Sprinkle the top with the brown sugar.

8) Bake 35-45 minutes until cooked through.

That's it! I promise it is easier than Sloane made it seem. If you do make this cake, please take a picture of it and post it on any of my social media accounts! I would LUV to see your creations!

Luvs,

Avery

ACKNOWLEDGMENTS

As always, I have so many people to thank. First and foremost, my family. To my husband who has been our rock even when I'm wondering what the hell I'm doing, I love you more than words can say. To my children who are still adjusting to having a working mom, I hope one day you'll see what I was able to accomplish with my own two hands. I love you with all my heart.

Beth-you continue to amaze me in all that you do. A phenomenal nurse during a pandemic, an even better mom, friend, and human. Thank you for always being my biggest fan and for pushing me when I want to quit. If it weren't for you, I wouldn't even be on this crazy journey.

Brittni-Where do I start with you? Thank you doesn't seem to cover it. You've been my biggest champion, my teammate, my friend. Your love and support not only as a PA, but as a friend means the world to me.

Rhonda & Kia-Thank you for jumping aboard when I made up a crazy name for a team with no questions asked. Your insight and input are invaluable to me. Thank you for being my support, my cheerleaders, my proofreaders, and my friends.

And finally, to you, my readers. Thank you for coming on this crazy ride with me. Thank you for your support, your encouragement, and your never-ending love for my group of chosen family, The Broken Heart Boys. I couldn't do what I do if you didn't read them, so thank you from the bottom of my heart.

Editor: Melissa Ringstead, https://thereforyouediting.wordpress.com/

Cover Designer: Emily Wittig @ Emily Wittig Designs. https://www.emilywittigdesigns.com/

ABOUT THE AUTHOR

A New-England girl born and raised, Avery now lives in North Carolina with her husband, their four kids, and two dogs.

A romantic at heart, Avery writes sweet and sexy Contemporary Romance and Romantic Comedy. Her stories are of friendship and trust, heartbreak, and redemption. She brings her characters to life for you and will make you feel every emotion she writes.

Avery is a fan of the happily-ever-after and the stories that make them. Her heroines have sass, her heroes have steam, and together they bring the tales you won't want to put down.

Avery writes a soulmate for us all.

Avery's Website www.AveryMaxwellBooks.com

ALSO BY AVERY MAXWELL

Standalone Romance:

Without A Hitch

Your Last First Kiss

The Westbrooks Series:

Book 1 - Cross My Heart

Book 2 - The Beat of My Heart

Book 3 - Saving His Heart

Book 4 - Romancing His Heart

Book 5 - One Little Heartbreak - A Westbrook Novella

Book 6 - One Little Mistake

Book 7 - One Little Lie

Book 8 - One Little Kiss

Book 9 - One Little Secret

Made in the USA
Columbia, SC
05 October 2024